TEESSIDE BLUES

TEESSIDE BLUES

JOHN NICHOLSON

Nick Guymer Series

No.5

Printed by Berforts Information Press Ltd

ISBN 978-0-9926640-8-4

http://www.johnnicholsonwriter.com

Big drinks are due to Robert and Janet for their editorial talents on this project. Cheers, you beautiful people.

Mucho love to Dawn for ideas, designs and sharp stick poking. Y'all help make me better than I am.

Thanks to my informal support network of rhinos, winos and lunatics and thanks also to all my readers. Your support means so much to this dislocated boy.

Teesside Blues is dedicated to my mam and to the blues.

"I love the blues
they tell my story
if you don't feel it
you can never understand
so many times I thought about it
and now I know just what it means to be a man

Everyday I realise
you can see it in my eyes
I never wait or hesitate
because I love the life I live
I'm gonna live the life I choose
but you've got to understand
I'm walking in the shadow of the blues."

CHAPTER 1

'How many times have you had sex?' said Julie Wells as she lay on the sofa, twirling a long strand of blonde hair around her index finger, a calculator on her lap.

'Sex? What kind of sex?' said Nick Guymer, bringing in two mugs of green tea. He sat down opposite her.

'Well, you know, the whole nine yards...' she laughed and poked her right-hand middle finger through a hole formed by her left thumb and forefinger.

'Nine yards? Bloody hell, I don't think I can manage that, Jules. Well, let's think...I lost my virginity when I was 17, so I've had about 31 years of red-hot lovin', but there have been some very fallow periods. I went at least three years getting nowt at one point.'

'But when we got back together we couldn't keep our hands off each other.'

'Yeah, early in any relationship is a time of massive amounts of sex, isn't it? So that'll balance out the fallow periods a bit. I dunno, Jules, err...maybe an average of once a week since the late 70s.'

She tapped at the calculator.

'My god, once a week for 31 years is 1,612 times. Not bad for an ugly get like you.' She laughed and made a face at him.

'Good grief. I've had it off over 1,600 times? I'm surprised I'm not dehydrated. It feels more like about 23. So come on then, what about you? Does the calculator go high enough?'

'You cheeky sod. Well, I'm 45 next week, so believe it or not, I think I'm up around the 3,000 mark now. That's about twice a week for 29 long years. I might be being conservative there an' all. Don't look at us like that...'

'Good god, Jules. You've had it off at least 3,000 times?!' He threw his head back and laughed loudly.

She almost blushed. 'Alright, alright...there's nowt wrong with that. Anyway, the number is still going up by three or four every week, isn't it?'

'True, especially if you've been drinking.'

'Ha ha. I do love a bit of drunk sex, me. But 3,000 does seem a lot. It's a wonder it's not like a clown's pocket down there, eh!' She sipped at her tea and laughed again.

'3,000. Amazing. It's no wonder you're so good at it,' said Nick, shaking his head.

'Flattery will get you nowhere, son', she said, raising an arched eyebrow at him.

'I dunno, Jules, those numbers suggest it probably does.'

She threw a cushion at him and crossed her legs dramatically. He laughed again.

'So why are you doing these sexual calculations, then?'

'Well, considering I've done it at least 3,000 times, it's amazing how few of those times I can actually remember. I mean, I can recall a few which stand out, mostly for very fizzin' embarrassing reasons, but the rest of them are totally gone from my mind, even though sex is supposed to be such a big, important thing in life.'

'I suppose so, yeah; I'd not thought of it, but that's true, isn't it? You remember the first one, though.'

'Oh yeah. Steve Vicars. He was such a nice lad. I cried afterwards. Don't know why, really. I'd been hanging on until I was 16, then we did it on my birthday and almost immediately I wondered what the fuss was all about. Ha ha. Welcome to the real world, Jules.'

'Oh, the romance of it.'

'It was the best 15 seconds of Steve's young life. We'd been working on his old MG. He had oily hands and I remember he left a big greasy thumb print on one of my nipples. I hadn't even got my motor running and he'd gone through the gears and blown his gasket.'

'Aw, blimey, 15 seconds? Is that all he could manage? That's a poor show even for a 16 year old. I was never that bad. You'd have to ask Diane Redmarshall, but I think I lasted a few minutes.'

'You've always had good self-control, you. Why is that?'

'I'm numb from the waist down.'

'Ha ha...do you remember our first time?'

'Of course. It was in my Harrogate flat after our first date.'

She laughed. 'We were snogging and half-jokingly I said, "I'd better go home" and for some reason you said, "Oh, alright then", which was exactly what I didn't want to do, so I had to say, "But I'd rather stay, get naked and have wild sex with you". The look of shock on your face. Eeee, I can still see it. Bless you. You'd clearly never thought that I might fancy you that much.'

'I've never had enough ego or self-confidence to think that, man. Not about you or anyone else, for that matter.'

'And as I recall you gave me what a less politically correct woman than me would have described as a damn good seeing to. I was quite shocked at how vigorous you were; you were like a rutting animal. It was mint. I remember looking up at you in the throes of passion and thinking, bloody hell, what's this bloke on?'

'Well, it had been a while. And I actually feel embarrassed now. Can we change the subject, please?' he said, putting his hands over his face.

'You have actually blushed.' She pointed at him. 'Was that Redmarshall lass the one who worked in the Rimswell pub? Dark hair.'

'Yeah, that's her. We were at a party. She had satin underwear on.'

'Satin? In the 70s?'

'Well it was some sort of soft, shiny fabric. I remember it clearly.'

'She must have planned that in advance, then.'

'You reckon? I never even thought of that. Maybe she did.'

'You only wear satin knickers if you think that someone is going to see them, don't you?'

'She just lay there. It goes without saying that, though I wasn't quick, I was utterly rubbish. How could you be anything else at that age?'

'Well we grew up with the belief that nice girls don't indulge in howling, bite-the-pillow orgasms.'

'Like the ones you had on our first night, you mean?' he said, trying to embarrass her now.

'Oh, I was faking those just to make you feel special.' She grinned at him and raised her arched eyebrows.

'Bugger. And I thought I was doing so well.' He tutted. 'I did think you were a bit too noisy. At one point I thought maybe I was hurting you.'

She gurgled a laugh and ran her index finger down her centre parting. 'Nah, it was the opposite of hurting, lad. And I'm kidding you, I've never faked it with you. At least, I don't think I have, but like I said, I've forgotten almost every single sex act I've ever performed.'

'Huh, well, I've faked it with you.'

'You have not!' She sat forward, turquoise blue eyes wide.

'I have. I told you this before, remember?'

'How the hell have you faked it? Quite obviously, I'd have known if you'd faked it.'

'It was about our fourth date. We went to a party. I got really pissed.'

'Jonny White's 40th party. Yeah, I remember that.'

'We went back to your flat. I wasn't too drunk to get it up, just too drunk to finish it. I was exhausted so after you'd done, I faked it. I'm sure I have told you this before. It's easy. You just make all the right noises and then whip off the Durex and go to the toilet and wait for it all to y'know...soften.'

She looked at him astonished.

'You've *never* told me that before. That's really shocked me. I thought faking it was a woman's prerogative. Mostly your lot are just trying to stop it being over too quickly.'

'I didn't have the energy and I may have vomited if I'd put much more effort in, which is always a passion killer. Maybe I'm the only man ever to fake it.'

'You're a loss to the female gender, you, Guymer.'

'It seemed only polite. Why are we even talking about this?'

'Just because it goes to show most of what we say and do, even if it's important at the time, fades quite quickly from our memory.'

'True. It's just the same with football. Think about how many games you've seen and how many you can remember even a little bit about. '

'I've probably seen the Boro at least 20 times a season for nearly 40 years. That's at least 800 games, bloody hell, I'm such an old sod.'

'And such a glutton for punishment.'

She slapped her leg to get his attention. 'No, but I had a bigger point to make. Me having a miscarriage was a big thing and it was upsetting for both of us because all those plans we had just amounted to nothing. That life we thought we were going to have with a little 'un just evaporated that morning. But now it's not happening, the whole pregnancy thing was just something we did for a while. Do you see what I'm saying?'

'I do. But don't you feel like having a miscarriage is a really big life thing? It's not like a Saturday night drunken humping that you drink off your mind by Sunday lunchtime.'

'All I'm saying is we just live on and do other stuff and soon enough it'll just become another bit of our history the same way Steve Vicars or Diane Redmarshall are. We haven't exactly forgotten them, but it's not like we pay them almost any thought now.'

'Aye, we're always moving on in life and we shouldn't dwell on it.'

'Yeah, exactly. Tomorrow matters more than yesterday. It'll always be there, but it won't feel anywhere nearly as big a thing in a year as it does now, three weeks after it happened. I mean, I'm 45 next week, I can't be dwelling on stuff too long. We've got our lives to live and anyway, it feels weird having my mam being nice and sympathetic towards me for these past weeks.'

It was a typically practical Julie Wells approach to life. She'd been pregnant for 14 weeks and they'd got used to the idea and were really looking forward to being parents when the miscarriage had happened. It was all over quickly and painlessly. She had already got on with life, Nick hadn't really been able to. Quietly, on his own, he had tried to deal with it, but the sense of loss he felt was profound, troubling and almost physically painful. It was on his mind almost the whole time and he'd begun to wonder if there would ever be a time when it wasn't.

He got up and went over to his desk, taking out two envelopes from a drawer.

'I'm glad you mentioned your birthday next week.'

'Why?' she sipped at the tea. 'Are we going out for a nice meal?'

'Oh yeah, definitely.'

'Where, like? Up in the Dales, maybe?'

'I had something a bit further away in mind. How about California?'

'What?'

He took out two plane tickets for Virgin Atlantic and held them up at her.

'We're flying to Los Angeles on Sunday, lady.'

She sat up and her jaw dropped open. 'Get out of here!'

'We're staying at the Hotel Carmel in Santa Monica for 10 days. We couldn't afford any longer, but I thought it'd be a nice change for us after everything we've been through.'

She leaped off the sofa and grabbed him around the waist. 'You lovely man. What a totally mint surprise. How did you afford that, like? We're more skint than a very skint thing.'

'I didn't. I just put the flights on a new credit card. We'll pay for it sometime in the future. No point in living within your means if it makes your life more shit, is there?'

She laughed and kissed him. 'In the past I'd have said that wasn't a very sensible thing to do, but now I don't care. The future can take care of itself.' She kissed him again.

'Well, it might have made more financial sense to go to Spain, but I was thinking about the holiday we had in LA way back when we first started going out and it was the best holiday ever. We had such a good time.'

She did a little offbeat jig with her hands in the air. 'This is brilliant. Yay! If I can face ripping my pubes out, I might dig out that black bikini I wore back then. It might even fit me now 'cos I was a right porker back then and it always was a size or two too small. Mind, you've got to do me one favour though, eh?'

'Yeah. What's that?'

'Don't wear your old Speedos from back then, there's a good lad.'

'Aw, no budgie smugglers?'

'They're not so much budgie smugglers as snake stranglers. They leave nothing to the imagination.'

'Ha ha...OK, I'll leave them at home.'

'Cool. Bring the snake with you, though. We'll be needing him.'

'Him? That's a bit sexist, Jules. How do you know it's not a she?'

'If you're thingy is female and my doo-dah is female, that'd make me a lesbian, wouldn't it?'

'Yes, obviously,' he laughed. 'You've been gay all these years and you just never knew.'

'I knew there was a reason why I liked the Indigo Girls so much.'

A couple of weeks later, after 10 days of eating, drinking and lying in the Southern Californian sun, as they waited in the queue for the Virgin Atlantic flight from Los Angeles International Airport back to Heathrow, Nick yawned and put his arm around Julie.

'I wish we could've stayed longer. I was just getting used to the lifestyle.'

'Aye, it's been class, though. I bloody love California.' She brushed his hair off his eyes and smiled at him. 'You've really caught the sun. You're all tanned and delicious like a well-roasted chicken. You look like you've been on Mary's sun bed.'

'Hardwick Mary?'

'Aye. Rent a video, get a tan for a pound. It's a killer deal.'

'Aye, killer is right. I'm sure that sun bed is actually some sort of low-rent nuclear waste facility. People come out of it glowing fluorescent orange.'

She laughed and stuck her hand in his jeans back pocket and leaned her head on his shoulder.

'This has been one of the best holidays I've ever had. I feel like it's really drawn a line under the baby and all of that. I feel proper rejuvenated, despite now being a 45-year-old slapper.'

He grinned at her. 'Good. That was the idea.'

'And are you OK?' She pushed a strand of his straggly hair behind his ear and stroked his ear lobe.

He nodded. 'Yeah, I'm fine,' he said, lying to himself as much as to her.

'Good. Well, you've been on very good form out here, lad. Top notch work in that department, I probably lost a few pounds off my thighs from all the exercise. Must have been the sun. All that vitamin D put some serious lead in your pencil.'

'On good form?'

She nudged him with her shoulder. 'You know what I mean. We must have increased our batting average a fair bit. I'll be well over that 3,000 mark now, you'll nearly be at 1,700.'

'Oh, that. Yeah, well, it was probably all down to your new minimalist holiday underwear. That was a nice treat for me, Jules.'

She laughed and rubbed his belly. 'Well you deserved a bit of indulging for arranging such a great trip and you're easy enough to please in that department, aren't you?'

'I suppose so. Sorry.'

She cooed at him. 'You daft bugger, you don't have to apologise. I've bloody loved it, too. It's been proper ace and it's a good sign, isn't it?'

'A good sign of what?'

'Of you being in sound mind. When you're down, there's not much action in that department, is there? I've been worried about you after the miscarriage. At times you've seemed a bit distant, or at least more away with the fairies than usual.'

'Have I? Sorry. You shouldn't be worried about me. It was you who had to go through it all physically. All those hormonal shifts and stuff. Can't be easy.'

'No, but even so, I was worried you'd go off the deep end, like.'

'Well, don't worry about me. I'm OK. Maybe they should issue that underwear on the NHS as an anti-depressant.'

'Ha, yeah, Prozac pants. Got to be a winner, those. Oh, look who it is...over there...coming out of the first-class lounge.'

She nodded at a large figure carrying a sports bag. He was at least six feet four, 22 stone and wore army trousers, an army-green 5XL t-shirt and big army boots.

'Huh. Steve "Big Fish" Salmon. Jeff never said his brother was in America. He plays east-coast clubs sometimes. He must have been working in LA this time. Can't see his humour working here, though. It's too parochial and British. I can't see anyone laughing about how pretentious it is to eat an avocado and they won't understand any of his "fanny" jokes, either. Without those he's lost about 75 per cent of his act.'

'Humour? I didn't realise he had any humour. He's just vulgar. And he picks on the weak and the vulnerable. And what was that routine he does...what's it called...the one he got banned from Channel 4 for doing last year?'

'I think it's called *On the Blob*. The one about having it off with women who are menstruating.'

'Aye, that's just plain horrible. He likes to think he's pushing the boundaries, but he's not, he's just being vulgar, which is about as conservative as you can get really. And all those rape gags...I'm sorry, I think it's just wrong.' She shivered and shook her head.

'He's no Lenny Bruce, that's for sure. He likes to play at being the common man who says what we're all secretly thinking, but he was born into money and privilege. I'm always amazed at how he's got away with that. Jeff gets on with him these days, though that may be as much due to the fact he's a multi-millionaire as his wit.'

'If I said he offends both my socialist and feminist principles would it make me seem like a right uptight prig?'

'It would to him. "Yerjokinarntya?", "Talk to the beard, darlin",' he said, in an approximation of Big Fish's Teesside accent, delivering his two most popular catchphrases.

'I'd like to set fire to the bloody beard and that's no bloody joke. It amazes me how those have stuck with people. They seem to enjoy shouting them at him.'

Nick laughed. 'Actually, it is puzzling. I was just reading the *Gazette* website before we left the hotel and there was a piece about the Teesside Blues Festival he's holding on the Blakeston estate in a few weeks' time.'

'Oh, is that actually happening now? It's been on and off more times than my holiday knickers.'

'Aye. The last minute objections were overruled - to the festival, not to your holiday knickers - so it's all systems go now. It'll be on in a few weeks.'

'Oh god, he's seen us. Shit.'

The big man nodded and made half a smile. Nick returned the acknowledgment.

'Is it me or does he look very nervous?' said Nick, into Julie's ear. She nodded and said,

'That's understating it. He looks like he's shitting a brick. Look at the sweat on him.'

The big t-shirt Big Fish was wearing had dark, damp patches down the centre of his back and under his arms.

'It's not that hot in here, is it?' said Nick.

'Nah. It's actually a bit too cold, if you ask me.'

They watched as he sat down, his back to them.

'Should I go over and have a word?' said Nick. 'Seems a bit weird not to since we're here together.'

'You can if you want. I'm happy not to have to speak to him. He'll only say something that'll annoy me.'

Nick walked over to where the big man was sitting and squatted down beside him.

'Now then Big Fish. Fancy seeing you here.'

He visibly jumped in his seat and turned to look at him with nervous eyes.

'Shit me. Don't sneak up on us like that, Nick. Alright there...'

He held out his big damp paw. 'Been on holiday, have you?'

'Yeah. We love it out here. Have you been working?'

'Yeah, yeah, just a few gigs at the Comedy Store on Sunset, like.' He ran his hand over his cropped, buzz cut ginger and grey head and then pulled on the exploding ginger, brown and white flecked beard.

'Ah right. Good.' Nick paused and looked around. He was already out of things to say. He was terrible at making small talk. 'Jeff never said you were out here, like.'

'Ah well, he probably doesn't know...I mean, it was all a bit last minute, so...' he nodded and looked around nervously again.

'Are you alright, man?' said Nick. He seemed really agitated, wobbling his right leg up and down. A sheen of sweat glistened off the stubble on his head.

'Me? Aye. 'Course.'

'Are you going first class?'

'Aye. Can't be doing with sitting in cattle class with all the pissed Scousers and other assorted shit munchers.' He said it dismissively, not even thinking that's where Nick and Julie would be.

'No, we're a right load of arseholes in economy, us, like,' said Nick with a shrug.

The Big Fish didn't pick up on his comment at all; instead, he rubbed his head and then his eyes, wearily.

'Not looking forward to getting back, really. Getting a lot of grief...' He was almost talking to himself now.

'Oh, aye? Who from?'

He winced and tugged at his beard. 'Just the usual anti-capitalist, lefty, liberal panty wetters. Have you heard of this anarchist group?'

Nick shook his head.

'Ironopolis Anarchists they call themselves. Stupid bloody name. Always having a pop at successful people...y'know...going on about tax and that...pain in the fucking arse. Should be glad we pay anything at all. We keep this bloody country afloat.'

11

It didn't seem like the time or place to have a debate about the nature and extent of taxation.

'Right. Well, I'll probably see you around, Big Fish. You're putting on that blues festival on your dad's land, aren't you? I was just reading that you've got the go-ahead.'

'Aye, aye...another pain in the arse, but needs must,' he looked around again, clearly either hoping to see someone or fearing seeing them. It was hard to tell which. 'It's costing us a fortune, like.'

'Can't be cheap, I suppose.'

'Christ, no. We'll have to cut a few corners. Just have one bog, maybe. Ha. The bloody insurance alone is ridiculous.'

'I suppose it must be,' said Nick, feeling that his input wasn't really needed in the conversation.

'I'm insured for acts of God. So if there's a plague of locusts, we'll be alright.'

'Well, we get a lot of locusts on Teesside, don't we?' said Nick, flippantly, but Big Fish wasn't even listening to him.

'Even the cheapo, economy insurance which covers the basic shit costs tens of thousands. You'd not believe it. I mean, anyone who falls over a cable and breaks a leg will be dipping his bread in my gravy.'

Nick had already had enough of listening to him moaning. 'Right. Well. Good. I might see you there then. OK, see you later.'

'Yeah, see you Nick.'

He walked back to where Julie was standing, arms folded.

'Is he a nervous flier or something?' she said. 'He looks in a total mess.'

'He's very distracted. Started moaning on about the cost of the blues festival. I couldn't think what to say to him, to be honest, not that he'd be bothered. He doesn't even listen to you.'

She turned her mouth down. 'I think he's on drugs or something...coked up, I think. Blokes like him are all on the cocaine these days.'

'If he is, it doesn't look much fun. He's got the air of a man who is waiting for a biopsy result. Maybe he just hates flying. People get like that, don't they?'

'Aye. It's never bothered me. It's always seemed much less dangerous than driving up the A19 on a rainy Friday afternoon in January. After you've done that, anything seems tame in comparison.'

At last they began to call first-class passengers onto the plane. Big Fish got up and made his way onto the plane. As he did so, a tall man ran up. He had telescopic legs and a small, short body. Big Fish turned to him and scowled and said something, angrily jabbing a finger in the man's chest. The man pushed him back, his face puce, then he pushed him again, then made a pretend slap of Big Fish's face. The big man gave a false laugh and waved a dismissive hand at him as they disappeared to board the plane.

'Who was that?' said Julie.

'I don't know, but they were not exactly in love, were they?'

'It wouldn't surprise me if he was smuggling drugs or something. He's that sort.'

'You reckon? He's a multi-millionaire, he doesn't need to do that.'

'Aye, maybe not, but blokes like him get greedy, don't they? And they think they're untouchable because all they hear is people saying yes to them.'

'He said he was getting a lot of grief from some local anti-capitalist type of pressure group back in the UK called Ironopolis Anarchists. Seemed pissed off about it,' said Nick.

'Oh, aye? Good old-school Boro name that, Ironopolis.'

'Yeah, it is. I love the Nops. FA Cup quarter-finalists and three time Northern League champions, albeit before 1900.'

'I think I've heard about this group. They've been trying to expose rich, powerful people, landowners and companies who don't pay tax or who screw the system somehow. They were in the news a few months ago because they discovered some landowner had put proceeds from a land deal into an offshore account and avoided Capital Gains Tax...I can't remember the exact details.

More power to them. I hate the way the rich elite gets away with things like that while the working class are demonised if they scam a few quid on the dole.'

They began calling 'priority boarders' to get on the plane first. Julie tutted as people walked up, eyeing them contemptuously as they did so.

'Priority boarding - what a pile of old shite that is. Why do people want to get on the plane before anyone else and pay for the privilege? The plane isn't going anywhere until everyone's on. It's not like you gain any advantage at all,' said Julie. 'It's pointless elitism sold as upmarket living. Trying to make out you're better than you are. I hate that. It shouldn't even be indulged by air lines.'

'Maybe we should get that Ironopolis lot onto them,' said Nick, his arm around her.

'Aye, unless Virgin want to give us a first-class upgrade and then I'm prepared to lord it over the plebs, obviously. Bloody scum bag working class oiks.'

They'd been in the air for a couple of hours and Julie had the window seat as they headed east over Canada. Nick turned to her after they'd finished their lunch, smiled, leaned over and pecked her on the lips, catching her by surprise.

'What's that for?' she said with bright eyes.

He shrugged. 'I love you,' he said. He all too rarely actually said it.

She looked at him, smiled, and put her hand on his cheek.

'I love you, too.' She kissed him again and then gave him a light push on the chest. 'That'll do. No, we're not doing it in the toilet, before you ask.' She laughed a little, pecked him on the lips again and squeezed his thigh.

'It's nice to see someone in love,' said a voice next to Nick. He turned around. It was a short, stocky woman with spiked up blond hair. She was pulling her small feet up underneath her. 'If you want to get it on, don't mind me. I'm not easily shocked. Sex in the toilets is not recommended though, trust me on that, you'll just end up getting cramp.' She made a toothy grin at him and wobbled her head at him in a silly manner, then gave a big arc of a wave of her hand. 'I'm Kaz Clarke, by the way.' She pointed to herself. 'Do you mind if I snaffle this empty seat, I'm all cramped up in the centre there? There's a massive fat bloke on one side with body odour so powerful it's got its own gravitational pull.'

'No, help yourself,' said Nick, amused by her.

Julie leaned forward and waved back. 'Hello Kaz. I'm Julie. This is Nick. Are you travelling alone?'

'No. See this bloke here,' She pointed across the aisle at a tallish thin bloke with long hair. He was tanned and dressed in a black t-shirt and old jeans. He looked like a roadie from the early 70s. 'This long streak of pish is my boss, Artie Taylor. He's a photographer. We shoot rock bands and other reprobates, don't we Artie?' She leaned over and prodded him. 'Artie, wake up, I'm talking to some real humans.'

He opened one eye and acknowledged them with his index finger.

'Are you going home?' said Nick, noticing the Yorkshire accent.

'Sadly, yeah. We just finished some work on the road with a band. Have you been on holiday?'

'Yeah, just 10 days in LA,' said Julie.

'We love LA, don't we, Artie?' said Kaz, turning to him again. He didn't respond. 'Excuse him, he was on a bender yesterday and he's also a moody sod.'

'So's he,' said Julie with a laugh, digging a finger into Nick. 'Which band was it?'

'Dry County. All big hats and tight jeans.'

'Cool. We like them, don't we, Jules?'

'Aren't they a bit like the Eagles?' said Julie.

'More like Poco,' said Artie, from across the aisle, eyes still closed. Kaz tutted.

'He's just trying to be smart,' she said.

'I'd have said they were more like the Flying Burrito Brothers,' said Nick, not wanting to be outbid in an obscure country rock bands competition. 'There's also a bit of International Submarine

Band about them.' He sat back, knowing this was a fine, nerdy reference.

Artie Taylor leaned forward and opened his eyes. 'One nil,' he said, grinned, leaned back and closed his eyes again.

'Oh, you're not one of those as well, are you?' said Kaz.

'One of what?' said Nick.

'A rock music obsessive,' she said.

Julie laughed. 'Yes, he is. A massive one.'

Kaz shook her head. 'How do we put up with them, Julie?'

'I dunno. If it wasn't for the mind-blowing sex I'd have left long ago,' she said and punched Nick on the arm, playfully.

'You haven't even got that excuse, Kaz,' said Artie.

'No, well, as you know, I consider you heterosexuals a bizarre bunch of pervs with very weird ways.'

'She must have been looking through the window at us, Nick,' said Julie, grinning.

'Can a man not wear a rubber cat suit in the privacy of his own home any more, without being judged harshly?' said Nick.

Later, as they disembarked at Heathrow, Kaz turned to Nick.

'You're from Teesside, you said?'

'Yeah. We live just outside of Yarm, near to Stockton-on-Tees.'

She nodded. 'Ah yeah, I know. That's right next to Middlesbrough, isn't it? We've worked at Middlesbrough Town Hall a lot over the years doing live stuff.'

'Yeah, you must have.'

'We'll be in your neck of the woods in a couple of weeks, actually,' said Artie Taylor.

'What are we doing?' said Kaz, turning to him.

'There's a blues festival somewhere up there.'

'Oh yeah. Teesside Blues. It's a new one being held on the land of my best mate's dad. Just north of Stockton,' said Nick. 'Should be good.'

'We'll come up and do some shots on one day, I should think,' said Artie. 'I'll have a look and see who's on. If it's anyone interesting, I'll make some calls.'

'We might see you there then,' said Nick.

He put his thumb up.

'You can stay with us if you want,' said Julie, putting her ruck sack over her shoulder. 'We don't live far from where it's being held.' She smiled from one to the other, wrote down their phone number on a bit of paper and handed it to Kaz.

'Cheers, Julie. That's kind of you. We might be two nutters for all you know,' said Kaz.

'Well, we are, so you'll feel right at home,' said Julie.

She and Nick stood and watched them walk away towards customs. One tall and thin, the other short and stocky.

'They're a funny pair,' said Julie, 'Nice. Like an old couple the way they go on at each other.'

'Yeah, they were. The bloke seemed like a right old grizzled rock dude. Straight out of the early 70s. Mind, she's right, they might be really big rock druggie types. A bit risky inviting them to ours, Jules.'

'Nah, they're alright, though our lives probably seem really tame and conservative in comparison to their sex, drugs and rock 'n' roll existence.'

'I don't know. We do alright for the sex. One out of three ain't bad at our age,' said Nick.

CHAPTER 2

'Hello Nick,' said one of the carers on the reception desk of the old people's home that Nick's mother now lived in. 'You're looking tanned. Been away?'

'Yeah, we just got back from California two days ago. I'm still quite jet-lagged.' He smiled back. 'Is mam in the lounge?'

'No, she's in her room. I took her a coffee in 10 minutes ago.'

'How has she been?'

'Bright in the mind, but a little tired though, I think.'

He walked through to her room and knocked. 'Hi mam, it's Nick.'

'Oh, come in, our Nick,' came her voice, still with an East Yorkshire accent.

He opened the oak door and peered into the small airy room which overlooked the gardens and out into the fields around the pretty village of Sadberge, a few miles west of Stockton. Outside a couple of old women sat on park benches beside some rose bushes, smoking and eyeing the stormy sky suspiciously.

'Hey, mam. How are you?'

She was sitting in her armchair by the window, the sun casting a shadow across her lap. It was a nice spot. She looked up at him, her fingers working yarns around knitting needles.

'Hello, our Nick. How nice to see you. Haven't you caught the sun. You're brown as a nut. Did you have a nice holiday?'

'Lovely thanks, mam. Yeah.'

'And how was Los Angeles? It sounds so far away.'

'It was fantastic. We didn't do much. Just walked around, went to some galleries and had a lot of nice food. We went to a steak house on Sunset Boulevard for Julie's birthday.'

'That's good. I'd have liked California, I think. I used to love just sitting in the sun.'

She looked papery-skinned and fragile, but definitely bright in the eye. The fact she had remembered where they'd gone on holiday was remarkable. It really was. For years she'd been adrift in a haze of confusion caused by paranoid schizophrenia and the drugs used to treat it. But now, somehow, the madness that had occupied her to one degree or another for over three decades was washing away. The tide had seemingly finally turned. Maybe it was improved medication or less medication, or perhaps her brain chemistry had actually changed with age. Whatever it was, in the past three months, it was as though she was coming back to life, like a desert plant after a storm.

It was disturbing in some ways because he'd long since adjusted to the idea that she was frail, old and little more than a shell. Now she was a proper person again, it felt like she'd been away from him for so long. It was lovely to have her back even though, in many ways, she was a stranger and not the mother he remembered as a child. The drugs and electro-compulsive therapy had changed her markedly.

'You used to go very brown when you were little. We had a week at Scarborough in 1966. It was early August and the sun shone and shone, do you remember? You went ever so brown that summer and your hair got all bleached from the sun as well.'

'I do remember that, actually. We stayed in a guest house, didn't we?'

'We did. They gave us grapefruit juice for breakfast in tiny glasses. You hated it.' She laughed a little at the gloriously random but detailed recollection.

'The weather in California was beautiful. Jules loves it out there, too.'

She looked at him and smiled with her washed out blue eyes. 'She's a lovely girl, Julie. And kind as well. A kind person is worth their weight in gold. Tell her I asked after her. I'm so glad you found a nice girl. You deserve someone nice, our Nick. You really do. You were always a sensitive boy. I used to worry you'd get hurt when you grew up.'

'Did you?'

'I did, aye. You were such nice boy. From the moment I held you in my arms you were always a nice kiddie. Oh, you'd grizzle and gripe sometimes, but mostly you'd look back up at me and gurgle and laugh. I used to think you were telling yourself jokes. You always seemed to be listening to something and being amused by it.' She smiled at the thought of those days.

'Actually mam, do you remember I said a while back that we were thinking of having kids?'

'Aye. I do.'

'Well...the thing is, Julie got pregnant. But only for 14 weeks. She lost it a few weeks ago. She's fine, but they reckon it'll be unlikely she'll get pregnant again. I didn't tell you at the time...sorry.'

She looked at him again and he saw something that he'd not seen in her eyes since he was 10 or 11, not since she'd begun to lose grip on her sanity: he saw sympathy. She reached out and patted him on the arm.

'Oh, dear. Well, not to worry, Nick. If it wasn't meant to be, it wasn't meant to be. You don't always get what you want in life. Tell her I'm sorry for her loss. I know what she's going through. Same thing happened to me. I was a lot younger than her, though.'

She'd never said this before. Nick sat up and looked at her square on.

'When was this, mam?'

'1959. A couple of years before we had you. 12 weeks I carried it for. People weren't as sympathetic in those days. They said it was because I kept on working. Blame the woman, that was the way back then. But it wasn't that. It was just one of those things. Not everything works out the way you think it might.'

'So I could have had an older sister or brother?'

'Could. But didn't. But that's life, isn't it? It's all a lot of could've but didnt's.'

He nodded and they sat quietly for a while looking out across the garden's summer flowers.

'And are you alright about it?' she said, the needles clicking. 'About Julie losing the baby?'

He wasn't used to his mother asking after him. She hadn't asked after him for over 30 years, so he didn't really feel comfortable answering, but felt that he should.

'If I'm being honest, not really...I'm really upset. I feel so sad that it really hurts. I so wanted to have a little one. I wanted to love them and I felt ready to do it, so I really regret us leaving it too late, but I know there's nothing we can do about it now. Julie would have made a great mother, as well.'

'I understand, but don't let regrets bother you, our Nick. Life is all regrets if that's what you let it be. You can only live one life and make one lot of decisions. You can't have everything, you can't do everything and it's wrong to regret the paths you didn't walk. Do you understand? Just get on with enjoying the life you have. You've got a clever, beautiful girl who loves you. Plenty don't have that.'

'I know and that makes sense, but I just can't seem to feel like that. I sort of accept that it's how I am. I wish I could just feel really happy more often. Even when we were in California and having a good time, there's always this...this...sadness in me...it just won't go away. The most I can do is to distract myself from it.'

She nodded. 'But like I said, when you were little you were a cheerful lad and always liked to chuckle and giggle at things. You were such a giggler. Anything would set you off. I remember you once saw something in a comic about a big dog trying to get into a small house and it just tickled you so much you laughed and laughed for hours. And you were always trying to make other people laugh. That was you. From day one, that was you. Whatever has happened since then, and I know you've had problems while I've been ill, underneath all those things, that happy, laughing boy is still there, Nick. I'm sure he is. I can still see him in your eyes. They're the same bright eyes that used to look up at me from that big old pram I used to push you around in. That's who you are. Just be who you are, our Nick. Remember that through all the bad times. Be who you really are. Don't let life take you away from that. It's like when you paint a door every year. You build up lots of layers of paint over the years but underneath the same door is there...do you get me, our Nick?'

'I do. That's a nice way of putting it, mam.'

'All you need to do is strip away all those layers to find the original door again and you'll find it's just as you last saw it before you started painting.'

'It's hard sometimes though, mam. Too hard. I want to be strong, but it gets exhausting.'

She was nodding while knitting. 'I know. I know it does. God knows, I know. And I'm sorry I haven't been all there for so long. I wasn't around when you needed me as a young lad. You had to cope with growing up on your own because your dad was no use to you, either. It can't have been easy.'

'It wasn't your fault, mam. You didn't get ill on purpose. Life was harder on you.'

She sat and looked out as sun shone through the dramatic rain clouds, casting a heavenly shaft of light from sky to the ground.

'When you were a small boy, you were my little Nick, my little bundle of joy, and I was *so* proud of you. This happy little thing with a nice smile and bright eyes. I was *so* looking forward to caring for you and seeing you grow up from a boy into a man. And...and I didn't. Well I did, I suppose, but I wasn't in any fit state to appreciate it. But now, thinking back to those early days in the 1960s and early 70s when things were still alright, I clearly recall how proud I was of you. It seems like it was literally just the other day now. Somehow, I left myself back there, but I never wanted to. It wasn't a choice I willingly made.'

Suddenly, she gripped his arm tightly with her arthritic fingers. 'I loved you so much, my lovely, lovely little boy and I loved you for as long as I was able to love you and I'm so sorry things didn't go better for us. Do you understand me, our Nick? I did love you. I just went away from myself. But I still loved you as much as I possibly could. Never forget that, you'll always be my lovely happy little boy.' She began knitting again, this time her fingers flying at a speed he'd never seen before, as though she was in a mad hurry to reach the end of the row.

With one final stitch, she stopped, closed her eyes and let out a huge sigh, the way she had often done when in hospital. It was a sigh so big and tired and final that many times when she'd done it, he had thought she had breathed her last breath.

...and this time she had.

In a split-second he knew she had died. It was profoundly obvious: felt rather than seen. There was no coming back. No resuscitation possible. The life that had been there seconds ago, had, in an instant, left. It was as though the air now moved in a different way and the molecules of existence were changed. Two lives in the room had been reduced to one. There was suddenly an unmistakable stillness to her. Wherever she was, she wasn't here now. There she sat, knitting still in her hand, eyes closed: gone.

His mother. Mam. Dead.

As if to prove that life is nothing if not unfair, at the very moment she had recovered some of her acuity and understanding, at the moment when her tortured mind had cleared, at the moment she was finally able to empathise and sympathise, her heart had stopped. The fight was over. The ticking clock, stilled. He put his hands on her warm hands and let out a silent sob, thick tears falling in heavy droplets from his eyes.

'Oh mam, mam...' he said quietly, under his breath, staring at her hands. 'I loved *you* as much as I was able to. If it wasn't enough, I'm so sorry. I missed the real you so much that I grew a shell to stop being upset by it. I'm still your little boy, even if I'm not happy any more.' The tears splashed onto her hands.

It was over.

CHAPTER 3

'I know I'll be in bits when my mam goes,' said Julie as they walked away from the short funeral service the following week. 'Even though we're at each other's throats so much of the time. I'll miss the old shitehawk when she's gone. You've only got one mam and she did bring you into the world. That makes it special even if you don't like each other.'

'Your mam will never die, Jules. She's the living dead, that one.'

'There is a touch of the zombie about her.'

She held his hand as they walked.

'Mentally, I've been prepared for mam dying for literally decades. When she was really ill, I thought she'd just top herself to stop the voices in her head. Either that or have a fatal accident ripping out some electrical wires that she thought were listening to her. It's funny how you run a scenario through your mind so many times that in one sense you're prepared, but then when it actually happens, you realise you're not prepared at all, really.'

'At least you managed to have a couple of good months with her at the end.'

He let out a low moan. 'It seems so unfair. No, not seems. It *is* unfair. Why did she have to suffer like that? She barely lived a life at all for decades. It's taking the piss, it really is, I don't know how anyone can have any faith in there being a god, because if there is a god, they must be a cruel one...they must be...why torture a woman like that? Why give her paranoid schizophrenia so bad that she ripped a clock apart, because she thought the cuckoo inside spied on her?'

Julie made a noise. He turned to look at her, she was smirking while looking at the ground.

'What?'

'Sorry. It is funny that, though. I know it was horrible for her and for you and everyone else - but all the same - pulling a wooden cuckoo out of a clock and wringing its neck...it is funny on one level.' She squeezed his hand.

'It is, like. Can't laugh just now, though. I've got no humour in me.'

They stopped beside her old blue Peugeot 206, climbed onto a field gate and sat looking out over open countryside.

'I keep hearing Johnny Cash singing, "Everything goes away in the end". It's right, isn't it? Three years ago my dad died, our child, now mam. Life feels really temporary.'

She didn't say anything. He let out another, involuntary low moan. 'Somehow, the fact there's a blues festival on Teesside seems very appropriate.'

Sadness is an imprecise thing, probably harder to put a finger on than most conditions. It doesn't really betray itself to the outside world until it is at the most extreme end of the scale and yet it is felt deeply, right down in the bowels of the soul as a palpable, all-encompassing, constant dull ache. It drains joy from things and, like a fractious child, needs to be attended to every hour of the day. When it becomes endemic to your life it casts its shadow over everything. Sometimes separate from depression, sometimes, as in Nick's case, it was part of it, nonetheless it seems an entirely justifiable reaction to life. A feeling of melancholy and loss doesn't feel out of whack with reality, it feels like the essence of it, regardless of whether you're a depressive or you're not.

As Nick dwelt on his losses, whilst he knew that this feeling of sadness was destructive, he knew it was a natural response to what life had delivered. His mother had been right, you can only take one route. You have to make choices all the way along, but how do you cope with the feeling that you'd made a lot of bad choices? How did anyone not have regrets? Not just one or two regrets, but a whole lifetime of them? People often said, as she had, not to have regrets in life and there was a logic to that - but they were just there, in his mind, in his make-up. You couldn't un-think them. You just had to live with them. Maybe it is the very nature of every life. Some people, like Julie, don't dwell, they forget and move on. He couldn't. All he could try and do was keep the blues at bay by any means available to him.

Nick dropped Julie off at the Teesside Women Centre, where she volunteered doing office work, and then drove to Stockton High Street to go and see Jeff in his store, parking on top of the Castlegate centre. Getting out he walked to the edge and looked out across Stockton High Street, the street which had witnessed his journey from childhood into manhood - from the innocence of the happy little, laughing boy, to the upset drunk who felt alone in the world, but who, he now understood, had kept up the happy face to the outside world to mask his deep loneliness. The same street that now bore witness to his deep, gut-wrenching sadness that he would also have to keep from the world. He let out a low, resonating groan in his throat without opening his mouth and trotted down the steps into the market. As he walked past a butcher's stall, a voice called out.

'Nick! Hello, stranger.' He looked up. A fair-haired woman about his own age smiled brightly at him with kind blue eyes. She had straight, shoulder-length hair, parted slightly to one side, even white teeth and a bright smile. She wore a floral blouse and jeans and spoke with quiet, soft Stockton accent.

'Eeee god. Shawn. How nice to see you again, lady.'

He gave her a light hug and took a look at her at arms' length. They'd gone to school together and had shared some classes. As a kid he'd been really attracted to her, but his home life had been falling apart, robbing him of any self-confidence, so he'd never quite plucked up the courage to ask her out properly. They'd met since, a month or two after he and Julie had split up and she'd left the Harrogate flat. They'd even gone on a couple of dates, including one where they'd gone back to her house and fooled around a bit. But he'd been in such a mess after the split from Julie, and had been drinking so heavily, he'd clumsily made his excuses and left before they actually had sex, unable to really deal with the degree of physical and emotional connection at the time. He still felt awkward about it.

Seeing her in front of him like this made his heart leap. In so many ways she was the very embodiment of the regrets that preoccupied him. He regretted not going out with her when he was young, he regretted not having her as a friend, he regretted not having sex with her. He'd always thought she was a lovely person, right back to their teens, but he'd been too dysfunctional to get it together with her at either time. Maybe it wouldn't have worked out, but it'd have been nice to have a go. Regrets. Regrets. One of his life's many what-could've-beens. He knew he was lucky to have Julie, but all those years of heartache before he met her, Shawn might have filled some of those.

'I can't believe I've run into you like this,' he said.

'How have you been?'

'Oh, y'know. Well...actually I just came from my mother's funeral.'

'Oh Nick. I'm sorry to hear that.'

She was one of those people whose feelings you didn't doubt or question, her sympathy always seemed genuine and not shrouded in politeness or affectation. Even when he was an overly needy teenager he'd felt that.

'Yeah. It's sad. She'd started to get a bit better too...y'know...after years of...'

'...paranoid schizophrenia, wasn't it?'

He nodded. 'Hey, let's go and get a coffee, if you've got time.'

'Yeah, OK. There's a place round the corner.'

They walked out of the market and to a café in Green Dragon Yard.

'So how are you, Shawn? You're looking great.'

'I'm fine, thanks, and so are you. You look a lot less chunky than the last time I met you. It looks like you've been working out a bit.'

'Yeah, well, a whole lot has happened since then. How are your boys?'

'They're fine, too. My eldest got married recently and they've just had their first kiddie.'

'So you're a grandma. Good grief.'

'I know. It makes you feel so old.'

'God. Where does the time go? It doesn't seem long since we were at school sitting through those bloody boring chemistry classes.'

'...and now I'm a granny! I know. It all goes too fast.'

She had a softness about her that was really appealing, but also a sadness. There had been problems with the father of the kids and they'd split up long ago. His heart was definitely beating a little faster. You couldn't forget how you'd felt about someone. It was as though he'd put it in storage all these years and seeing her again simply unlocked the box it had been kept in, even though it did seem inappropriate, really.

'So where are you living these days?' she said. 'Still down in Harrogate?'

'No. We live south of Yarm in an old farmhouse.'

'We?'

'Me and Julie.'

'Julie from before?'

He nodded. 'We got back together about three years ago now and moved back up here. It's a run-down old place we're renting, but we like it. It's quiet and rural. How about you?'

'I still live in Norton in the same house. It does fine for me on my own.'

'You're still single, then?'

'I'm not interested in a long-term relationship now. Not at my time of life. It's all too much trouble, too much heartache. I can't be doing with it. That probably sounds a bit mad cat woman-ish...or dog woman, in my case.'

'Not really. No. Not at all. I totally understand. There's too much obsession with being paired up in life.'

'But some things have changed. I gave up smoking.' she grinned at him with an even, white smile.

'Wow. But you loved smoking.'

'I know. But I wanted to get a bit more fit and it was the obvious thing to stop doing. It wasn't easy. I still fancy a fag from time to time. The smoking ban has helped, like.'

'Well good on you, man. It's good not to have your life controlled by something like that, I reckon.'

She nodded. 'So you made it up with Julie, eh. I did wonder what became of you. Must have been five years or so since we last met. When I last saw you, you were...'

'...in a bit of a mess? Yeah. Sorry, Shawn. I had a lot of issues going on. I don't think I behaved very well. I still feel bad about that.'

'No need to apologise.' She grinned a little. 'It was obviously a difficult time for you.'

'Last time you saw me, I was a bit of a drunk. Well, a lot of a drunk.'

'You were, all right. You were a good listener, but mostly just very pissed. A lot of us are a bit like that in the northeast, aren't we? We grew up with it being normal.'

He wasn't sure how much to tell her really and he feared making himself look bad. *"Just be yourself, our Nick"*. His mother's voice was right in his ear as though she was alongside him. He looked to one side, half expecting to see her there. How could it be so loud and clear? As loud and clear as if it was a recording playing in his ear through headphones. He cleared his throat.

'I've stopped drinking now. I changed my life around to try and get healthy. I eventually realised I'm some sort of depressed person and that's what was the root of all my problems. So I went into therapy.'

She raised her eyebrows. 'Really? What's that like?' She put her teaspoon down quietly as though not to interrupt him. It seemed such a small but nice, thoughtful gesture.

'It helps me keep my darkest moods at bay a bit and slowly I've got less depressed more often.'

'I didn't actually realise you suffered like that.'

'I didn't understand it very well back then and had no way to talk about it even if I had. I see it all more clearly now.' He pushed his hair behind his ears and smiled at her.

She nodded. 'Did you two have kids then?'

He winced. 'No. Sadly not. Nearly, but...it didn't work out. I'm sad about that. I envy you having two grown-up lads. Two young men that you've nurtured and supported and given unconditional love to. I wish me and Jules could have shared that.'

'It's not exactly a bed of roses. I envy you having a partner. It must be nice to be able to share things with someone special.'

'Yeah. I am lucky. We are really daft about each other.'

'See, I've never had that. Not that real big intense love that people talk about. Not even with the kids' dad. It was something, but it wasn't that, like.'

'Well, I was daft about you at school, you know.'

She smiled nicely. 'I knew you liked me. You were quite shy.'

'I wanted to ask you out for about three years.'

'Well, you should have. I'd have said yes. I really liked you. You knew I liked you. My friends even told you.'

'Yeah, I did. I was emotionally paralysed somehow. I just couldn't do it. Here's a mad question. What do you think would have happened to us?'

'What? If we'd gone out? I don't know, do I? I remember I liked you because you were quite a gentle soul and you made me laugh. You were a bit different to normal lads, but it's impossible to tell, isn't it?'

He smiled. 'I liked you for the same reasons. When we met again, I thought you'd not changed at all. It was like meeting the same girl. Maybe we don't change much, not fundamentally.'

'It doesn't seem likely that we'd have lasted, does it? We were just kids.'

'Yeah. Of course. Lately I've been wondering a lot about the paths I took in life and feeling like I took some wrong ones, a lot of wrong ones. Not going out with you was one of those. I always thought we had something between us. A connection. Did I imagine that?'

'Probably not,' she said, quietly with a reflective smile.

'Even if we had crashed and burned, which as you say, is more than likely. Then at least we'd know.'

She gave him an almost winsome look.

'That sort of thinking can really mess you up, Nick. If you don't mind me saying, it's sort of immature. Childish, really. Almost a bit creepy. We could have fallen madly in love and had lots of kids for all you know or we could have ended up hating each other. But it's all bit silly to think about, isn't it? A waste of time. Life has beaten romance out of me, I'm afraid. So, you know...I don't give such things much thought at all.'

'Yeah, I know what you mean. And you're right...this is just how my mind works. I dwell on things, I don't seem to have a choice in the matter. You know, you don't really look any different from when we were 15.'

'Oh, I'm sure I do. I'm a crumpled old bag these days.'

'I dunno. Some people turn into unrecognisable older people. You just look like an older version of your young self.'

'I remember you as being very boyish. You really don't look boyish any more. You look like a middle-aged man now.'

'I'd give anything to get some boyishness back, but you can't.'

She brushed hair from her eyes and sipped at the coffee.

'You can't live in the past or wish for things to have turned out different. It'll bugger you up good and proper if you do. What's the point? Just learn your lessons and move on.'

'That's a good attitude to have.' He tried to shake himself out of this frame of mind. He was being too intense and probably a bit weird. You didn't launch into serious shit like this as soon as you met someone.

'Are you having a mid-life crisis of some sort, Nick?' She smiled sympathetically at him.

'Ha, well, if it is, I think I've been having it since I was 15.' He shrugged.

'Men seem to suffer from this more than women. I wonder why?'

'I don't know. To me, it's nothing to do with being male, it's just a human thing about feeling you've less years left than you've had. Mam dying has just made me more reflective.'

She shook her head and dabbed a gentle touch on his arm. 'No, it's how you're made up, really. It's not a general thing. A lot of people, most people probably, they don't feel like you do. They just get on with life and don't dwell on things. You...you go too deep. It doesn't get you anywhere.'

'Yeah. I know it's not an attractive quality to have - introspection.'

'I don't know. You're just sensitive and that's nice. You were always like that as a teenager, as I recall - but there's sensitive and then there's self-obsessed and, y'know, there's being downright soppy and daft. And you're right, that's not an attractive quality. Like I say, it's a bit creepy.' She poured them more coffee. 'Have you tried anti-depressants?'

He shook his head. 'No. They've got such a poor success rate. I don't want to go through a suck-it-and-see thing, then end up taking the wrong one, get suicidal and top myself. It happens to enough people to make it a big worry.'

'They helped me a lot when I was depressed after breaking up with the kids' dad. But you can become reliant on them. Still, don't rule out something that might help you.'

'I just mistrust doctors, that's my problem. I've seen some really bad ones - so much so that I think at least two of them were actually just people off the street who had sneaked into a doctor's office. Then again, they'd probably have been more sensible than the doctors, when I come to think about it.'

She smiled. 'We've all been there, I think.'

'But you're right. I should be more open-minded about it. Since Julie had the miscarriage...'

'...did she miscarry? Aw, poor lass.'

'Yeah, it was just a few weeks ago, actually. Since then I've really felt sad. Really had the blues, y'know? Feels like they'll always be with me. Sorry, I'm being a self-indulgent, boring sod again, I know.' He shook his head and looked up at her. 'So where are you working these days?'

'I work for a women's charity in Middlesbrough.'

'Oh, right. That's funny, Jules volunteers at the Teesside Women

Centre. She's hoping to get a job there later in the year if their new funding comes through.'

She nodded. 'Oh yeah, well, I know it well. I've probably met her, you know. There are lots of events that we do together. What does she look like?'

'Blondish longish hair, about your height, she has very turquoise blue eyes and these sort of arched eyebrows which make it look as though she's rather bemused with whatever you're saying. You'll have heard of the Wells brothers when we were kids - legends of the Hardwick estate.'

'Oh god yeah, that rings a bell. They were always fighting.'

'Yeah, well, she's their younger sister. They're not much less scary now. Jules is the only person they take notice of.'

She sipped at her cup. 'Does she by any chance like rock music, can't dance to save her life and have a terrible singing voice?'

'That's her. Dances like a robot on a magnet and makes the noise a wounded animal might make after being caught in a trap. Bless her.'

She nodded. 'I was at a do at the Penny Black when she was there. She "sang" something I'd never heard of on the karaoke.'

'It'll have been by Heart or Pat Benatar. She loves Pat Benatar.'

She laughed a little. 'I do remember her, actually. I remember she was wearing black jeans and a white denim jacket.'

He nodded. 'That's definitely her.'

'Eeee, that's funny. So that's your Julie, is it? She's more glamorous than I thought she'd be.'

'She does scrub up well for a hard lass.'

'Eeee, well I never. She's very good looking...'

'...to be with a scruffy git like me...?' he interrupted. 'People do say that. I agree, though Jules would complain that they were objectifying her and there's nothing she hates more than women being objectified. And to be fair, her admirers don't have to put up with her broccoli farts, or hold her hair back while she pukes up in bog after too much wine. So they see the best of her.'

She laughed loudly and threw her head back. 'Well, she seemed very nice at the Penny Black. A good laugh, like, and not afraid to make a fool of herself. I'll probably see her next week actually. There's another do up there...'

'I'll tell her to say hello.'

'Well, it's been lovely to see you again,' she said, finishing her coffee and picking up her bag. 'I'd say we should go out for a drink, but that'd probably not be appropriate now, would it?'

'Maybe not. Look, here's my email and contact numbers. Stay in touch, Shawn. I've lost touch with far too many good people in my life for no good reason other than lack of effort due to self-absorption and I don't want you to be another one of those.'

She took the card. 'OK, I will.' She kissed him on the cheek, gave him another smile and left. She still had a distinctive way of walking: a kind of fast shuffle. He'd always liked that. And he was still really attracted to her. He couldn't help wondering what sex with her would have been like. Really bloody good, in all probability. She had that quiet but passionate thing going on. Yeah. Bloody regrets. She seemed so sensible. Sensible people were to be admired. They were the quiet heroes who went about keeping the world together while the flaky lunatics like him messed about like overgrown children. And she wasn't that different to Jules. Maybe he was just attracted to women with blondish hair and blue eyes who quietly looked like they could give you a good time in bed. It wasn't his worse character trait.

He was about to walk down to Jeff's record shop on the High Street, but then realised he didn't have time because he had a session with Marc Lewis, his therapist, and had to get to Harrogate within an hour and then see Mike, his accountant. He took off down the A19, taking the A59 outside of York and heading west to the well-to-do town where he'd lived for nearly 20 years.

It was nice to come back. The bad times when he and Julie had split up still haunted him a little, but he'd had some good times in the town as well. It all felt like an entirely different life now.

He'd been making twice-monthly visits to Marc Lewis for over two years. All he did was talk about himself and his life, which naturally felt massively self-indulgent and went against his instincts even now, but somehow, it did help with his depression. It worked as a pressure valve even when he wasn't actually there. He always knew that whatever happened to him or however he felt, he could always talk to Marc about it. OK, he paid him to listen, but that was better. It was an honest relationship. If you talked to a friend they were emotionally obliged to be on your side or to be supportive, even if they didn't want to be or couldn't be. That was far too much of an imposition. At least if you paid someone to listen to you they had to do it and both parties knew where they stood.

He'd missed the last appointment because of their holiday, so this was his first visit since Julie had the miscarriage.

'Come in, Nick. How are you doing?' said Marc Lewis, ushering him into his airy, bright, tall-ceilinged office and gesturing him to sit down on a leather chair, while he got coffee for him from a machine. He was in his mid 30s with a receding hairline, but disturbingly hairy arms and a rather unctuous, accentless voice.

'I've got a double dose of bad news, Marc. My mother died last week right in front of me and Julie had a miscarriage a few weeks ago. I should have emailed you but I couldn't face it.'

'Oh, Nick. Gosh. Quite a few weeks. I'm so sorry to hear both of those things. Your mum was unwell for some time, wasn't she?'

Nick hated her being called mum. It was mam. It had always been mam. Mum was too middle-class. Mum was a whole other culture to his.

'Yes. Ironically, she'd improved a lot in the last few months, but she was tired and...well...her time was up. She died right in front of me. I'm sort of glad about that.'

'Interesting. Was it not upsetting for you?'

'Yes. But it was...real. Does that make any sense? It's been easier to deal with because I saw her go. She wasn't in pain. It was as though her switch had just been turned to off. The best way to go, I think. She died knitting as well, which she loved. It'd be like me dying just as I put a Little Feat vinyl album on.'

Marc Lewis nodded, though he almost certainly had no idea who Little Feat were. 'And how is Julie after the miscarriage?'

'She's fine. It was all over very quickly and painlessly.' He wobbled his leg agitatedly, then stopped as he saw Marc Lewis had noticed it. 'She just woke up one morning, got up to go to the toilet and...and that was it.'

'Poor lady. How upsetting for her.'

Nick nodded. 'She was upset. I've tried to be strong for her, y'know. Be supportive, like. We both knew it could happen, that it was likely to happen, really.'

'Even so. I know how much you were looking forward to being a dad.'

'I was, yeah.'

'How has your mood been since?'

He didn't reply for a minute, weighing up how to express it. He held out his hand and wobbled it.

'A bit odd really, to be honest Marc. On the surface I've been keeping cheerful for Jules. I don't want her worrying about me, even though I know she does.'

'That's thoughtful of you. But underneath?'

Nick cleared his throat. He'd long since learned that he got the most out of his talking therapy when he was totally honest with himself and with Marc. The trouble was, being open and honest was bloody painful. He rubbed the stubble on his chin and let out a low moan in his throat.

'Underneath...' He shook his head and stared at the patterned wool carpet. 'Underneath, part of me feels utterly crushed and I feel guilty about that. I feel like I should be able to be stronger and just move on. I want to, but I can't seem to let myself. I don't know how to.'

In saying the words, the emotional seal broke which had kept his feelings about the miscarriage at bay for weeks. The tears welled up in his chest and were out of his mouth in big heaving sobs before he could stop them. It was embarrassing but briefly uncontrollable. He put his hands over his face. All the upset and disappointment leaking out of his eyes.

'Don't be ashamed to cry, Nick.'

No, no. Shut up. He didn't want to hear that. He wanted to be told to pull himself together. That's what he needed to do. Get it together. Come on. This was no good at all. Letting yourself get crushed by your emotions achieved nothing. Sometimes you just needed to swallow it down and be strong. Sometimes you needed to be sodding repressed and Northern. Sometimes you just needed to be a man, in the old-fashioned meaning of that word.

He wiped at his eyes with the back of his hand. Marc Lewis handed him a tissue. Nick tried to calm himself. This was pure self-indulgence. Pull yourself together, man. He took a drink of coffee and let out one slow, shuddering breath, getting control back.

'Sorry, Marc. It's just that we had this new future ahead of us and now we don't. I feel empty in comparison to how I felt before. The thought of being a dad had made me really happy and fulfilled. I really wanted to look after our own child. To see them grow up into an adult. To feel proud of them. To love them. Now...I just wonder what it's all about.'

'"It"?'

'Life. What's it all about if it's not about that?'

'That's quite an existential question, Nick. It's understandable you might feel like this, though. It may be a cliché, but time is a great healer.'

He nodded. 'I just feel this really deep sadness in me now...it's not like my worst depression, though. If it was, I'd probably know how to deal with it better these days. But that's definitely not it. It's just...I don't know any other word to use other than the blues. It's the blues, Marc. No matter how I try to dress it up, this...' he thumped his chest with his fist, '...this empty feeling is in me because that future with a child has been taken away from me. It's no-one's fault, it is what it is, and I have to just put up with it, but I know now I'll never really be happy again. I'll have moments of happiness, and joy and pleasure, I know that. But that feeling I had when I thought of raising our own child, that won't come back. It's gone now. So I think, all in all, feeling really fucking sad is a sensible reaction to all of that. How the hell else should I feel? If I can't be sad about that, what can I be sad about? But I don't want to talk to Julie about it because it'll upset her. And to be honest, I don't think talking about this will help. Even talking to you about it here won't help. It's just life, isn't it? You can't always get what you want, sometimes you've just got to try and get what you need.'

Marc didn't spot the Rolling Stones reference. Typical. He lost more credibility points for that.

'Is Julie coping?'

'Jules is strong and pragmatic by nature. She was upset initially, of course, but she's already moved on. I'm not sure that I'll ever be able to do that in the same way.'

Marc Lewis nodded, fingers placed together to a point.

'I've...I've even tried to...this will sound mad...I've tried to wipe the feelings away...by...by having a lot of sex. I thought it might help somehow and, as mad as it sounds, it does. For a while, or for a few minutes, anyway.' He felt embarrassed even talking about it, aware it made him seem like some sort of pervert or weirdo

'I take it you mean with Julie.'

'Yes. Of course with Julie,' he said, a little bit indignant and a little bit annoyed that he thought anything other than that. How well did he know him, really? He wouldn't go seeking it with anyone else, would he? Good god.

'I think that is understandable, Nick.'

'Is it?'

'I think so. Intimacy is much to be valued in relationships. It would be easy after something like a miscarriage for that to fall by the emotional wayside. I hear what you're saying that it's a...a distraction technique if you will. I understand that. It's a way to make yourself feel better. You could do a lot worse, more destructive things.'

38

Nick winced inwardly. Emotional wayside? There was something so monumentally poncy about Marc Lewis at times.

'It won't take away your pain or sense of loss, though. At some point you do need to address that. Maybe not now, but sometime.'

'No. Well, it hasn't taken away the blues except for the few minutes we're actually doing it or thinking about doing it. But to be honest Marc, apart from sleep, that's the only time I don't feel upset. Otherwise it's with me from the first seconds of consciousness to the moment I fall asleep. So I've sort of relished it really, for that reason as much as any other.'

'As I say, I don't think it's the worst idea as long as Julie is fully on board and doesn't feel bullied by you.'

'Oh god, no. I'd never do that. We're very...y'know...compatible, in that regard, like. She's always keen. Sorry, that makes it sound like she's a bit of a....I just mean we've always enjoyed each other, physically.' He inwardly cringed at that expression and felt awkward beyond belief.

Marc Lewis nodded and gave him a sickly smile. 'Good. But if you've not discussed this aspect of your relationship recently, I think you should, at some point, tell her about this. When you feel you can.'

'Yeah, I will. I just...it's a hard thing to talk about, really.'

'I know. But from everything I know about her, she's on your side. She'll understand.'

Nick nodded, but feared it was all a bit too weird for Julie and that it'd seem like he was disrespecting her by using their sex life as a kind of psychological balm.

'But what I've realised, Marc is there are nice things, good things and happy things, but they're always fleeting. Most of it is just getting by, getting through and trying to be at ease with your lot at any given moment. It's just an endless parade of ifs, buts and what might have beens. All the different routes you might have taken, different decisions you could have made - it can eat you up inside. It does really eat me up if I let it. So for all I know you tell me it's good to talk about stuff and talking has helped me deal with my depression, outside of that, I think there's much to be said for swallowing your blues down and just trying to get on with life. Dad dying, mam dying, the baby...not making it to term...this is life. Death is life. I don't like it. That's the problem. I want life to be nicer. But it isn't. So I don't want to talk about it any more.'

'OK. Fine. But my advice to you would be not to just try and bottle this up, Nick. Don't just try and ride it out.'

Nick snorted the beginnings of a laugh, but then stopped because he could see Marc Lewis hadn't got the pun.

'Talk to Julie about it all. Find a place to resolve this feeling you have.'

After he'd left Marc Lewis' office, he sat in his car, closed his eyes and took a nap for 10 minutes. He was exhausted. Exhausted by the therapy session, exhausted by life. Sometimes it felt all too much to bear and if there was a chance it would suddenly all stop, he wouldn't put up any fight at all.

CHAPTER 4

He went into a Costa for some green tea, then popped into Jeff's store on Commercial Street and said hello to Luke, who now ran it full-time for Jeff. His accountant, Mike, had asked him to look in at his office when he was next in town, so that was his next stop.

Nick liked Mike. He was a phlegmatic East Riding Yorkshireman, not easily impressed by money or by lack of money or by anything, really. For Mike, life was to be endured, sorted out and a line drawn under it. He hated disorder or lack of planning and couldn't see why anyone tolerated it. His idea of a holiday was to go to Poland to see the sites of the Nazi concentration camps. Perhaps accountancy forced you to confront man's greatest inhumanities to man.

In the 13 years he'd been Nick's accountant he'd often had to negotiate payment plans with HMRC to sort out tax Nick owed. He'd had to advise him on bankruptcy and even tried to show him how to keep records of his income and expenditure. All to no avail. It was a foreign language and no amount of exhortation to do it made it any less incomprehensible. It was hard to take it all seriously, really. The fuss and bluster the revenue made if you didn't pay them was all hot air and everyone knew it. If you had no assets and no money to pay them, there was sod all they could do about it.

Above all else, like Shawn earlier in the day, Mike was sensible. Nick liked that about him, admired it, even. He was blunt, prosaic and well organised. You need the Mikes in your life. As he got older, he appreciated the quality of sensible more and more and had often wished he had a little more of it in his own character. It was the sensible people who created the warp and weft of life's canvas that creative, messed-up people like him could embroider on. He'd been slow to appreciate that.

Nick wandered into Mike's office, sat down and waited for him to come in. He had a small shelf on which two vinyl records rested. He wasn't a collector like Nick, he had just refused to change to any other format on the principle that it was a great way to listen to music, so why change? Nick looked at the two records. One was Dylan's *Highway 61 Revisited*, the other a copy of Jefferson Airplane's *Volunteers*. He slid it out of its sleeve as Mike came in.

'It's a nice original UK copy this, Mike, first pressing, too. Worth a bit of money. Their political album. "Up against the wall muthafuckers" and all that, though ironically, they were coining it big at the time and moving out to some nice big place in Marin County.'

He was a sombre-looking man, about the same age as Nick with a salt-and-pepper beard and close-cropped dark hair. It was as though he had modelled his look on the 1970s political exiles from the former USSR.

'I always thought the Airplane were more cut out to be revolutionaries of the mind rather than the streets. You can't exactly riot while you're off your head on LSD, can you? Still, some decent sentiments on that record. I just bought them from Jeff's. Luke gave me a discount. Nice lad, him. Skin like a five-day-old pizza though. Sorry to keep you waiting. You didn't come down just to see me, I hope.'

'No, I was in town, anyway. How's it going, Mike?'

'All good. I asked you to come in to sign this. It's just your finance deal so you can keep paying a monthly amount to us for our work and you won't just get a massive bill one day. HMRC have gone quiet since you settled your debt to them three years ago. I had feared they might want to audit you, but they seem to have found some other poor sod to harass.'

'I don't mind paying taxes, I just mind what the governments do with it...or don't do, more precisely. And I object to being hounded by them for a few quid, whilst the millionaires and billionaires get away without paying anything.'

Mike raised a dark eyebrow and nodded vigorously. 'Indeed. Who amongst us does not feel like that? Bastards, eh. Talking of which, Jeff's brother is actually Stevie Salmon, the comedian, isn't he?'

Nick nodded. 'It's a bit complicated, but they only realised they were brothers a couple of years back. Why do you ask?'

'Yes. I remember you telling me about all that. The thing is, right, you get to hear things unofficially on the grapevine in this business. Tittle tattle mostly, but strictly between you and me and these four walls, a little birdie tells me that Mr Salmon might be a naughty boy when it comes to his money.'

Nick sat back in his chair and put the record back into the cover and laid it on his lap. It seemed an odd thing for Mike to say.

'Should you be telling me about this, Mike? Isn't it all confidential accountant-type info? In fact, doesn't the Data Protection Act cover this sort of thing? I mean, I'm not going to tell anyone, but...'

Mike shifted in his seat and raised a dark eyebrow again.

'Let's just call this a bit of gossip. An off-the-record chat. What do you know about him? Stevie, that is. I seem to recall you talking about him in less than glowing terms.'

'Oh, I just can't stand him. He's a boorish wanker. Exactly the sort of bloke I dislike the most. Big Fish - that's what everyone calls him - is probably a multi-millionaire. He earns a fortune off his DVDs and he does massive tours which sell out to people who think he's telling it like it is, when in reality he's just playing to their bigotries. And he's got these terrible catchphrases...'

'"Yerjokinarntya?" and "Talk to the beard"?'

'That's them. I mean, what do they even mean?'

'Peculiar. They're some sort of rhetorical device that means, you're wrong, I'm not listening to you, or I think you're talking rubbish. I was watching something online and I just don't know what people get out of it. He was telling this joke, "How come fat people have got a chip on their shoulder about being fat? Surely they've eaten all the chips." And it gets a big laugh and people yell out "talk to the beard" afterwards. I think they must all be hypnotized.'

'Yeah, it's not exactly Chris Rock. He's started using the Boro's match-day music "Pig Bag" when he finishes his set. The crowd all sing the catchphrases in tune with the music. It's totally bizarre, but they love it. He's mega-popular these days.'

'My favourite comedians are George Carlin and Bill Hicks, so maybe I'm not exactly in his target demographic.'

'Good choices, Mike. Hip even.' Mike ignored that. Such a thing would mean nothing to him.

'There was another joke about farting during sex. Not my thing. The jokes, I mean. Or farting during sex.'

He spoke in such a dry, flat Yorkshire monotone that at first it wasn't at all obvious when he made a joke.

'Well regardless of what we think, he's massively successful. And on top of that he's just opened a chain of chip shops all over the northeast called, inevitably enough, "The Big Fish".'

'Yes, indeed, so I understand. It's an all-cash business is a chip shop. Very useful, that. They were always a favourite target for tax inspectors back in the day, along with fruit and veg shops. When it's all cash you can keep as much back as you like and who is to know? They were only ever nabbed when they got greedy and were living in a big house while declaring tiny profits. A few grand here or there was hard to spot. Many a good working-class fortune has been built that way.'

'Well, like I say, Big Fish really must be worth a fortune, Mike.' Mike shrugged, his mouth set on the expression dial somewhere between grim and sour.

Nick had always liked how money didn't impress Mike at all. In an age so obsessed by defining itself by what it had acquired, from cars to houses to overpriced designer clothing, meeting someone who couldn't be hypnotized by big numbers was rare and very refreshing. Nick had the feeling that even if he turned up one day having won a 100 million quid on the lottery, Mike would just shrug, scratch his beard and say, 'That's not that much really, not when you put it into perspective,' or he'd come out with one of his favourite expressions, 'How much money do you really need?'

The accountant sat back in his chair, arms folded across his chest. 'See, the thing is, I'm all for everyone paying their fair share. An old-fashioned notion, I'll grant you, but the way I see it, we all have to live here together and so we should all support each other in proportion to our income. Nobody should be left behind or excluded.'

Nick nodded. 'Jules would kiss you if she heard that. Very much her way of thinking.'

'But not yours?'

'It is, but I'm more pragmatic. To be honest, if I could screw HMRC for a few hundred quid I bloody would because I feel like the system is basically unfair. In the same way, I'd never rob from a small business, but if it was from a big corporation, I'd not think twice if I knew I could get away with it.'

'Like most people in that regard, I imagine. As you say, the system is unfair. It takes too much from the vulnerable, the poor and the defenceless and leaves the rich to pretty much do what they want. When I hear about someone as wealthy as Mr Salmon potentially not paying his share and hiding money from the public purse...or worse...it rather annoys me. We've got people on 400 quid a week having to cough up money they can barely afford in tax, so why should he get away with not paying up? It's just greed. That's all it is.'

'I agree. Plus, I don't like the man. He's crass and he likes banter.'

'Banter? What's banter?'

'You know. Blokes being blokey with each other - especially blokes being blokey about women, drink and sport. Piss-taking and that...'

'Oh, aye. My old dad used to say that it was the stupid people that always have the most to say. He wasn't wrong.'

Nick laughed a little. It seemed a typically dour Yorkshire view of life, but not far awry of the truth for all that.

'Why are you telling me this, Mike? Other than as a bit of gossip.'

He took out some papers from his folder and pushed them across his desk. One was a publicity poster for the Teesside Blues Festival stating who was playing, ticket prices, location etc.

'I was sent this by a contact. He thinks there's something iffy about it, he thinks Salmon is laundering money by putting this festival on. That's what he's heard. I was wondering if you'd heard anything similar?'

Nick shook his head. '"Laundering money"? What does that actually mean in reality?'

'In this case, that he's got a lot of cash that he wants to legitimize. Say you put a band on and their fee is 30 grand. You agree to pay 20 of that in cash and 10 into their account, but state in your books that their fee is 10 grand. The band pockets the 20 tax free and you get to understate your costs and thus inflate your profits. That way you achieve two important things. You get rid of a lot of your dodgy money and in doing so you create a company - or in this case a festival - that looks far more profitable than it really is, thus allowing you to sell it on at a value far above its actual worth, usually before the tax is due on those profits. The money you get for the sale pays off the tax owed, you pocket the difference - a tidy profit - and more importantly, all that dirty money you had has now been cleaned up and legitimized. As long as you keep it all paper free and no-one blabs about cash payments and why would they? It's hard to detect and quite simple to do. Even if someone does talk, as long as there is no hard evidence of cash changing hands, nothing much can be done.'

'Wow. I find it hard to keep track of the money in my bank account, let alone anything more complicated or devious.'

Mike drummed his fingers on his desk, stared at the desk, thought for a moment and then looked up at him. 'A lot of people are rightly pissed off, that after the banking crisis, the public are being asked to cough up to solve fiscal problems that are not of their making, while the rich bastards that largely caused it busily stash away cash and cheat the system out of millions. A lot of people think it's wrong. There's a lot of bitterness. There's a general feeling that life is significantly more unfair for regular people than at any time in the recent past, isn't there?'

This was as animated as Nick had ever seen Mike. He obviously was talking very personally. He was in danger of showing passion and he never did that. Like many Yorkshiremen, he mistrusted displays of emotion and saw them as the province of the weak, the deranged and the Southerner.

'I agree. Me and Jules have been talking a lot about it. How come we bail out banks for billions, but can't find a few quid for things that really help people in need, like the Teesside Women Centre Jules volunteers at? It does just seem fundamentally wrong to the point of immorality. It's nakedly the case that the elite are getting rich at our expense and worse still, it feels like the government is either encouraging it or is powerless to stop it. It is depressing. I grew up with the idea of a meritocracy being the gold standard for a society, but now it feels like the money keeps the money, the old boys' act drives it and the rest of us can go to hell, regardless.'

Mike nodded vigorously. 'That old tradition of the banks being bastions of responsibility and civic status that we grew up with has been wiped out. They look worse than bookies, much worse. I have no faith in the system any more. It just seems fundamentally unfair. I see people here every week who are being shut down because the banks don't want to help them to the tune of a few 100 or 1,000 pounds, the same banks that simply threw good money after bad just a few months ago. They're breaking people's lives on the back of utterly discredited economic and moral thinking. We're penalizing the poor in order to bail out the rich and we're all just supposed to just look the other way while it happens. People are right to be angry.' He looked at some papers on his desk and went on. 'You know, the Salmon family own a lot of land around Teesside and right up into Durham. On top of that they have one of the most successful racing stables in the country.'

'I know Brian Salmon a bit. He's a really nice chap.'

'Is he? A nice chap, who is resident in the Bahamas much of this year.'

'Really? I didn't know that.'

'He has a residency at Sandy Lane. He's richer than God. Between him and his son they are easily one of the richest families in the north of England, which is why attention has fallen on Stevie being behind this festival. Will you be working there in any capacity or meeting up with him?'

'I've not been asked. Me and Jules will go. It's only a few miles from our house and I want to support a Teesside music festival.'

'Pity. Will Jeff know anything? Is he close to his brother?'

'No. Not close as such. He sees him regularly. That's not quite the same thing. I'll ask him if you want.'

OK. Thanks. Just keep your ear close to the ground. The things to look out for are bills being settled in cash...'

'...in fairness, I'll not see anything like that happening, Mike,' interrupted Nick, feeling this was all a bit odd and un-Mike-like.

'People get careless. You might get talking to someone in a band who has been paid cash. Of course, it's not illegal to pay people in cash - only to not declare you've done so. All we're doing is trying to gather any evidence we can, if indeed there is any evidence to be gathered. You're under no obligation, obviously. I just think this sort of scam is despicable. It means all the honest, law-abiding workers have to cough out more for the government to waste on shit that none of us want.'

Nick grinned at his bone-dry humour.

'There's nowt in it for you apart from the satisfaction of doing the right thing, though considering some of the scrapes you've got into, doing the right thing seems to have always been quite important to you. That's why I asked you.'

Nick considered it for a moment. Julie would certainly approve. Jeff almost certainly wouldn't, but more importantly, who was this 'we' Mike was almost sub-consciously referring to?

'Well, it's funny really because coming back from California, on the flight home from LA was your man, Stevie Salmon and at the time we said he looked really nervous. We joked he was probably smuggling drugs. I mean, obviously, he wasn't...'

'...you don't know that,' said Mike quickly and pointed at him.

'Well no, I don't, Mike. But it seemed unlikely.'

'Why?'

Nick shrugged. 'I dunno, really.'

'Someone must be doing it. Why not him? I bet he was travelling first class.'

Nick nodded.

'Aye, his sort always do.'

Mike didn't approve of First Class, either financially or morally. He'd mentioned it before.

'More likely is he was bringing cash in from an offshore account.'

'That's a bit fanciful, isn't it, Mike? California isn't even offshore as such, is it?'

'No, no. He goes to the Cayman Islands, takes out his money, flies to Brazil, then the USA and then back home. You can get a lot into a well-hidden money belt or strapped somewhere. Not 100 grand, but 10 or 20 thousand on every trip would be a cinch. He could have been bringing cash in for this festival. Or he's just got money stashed in safe deposit boxes all over the world, from one venture or another. That'd work, too.'

'Well, he's a massive fat bloke so there'd be plenty of room to hide rolls of notes under his fat.'

'I know you're joking, but that could be true. Anyway, just keep an ear open would you, Nick? I'd like to help this contact out on this. He's very much on the side of the little guy.'

'Yeah, OK Mike. I can't guarantee I'll be of any use, though. Me and Jules don't ever spend any time in his company, precisely because we don't like him, so I'm not sure we'll hear anything.'

'Fair enough. But if Salmon is laundering dirty money, you'd want to hammer him for it, wouldn't you?'

'Totally. Yeah. If he's screwing us, let's bloody nail him.'

'Good lad.' They shook hands and Nick left feeling like he'd agreed to something, but wasn't quite sure what.

The following morning Julie greeted him as he came down from breakfast. She was holding a piece of paper.

'You are now looking at Julie Wells, MA,' she said, her face alight with pride. 'And no, MA doesn't stand for Massive Arse.'

'Yes! Get in! Not in the massive arse, obviously. You got the notification then? Was that the postie just now?'

'Yup. I passed it with a distinction, which means I'm officially a dead smart lass, me, like.'

He scooped her into his arms and lifted her up. 'Aren't you clever? Well done, Jules. It'll be funny you not going up to Durham University any more. Unless you're staying on.'

'Time to get a job, I think. We need money. I just got an email from Diane Edwards congratulating me though, which was nice.'

'That was nice of her. How is she?'

'She took a long time to get over the breakdown, but she's in a good place now. She's going to resume work in the autumn, I think. Yeah, it'll be strange to leave it all behind. Going there changed my life, or it coincided with my life changing; getting back with you, moving here and everything else that's happened to us.'

'So are you still going to try and get a job at the Teesside Women Centre?'

'I'd like to, but there's nothing available that I'm qualified for. I'll need to do some more training - preferably while working there. I might have to wait a while until the next round of lottery funding. If they get what they're after, they can employ a couple more people. I might have to do a bit of temping until then. I can do that with my eyes shut and at least it'd bring us some dosh in.'

He nodded. 'Cool. OK. It feels like we should do something to celebrate your degree, but we're totally skint after California. In fact, skint would be living high on the hog compared to what we are.'

She looked out of the window. 'It's a lovely morning, why don't we just go for a bike ride? I stripped, cleaned and repaired those old push bikes we got from the auction rooms. We should take them for a run.'

'Alright. I tell you what, let's go and look at where they're putting together the Teesside Blues Festival outside of Norton. There and back is about 20 miles. That'll be plenty for us. I've got something to tell you about the festival. I've been talking to Mike the accountant. For one reason or another, he thinks it might all be a big scam to launder money.'

'Really? I hope Big Fish is going to get busted. Hold on, I'll pack us some scran and a flask of tea. We can pretend it's the 1950s.'

They took Yarm Back Lane and went north towards the western edge of Norton, joining up with Junction Road and stopping at the Blakeston Lane turn off, which ran out of town and into open countryside. Nick wiped the sweat from his brow and looked up at the sky. It was almost cloudless and now a classic hot, blue July summer day.

Julie took off her baseball cap and took a drink of water from a bottle strapped onto her bike.

'God, we've hardly gone far and my thighs are aching. You wouldn't think it was such hard work, would you?'

'Even the slightest incline seems tough, and not getting crushed under the wheels of a lorry, even harder.'

They cycled out of town into open countryside and stopped to look at the open fields on Brian Salmon's land where the festival was due to be held. Construction of the main stage was already well underway as was the fencing in of the land so that people couldn't get in for free. A smaller stage for acoustic and comedy acts was already built and a marquee being erected around it. In the distance a field was being readied to serve as a car park and beyond that land set aside for camping.

She poured them some tea from the Thermos flask. 'God, I didn't realise this was going to be such a big thing. How many are supposed to be coming?' said Julie.

'About 15,000 a day for three days. All paying £75 per day. It's the best part of four million quid in gate receipts alone, before you even look at the money from licencing, media stuff, renting out merchandise and food stalls. I bet he'll pull in six or seven million in total.'

She drank her tea. 'Christ almighty. That's amazing. Must be a good profit when you don't even have to rent the land or anything.'

'He'll coin it big style, man,' said Nick, enjoying quenching his thirst.

She rested on her bike. 'Eeee fizzin' hell. It stretches right to the north and the east. They're putting up toilet blocks here an' all. I suppose 15,000 people is a lot to accommodate, really. We won't get a lot more than that at the Boro next season now that we've been relegated.'

'They're doing a campsite on the other side of the woods and there's going to be a helipad in one of the fields on the eastern edge of the farm to bring the bands in and out. It's Teesside's Woodstock this, man. It's dead exciting, I reckon. I was reading last night that it's almost sold out already.'

She took a drink of water again and nodded. 'Aye. We need a bit of rock n roll on Teesside. It's really progressive of Brian to use his land like this.'

'Well it's all Big Fish's idea, isn't it? Brian is living at Sandy Lane in the Bahamas, according to Mike. I do wonder how much he knows about what is going on.'

'I always liked him. He's a gentleman in the old-school style. I wonder if he knows his son is up to his neck in dodgy money, if what Mike told you is to be believed.'

'I bet he's totally coining it from those chips shops he's opened, imaginatively called "The Big Fish". No-one loses money selling fried potatoes, do they? Not in the northeast, anyway.'

'It's immoral, if you ask me,' said Julie, squinting into the sun.

'What? Selling fried potatoes?'

'Ha ha. I mean, screwing your tax, especially when you're loaded. I hope he gets found out.'

'Alright Jules, I'm sweating too much to listen to a socialist lecture about taxation.'

She curled a lip up at him in the manner of Elvis Presley.

'What's right is right, baby.'

'I know. But it's all a bit out of our league, isn't it - high finance, I mean. Last time I looked, I'm £2,230 overdrawn, so if he wants to divert some ill-gotten gains into my account, he's quite welcome to. It's hard to keep your principles when you're skint.'

'That'd just be redistribution of wealth. I'm all for that, like.' She gave him a cheeky wobble of the head.

They finished their tea and rode around the narrow country lanes that formed the boundary of the site, arriving at a big field north of Norton which was going to be the car park. As they did so a small, two-man helicopter, the sort used for crop spraying, came into view, heading up from the south and circling the site. They watched as it came in to land at the far end of the car park. The rotary blades were cut and once they had come to a stop, two people got out of the chopper.

Nick pointed in astonishment. 'Look who it is! It's bloody well Jeff!'

'Fizzin' hell, it is an' all!' She jumped up and down and waved at him, shouting his name. He stood for a moment, surprised to see them there, then waved back. He slapped his companion on the back, who headed in the other direction towards the Salmon farmhouse and stables, and then came over to them.

'Now then, big man!' shouted Nick as he approached the fence where they were standing. 'Is this how you're getting around these days?'

Jeff grinned, his long greying hair tied back in a pony tail, a blue collarless shirt worn loose over jeans.

'Not bad, eh. He picked me up just outside Harrogate.'

'So how come you get this special treatment?' said Nick.

'I'm working for the festival, aren't I?'

'Are you? Eeee. You look like Harvey bloody Goldsmith or someone,' said Julie, excitedly.

'You never said. How long has this been going on?' said Nick.

'Not long. Just since you were on holiday. I've not seen you since you got back, have I? I was going to email you about it, but it's all been a bit hectic. The festival has been on and off, but when they got the go-ahead from the council after some legal objections were overruled, suddenly it was all systems go and as a result they were short-staffed. Hence, I have been recruited. That's El Fat Fisho's chopper. I was shitting myself up there. You feel like you're floating and could just fall out at any minute because the sides are open.'

'Well we're on push bikes. You're putting us to shame,' said Julie. 'Hey we saw your brother at the airport with some other bloke. Did Nick tell you?'

'Aye, you said in your email.'

'We thought he was smuggling drugs. He was dead nervous.' said Julie. 'Sweating buckets, like.'

'That wouldn't surprise me at all. That'd have been his business manager that he was with, Simon Garbutt. Wouldn't surprise me if they were dodgy.'

'You reckon?'

'Oh, aye.'

'Got any evidence of that?' said Nick, thinking about what Mike had said.

'Best not to ask or look too closely. There's got to be a lot of slush money around the comedy game, hasn't there? And even more around those fish and chip shops he's opened all over the place...or the plaice - ha - bloody hell, it's wasted on you, this level of sophisticated comedy. I mean, it's all cash-in-hand, isn't it? So who knows where all the money goes?'

'Is he screwing the tax, do you reckon?' said Nick.

Jeff laughed. 'Wouldn't surprise me if he was screwing the tax with the help of the actual tax people, HMRC, like. He's always taking tax bloody inspectors out for expensive dinners and to that titty bar in the Boro that he's invested in, the GC.'

'I think that's disgusting,' said Julie, flatly. 'On all levels.'

'No-one wants to have to pay more tax than they have to though, do they?' said Jeff with a shrug.

'I don't bloody care. We've got this thing called society, right, and we're all in it, so we all have to pay our fair share,' she said, scuffing the ground with her Adidas trainer.

Jeff held his hands up. 'Alright, Lady Lenin. Come the revolution and all that. So just having a bike around the site are you? What do you reckon?'

'We were just saying how big it is,' said Nick.

'Yeah, it's a big site, alright. There are so many regulations to follow and admin to sort out. All I'm doing just now is finalising the bands that are on, largely because The Fish couldn't tell the difference between B.B. King and Burger King.'

'Is it not all sorted yet?'

'The top bands are, it's just a few of the first and second on the bill to get sorted and the acoustic stage where we're putting on comedians and one-man bands...'

'...and one-woman bands as well, I hope,' added Julie.

'Yeah, yeah, don't worry about that...we've got three folky strummer lasses with long straight hair, severe fringes and floaty dresses doing that oh-my-god-I'm-so-fragile thing. The sort of shite that John Lewis use for Christmas adverts.'

Julie tutted and rolled her eyes.

'Oh god. I wish more lasses would just play rock 'n' roll. That wimpy, "Oooh look at me, I'm such a delicate little thing" really gets on my mammaries. You wouldn't catch Pat Benatar doing that.'

Jeff hi-fived her. 'Amen, sister. Sadly, we couldn't get the Benatar and anyway, the younger generation likes its music overemotional and fringe-based and we've got to think of them for this festival. We can't pack the bill exclusively with the sort of old farts we'd like to see. After all, we've got Blues Machine headlining on Friday night all the way from Macon, Georgia, they're fantastic southern rock. YYZ on Saturday, who are about 24, but play like a power trio you might have seen in 1971 and T-Bone Boogie Band are winding it up on Sunday night with their heads down, no-nonsense grindcore boogie.' He did an approximation of The Twist.

'Nice moves, son,' laughed Nick.

'We've got the new YYZ album,' said Julie. 'On vinyl an' all. They stuck in my brain because it's one of my favourite Rush tracks is YYZ.' She made an air guitar pose.

Jeff made a nod of his head at her. 'What's she like, her? My Rita wouldn't know Rush from thrush.'

'Sadly, not all women are red hot rock chicks, like our Jules, she'll be wanting a backstage pass to hang out with all the bands,' said Nick.

She laughed and punched him on the arm. 'I went through a phase of dating blokes in groups, actually. Every single one of them was a total shagger. Would do it to anything with a pulse. Some of them would have done it to road kill.'

'That's not so much because they were rock musicians, Jules, that's because they were men,' said Jeff.

'True. Are you coming over to ours for your tea then?' she said.

'Aye, I will, as I've not seen youse two since...err...you know...so thanks Jules. Are you OK now? After the...'

'I'm fine, thank you Jeffrey,' she said, expressing their mutual awkwardness by addressing him formally. 'But it's not like I was ill.'

'Aye. I mean no. Good. Err...not good, I mean...so California was good, then?'

'We had a great time, aye,' said Nick. 'I tell you what though lad, those jeans are hanging off you. They just about fit where they touch. You must have lost more weight since we last saw you,' said Nick.

'Nowt fits us any more. I need a whole new wardrobe. Rita keeps saying we should go shopping, but that way lies madness.'

'Shopping for clothes is a deeply upsetting experience,' said Nick. 'It can break even the strongest relationship, can't it, Jules?'

'He goes all sleepy and sits there like someone's grumpy dad while I try on clothes. It's embarrassing. We don't do it together.'

'I like the clothes you buy, I just don't want to be there when you're buying them. Not unless you're trying on underwear, anyway.'

'You're not allowed to do that,' laughed Julie. 'It's unhygienic and especially unhygienic if you were sitting there watching me.' She raised an arched eyebrow at him and laughed happily again.

'Cool. OK. Right. I'll be done by about seven, so I'll get a lift over to yours after that.'

'How's he getting on with that Rita lass, do you know?' said Julie as they watched him go.

'He doesn't talk much about her, but I have the feeling it's getting quite serious. He spends a lot of time over at her place in Hartburn and I know she's been staying down at his flat in Harrogate. So I don't think they spend much time apart, one way or another.'

'Aw, that's nice. Will they get married, do you think?'

'Jeff? Yeah. Well, I reckon Jeff would in time, maybe. Not yet. They've only been going out for about four or five months. It's too early yet, I reckon.'

'Maybe if they do, we could have a double wedding? Me and you and him and her, like.'

He turned to look at her. 'I thought you were against the whole idea of marriage.'

She shrugged. 'I'm against what it traditionally means, but I know that's not why you want to do it. If it'd make you happy, I'd do it. It'd be a laugh. Mam and all my family would like it as well and we'd have a massive party. There are positives about it. You talked about it a while back. Do you still fancy it now that we're not having a bairn?'

He got onto the bike and rested on the saddle. For no reason he could understand, his long opposition to marriage had melted away in recent months. It was something he felt awkward about because he could make no logical argument as to why marrying Julie would make the slightest bit of difference to them and he assumed it wouldn't. It was irrational but then, love was irrational.

'I do, aye. But not a big grand affair in a church with bridesmaids and all that. Just a registry office thing would be good.'

She smiled. 'Alright then, well, why don't we sort it out?'

'Really?'

'Yeah, really. I'm not taking your name though. I want to remain a Wells. Julie Guymer sounds....weird...and anyway, it's totally out-moded, isn't it? Taking the bloke's name. Positively medieval.'

'No. Of course not and I wouldn't want you to. I love you as a Wells, not as a Guymer. But I don't want you to do it just as a favour to me. I want you to want to do it.'

She shook her head. 'You're a funny bloke, you. I'll love you either way, won't I? Legal contract or not. Is it because you're insecure or something? About us, like?'

He took a drink of water from a bottle and thought about it. 'Yeah, I think it is a bit. Is that mad? Mam dying has made me realise just how ephemeral life is. I think I want something to anchor us and tie us down together.'

'Oooh, err...are we having a bondage wedding?'

'No...but...you know what I mean though, don't you?'

'Sort of. But I'm going nowhere, am I? And anyway, being married wouldn't stop me if I wanted to, would it?'

'No. I know that. Maybe it's more to do with acknowledging how special we are, to myself as much as anyone else. But as I've said before, I can't argue you a case for it. Anyone that says they can is lying, at least if they're not religious. There is no logical case to justify it other than as buying into it as a social construct. It's really just a mental thing.'

'I sort of understand. I do kind of like the idea of us officially being a couple. And I'm happy to do it for you, but I can't pretend it's mega important to me, 'cos it just isn't. Sorry. It never has been. All that gooey shit about weddings has always gone over my head since I was a kid. The whole institution has always seemed mostly to do with subjugating women to men. I know that's not how you see it, obviously, but that's why I never liked it. On top of that, as over 40 per cent of people who get married get divorced, it's not exactly working very well. Sorry.' She smiled at him and flapped her arms up and down as though to express her indifference.

'That's fine, man. I know where you're coming from. I really do. We don't have to.' He took another drink of water.

She shook her head. 'You obviously want to. So let's do it. But you've got to propose to me first.'

'Eh?'

'You've not actually asked me to marry you.'

'What? I've got to actually ask?'

'Of course you do. I can't say yes unless you ask me, can I?'

An idea struck him.

'Alright, but I want to do it somewhere special.'

'Where's that, like?'

'Follow me.' He got on the bike and pedalled off.

CHAPTER 5

This was a big moment in his life. He'd never asked anyone to marry him before and damn well knew he'd never ask anyone again. It was such a strange feeling. Somewhere in his heart he wanted them to be the married couple his parents hadn't been. Loving, communicative and happy. Maybe he wanted to prove he was not like them. It was stupid, really but then life isn't always logical nor sensible. You just coped with it the best way you could and the thought of marrying Julie gave him a feeling of warmth, pleasure and security, even if there was no obvious reason why it should over and above living together. So if he was going to propose, there was only one place he could really do it. The place which symbolised where he was from.

'Where are we going?' shouted Julie from behind him as they headed east towards Billingham and up Haverton Hill Road. He pulled into a bus stop lay-by alongside the prilling tower; an industrial obelisk that was part of ICI Billingham when he was kid. It was 100 feet tall and made of almost featureless concrete slabs. The top fifth was an offset block, giving it its distinctive shape. You could see it from a distance all over the area. All around it was industry. Even on a warm blue summer's day, it looked hard and industrial. In the distance were the Cleveland Hills. Nature was always somewhere close on Teesside, that's what made it so special.

They got off and looked up at it.

'We're stopping here?' said Julie, taking off her baseball cap and wiping sweat from her forehead.

"Just be who you are, our Nick". His mother's voice was in his ear again. It sent a shiver down his spine. It was so clear and so intimate. Closer than close. He had to turn around again, just to make sure she wasn't standing there, but of course, there was nothing but the industrial architecture.

He looked up at the prilling tower and took her hands in his.

'This is Teesside to me. When I see this thing, it takes me back to being small, to being who I was, or who I really am, or something. This is the essence of me and of the region. This is sort of what made us who we are...so...' he got down on one knee, held her hand and said, 'Will you marry me, Jules?'

She laughed and looked away from him for a moment, her eyes glazed with a tear. 'Eeee god. I feel a bit choked-up. Must be the ammonia fumes around here. Trust you to get all romantic with me, standing there with a massive erection.' She pointed at the tower.

'You don't normally object.'

'Ha, ha. No, I don't, do I? And I'm not going to object to it now. Of course I'll marry you, you big soft clart. You're the only man I've ever properly loved; the only man I'll ever properly love.'

He stood up, took her around the waist and lifted her feet off the ground

'Thanks, Jules.'

'Eeee fizzin' hell. You know how to woo a lass you, eh? Smoking chimneys, industrial wasteland and gas pipes.' She kissed him on the lips. 'That's proper Teesside love.'

He held her close, feeling the heat radiating from her skin, feeling almost embarrassed by how much love he felt for her in that moment.

'C'mon, let's get home,' she said, after a few seconds. 'I can already feel your love is inevitably turning to lust.' She brushed his hair out of his eyes and gurgled a laugh. 'Either that are you are getting turned on by noxious gases.'

By the time they got home, neither of them could walk properly.

'Every muscle on me hurts.' said Julie, struggling to walk through their front door. 'And my arse is red raw. God, I'd forgotten how bloody knackering cycling is.'

'I'm seizing up. My legs don't work properly,' laughed Nick. 'We're such old, knackered bastards.'

Jeff turned up at 7.30.

'Hello my lovelies. How are we?' he said putting a bottle of wine down onto the kitchen table.

'We're both shagged out from cycling. We hurt in places we didn't know we had,' said Nick.

'It's cruel and unusual punishment is cycling. That'll teach you.'

'But we've got some good news', said Julie, taking the wine bottle and getting a corkscrew.

'Oh, aye. What's that?' said Jeff.

'We're-gettin'-married,' said Julie in a sing-song voice, while doing a little jig.

Jeff looked from one to the other, mouth open. 'Bloody hell. You're not, are you? I thought you weren't into that.'

'It's my idea. I wanted us to,' said Nick. 'I really fancy it now.'

'Cool. Well, congratulations,' said Jeff. 'I know you'll both be happy because you're already happy. I take it I shall have an invite to the piss up?'

'Of course. You'll be my best man.' said Nick.

'Yup. In charge of wrapping him in cling film naked and tying him to a lamp post.' said Julie. 'If you do that I want photos, by the way. I fancy seeing you wrapped up in clear plastic.' She pulled a lustful face a him while laughing.

'I shall look forward to that. You can't beat a bit of cling film-based bondage. And while we're dishing out happy news, I've got something to tell you.'

'Are you opening a third shop?' said Nick.

'Better than that. Me and Rita are with child. She's having a baby.' He made a big wow face.

Julie let out a howl of shock. 'Eeee fizz me, Jeff. You! A dad! Eeee my god. Eeee, come here you big lummock.' She gave him a hug. 'Well done. You must be delighted, like. You are, aren't you?'

'Aye, I'm well chuffed. I've known for a couple of weeks, but I didn't want to mention it because...you know...'

'Oh man, I can cope with other women being pregnant, even if I'm not,' she said, slapping at him.

Nick stood up and held out his hand.

'It's a turn up for the books this, man.'

'Aye. Just a bit. Obviously, as you well know...there are issues and that.'

'How far on is she?' said Julie.

'Well she's already 16 weeks gone. She thought all that sort of thing was done because she's 48. She was in me and Nick's year at school, after all, like. So it's all a bit dodgy really, but she seems healthy enough and we're over the most dangerous period, apparently so...fingers crossed. Her doctor had a 50 year old give birth to a healthy baby this year, so there's a chance it'll all be OK. Well, you two know all about this.'

'Eeee well, send her my best,' said Julie, grinning. 'You'll make a good dad, Jeff.'

'Aye, I hope so. I'll be an old dad though so I'll have to be as immature and childish as possible to compensate. I'm probably like you were, Nick. I don't want to get too hyper about it in case something goes wrong.'

Nick nodded. He felt so bloody conflicted. Pleased for Jeff, but instantly quite insanely jealous, and he'd never felt jealous of Jeff in his life. 'Well, what will be will be,' he said, then immediately felt that was a little too fatalistic and didn't have the right degree of warmth about it. 'I'm sure it'll all work out well for you both. Are you going to move in together?'

'Aye. I'm coming up here. Lukey will run the Harrogate shop and I'll run the Stockton one. It'll work out well, I reckon. So I'll be around a lot more after the summer, if you'll have us.'

'Cool. Well you'll have to get everything ready for the little 'un,' said Julie, taking some ham salad out of the fridge. She looked at him and grinned again. 'Eeee, well I never. It's all change, eh.'

'Aye. It is. Never thought it would happen to me and a girl from Stockton, to mis-quote Squeeze. I ran that Harrogate shop for years. I thought I'd be there forever, living the bachelor life, pissed every night. In a way, the heart attack was the best thing that happened to me. Forced me to change my life.'

'Yeah, it's funny how things like that work out. We probably wouldn't have got back together if the Boro hadn't done so well in that 2006 UEFA cup campaign. You never know what's around the corner, do you?' said Julie.

'Oh hey, while I remember, I can get both of you work at this festival if you're up for a little bit of nepotism. If you can't give work to your mates, who can you give it to?'

'Oh, aye. What's that?' said Nick.

'They need someone to do admin in the office. Answer the phones, do email, organise things. Obviously it's only for the next few weeks. Brian's house has been converted to admin office central.'

Julie put her hand up eagerly. 'Please sir, I can do that.'

He laughed. 'Aye, well I wasn't going to ask Nick, was I? I've seen the state of your computer - nothing filed where it should be filed. It'll be 500 quid a week. Alright?'

'Brilliant. Thanks mister. It'll be fun to be involved, actually. A bit different from volunteering at the Teesside Women Centre.'

'I dunno. You might find a few abused women at the festival...sorry, that was in bad taste,' he said, hastily apologizing after seeing Julie raise an arched eyebrow at him. 'And I can get you some work doing website, social media and press work if you want, Nick. You know all the bands and musicians anyway, so it won't be hard.'

'Sure. I can do that.'

'Cool. I'm, not sure exactly how much work there'll be for you to do, so can you just stick an invoice in at the end of the festival and I'll get you paid out? It might even be cash in hand.'

'Great. I love a bit of cash.'

'You'll both need to turn up to the admin meeting tomorrow. The gaffer will sort it all out and show you what's what.'

'Ah. No problems. The gaffer? You mean Big Fish?'

'Nah. It's El Fishy Boy's company that is putting the festival on, but he's not running it. He'd be rubbish at that. He's as thick as gravy, him, man.'

'Yeah, he was never the brightest at the *Echo* when he was there with me.'

'He's contracted a company to do the whole thing, or rather, Simon Garbutt has.'

'And what are you responsible for, exactly?' said Nick.

'I'm going to find that out tomorrow as well. Like I said earlier, I'm co-ordinating the booking of bands, finalising the running order, humping gear and err...what's the wanky word for talking to...'

'Liaising,' said Nick. 'Everyone who wants to make themselves look important, calls talking to people "liaising".'

'OK, well I'm liaising with the security team to get all the gear and the musicians in and out. It's hardly sophisticated stuff or they'd not even be letting me near it. Mostly it's pointing at people who are humping boxes and shouting, "Put that there!". The Fish is a bit paranoid, likes to get people he trusts or who owe him favours on board. I think I can do it. I used to run the Entertainment Society gigs at Poly, remember? And that largely involved organisation of box humping and the hosing of lager into failing rock bands' open mouths. Plus I can point with the best of them. Look.' He pointed a few times into the air at random. 'See, I'm a natural.'

Julie laughed and rolled back and forth on the balls of her feet.

'That's true. I always thought you'd go into pointing work. You're a natural for walking around with a massive bunch of keys clipped to your belt like every self-important sod who works in rock venues,' said Nick, warming to the idea.

'Ha, ha. I do love all that, actually. Keys maketh the man. Anyway, point is, it's not going to be that difficult a gig. The guy responsible for putting it all on is Mel Stephens from Showstoppers, who I know from way back at Newcastle Poly. Remember him? His mob of roadies and sparks used to help out our mob of beer-bellied reprobates and feckless HND electronics students when they could. We always got on OK.'

'Oh yeah, the Mel Stephens who used to organise the roadies at Newcastle City Hall back in the day?'

'The very same. Only he's about twice the size he used to be, is now bald, has a tattooed head and he smokes a cigar constantly. He looks like a total lunatic, but he's actually alright. I met him earlier this week, briefly. He comes on like a Geordie WC Fields crossed with a Hells Angel these days. His team know how to run a thing like this with their eyes closed. It's only 15,000 - not exactly the Isle of Wight Festival.'

'And you're full time on payroll as well, then?' said Julie.

'I am indeed. I'm getting some mega wedge for all this. Five of your English grand.' He held his hands out and made a face. 'I know. Great money for basically telling people where to go, but then I am family and the Salmons are collectively probably the richest people anywhere from here to Edinburgh unless the Duke of Prunes, or whatever his name is who own all that land out by Skipton, is visiting.'

'Duke of Devonshire, I think it is,' said Julie. 'I'd dispossess the old fart and give his land back to the people he stole it from in the first place. It might have been 500 years ago when he took control of it with a private army, but that still doesn't make it right.'

'Bloody hell, comrade. I didn't realise you were such a Commie, Jules,' said Jeff.

She frowned and dismissed his comment with a wave of her hand. 'Oh, it's all bollocks that, putting labels on stuff. I just hate the way the rich coins it off the back of the working class and then blames the working class for being skint and goes after them. Seems like if you scam £20 on the dole you're a criminal, but if you scam 20 billion you're free to do whatever you want.'

Nick nodded, adding, 'Like Dylan said, "Steal a little and they throw you in jail, steal a lot and they make you king".'

'I wouldn't tell the Big Kipper that...' said Jeff.

'...the Big Kipper?' laughed Nick.

'Aye, or whatever...I can't call him Stevie, can I? As I say, no mention of left-wing stuff in his presence if you want your money. He knows as much about politics as I know about hallucinogenic frogs...'

'...you know quite a lot about hallucinogenic frogs, don't you?'

said Julie. ' Didn't you try licking a load of them up by Cow Green Reservoir when we went up there looking for magic mushrooms that time?'

'I was bluffing. The only toad I know is the drum solo of the same name by Ginger Baker. In the same way, the Big Bloater there, he wouldn't know free market capitalism from free Matalan carpet, but he likes to think he's some sort of entrepreneur and all left wingers are hell bent on redistributing his wealth, preferably at the barrel of a gun.'

'I'd put my hand up for that job, like,' said Julie. 'After he'd paid me my money though, but.'

'Rightly so. But until the revolution happens we'll all meet up at Brian's farmhouse tomorrow at 10, OK?'

Nick wondered if he should tell him about what Mike had said about money laundering, but it didn't seem like the right time. And what could he actually say, anyway? Plus, he was pretty sure Jeff wouldn't care one way or another if Stevie Salmon was defrauding HMRC of millions of pounds and since he and Julie were about to benefit in a small way from his largesse, maybe it'd be churlish to say anything. They badly needed the money, without it they probably won't be able to make the next rent payment.

Later that evening, after Jeff had left, Nick was in bed as Julie came into the bedroom and took off the band that had held her hair in a pony tail.

'I feel so bruised up me doo-dah, off that saddle,' she said, pulling down her trackie bottoms. 'Amazing how cycling can knack you so much when you're not used to it.'

'Aye. I still hurt an' all.'

She went into the bathroom and shouted through to him.

'What a shock about Jeff, eh?'

'I was stunned me, like. And jealous as well.'

'Are you? It seems unfair. They weren't even trying and it happened anyway. Is there any reason why he's not brought Rita around yet? I've not even met her in the pub yet.'

'Neither have I, man.'

She reappeared at the door brushing her teeth.

'Have you not?'

'Nah. I do remember her from school.'

'What was she like back then?'

He put his hands behind his head. 'She was nice. Quite exotic really. I remember she had soft brown eyes and was quite tea-coloured. I think her dad might have been from the Middle East. She had lovely straight dark mahogany hair. Anyone not 100 per cent white seemed exotic back then, though, didn't they?'

'Oh god, aye. I went out with a lad whose grandma was from St Kitts. He was ever so slightly not white and I was disappointed when I found out both he and his parents were born and brought up in Port bloody Clarence. Thought I'd bagged a proper foreigner.'

'Rita always seemed quite knowing, if you know what I mean. Like she was more worldly-wise than me or Jeff.'

'Lasses always tried to affect that air, man. We knew no more about owt than you did. I bet you'd have thought I was like that.'

'I bet you *were* like that.'

She laughed. 'I liked to think I was...but I wasn't really.' He went back into the bathroom. He heard her gargling mouthwash.

'Do I need to put any pyjamas on?' she said, coming back in, unfastening her bra and idly scratching a nipple with an index finger.

'Aye, it's not that warm tonight, Jules,' he said, throwing her pyjamas towards her, his mind unable to stray far from thinking about Jeff becoming a father. It seemed really bloody unfair, somehow. He wanted to be a dad. Why couldn't he be? Jeff wasn't really bothered, either way. That was uncharitable and selfish, he knew that, but it was how he felt, all the same. It was really troubling him and he didn't know how to shake feeling upset by it. He needed to untie his mind from the knots he was twisting it into.

She took off her underwear and stood at the end of the bed, hands on her hips. 'Do I have to spell everything out to you?'

He looked up from winding his old bedside clock. 'Eh?'

She stood and looked at him, shaking her head, a wry look on her face.

'What?' he said again, still dwelling on things.

She pointed at herself up and down. 'Do you want to have it off with us, like? Eeee fizz me, it's a good job I'm not big on romance, isn't it? Since we just got engaged I thought we might celebrate it with a bit of the old naked in 'n' out business. Is that clear enough, or do I have to get a film of it off the internet for you?'

He let out a sigh as she got onto the bed. 'Sorry. I get you now. In and out, you say. Right. I'll try and remember that.' He was trying to make a joke of it, but was fairly sure she hadn't been fooled.

She looked at him quizzically. 'Are you alright?'

'Yeah, I'm fine,' he lied.

She looked back at him as though searching for something in his eyes.

'Alright then...' She turned onto her belly on top of the bed and lay flat out. '...you can start by massaging all my sore bits, which is basically all of me from the waist down.'

He straddled her across the back of her legs and rubbed at the back of her thighs with his thumbs. 'They're quality bits these, mind.'

'Aye well, go gentle, remember, I've already had one painful ride today.'

Ten minutes later he looked down at her a little breathlessly, a bead of sweat rolled down his temple and dripped onto her left nipple. She opened her eyes as she felt it splash onto her and looked back up at him, frowning and then put the flat of her hand on his chest to make him stop.

'What's up? Is everything alright?' he said, slowing down.

'What's going on?'

'Eh? I don't understand. We're...you know...making love.'

'No. We're not making love. You're just having sex with me. That's not the same thing. You're doing it to me, not with me. That's not you...you're not like that. I don't like it. It's so....so blokey. Gerroff us. What's the matter with you?' Her tone was one of confusion more than annoyance.

'Sorry, Jules.' He rolled off her and lay on his back, suddenly feeling guilty. She turned onto her side and propped herself up on her elbow.

'Come on then. Talk to me about it. I know something is going on in that weird brain of yours. You've got some daft idea going on...I know you have. Don't try and hide it from me. Is it Jeff having a baby or something?'

He didn't say anything. She'd pin-pointed it in one.

'Nick, man, if something's wrong, you have to tell me. Is it me? You just...just...doing me...it's like you're just thinking about yourself and you've never been like that with me.'

She brushed hair out of his eyes and kissed him on the cheek and gave an encouraging little laugh.

'Owee mister, you're usually a class act in bed, you. I want that Nick back or I'll have to resort to self-abuse and I don't want to do that, not unless you're there to watch me, anyway.' She stroked his chest. 'C'mon, tell us what's wrong.'

He closed his eyes and licked his lips. He had to, now. He couldn't pretend any longer - it wasn't fair to her. *"Just be yourself, our Nick"*. He took an involuntary, sharp breath as he heard his mother's voice inside his head again. It was so shocking and briefly upsetting to feel like she was there beside him.

'Oh, alright. But this will all probably sound very weird.'

'Don't worry about that. I'm very open-minded, aren't I? I mean, remember what we did in the hotel in Santa Monica? You don't do that if you're not open-minded.'

He made his mind up just to be honest with her. Be himself. 'Yeah. Well, what it is...the thing is...sex helps me forget. It takes my mind off things. It stops me from thinking and it makes me feel a bit better. It's become a way to get a bit of relief from myself and I'm sort of using it like...I dunno...like a kind of medicine.' He looked away from her. 'I know that's very messed up. I'm really sorry.'

She furrowed her forehead.

'To forget what? Forget the baby?'

He nodded. 'To forget that and the road that future led down...everything that lay on that path - all the things we're now never going to experience. Just now I was thinking if I did it faster and harder, then maybe it would knock the jealousy I feel for Jeff further to the back of my brain or that it would drown the sad feelings. The more intense the sex, the more it blocks out the bad stuff, y'see. Sorry, Jules.' He felt stupid even saying it. It was so selfish and so self-absorbed and so typical of him.

'So it's like doing a physical thing to forget the mental thing? Is that it? It's a distraction for your brain?'

'Sort of, yeah. And it relaxes me and briefly unties the knots in my brain. It's almost like I can get away from myself for a few minutes. You know that moment when you come? When the orgasm is at its peak, just for those few seconds, it's like I'm living in a different body and I'm free of all the emotional clutter of life. It wipes all that away for however many seconds it is and, honestly, that's such a relief.' He let out a sigh. 'Sorry. It doesn't make much sense. I don't really understand it myself.'

She made a small groan.

'Well...it does make sense, man, in one way at least. It's raising your dopamine or serotonin level or whatever it is. Sex makes you feel nice, so it's not that hard to understand that you might do it to take away feeling sad. I get what you're saying. But it's no good when you get so obsessed with it that you're just pounding away on me like I'm almost not even here. It's really...it's really unpleasant and I don't want it to happen again, right?'

'Sorry.'

'Don't keep saying sorry. I'm not mad at you. I just wanted to understand what was going on and I want you to know how I feel.' She curled a strand of blonde hair around her finger and thought for a few seconds. 'Is this actually why we've been doing it so much in the past few weeks?'

He sat up and put his arm around her bare shoulders. She leaned into him. 'It's how it started. So, yes, sort of, but also, obviously, me and you have always been good together like that, and the more you do it the more you want to do it. So it's all mixed up, really. But yeah, it is.'

'I knew something was going on in here.' She knocked on his head with her knuckle. 'I just couldn't work out what it was. But not even you can shag enough to keep all those thoughts at bay for long. You do know that, don't you?'

'Yeah. I know. It's not a solution. Like you said, it's a diversion tactic. I can't focus on the sex to exclude all the other ghosts in my head forever. I really wanted it to work again because I couldn't shake the thought of Jeff having a bairn and us not...'

'...and did it?'

'No. Hence my imitation of a Black and Decker. God, I feel like I'm a sicko, even just talking about this.'

'But you're not depressed, are you? I know when you're depressed. When you're down, you don't want to have any naughty at all. In fact, you've been in an upbeat mood if anything.'

'No, this feeling isn't like my old depressions. It is related to them, but it's something else. It's a layer deep inside - all the other stuff - the day-to-day moods are on top of it. It's the blues. That's what I've been calling it to myself and to Marc Lewis. It's the pain of life, if you want. That's wanky, I know. I can't think how else to express it. The pleasure of sex relieves it, if only briefly...and honest Jules, just to have a few minutes away from the hurt is more important than anyone with a non-tortured brain can imagine. Just to stop feeling the ache inside for a short while is such a relief. I just wish I could live without having to feel it at all.'

She didn't say anything for a couple of minutes, content to just rub his belly as though to comfort him. He went on. 'And, while I'm confessing everything, this is just really embarrassing, but I'm just going to say it anyway. Just anticipating us doing it, is a kind of distraction as well...that's how it all started. Before we went away I was thinking about you...you know...when I was on my own...' He cocked an eyebrow at her.

'...oh you dirty little sod.' She said it with a laugh in her voice though.

'...and while I was doing that, all those worries and regrets all got pushed to one side in favour of thinking about you in the holiday underwear.'

'You're mad for that underwear, like.' She drummed her finger on his belly contemplatively and looked at him fretfully, 'I wish you'd said about this before. I've *told* you not to keep stuff to yourself.'

'I was embarrassed, Jules. And it is weird, isn't it? I'm not wrong in thinking it's weird.'

She shrugged. 'I dunno if it's weird or not and I don't really care either way, I'm more bothered that you actually feel like this. You've been through a lot recently with the miscarriage and then the loss of your mother.'

'When I was a boozer, I'd try and drink things off my mind. Try to drink away my blues. I'm probably trying to do that with sex instead. Addictive personality and all that jazz.'

'Well at least you don't get a hangover from sex. Well hung, but not well hungover. Ha ha...I should sell that joke to Big Fish.'

He put his hand across his face and covered his eyes. 'I feel monumentally bloody awkward even admitting to any of this, but Marc Lewis said I should. He didn't think there was much wrong with it.'

'Well, I know you don't like him but he's often right. You don't need to be...y'know...uptight about it. I know you're a loony, don't I? I expect you to do weird things. Sometimes, I'm surprised you don't behave more oddly and ask me to dress up as a nun or something.'

He pushed her hair behind her ears and looked in her eyes. 'Well, if you could put on a curly wig and pretend to be Graeme Souness in 1976, I'd be very grateful'

She shook her head and laughed her woody, rolling laugh. 'I might say the same thing to you. Look, I'm happy racking up another 3,000 on my sex-tastic total in the next month, if it would help you, but I don't think it will. It's not really a solution to these blues, is it? I really think you need some help. You need some drugs to support you. I know you don't like the idea, but I just knew the miscarriage and your mother dying would affect you somehow. I knew it'd stew in your brain and I just can't bear you suffering like this, it sounds like torture and you shouldn't have to suffer it, luv, you really shouldn't.'

'I'm just not going on Prozac or anything like that, Jules. It could make things a hell of a lot worse. You know it could. I don't want to go back to feeling suicidal. That was such a deep, black void I just can't revisit...I'll never come out of it if I do. I've been one small step from suicide once before and that was one too many times.'

'No, no, I don't mean Prozac. Don't go mad, but I've ordered you something. They're called Phenibut. I've read up on it a lot because I've been worried about you. A lot of people swear by them. They raise your dopamine, but aren't addictive and don't have bad side effects like the Prozac-style anti-depressants. Some people don't get anything out of them, but a lot of people do. They might help you cope. I looked them up because, like I said, I knew you'd suffer with the post-baby blues sooner or later, not to mention losing your mam as well.'

He sighed and just didn't have the energy to resist. 'If you think they're OK I'll give them a go. I do need to get into a better place in my mind with all this, I know that. It's starting to really worry me that I might go back to my worst days again. I need to find a space it can exist in comfortably, or at least find somewhere I can park it for a while.'

She nodded keenly. 'If for no other reason than you'll wear me out if you go on like this!' She smiled sympathetically at him. 'It's all to do with your brain chemistry. It is. I'm sure of it. I mean, I miscarried and though I do feel sad about it, I just feel able to look forward and not dwell on the past. I feel the sadness, but it doesn't destroy me. That has to be to do with my brain chemistry, doesn't it? It really crushes some women. I've been lucky like that. It's not that I'm better or superior, I don't even feel like I even have any control over how I feel. It's just how I'm made.'

'All consciousness is to do with brain chemistry. It's all hormones, chemicals and what I think a biologist would call, like, other stuff.'

'Well, give them a go when they come. I bookmarked them on your laptop so you can read up.'

'Thanks, Jules, I should've known you'd understand. I should've talked to you about this before now.'

He suddenly felt really emotional and pulled her into him, so that they lay face-to-face breathing in each other's air.

'I don't deserve you, sometimes. You know that? All my life I've fought this shit in my head on my own...whatever it was...I lived with it for so long, most of the time not even knowing what it was. I find it hard to talk about, even now.'

'Well you didn't have a mam or dad to turn to, did you? I'm the only person you've ever been able to talk to about it properly and I wasn't exactly sympathetic back in the day. I had to learn too.'

He nodded and kissed her lightly on the lips.

'Y'know, just before mam died, she said she'd loved me as best as she'd been able.'

'Aw, god. Bless her.'

'I'm so glad she said it. That is as much as you can ask of anyone, but talking to her in the last few weeks I realised that with her being ill and dad being...well...dad, I had just been alone most of my life. It was a way of life. Even when *we* met, on some level I was still on my own, still wrestling with the things in my brain or more often, the things that were *not* in my brain. Until we got back together and I began to deal with it, I was isolated and it's why I still tend to go into tortoise mode, pull my head in and try to sort things out on my own, even now. That's why I didn't talk to you about this. Sorry.'

'OK, but if you're looking for silver linings, it's good that you know this about yourself now. And as *my* mam always says, who said life would be easy, eh? No-one. I reckon we deserve each other. I mean, who the hell else would put up with us? You with your wonky head, me with my broccoli farts and decidedly unsensible underwear for a woman of 45.'

'Yeah. We're not sensible, us, are we?'

'If we were sensible, our lives would be very different and much less fun.' She sat up. 'I've spent quite a lot of time around sensible people when I was a legal PA and I wasn't far from getting hooked up to a sensible bloke before I met you, remember? James.'

'Doesn't any part of you wish you had, though? Instead of me and my shit-for-brains?'

She sat up and took a drink of water. 'Nah, not even for one heartbeat. I mean, life with him would have been perfectly fine, I'm sure. He was decent and solid and we'd have had a good income, a nice house and a nice car. He'll be on bloody good money now. Materially we would have had everything anybody could want, but I know fine well I'd have left him in the end, because he'd have been passionless and I'd have been bored. I'd have left him and come in search of you, wherever you were, because whatever else you are darlin,' you are not boring or passionless.'

He smiled. 'Sensible is underrated though, I've kept thinking that recently. We need the sensible people to sort our lives out.'

'True, but we don't need to marry them. Imagine if you'd married someone like that. From the start with me you were messy and odd and funny and could quote bits of books and songs. That made you funny, sexy and attractive to me, but I know that's exactly what a sensible, straight up and down woman would find repulsive about you. You would drive a sensible, straight woman mad.'

'I know. You are right.'

'There you go, then. So like I said, we deserve each other. Let the sensibles get on with their life and we'll carry on being mad, flatulent shaggers.' She pulled the covers down, straddled him, pressing down on his chest with the palms of her hands and fiddling with his chest hair. 'Now, we've got a bit of unfinished business, haven't we?'

CHAPTER 6

Nick ate bacon and eggs as he read the *Gazette* website the following morning. The headline on the front page read, 'Festival Under Fire.'

The postman arrived and handed him a small packet, along with the junk mail. He held onto the Jiffy bag and dumped the leaflets into the recycling bag in the kitchen without even looking at them, as most people probably do, pausing briefly to wonder if those paying for the junk mail realised this was what usually happened.

'Do I look alright?' said Julie, coming into the kitchen, tying her hair back.

She was wearing a tailored, cream Nicole Farhi suit, cut close on her legs and hips, with a turquoise blue top and white trainers.

'Very business-like, Jules. Is this you, back in your sensible, legal PA mode again? I still think it's weird you did so many years at that coalface.'

'It does to me, now. Well, you've got to look the part, haven't you? At least at first. When you've got your feet under the table you can just turn up in old jeans.'

'It's a quality suit, that. Must have cost a bomb.'

'25 whole English pounds. It would have, if I'd not bought it second hand from an Oxfam shop. I've had to take the waist in - I say take it in, I have no idea how you do that properly, so I've pinned it.' She lifted up the jacket to show a fold in the waistband fabric anchored from inside with a safety pin. 'I thought I'd wear this for our wedding. What do you reckon?' She pulled the door shut as they went outside to his old BMW.

'Definitely. Yeah. I like it with the trainers. Gives you an arty but smarty sort of look.'

'Aye. Well, it's still a music festival, so I thought the trainers made it a bit less formal. I think it's a bit lesbian-ish meself, like, but I don't mind that.'

He laughed and started the engine. 'Don't let me stop you

expressing your inner lesbian.' As he spoke, he tore open the packet. It was a white plastic tub of pills. He held it up to her. 'It's those pills you ordered for me.'

'Ah good. Are you going to take them now?'

He snapped the seal and took two green capsules out and swallowed them.

'Wahey! I already feel amazing!' he said, bouncing up and down.

'Don't take the piss. Give them a few days to get into your system and start to work.'

He didn't expect them to, but just hoped they wouldn't have any side effects.

They drove up Yarm High Street, heading north towards Stockton.

'Did you see that piece on the *Gazette* website?' he said.

She shook her head while looking in the vanity mirror, trying to pluck a nostril hair. 'What was it about? Ow. Gotcha. Oh god, I'm going to sneeze now.' She barked out a wet explosion and wiped her hands on a tissue.

'It was about the Ironopolis Anarchists calling for a full investigation by HMRC into the Blakeston Estate's financial affairs and into Big Fish's company, too. The implication was, that they think they're either avoiding paying tax or evading paying tax - which they seem to see as one and the same thing - and that the festival is another money-making racket. They stopped short of accusing Salmon of being dodgy, obviously, or he'd sue them, but it seems to back up what Mike was saying to me, about Big Fish laundering money.'

'Well you know my feelings about such things.'

'The local MP seemed keen to be on the Ironopolis Anarchists' side and they even had some HMRC big wig to say they take these matters very seriously, blah blah blah. It was all the sort of stuff Mike was telling me about. There's a real mood to hold the elite and wealthy to account right now.'

'Yeah, suddenly everyone is anti-corporate, anti-fat cat, but I worry it's all so phoney, though. Everyone is only pissed off because there's a recession on. As soon as there isn't and people feel a bit better off, they'll forget all about these sort of abuses. I wouldn't mind betting there'll be no real change and that it's all just hot air for HMRC to appease the public's anger.'

'I dunno Jules, I think these anti-capitalist groups are getting some real traction now. I think people see them as being on the right side of history. No-one can stand against what they're saying because all they're really saying is "stop taking the piss and pay your fair share". As far as I can tell, that's pretty much their agenda and somehow they're getting tip-offs about who to go after.'

Brian Salmon's farmhouse was about two miles north of Norton, set off the road; although very close to urban Teesside, somehow, as soon as you drove up the gravel path towards it, you felt like you were very rural.

'Eeee, it must be three years nearly since we were last here, remember?' said Julie as they parked up alongside a long line of four-wheel-drive cars and farm vehicles.

'I do, yeah. They were doing that Boudica dig over there.' He pointed to a copse of yew trees to the east.

'Yeah and we'd just fallen back in love. It was a nice time, that,' she said, her hand on the small of his back.

They walked around to the front of the house and past the stables. Four horses stuck their heads out at them as they passed by. Nick went over and stroked a dappled mare on the nose.

'Now then. You're lovely, you, aren't you?' he said, chatting to it as it nodded its head up and down.

'Must cost him a fortune to run these stables,' said Julie looking around. 'There are eight of them here and some more round on the other side of the farm. Must be a full-time business.'

'Jeff told me it's quite successful. They've had some big winners on the flat, I think. Not that I know anything about horse racing.'

'They all go around in a circle for a bit and then the fizzin' brown one wins. That's how it goes, isn't it?' she said, walking off to ring the bell by the large green double front doors. He joined her, looking out across the countryside, a warm breeze blowing rain in from the west. From inside, the sound of heavy guitar music was already audible. It blasted out as the door opened.

A tall, fat, bald man with a tribal tattoo over his head in dark blue, green and yellow, and both large, drooping ear lobes pierced with what looked like Newcastle Brown Ale beer bottle tops, pulled open the door and looked at them quizzically. He looked so incongruous in this polite, rural setting. Nick took a step back as he loomed over them. Julie didn't.

'I'm Julie Wells, this is Nick Guymer, Jeff Evans said we should come over for the meeting. He wanted us to do some work on the festival,' she said, as though the man in front of her didn't actually look like the biker from hell. Nick grinned to himself.

The man just grunted and gestured at them to come in. Inside the house, it was noisy and messy. The neat and tidy and respectable Georgian interior had been turned into a makeshift office and media centre. Two large downstairs reception rooms, either side of a long, wide hallway, were littered with phones, computers, wires and TV screens. People sat looking at the screens while the Guns 'n' Roses song 'Paradise City' played at a volume too loud to hear the phones if they rang. They walked out up some stairs to the relative quiet on the first floor where there were four more rooms.

'We're using the big room along there for meetings,' said the tattooed man who Nick was now pretty sure was Mel Stephens. 'I'll be back in a bit.' He left them and went up another flight of stairs.

Nick peered around the door. The high-ceilinged, airy Georgian room was mostly taken up with a huge oak table, around which chairs were arranged. It was empty so they took a couple of seats at the end by a window overlooking a gentle slope of land north into County Durham.

'It's no wonder Brian's gone abroad,' said Julie. 'He would hate all that noise downstairs. His house has been totally taken over.'

'Yeah. He must be 69 or 70 now. I'm surprised he agreed to this, really. I hope he wasn't bullied into it by his son.'

'Wouldn't surprise me. I feel really overdressed now after seeing that lot downstairs. Like I've come as a prim secretary. Good god, that music downstairs is loud. The floorboards are vibrating. What's that they're playing now? Velvet Revolver's 'Slither', isn't it?'

'It is. Best track on that album.'

As he spoke Jeff walked in playing air drums. 'Ah ha, welcome to the jungle, baby,' he said, rolling his eyes up into his head to leave only the whites showing. 'It's a bit bloody mad in here, isn't it? Enough to frighten the horses, quite literally.'

There was shouting from above and then footsteps running down the stairs

'Where is that fucking toe-rag Benny?' said Mel Stephens, appearing at the door, his face puce with anger, his Geordie voice bellowing out every syllable of each word.

'I dunno Mel,' said Jeff.

'What's up, boss?' said a small, thick-set man coming up behind him. Stephens swung around and grabbed the man, presumably Benny, by the t-shirt and lifted him off the ground.

'What did I fucking tell you about renting out concession stands? Eh? You useless shite!' he threw him down and the man staggered backwards, a look of genuine fear in his eyes now.

'Hey, that's enough mate...don't hurt the bloke, whatever he's done,' said Nick, getting up and striding across the room, followed by Julie.

'Eh? You can fuck off for a start, and you can take Miss Moneypenny with you as well.' He pointed at Julie.

'Hang on Mel, don't kick off, these two are my mates and they're top-notch grafters,' said Jeff.

'Oh aye. You're fucking give me beef now, are you? Do you wanna go outside and fucking sort it out? Eh? Well do ya? No. You fucking don't because you're full of shite, like this short-arsed cunt.'

'There's really no need for that sort of language,' said Julie, drawing herself up to her full height. 'And there's no need to threaten people with violence either. That won't solve anything will it? I'm sure whatever...'

'...oh dear me, what have we got here? It's not Miss Moneypenny, it's Little Miss fucking Gandhi, is it? Fuck me, darlin'. Let me tell you this, if I didn't shout at this little twat here, nothing would get done right, would it, Benny?

'No boss.'

'Aye. No is right.'

'You're just bullying him now. He can't say anything different, can he?' said Julie, indignant on the man's behalf. Nick looked at her, jaw set against Mel Stephens defiantly. The jaw of doom. She was blowing their chance of any work, that was for sure, but there was some pleasure in seeing her go after bullies like this.

'Are you his union rep or something?'

'I doubt you'd have unionised labour here, somehow. But you know I'm right.'

'Do I now? Thanks for informing me what I think. One thing I do know is you're a pain in the fucking arse, darlin'.'

'My name is Julie Wells. Not darlin'.'

'Wells is it? I might have known. Fuck me.' He shook his head, turned around pushed Benny away. 'Get downstairs and re-do all those concession contracts at the proper rate. The details are on Angie's desk.'

Some other people had come up the stairs. A middle-aged women in brown slacks and a cardigan and a younger woman with rock 'n' roll hair that looked like it belonged in the mid 70s: a Rod Stewart-style scrag cut. She wore white skinny jeans, baseball boots and a white t-shirt with a Gibson Les Paul gold top printed on the front. Behind them came two young blokes in tight, shiny slate blue and black suits and long pointy brown leather shoes and a man in his 70s who looked like Old Father Time, with hair as white as January snow. They stood nodding at each other and looking a bit awkward in the tense atmosphere that Mel Stephen's rage had caused.

Benny went downstairs as three more people came up. They each had a goatee beard, scruffy long hair, black t-shirts, black jeans and big bellies and big sets of keys. Classic roadies.

'Right, you ugly bunch of cunts. Get in here, sit your fat arses down and let's get this shit sorted. You too Cheryl fuckin' Guevara.' He gestured at Julie. She pursed her lips together and scowled at him. This made Mel Stephens laugh.

'Oh, stop getting shit on your G-String, pet. I'm just winding you up. Howay you too, twat features,' he said to Nick. They walked in. Behind his back Nick mouthed, "twat features, me?" and made a silent laugh at Julie, who pulled a face in return.

'Fuck me, this is like looking at an army of zombies. C'mon people, we're putting on a big fucking blues show here in nearly three weeks time, we haven't got the stages finished, we've got 50 per cent less bogs than we need, we nearly undersold all the concession stands and the contractor that was putting up the fence has pulled out on us. So cheer up, everything that can go fucking wrong, has already gone fucking wrong. Alice, what's the situation with the PA system?'

One of the long hairs, presumably not actually called Alice, spoke up. 'It's all cool, boss. It's already all on site. As soon as the sparks gets the juice flowing, we'll hook it all up.'

'Hook it up? That's just a fancy way of saying you'll plug the fucker in, you mean. And what about your team - have you got enough hands?'

'We will have.'

'Arthur - budgets? Are we over or under?'

The grey haired older man had a laptop open in front of him. 'I've got all the spreadsheets here, if you want to see them.'

'Of course I don't want to see them, I wouldn't know a spread sheet if it came up and bit me on the balls, that's why I've got you here. Not to bite me on the balls, don't get us wrong, I like you Arthur, but some things are off limits.' The whole room laughed at that one. He had a nice line in aggressive patter.

'The budget is fine. Cash flow is good. The event is all but sold out, with ticket receipts of over 3.75 million sterling.'

'Fuck me. Already? Really?'

'Yes and we've got merchandise sales, broadcast rights and concession rental income to add to that. One concern, we haven't had the insurance documents yet. I'd like to get them in place this week. We need to be covered for all eventualities and at the moment we are not.'

'Aye, good thinking Arthur. We don't want to have to call off the festival due to Teesside being invaded by aliens or something and then ending up with a big bill. Angie, can you get onto that?'

The woman in the cardigan made a note on her pad and nodded.

'How much money will it make, do you think?' asked Nick.

'Why the fuck do you want to know that?' said Mel.

'I thought I might build some numbers into a press release...success breed success, doesn't it? There was also a lot of local opposition to this, so if they hear it's a big success it'll calm everyone down and make them think it's a big hit for the region. Puts Teesside on the festival map, like.'

Mel pointed at him with a Biro. 'What's your name again?'

'Nick Guymer.'

'And what exactly the fuck are you doing here?'

'Jeff said you wanted a writer to do social media, press and publicity.'

'You did, like,' added Jeff.

'I did aye. And do you three come as some sort of team, like a Smoggy Batman and fucking Robin and Wonder sodding Woman??' He pointed at Nick and then Jeff and then Julie with the Biro.

'We're old mates, like,' said Jeff.

'Good. Well I like it. Yes. Do it, Guymer. Get the numbers off Rumplestiltskin here. Make us look better than we sodding are. I want to come out of this smelling of roses. That's all I ask.'

He pointed at the woman in the cardigan. 'Your turn Angie. Angie baby, you're a special lady, living in a world of make-believe. Fucking hell, I'm quoting Helen Reddy songs.' She laughed a little, clearly feeling nervous. Her voice was soft and quiet and put Nick in mind of the Mavis Riley character off *Coronation Street.*

'Well, Mel, all the phone lines are in and the extra broadband, but we've simply got no-one to do any admin at all. I'm absolutely swamped and phones are going unanswered and we can't hear them anyway because they play the music so loud down there that you can't hear yourself think, let alone pick up a phone. I can't really work in there...'

'It's a rock festival, not a kid's play group, Angie. Why don't we stick the phones up on the top floor then? Is that so hard? No. Problem solved. See, I'm a fucking genius.' He pointed at Julie. 'Take Left Wing Wanda here with you, then you'll have 100 per cent more admin staff to help you. OK? Good. Now, you two lavender-scented gay boys in your suits with your waxed fucking eyebrows, dear me what do you look like? What's your names again? Nevermind, I've realised I don't care.' The two blokes in tight suits laughed a little at his craic. 'Have we got any media deals in place yet? By the look on your face, I'm guessing that's a no. Well go and fucking well get it sorted. We want this broadcast live on Radio 2 and I want film of it on BBC4, so go and bum whichever double-barrelled, limp-wristed BBC arse-bandit you need to bum to make it happen. Take some petty cash and buy them an alfalfa sprout and soya bean dinner.' One of them was about to speak, but he held up a hand at them. 'I don't want to hear it, son. The only thing I want to hear you say is "Mel we've got a deal in place, thank you for punching me in the face until I realised I was shit." OK that's us done - are there any problems at all that I should know about? Emily, is the website OK and the FaceTweet bollocks all set up?'

He was addressing the girl with the guitar t-shirt. She nodded. Her narrow pink lips pulled back in a smile to reveal uneven, wonky white teeth, with a gap between her front two. 'We just need to populate them with content now,' she said in a flowery, light voice.

'By populate I take it you actually just mean bloody well write?'
She nodded and giggled in a girlish sort of way. 'Aye, I thought so.
Well get Nick here to help you on that if I haven't punched him in
the face by the end of this meeting.'

'Me? What have I done, like?' said Nick.

'You've not got a beer gut and you're alive. That is two very
good reasons,' said Mel.

'The additional toilet blocks are arriving on Wednesday. I'm
worried that if we get let down on those, we'll have no time to
organise replacements,' said Angie, her brow furrowed, making
her look older than she probably was.

'Well, just approach another company, establish that they can
supply us if needed, tell them they're on reserve. Job done. Are
you three hairies happy with the stage and your routes in and out
for equipment?'

All three nodded.

'Jeff - have you got all the bands sorted now? If so, get all the
bands' contracts from Simon Garbutt and make sure Angie has
them.'

'Will be done by the end of today, boss,' said Jeff.

'Good. Right. That's us done then.' He banged the table with his
huge hands. They all got up and left the room. The woman in the
cardigan came over to Julie.

'Hello, I'm Angie Page. I think we'll be working together,' she
said.

'Hiya. I'm Julie. He's a bit of a volcano, him, isn't he?' she
nodded at the exiting Mel Stephens.

Angie page scrunched up her face as they shook hands. 'He's a
bit scary if you ask me.'

Mel stopped and reversed into the room, walking backwards.
'Me? Scary? I'm a pussy cat. If you're lucky I'll show you my
prehensile tail. So you're Julie Wells, blondie?'

'Yeah. I'm also a pussy cat, but I've not got a prehensile tail to
show you though, sadly,' she said.

He lifted up the back of her jacket and looked at her backside.

'What a shame. I can see that, like. Tell your Kev and Ricky that if they want a gig doing security, to turn up here early on the first day.'

'Do you know them, like?'

'Who doesn't know the Well's brothers? No surprise you had a pop at me. Must be in the genes, pet, eh. I'm just grateful my balls are still intact. I'll make sure you get paid on time or I know I'll have those lads so far up my arse they'll be looking out my eyes.' He grinned and stuck a fat, unlit cigar into the corner of his mouth. 'Cheer up, you'll learn to love me.' He whacked her on the shoulder, spun on his heel and marched back out.

Nick stopped the grey-haired man. 'Can I get those profit projections for that publicity piece? I'll get it into the *Gazette* and the *Northern Echo.*' He handed him a card with his email address and mobile number on.

He looked at it.

'I shall email some headline figures to you. Obviously some thing are confidential, fees and such for groups. We can't release those to the press, except in collective terms.'

'Of course. All I need is something to back up how successful it's going to be despite fears from locals. Generating money for Teesside business, progressive council, putting the region on the musical map, blah blah, you know the sort of thing. Classic bit of local news reporting.'

'Not a problem.'

Someone tapped him on the shoulder. He turned around. It was the rock 'n' roll girl in white. 'Hiya Nick, I'm Emily Davids,' she said, head on one side, a friendly smile across her face as she chewed gum. She had proper green eyes. You hardly ever met anyone with proper green eyes. Hers were the colour of summer grass. She held out a small hand which he feared he could break if he held it too tightly. With her old-fashioned rock hair, tight clothes and cheeky, toothy grin, she looked like fun. 'Can you write me some short biogs of all the bands that are appearing for the programme, just to start with?'

'Yeah. Easy. I love your t-shirt by the way. Are you a guitarist?'

'No. I just like guitars...and guitarists.' She made a fluttering hiccup of a laugh.

'They're a good lifestyle choice, man,' he said.

She smiled at him again and rested on her left hip, her finger tip on her chin. 'Err...we've also got two local bands on the bill opening Saturday and Sunday and we thought...or rather...I thought it'd be a good idea to get an article in the local press about them. The locals never do anything unless it's got a Teesside angle. Could you knock something together do you think? By this afternoon? I know it's all very short notice. I'll need the biogs by end of tomorrow, 'cos it's got to go to the printers asap.'

'I'll get it all done.'

"Aw thank you. Aren't you lovely?' she said and laughed a little again. 'I'm liaising with all media so everything you write should come through me. My email is just emily.davids@teessiderblues.co.uk.'

He raised a thumb and nodded.

'I'm going to organise the office upstairs with Angie,' said Julie. 'We might as well get it sorted now. You can get off and get a start on that writing. I'll ring you when I need a lift.' She gave him a quick smile and wiggled her fingers at him. 'See you, Emily.'

'Bye, Julie.'

He went downstairs with Emily.

'So are you local?' she said.

'Yeah, I was brought up in Stockton. We live just south of Yarm.'

'We?'

'Me and Julie. The woman in the inappropriate cream suit.'

She gave the fluttering little laugh once more and ruffled her hair up, a little habit she had. 'She did look like she had come from the planet Well Dressed. Oh, but I mean, she looked cool,' she said, holding her hand up, not wanting to offend him. 'Well, we're all one big team here. I think it's going to get really manic in the next few days, though.'

'Just keep some strong drink on hand, everything will seem

much better if you're drunk.'

She laughed louder this time. Somehow, it was flattering.

'I shall bear that in mind. Thanks for the tip. Oh, listen to that - Zeppelin's "Heartbreaker". I love this.' She pointed into thin air as the riff from the song blasted out of the office. 'I'll see you around, Nicky boy.'

She turned right at the bottom of the stairs and went back into the loud music room, doing a little hip-shaking dance as she did so. She was quite the rock chick.

'She's as cute at they come, isn't she? Can you imagine? Ooof, dear me. I would beg her for some sweet poontang, wouldn't you?'

Nick turned around. It was Stevie Salmon coming in the front door. The Big Fish. He beamed at him and tugged on his ginger biscuit-coloured beard, now flecked with white and grey and brown. 'Now then, Nick. Alright?'

'Alright mate. Aye. Thanks for the work. Jeff's sorted us out.'

'Has he? I don't know nowt about the business side. I leave it all to the virgins and nerds to sort out.' His ability to be rude about and to people remained undimmed. 'She's a student at Teesside Uni, that one. Proper little stunner. Lovely little tits and arse on it. I could fucking wear her like a glove puppet.'

Nick inwardly winced. She was attractive, but Big Fish took all the pleasure out of such a private observation. It was particularly horrible the way he said 'that one' and 'it' instead of 'her'. They were only small words, but somehow it dehumanised her and was probably the very definition of objectification. How did you respond to such words? A lot of men just join in, even against their inclination. He used to when he was younger, but he damn well couldn't do it any more and he didn't see any reason why he should.

'She has all the qualities traditionally desired by the superficial male,' he said, quoting Jerry Seinfeld. Big Fish didn't 'get' Seinfeld. Not his sort of comedy. He seemed to think this comment was actually a compliment to his taste in women.

'I should say so. Dear me. Talking of which, is your Julie here as well?'

Nick looked at him incredulously and almost laughed. 'Yeah. She's upstairs.'

'Cool. She was looking tanned and gorgeous at the airport, like. Bet she looks mint in a bikini, like, even at her age. She's still got great tits that one, you can tell her that from me. This place will be full of wall-to-wall quality fanny for the next couple of weeks, I should think. At least that's one good reason to put up with the fucking thing.'

Nick looked at him again, astonished at how he trampled over everything like a rampaging bull. God knows you grow up on Teesside without a lot of airs and graces, but by any standards, Stevie Salmon was vulgar. Yet he was totally unaware and totally thoughtless about how rude he was, because it was so ingrained in him. Money and power had only given him less reason to choose his words carefully, let alone politely.

'I wouldn't say any of that to Julie if you see her. Not if you don't want your bollocks ripped off and stuffed down your throat,' said Nick, serious, but trying to pretend it was a joke.

The big man pulled on his beard, a habit he had of doing virtually every minute of every waking hour. 'Are you saying she'd touch my balls? I might give that a go then.' Then he laughed and pushed at Nick in the alpha male, roister doister manner that he hated most.

'It is a royal pain in the arse, though. There's so many regulations and health and bloody safety bollocks. It's not like the old days when the money talked and the bullshit walked. Everyone wants a piece of you these days.'

He obviously had no recollection of going on about this to him in LAX.

'And the liability insurance is absolutely sky high. I said to Si, why can't we just get everyone who turns up to sign something which says if I fall over and break my face, it's my own fault? Apparently it's illegal to do that and then we've got to get some council idiot to approve it all...I mean, fuck off, it's my land, I'll do what I want on it. So I've put the red pen through as much as I can while staying legal. It's literally the least I can do. Ha ha...not bad that, I'm writing it down...' He took out a small notepad and pencil and jotted a note down.

Nick knew Big Fish wasn't interested in hearing his views on anything so he made his excuses and got away. As he left the house and walked down the gravel to the car, he spat out of gob of saliva as though to expunge Salmon from himself.

This was the trouble with being freelance, you pretty much had to work for anyone who would pay. There wasn't enough work around to be choosy, not with the recession and the general collapse in advertising revenues in newspapers and magazines. Had he anything else on his books, he'd have told Salmon to stuff his writing job up his arse, right there and then. 'She's still got great tits'. Jesus Christ. But the money that he and Julie could earn across the next three weeks might total the best part of three grand which would cover their rent and food for three months. That was significant cash. In fact, if he was careful, he might be able to put in an inflated invoice and no-one would even realise, especially if the venture was awash with money. He'd take pleasure in that small victory. But even so. Fucker.

He was just about to get into his battered old BMW when an old Land Rover pulled in alongside him. A man with long, flowing hair and a heavy beard line got out and gestured to him.

'Nick! Nick you old rocker. I thought it was you...what are you doing here?'

'Bloody hell, Bertie...I haven't seen you for...god knows how long.'

He held out his hand and the man gripped it tightly, grinning at him.

'Not since we had that drink in Jack and Danny's when we played down in Leeds and stayed over in Harrogate. What happened to you? You look like you lost three stone and took up boxing.'

He looked him up and down.

'Ah, it's a long story. I quit drinking to get healthy in my head. Took up resistance training.'

Ian Bertram nodded. He was leathery skinned, tanned and looked as lean as he'd been in 1979 when he'd first met him at Newcastle Poly, where they both studied English literature. He'd gone on to have a career in the music business, managing bands. He'd started when at college and had done very well since, with a roster of popular rock bands on his CV.

'Well, you look good on it, man. As I recall you were a bit pissed off last time I saw you. Things were not good at home with your missus.'

'Yeah. I was breaking up with Julie. We've got back together since, though. I wasn't in a good place back then. Things are much better now.'

Bertie held up a hand for him to hi-five.

'Good on ya. So you're involved in this festival?'

'Yeah, I'm just writing publicity material and press releases. Have you got a band on?'

'Yeah, Blind Belief are potentially on the first day. Do you know them?'

'Name sounds familiar. Didn't they do a Paul Jones session on Radio 2?'

He nodded. 'Yup. I've been managing them for a couple of years. I got them on a tour supporting Joe Bonamassa. Things are going OK. Hard to make a decent living being a blues band in Britain, though. They're always on the road in Europe. But they're actually really good guys. All in their 20s and very keen.'

'Cool. I look forward to seeing them. Big Jeff's working the festival too, y'know. You remember him, don't you? The gaffer is his brother.' He gave him a brief explanation.

'I've come to see him, actually, as I was in the area visiting my old mother. She's in a home just off Fairfield Road. I'm going to sign the contract for the band, if we can sort out a fee. They've only offered us five grand. We'll do it for that but is there decent money to be had, do you reckon?'

'Yeah. It's sloshing with money. You should be able to get a lot more than five, one way or another. It might just be five on the books. Hey, do you get paid in cash much, Bertie?'

He shook his head and pulled some strands of his hair off his lips. 'Never. It's all bank transfers these days. The era of getting a packet of money behind the bar is long gone, at least at the level I operate at.'

'What would you do if someone offered to part pay you in cash?'

He looked out across the open fields and raised a dark eyebrow.

'I'd take it and use it for expenses. I wish that actually happened. Keep some of the money out of the tax man's hands.' He rubbed his tanned bare arm. 'Why do you ask?'

'I think Big Fish - Stevie Salmon that is, I reckon he might offer to pay you cash either personally or through his manager. I think he's a bit...' He made a wobbling gesture with his hand '...y'know...a bit dodgy.'

Bertie laughed. 'I bloody hope so. I don't meet dodgy promoters any more. I used to love a dodgy promoter. The business is so clean compared to how it was in the 80s.'

'If he does, will you let me know?' He handed him one of his cards.

'Are you working for HMRC then?' he said, with a laugh.

'Not exactly. But, as you'll see if you ever meet Big Fish, he's a monumental twat and it never hurts to have something on monumental twats, does it?'

Bertie slapped him on the shoulder.

'You're a loss to the world of rock 'n' roll management with an attitude like that, Nick.'

Later in the day, he'd just finished the press releases on the local bands for the local press and for Emily Davids when Julie called. It was still a sunny blue afternoon when he picked her up. She looked pink-faced and sweaty.

'Fizzin' hell, it's hot up there, I'm bloody roasting. Fizzin' bloody suit.'

She threw the jacket onto the back seat, turned to him and lifted her arms up to reveal a large sweat patch under each armpit of the turquoise top.

"Look at the state of me. I'm sweating like a Teessider buying lager in London.'

He leaned over and kissed her. 'Aye, but I like a sweaty lass, me.'

'Aye, but you are a perv,' she said, dabbing at her forehead with a tissue as he drove off. 'If this warm weather keeps up I'm going to have to come to work in my California bikini. All the heat rises up that house so it's about 15 degrees hotter at the top. It was 91 degrees in there. 91!'

'Big Fish might pass out if he saw you in a bikini, though you might get a pay rise.'

'Oh god, what's he been saying? He *has* been saying something, hasn't he?'

'Nothing you want to hear. But as you've still got your Californian tan, you should at least get your legs out tomorrow. It seems set fair again.'

'Aye, I will. Seems a shame to waste a leg waxing. You don't ever get your legs out, do you? I don't know why not. You've perfectly decent legs. They go from your hips to the floor in the traditional style and everything.'

'I consider a man showing his legs to be bad form. No British bloke looks any good in shorts and even worse in those three-quarter length monstrosities.'

'At least you don't wear socks and sandals. I'd dump you if you did. God, it was a busy day. I met that lass, Emily this afternoon. She came up to introduce herself. I love her hair. Looks a bit like Suzi Quatro in 1974. I might get mine done like that, sometime.'

'It is great hair, isn't it? She's got an old-school rock thing going on. And she has the green eyes, which you never see. She seemed a cheerful soul, quite posh I'd say. No accent, anyway. She called me Nicky boy, like I'm 12 years old.'

'I always wondered who petite clothes were designed to fit. Must be her. I could hurt her with one good fart.'

'Yeah she is very slight, isn't she? Best be careful if she's nearby after you've been eating broccoli then. Your broccoli farts are especially vicious.'

'I could broccoli fart for Britain, me. Did you get any work done?'

'Yeah, quite a bit. What do you make of it all over there? Mel seemed to think it was all as organised as it needed to be.'

'It remind me of a student gig. When I was at University we'd put on one thing or another and it was always messy, until someone took charge.'

'Until you took charge, you mean?'

'Aye. I'm well organised, aren't I? And I don't mind giving out orders. That woman I'm working with, Angie, she's nice enough, but dear me, what drip. She's so...' she lifted up her hands in an ineffectual way and put on a whiny Yorkshire voice. "I don't know what to do Julie. Should I put the phone here on the desk or here on the table?" Dear me, lady. Just do something.'

Nick laughed. 'She did sound like Mavis off *Coronation Street*.'

Julie burst out laughing at that and slapped the seat. 'Yes, yes, she's just like that. Ha ha. That's spot on.'

'You'll soon whip her into line.'

'If she doesn't shape up I'll put her over my knee and give her a damn good thrashing!'

'That might be more fun than she's ever had, Jules.'

'Ha. Yeah. She isn't exactly a raver. She was wearing a cardi even in the heat. I like a cardigan as much as anyone, but some people have cardigan minds, don't they? Mind, you know what they say, the cookers with the coldest tops have the hottest ovens.'

He looked at her incredulously. 'Do they? Who says that, like?'

She gestured airily. 'It's a saying.'

'No, it's not. You've just made it up, man.'

'Might have done.' She stuck her tongue out at him and winked.

'And anyway you've got a red hot top and a roasting hot oven as well...' he laughed, '...which makes it sound like you've got cystitis.'

'I bloody will have if I don't get these pants off and something cool and loose put on. I need an ice pack in me knickers.'

He laughed again. 'Oh hey, do you remember Ian "Bertie" Bertram?'

'Remind me who he is.'

'He manages bands. I went to Poly with him and you met him once in Harrogate. Longish hair. Handsome, windswept sort of bloke.'

She shrugged. 'Sorry, doesn't ring a bell.'

'Anyway, I met him outside as I was leaving. He's got a band on the bill called Blind Belief. He was going to sort out their contract and fee. I told him to let me know if he's offered cash.'

She nodded. 'Good idea. I hope Big Fish gets nailed for tax fraud or whatever. Mind, even if he gets caught, they'll just fine him some amount he can easily pay. The rich have it stitched up every which way in this country. It stinks. Meanwhile they'll spend thousands on hunting some poor sods down for the 20 quid they scam on the dole. It's all wrong.'

When they got in, Julie took a shower while Nick made chicken and olive salad. She came down in a long white linen dress, combing her damp lightened-to-blonde hair.

'God I feel positively middle class in this thing. I should be called Jocasta not Julie,' she said, wafting it around. 'Feels lovely and breezy though.' She lifted it up and flashed at him.

'No underwear Jules. You brazen hussy.'

'Not really, it's just that all my knickers are in the wash and I'm not putting them on inside out like I used to when I was a student.'

'I'll do a wash in a bit.'

'Thanks, luv. I could do it, but I hate to conform to gender stereotypes by doing washing.'

'I know and you're also a lazy get.'

'This is true.'

They ate in the back garden with blackbirds singing noisily in the hedge and a skylark hovering above the nearby field, singing its timeless, mellifluous song.

'Do you think we'll hear the festival from here?' said Julie, eyes closed after their meal, taking in the evening sun.

'Nah. It's 10 miles away. Even on a stiff breeze you'd not hear it. They've capped the decibels you can play at these days. It's not like the 70s when you could sonically assault people at high volume with impunity and a perforated ear drum was a rock 'n' roll badge of honour.'

'I'm really looking forward to it, though, and it's great to be involved. I mean, I know it's only being done by that sexist bugger Salmon as a tax dodge or whatever it is he's up to, but it's still great for the area to have something like this on. It's exciting. I just hope the weather stays dry. It'd be a disaster if it rains for three days solid.'

Nick's phone rang. He looked at it. 'It's Jeff. Your hair has dried nicely in the sun y'know. It's gone into long ringlets. A touch of the 1970s Goldie Hawn about it.'

She sucked her cheeks in, pulled a face and shook her tousled head at him, her hair now well past her shoulders.

'Ask him to come over with Rita for a meal and drinks sometime soon. I want to meet this lass that's won our Jeffrey's heart.'

'Hey big man,' said Nick, watching a wren skip under a hedge.

'There's been a bomb threat.' He said it with a flat certainty.

'What?'

'There's been a bomb threat. The whole site has been evacuated.'

CHAPTER 7

'A bomb threat? It's a joke, surely?'

'Nope. I fucking saw it, Nick.'

'Eh? What?'

'They rang it in. That woman Jules was working with, Angie, she took it. They said there's a bomb under a horse box outside the stables and it'd go off at 9pm. They called themselves The Ironopolis Anarchist.'

'Really? The Ironopolis Anarchist? That's the name of a pressure group. They're not terrorists, though.'

'Well, they bloody are now.'

Jeff was breathless, clearly walking at high pace as he talked. 'I thought it was kids just pissing around so I went out and looked and fuck me if there isn't a device underneath there. A black box with a light blinking on it.'

'Shit. You've called the cops?'

'Yup. Mel got them. They sent for a bomb squad from Catterick. Hang on...that's them...they're here now. The whole place has been cleared. Horses and everything.'

He sounded panicked.

'Is it for real ?'

'Looked fucking real to me. Couldn't risk it.'

'But who would do that and why?'

'Like I said, the bloke said he was the Ironopolis Anarchist. He said he wanted the festival to be called off. Shitting hell. I've gotta go.'

He rang off. Julie was sitting up, sunglasses pushed up onto her hair.

'This doesn't sound good at all,' she said. 'If it is a bomb, will they cancel the festival? They'll have to, surely.'

Nick thought for a moment, rubbing at his chin. 'Maybe. I mean, Health and Safety is worried about uneven paths, so I can't see them being happy with the threat of high explosives on the site.

God. I hope they don't. It'd be giving in to terrorism. I can just imagine Mel Stephen's reaction to this. He'll be apoplectic. His head will be a fluorescent beacon of fury.'

He went and got his laptop, moved his seat into the shade and looked up Ironopolist Anarchists. Julie stood in front of him, sipping the last of her wine.

'Anything on them?'

'No website, but there are 9 or 10 news stories about them. Stuff we'd heard about, actually, now I think about it.' He went through a few pages. 'They're all pieces criticizing wealthy landowners and corporations on Teesside and in North Yorkshire that they think are underpaying tax or paying less than the minimum wage and other injustices. They must have been formed 12 months or so ago, there's nothing any older in the archives.' He kept looking through Google's pages. 'Hold on...there's something here. There's a couple of mentions of the term Ironopolis Anarchists on forums. This one is an anti-capitalist, Occupy Movement type thing. This is what they say. "The powerful are rich and the rich are powerful and governments will not tax the powerful properly. So the only way we can reduce their power is to rob them of their wealth. Then they will cease to be powerful. But we can't steal their wealth because it exists purely digitally as a number in banks or it is insured land or property which, even if we destroy, will not de-wealth them. So how do we de-wealth the wealthy for the greater good?"'

'Whoever wrote that isn't wrong. It's like we were saying to Jeff, the whole country is run by and on behalf of a tiny elite of people. The rich are getting richer and the poor are making them richer, while getting poorer themselves. It's a double piss-take. I was reading that about 10 per cent of the population own about half of all the wealth and that the gap between rich and poor has never been wider.'

Nick nodded his head. 'There was a totally insane statistic I read from Oxfam that the 85 richest people in the world have as much wealth as 50 per cent of the poorest people on the planet all put together. I mean, let that sink in for a moment. It's a terrible indictment of how we economically organise ourselves. And it just can't be justified. It's wrong, but it never feels like something we can do anything about, does it? We have to live our lives and try and get through somehow. We're too busy to address these big issues. How do we do anything about inequality of income? I mean, this post has a good point about how do you de-wealth the wealthy, though it's a clumsy expression. They always manage to hide their money somehow. It's like Big Fish. He'll have money stashed all over the place that HMRC will never touch. The government encourage the poor to grass each other up for fiddling the dole while ignoring the bigger picture.'

'What's their solution then? Do they say?'

He scrolled down another couple of threads. 'Here we go. In response to someone they say, "We de-wealth the wealthy by devaluing them as people." That's a bit vague, isn't it? Not sure what that means. Sounds like another way of saying "...err...I don't know". '

She tapped on the screen. 'Is the pressure group referred to in the plural or singular?'

He went back to the news stories. 'Always plural. Anarchists.'

She turned her mouth down. 'Funny, didn't Jeff just say it was singular? That the bomb hoax was from the Ironopolis Anarchist.'

She rolled a thick strand of hair around her index finger as she talked.

Nick stared at her, thinking. 'Yes. Yeah, he did. I repeated his words out loud, didn't I? It was Ironopolis Anarchist.'

'Since those posts are plural, they might be nothing to do with this bomber. This might be an individual taking almost the same name.'

'Good point, Jules. That would be an easy conflation to make.' He read on. 'Whoever it is makes good points about the upward spiral of property prices and how that distorts the economy and creates a two-tier society.'

'House prices are mental in this country. The only way to reduce them is to build loads more houses for the next 20 years and no-one seems to want to do that exactly because no-one wants their house prices to go down. It's a one-way street to the town of Screw Up, that is.'

'Is that a Springsteen line?'

'No - but it should be, eh?' She looked pleased with herself. 'Thank god we don't have massive house price inflation on Teesside though, not compared to some places, anyway.'

'Aye, but if we did you could have coined it on your flat.' She'd sold her flat in Norton the previous year for 15 grand more than the mortgage. It had helped pay her university fees debt, but was now all gone.

'I know and that's the sick thing, isn't it? It encourages us to be greedy and keep the status quo. It's most people's only chance to make some money. But I bought that place as a little home for me to live in after we split up, I didn't buy it as an investment. As I get older I'm not even sure I agree with the whole idea of unearned wealth from property. It's not like it takes any skill or effort to benefit from house price inflation and it only happens because there's a housing shortage, which means everyone who can't buy a house has to pay high rents and anyone that can buy a house has to pay over the odds. It seems a mad thing to base your whole economy on, but we all get sucked into it because it's our only chance to have any financial asset at all.'

'People are all into the culture of home ownership in this country though, aren't they? Rent is money down the drain, that's what they'd say.'

She wafted her dress around her a bit to cool off. 'As I get older I realise more and more that it's your quality of life that matters, not the monetary value of your possessions. It's not about what you own. It's about wanting what you have, not having what you want.'

Nick pulled at his lip in contemplation. 'You are turning into a hippy.'

'No, I'm not. You can't be a hippy on Teesside, can you? You've just got to find a path through life that makes you happy. I had my Yuppie phase in my late 20s and 30s when I lived in bloody Camden and it was awful, really. As soon as you try and give yourself status by what you can buy, you're always going to lose, because there's always someone with more than you to feel envious of. So you end up trying to stick it to the people with less than you, in order to make yourself feel better about the choices you've made. It's all so negative. Now I'm middle-aged, I'd take love over gold every time. And really, it's not wrong to feel that no-one wins unless everyone wins, is it?'

'It's probably a bit idealistic, Jules. But I do know what you mean. You know, I can never imagine you living in London. You're so, not London.'

'Genuinely, it's more like living in a foreign country than living in a foreign country is. It was good in lots of ways because of that and I liked it for quite a while, but it wears you out on every level, eventually.'

'Yeah, well, the whole house ownership thing never made any sense to me, largely because I have never trusted in the future even happening, let alone being something I should plan for. Life is now, not in 25 years time when you're retired. Also, your depressive tends not to have a long-term vision...it's all you can do to get through another day, sometimes. I've always looked at those TV programmes about buying dream homes with the same disinterest as I would programmes about algebra.'

He pulled at his lip again and looked at the computer. Was this written by the person who had planted the bomb? Was it a lone individual or was it the pressure group? It was a cool name. Middlesbrough Ironopolis was a late Victorian football club that won the Northern League three seasons running and had even reached the quarter final of the FA Cup before going into liquidation after a season in the Football League. Ironopolis was a name coined to express the industry of the area, industry built around iron and steel. It still had an almost futuristic, powerful vibe to it.

103

'There are a few posts from the Ironopolis Anarchists. I'm sure the police and security people will find them from the IP address.'

'Maybe. Unless they use the Darknet and then the IP won't be traceable. Will DI Colin Harcombe be in charge, do you think?' said Julie, collecting their glasses and walking towards the back door.

'Not of this. It'll be classed as terrorism. It'll be a specialist security thing. This sort of thing must happen all the time at all big events though, mustn't it? Bomb threats, I mean.'

'Yeah, you'd imagine so. The difference is someone has put an actual bomb under the horse box. So someone knows Brian's farmhouse and knew there was a horse box there. It's not just someone making a prank call, is it? Even if it is a prank, they've made a lot more effort.'

'No. Jeff will know more when he gets here, I should think,' said Nick.

'I suppose I'd better change and put some pants on if Jeff is coming over.'

'I'll stick the smalls in on a quick wash. He won't be over for a while. There'll be time for them to do and dry.'

'Thanks, darlin'. You're a good gusset washer, you.' She ruffled his hair. 'It's always a social faux pas to show your fanny to your blokes' mates, I reckon.'

'In all except the most liberal of households, certainly.'

She was about to go inside but stopped.

'Hey, how's those drugs doing in your brain? Do you feel any different? You've only had a few so far, so it might take time yet.'

He stood up and looked around himself. 'I think I feel quite good, Jules.' He let out a sigh. 'Yeah, hey I hadn't noticed, but I'm OK. I don't feel stoned happy or anything though...just OK.'

She grinned. 'Good. OK is good.'

The sun had gone down but the sky was still bright in the northwest when Jeff came down the track to their farmhouse in his white van. Rita was alongside him in the passenger seat.

'Aloha, my pretties,' said Jeff, getting out and giving them a wave as they stood at the door.

'Hey, man,' said Nick.

'Hello. You must be Rita,' said Julie, with a wave.

'Hiya, Julie. Yeah. I thought I'd tag along with him and say hello, since we've managed to avoid each other for a few months.'

She had long dark hair and wore a knee-length floral cotton dress with a gold ankle bracelet.

'It's nice to see you. Congratulations on the baby, by the way,' said Nick.

'Yes, congrats Rita,' said Julie.

'Cheers. Yeah, it was a bit of a shock to say the least, but we're looking forward to it now. I was sorry to hear your news, Jules.'

Julie held up her hand. 'Thanks, but there's no need. It is what it is.'

'So, what's been going on, Jeff?' said Nick, ushering them in.

'Well the good news is, it *was* a hoax. The bad news is that it almost wasn't.'

They went through to the back garden and sat around a white wrought-iron table. The air was warm and still. Julie made green tea and brought it out on a tray.

'That box I saw with the blinking light on - apparently that was exactly what a bomb would have looked like. It just didn't have any explosive or a detonator in it,' said Jeff, scratching at his beard. 'But it was "real", if you know what I mean.'

Nick pushed his hair behind his ears. 'Right, so they're saying, look we know how to do this...next time it'll be for real.'

'Aye. Exactly. It's a case of don't mess with us, we're serious and just to emphasise that point they sent an email to Mel Stephens...'

'...to Mel? How did they have his email address?' said Nick.

'Easy. All festival emails are first name dot second name at Teesside Blues dot co dot uk.'

'But they must have known he was in charge,' said Julie. 'That's some sort of inside knowledge.'

Jeff pointed at her and nodded. 'Exactly. Yes. You're right, Jules. They had insider info. No civilian knows Mel. You'd have to be working here, be contracted here or have contacts in the music business to find that out. Not impossible, but it does narrow it a bit. The email said something like, "You have 24 hours to call the festival off or the next bomb will be real". I saw Mel afterwards and he was raging. All sorts of top brass law enforcers and security types are over there now. The whole place is on lock down. They're deciding if it can go ahead.'

'Bloody hell. Were there any more demands made?'

'Apart from the cancellation of the festival, they demanded an investigation by HMRC into the Blakeston Estate and into Big Fish's company which, unimaginatively enough, is called The Big Fish.'

'I'd like to string them up by their bollocks,' said Rita. 'It's disgusting. What have they got to gain by just scaring everyone?'

Jeff held a finger aloft. 'Ah, you say bollocks, but it could be a woman behind it. It was bloke on the phone though, Angie said.'

'She must be a nervous wreck after this,' said Julie. 'She didn't seem the most robust type of woman.'

'She was shaking like a jelly in an earthquake when I saw her. I don't even know if she's going to come back to work, so you might be on your own in there from now, Jules, at least for a few days.'

'To be honest, I'd prefer to do it alone if I can.'

'Mel would like to send out a posse on horseback to lynch whoever did it, if he could,' said Jeff. 'But he's vowed to keep the festival running if they let him.'

'You can't give in, can you?' said Nick.

'They won't risk people's lives, will they?' said Rita. 'Also, no-one will turn up if they think there'll be a bomb.'

Julie poured the tea and shook her head. 'I actually think the opposite is true. I think most Teessiders would want to come even more, just to stick it up the terrorists.'

'Do you reckon?' said Rita, in disbelief.

'Aye. We're an arsy bunch. Sod 'em. I'd go just to make the point even if it was rap music and I can't stand rap music,' said Julie.

'The thing is, this is quite a change of tactics for the Ironopolis

Anarchists. They've been about research and investigation before. Every single case they put into the media was 100 per cent correct. Every dodgy deal, every tax evasion, every underpayment. Bombs seem crude in comparison to that,' said Nick.

'Mel is already planning to beef up security massively. Just about anyone with a decent bicep within 50 miles is being drafted in. He's getting a security firm in as well - blokes in uniforms patrolling around. I mean, someone put that mock bomb under the horse box, so someone must have seen them do that. But we've no idea how long it had been there or even if it was put on there, it might have been done elsewhere. He's putting CCTV cameras all around the house and stables and he'll have them in the campsite as well, I reckon.'

'This'll make a dent in the profits,' said Julie.

'A bit, but muscle isn't expensive, is it? Half of them would do it for the pleasure of bossing people around and the occasional fight,' said Jeff.

Nick told him about the Ironopolis Anarchists he'd found online. 'Let's clear this plural or singular thing up,' said Nick. 'It's bothering me. The forum poster and the campaigning group is plural...'

'...the caller was singular. Angie said anarchist, I heard her telling Mel and the email to Mel was singular as well,' said Jeff. 'Definitely singular because they both assumed it was a lone wolf whack job.'

'Hmm, there's something weird about that. Why would they change their name?' said Julie. 'I suppose it could just be a typo.'

'Not when it's done more than once,' said Nick. 'You'd spot it, wouldn't you? I think it's someone different. Someone who is just using their name to describe themselves.'

'What exactly is an anarchist?' said Rita.

'It's usually a bloke with a big A on the back of an army jacket carrying a few Gang Of Four albums,' said Jeff.

'That means nowt to me,' said Rita with a shrug.

'It's a bit vague in reality. Usually it's someone who doesn't believe in the prevailing system,' said Nick.

'Well I don't believe in the prevailing system, but I'm not an anarchist, am I?' said Julie.

'Are you into politics then, Jules?' said Rita.

'She's as red as they come, this one,' said Jeff scratching his beard.

'No, I'm not. Not in a party politics way. I just believe in people being respected and not being exploited for profit by people with all the money and power. I just believe in equality of opportunity. Everyone deserves a decent chance in life, not just those born into money. If that's left wing then shoot me, but I think it's only, I dunno, it's humane, isn't it? None of us want to be exploited and the way this country is going, it's getting more and more unequal. The rich are getting super rich and the rest of us are left to fight it out for the crumbs.'

She leaned forward and tapped the table with his finger.

'Did you know that top executives now typically earn in three days what their workers earn in a year? In a year! I'm just not having that. It's wrong and you can't tell me it isn't. They're not worth that, they've just awarded themselves big money because they can. More galling still is that these blokes - and it is almost always blokes - go from one big job to another, regardless of if they're any good. It's like they're in the club so they get the next highly paid gig that comes along. Look at the people that used to run the FA. They made a right bollocks of that but went onto to run other massive public bodies as though they were any good.'

Nick cheered and applauded. 'Top-class ranting, that, Jules.'

'You should stand for Parliament, you. Like I said, red as they come,' said Jeff, with sarcasm. Julie pursed her lips but said nothing more. 'But it's one thing to have political ideas and theories but another to start bombing people, isn't it? I mean, that's the work of total nutters.'

'It is, I agree...' said Nick, '...but don't forget, a lot of major landowners in this country first got their land hundreds of years ago by force. So getting what you want by violence has a long tradition in the establishment, they've been at it longer than anyone else. I was reading about how when they built Castle Howard down near Malton, they just booted out everyone from a nearby village and razed it to the ground just so they could build their big fuck-off house. They'd like us to all forget about this sort of stuff or just laugh about it because now they've got the money and land and respectability they don't want us taking it off them the way they took it off the people in the first place.'

'Totally right,' said Julie, nodding. 'They nicked the land with private armies, they got themselves and people like them elected to Parliament, often corruptly, and then made laws to enshrine and protect the power and wealth they stole from the people, and now they want us to respect them or even look up to them?! Sod that. I'll respect a steelworker or a miner or a nurse, but I'm damned if I'm looking up to some chinless wonder who's just inherited money and land and power. How fair is that?'

'I know what you mean but that sounds dead left wing to me,' said Rita. 'It sounds like union leaders sounded in the 70s and 80s.'

She seemed to disapprove of this.

'I don't think you need to be left wing to see that the money keeps the money,' said Nick. 'What annoys me most is how the rich elite gets the people to turn on each other while they're getting away with any amount of tax dodging, awarding themselves huge pay increases and generally taking the piss on a grand scale. I don't even care about the money really, it's the principle of it that really winds me up.'

'Aye, I know what you mean,' said Jeff. 'But like I say, threatening to kill people with a bomb isn't right, is it? It's not the way to change things. Not in the 21st century.'

'No, of course not. It's totally bloody disgraceful and I hope they catch whoever made that threat. But it's not said enough, that the rich and powerful stick the boot into the regular people without any guilt or consideration to the devastation they cause,' said Nick.

'The problem is, people don't mind just having enough to get by on - we're used to it as a way of life - but when they see other people rolling in unearned, undeserved wealth and then they get told what to do, how to behave and what they should or shouldn't be prepared to do in life by those people, they stick two fingers up at them and rightly so,' said Julie, her cheeks now flushed pink with righteous anger.

Jeff finished his tea. 'Right, we'll get off and leave Mr and Mrs Red Revolution to plan the overthrow of society. I'll see you both at the festival site tomorrow, providing it's still there and hasn't been blown up.'

The whole of the festival site was crawling with security and police officers in the morning. Overnight the *Evening Gazette* had run a quick opinion poll and found that 91 per cent of the people wanted the festival to go ahead. A decision had been made. The show would go on. There was a sudden rush for the remaining tickets on the website. By 8am, the whole three days were sold out.

Angie had called in and refused to come back to work in the office, fearing an explosion, leaving Julie to organise things as she wanted them. Nick lent a hand doing some heavy lifting before writing more content for Emily Davids. Mel Stephens called everyone together and made sure everyone knew that it was business as usual.

A couple of days later, Nick was up early as usual for his walk around the fields. A warm, sticky night had given way to low haze and a humid, damp morning, the Cleveland Hills in the distance obscured by low cloud. The summer birds were all in full chorus. He stopped at a wooden gate and perched on it for a few minutes just to take in the early morning peace. It was strange how every morning seemed to be a new, fresh start, as though the previous day hadn't happened at all. Every day was fresh out of the box: a total reboot. By 10am it was already being sullied and used, but at 6.30am it was still uncreased and unstained. Beautiful. It'd have been nice to enjoy it whilst holding the hand of their girl or boy.

He let out an involuntary groan as he often did when something came into his head that made him feel awkward or that he didn't really want to think about. Taking two green Phenibut capsules from his pocket, he looked at them. Were they helping? Even though he felt stronger since taking them, they hadn't stopped him dreaming about what might have been. He still imagined pointing out the birds and plants along the route to their daughter or son. The cheeky robin that was always flitting from fence post to fence post, the noisy wrens, the tall purple and white foxgloves about to come into flower, the occasional mouse that scurried under some butterbur.

Wandering back at a dawdle, he hummed loudly to himself - another distraction technique he'd started to take himself away from his thoughts. In the past he'd pinch his skin or dig his nails into the palms of his hand to the point of drawing blood in order to get relief. At least he didn't do that any more. Things were better. Humming was less destructive and you have to embrace the small victories when you are prone to depression, or the big losses can really bloody drown you.

Still, it was a lovely early morning and although his mind was prone to re-inhabit the same old places, the deep ache in his bones seemed to be forgetting to hurt him the way it had done. It wasn't something you noticed as you went about your daily business, but in the quiet of an early Teesside morning it was more clear. The thoughts were still there, but the reflexive melancholy that had accompanied them was diminished. Yeah, the pills had to be working.

'What's it like out?' said Julie as he got back into the kitchen.

'Humid and damp. You'll be hot in that office again.'

'Bugger. Are you working at home?'

'Yeah, I've got to finish more band biogs by this afternoon. Shouldn't be overly stressful. When's your lunch break?'

'1pm for an hour.'

'I'll come over and take you to that tea shop on Norton Green then.'

'Aw, that'll be nice. I'm going to eat my body weight in their delicious lemon cheesecake.'

She dressed for work in lightweight pale blue cotton pants, baseball boots and a cropped black Guns 'n' Roses t-shirt which revealed her tanned midriff. She pulled on an LA Raiders baseball cap bought on holiday.

'How do I look? Mutton dressed as...?'

'I know you're always worried about that, but you look cool to me and more importantly you're less likely to overheat in there.'

'And I want to look a bit rock 'n' roll, don't I? I felt like a right Little Miss Prim in my suit on the first day. Right, I'll see you later.'

Writing 200 words on every band on the bill wasn't hard, but it took him all morning. He sent an email with them all in to Emily and then set off for the festival site.

There was a high police presence on the approach road to the farmhouse and as he turned off the road to drive up the long gravel path, two officers flagged him down.

'Do you have business here, sir?' one said.

'I'm picking up my missus, Julie Wells. I'm Nick Guymer. I work here as well.'

The copper turned away and spoke into a lapel radio. A minute later he was allowed to proceed. There were cars everywhere, parked seemingly at random. Some yellow police tape cordoned off the entrance to the stables where the horse box had been. As he got out the car and threw his bag over his right shoulder, he could hear Mel Stephens' booming Geordie voice, shouting.

'Do I have to do everything here myself? Do you want me to build that bloody stage with my own bare hands?' He emerged from the house carrying a large rubber mallet with two hairy men in pursuit.

'Everything OK, Mel?' said Nick as he approached.

'No, it is not, Guymer. I've got a loony making bomb threats and I've got a bunch of useless bastards constructing a stage for me out Sellotape and matchsticks and everyone in there seems to have nicked off for their dinners, skiving bastards. Apart from that...'

Nick grinned at him, Mel had turned moaning into a sort of art form. He pushed open the large glossy black Georgian front door and walked into the hallway of the house. As he did so, Simon Garbutt and Big Fish were coming out of a big room on the left. Their voices were raised and seemed to be arguing about something. They didn't seem to notice him despite his attempts to acknowledge them. It was quite a relief, as he had no idea what to talk to them about.

As he walked in the sound of Soundgarden's *Superunknown* album was blasting from the office on the left - his favourite album from that era. He put his head around the door. Jeff was in the far corner talking to someone.

'Alright Jeff!' he shouted, above the music, putting his bag down behind a desk.

'Now then! Sounds bloody great, doesn't it?' shouted Jeff. 'Everyone is on their lunch so we thought we'd crank it up a bit. You here to see Jules? She's on the top floor.'

Nick put his thumb up and went back out and up the stairs. The air got noticeably warmer as he got higher up. Originally four bedrooms, it was now two offices and two locked rooms; presumably they were still bedrooms. Julie was sat behind a large Queen Anne oak desk at the far end of the first room, right beside an open 12-pane Georgian window. She looked up from her screen and held up a finger.

'I'll be two minutes. Just need to make a call.'

He walked out and along the landing to the second room. The slight figure of Emily Davids was also sitting at a big desk. 'Hi Emily,' he said looking in the door and waving.

She ruffled up her scraggy hair and looked at him with sparky eyes.

'Hey, Nicky boy, are you here to pick up Jules? Thanks for your biogs, they were ace.' She smiled generously at him.

'No probs. It's what I do, baby cakes.' He said, affecting an American accent. 'Bad business with that bomb threat.' He smiled to himself for using Detective Inspector Colin Harcombe's favourite phrase and walked into her office.

'Awful, yeah. We're all on pins wondering what's going to happen next, but Mel rallied the troops, as is his way.' She fiddled with a silver skull pendant around her neck, got up and walked to an open window to let the breeze cool her off a little, tugging at her black vest adorned with the X-Ray of a skull, a short white cotton skirt fluttering around above her knees. 'Gosh, I'm so hot. I think I could sit here naked and still be sweaty.'

'Well don't let me stop you, Em,' said Nick.

'Ha ha. I will if you will, mister. You go first. Ha ha. I mean it...go on...oh alright, I'll go first.' She quickly lifted the skirt up to her belly, revealing her slim thighs and hips and underwear, giggling in a teenagy sort of way as she did so.

Nick felt almost beyond awkward and put his hands over his eyes. 'I'm too young to see this,' he said in mock horror.

She seemed to enjoy his discomfort and hooked her thumbs into the string of fabric at the side of her underwear and rolled it down a little, saying, 'And now to cool off properly.'

'This is probably illegal, Emily. I might have to make a citizen's arrest.'

Still laughing, she pulled her underwear up a little and let the dress fall.

'Oh, you're no fun, are you? Well, another time, maybe,' she said, cheerfully straightening herself out and sitting back down.

Julie came in and smiled at him. 'Right, let's go and get some tea. We're proper mafted up here, aren't we, Em?'

'Yeah. I was just showing Nick how hot I am.' She pushed her tongue into the gap between her front teeth and grinned to herself as she said it. 'I'm sweating from places I didn't know I had, Jules. We should grow tomatoes in here.'

'Or cannabis maybe. Just so we can calm Mel down a bit. He's been raging about the place like a bull with haemorrhoids. The irony of it is, the bomb thing apart, everything is really well organised. It might look chaotic, but everything is right on the money. As far as I can tell, everything that needs sorting is being sorted. I've not had one raised voice on the phone this morning.'

Emily nodded. 'That's all down to Mel. He runs this thing with a rod of iron, but only so things get done. His bark is worse than his bite.'

'Have you worked with him for long, then?' said Nick.

'This is my third summer holidays on his books. I've just finished my degree at Teesside Uni.'

'Oh yeah? What did you study?' said Nick.

'Computer Science.' She ruffled her hair again and took a drink out of water bottle.

'That sounds really 1970s-ish, Computer Science. Jules has just got her MA, you know. Has she told you?'

'No. Oh, well done. What was it in?'

'History. Much good it'll do me in the job market.'

'It's not all about jobs though, is it?'

'No. You're right. Come on mister, my lunch hour is already down to 50 minutes. There's just you up here now, Em. If the breeze picks up any more, will you shut the window in my office? It'll make every door in the building slam otherwise.'

'No worries.' She waved a hand at them as they left. 'Have a nice lunch.'

Nick took Julie's hand as they walked downstairs.

'What's that for?' she said, looking at their hands intertwined.

'I don't know. It just feels nice coming here to pick you up in the sunshine, going out for some tea and cheesecake. It's like I say, it feels nice.'

She kissed the back of his hand and grinned at him happily. 'Eeee, you're a funny lad you, must be those happy pills,' she said, swinging hands to and fro like they were teenagers.

'You know, just before she died, mam said I was born a happy little boy who was always giggling and laughing; maybe I'm just starting to find which bus stop in life I left him at.'

'Aw man. How sweet,' she said, touching his cheek a little.

'Oh bugger, I've left my bag in the office, I'd better just pick it up,' he said.

They got to the first floor landing and had turned to take the last flight of stairs down to the hallway and the front door.

He felt it before he heard it.

Holding onto the banister as they took the first steps on that final flight of stairs, without warning, it shuddered unnaturally. A micro-second after he felt it, a huge, gut-wrenching, deep, resonant, almost comedy boom, exploded. It seemed like there should have been warning, a preamble to the explosion, but there wasn't. One second everything was normal, the next second everything was devastation. Both of them knew in half a heartbeat what it was and what it meant.

CHAPTER 8

It had gone off in the room where Soundgarden had been playing. The explosion was followed by the roaring noise of masonry, plastic and god knows what else falling down. The force of it pushed a fierce sideways mushroom cloud of smoke out of the large, wide door and into the hallway below Nick and Julie. A powerful belch of air pushed up the stairs. What do you do? Do you run away from it or run towards it to help people?

'Jeff was in there! Jeff!' he yelled. What if there was a second device? Fuck it. It would kill them. So be it. Instinctively they ran down the stairs two at a time and into the billowing clouds of smoke and dust and crap.

Weirdly, the room was suddenly quiet except for the sound of falling plaster from the roof. It was impossible to see anything and even harder to breathe. Nick pulled off his t-shirt and wrapped it around his mouth to create a makeshift filter. Julie did the same with hers. Where was Jeff? No-one could have survived, surely. 'Jeff! Jeff are you here?!" he screamed, muffled by the fabric. No reply. God help him, the room was devastated.

Right beside the door was a figure, male. He was lying flat out, having been blown off his chair. Unconscious or dead, he lay motionless.

'Let's get him out!' shouted Nick and pointed to his feet. Julie lifted them up as he lifted the shoulders. Fortunately he was a skinny kid. They took him out into the hallway and then a right towards the foyer and the front door.

Emily Davids was screaming at the top of the stairs, looking down on the devastation with uncomprehending horror, her hands over her mouth.

'Emily! Come down! Get outside!' he shouted. 'Come down the stairs and get outside. Do it! Now!' he yelled. She seemed frozen with fear. They got the body to the front door and then heard a familiar Geordie voice bellowing at high volume.

'Who needs help? Shout out. I'll get you out. Don't fucking worry. Don't you fucking worry. Hang on in there. We're fucking coming for you!' It was Mel Stephens. He emerged out of the swirling miasma of dust like a tattooed apparition.

'Mel. Mel! We've got one here. Give us a hand,' yelled Nick.

Without a question or a moments hesitation, he hoisted him onto his shoulder and ran out. Nick turned and ran up the stairs two at a time, grabbed Emily around the waist and put her over his shoulder just as Mel had done. She seemed to weigh nothing as he ran back down through plumes of dust and disaster and outside to the bright light of a summer's day.

He lay her down on a strip of grass.

'Are you alright?' he shouted, she nodded, tears streaming down her face, her green eyes distraught and uncomprehending. He put his hand on her cheek and kissed her once on the head.

The police and security teams that had been on site were now massing outside the house, clearly awaiting instructions on how to proceed. Someone shouted in an attempt to stop him going back in. Screw that. This was no time for procedure. This was life or death.

Julie was already in the exploded room as he returned at speed, Mel hot on his heels. The three of them waded almost blindly through the gritty, charcoal fog, the floor littered with debris. Julie let out a yell. She'd kicked an arm; an arm that wasn't attached to a body. It didn't look real, it couldn't be real, but it was real. No time to think about it. Now was for the living, not for the dead. The dead had had their day. This was the one marked on the cosmic calendar for them. We've all got a last day. Every single one of us. We could turn the pages of a diary and put our finger on it if we did but know when. This was their last.

Sirens in the distance now, lots of shouting and raised voices from outside. Nick turned around and looked across the room as the dust settled. Was Jeff here? Please let him not be here. But the bomb had gone off in the far corner where he'd just been talking to him and had taken out an 18-pane Georgian window in totality.

Outside the humid, damp day continued as though this hadn't happened. As though there had been no ripping apart of the normality of the day. Inside it was devastation. He glimpsed more body parts, trying not to let his eyes rest on them. What was Jeff wearing? Black jeans and a red checked shirt.

Oh fuck. A torso was propped up against the back wall, blood oozing out where limbs had been severed from it. It was red...oh god, oh god. It was Jeff. It was what remained of Jeff. He stepped over a detached bare arm and approached the bloody mass of flesh. No. Whoever it was, it wasn't Jeff. The red was blood on a white shirt. At the same time that he felt revulsion and numb fear, he also felt relief.

Bodies had been ripped into pieces. A roll of bloody blue denim lay under some big chunks of plaster, it had to be a leg. People had been reduced to butchered meat: the office now some sort of improvised slaughterhouse. There were no other bodies to rescue, not whole bodies, anyway.

'Jules! Mel! Come on, let's get out of here! There's no-one left alive.'

She pointed at a green army canvas bag. Jeff's bag. The one he used to carry albums around in. It lay on its back against the far wall, a copy of Johnny Winter's *Still Alive And Well* ironically enough, spilling out of it.

Nick looked around again, desperate not to see anything that might be a piece of his old mate, but maybe he had been atomized by the explosion. No, surely not. It hadn't been that big an explosion.

He walked out, pushing past other people now crowding into the scene, horrified at what they were seeing, catching up with Julie as she forced her way out. He took his t-shirt off his face and spat out gritty dollops of greyish saliva and blew snot and dust out of his nose.

'Are you OK?' he called to her.

She took her t-shirt off her face and pulled it back on over her black bra. Her fair blonde hair had a thick layer of steel-coloured ash on it, her face a full-make up of filth. Only her turquoise blue eyes remained clean and bright.

She nodded, spat twice and wiped her mouth, standing hands on hips, shaking her head.

'The fucking bastards that did this...we'll fucking 'ave them,' she said it with a quiet, determined viciousness and spat again. 'No excuses. Nothing. This is so fucking wrong. Fucking bastards. How the fuck dare they?!! How dare they do that to...to...to those poor people!' She squatted down and put her head in her hands.

Nick stared at the ground, at his feet on the gravel. Was there no limit to the evil humans could inflict upon each other? What could possibly justify this? What sort of mind would think it was in any way at all acceptable? Killing people in the name of what? It was profoundly shocking in a literal way, but then, in another, it was despicably familiar human behaviour. He patted her on the back; an utterly impotent gesture. He spat out more gritty saliva. They had nearly died. They were a few feet from dying. It was just luck. If Julie had been ready sooner, if he hadn't stopped to mess around with Emily. If...if...if...their lives hung on these random chances. Whoever had planted this had tried to kill him, tried to kill Julie, tried to kill Emily and Jeff and everyone in there. This was personal. He hockled up dirty phlegm once more and spat it out again. Very fucking personal.

The house now embodied two different realities. The northwest corner of the building now had no windows and plumes of dust drifted out of the gaping wounds in the building where they had been. The eastern and southern parts were untouched by the trauma of the explosion. If you shielded your eyes from the broken side, everything still looked normal.

No-one could speak. Words seemed inappropriate or inadequate. The staff that were on the site now sat out on the grass, backs against a stone wall and watched as emergency and security services went about their business. Still no Jeff. Nick tried phoning him. It went to voice mail. Fuck. Come on, Jeff.

'Jules! Jules! Thank god...' Kev Wells came running up, with his brother Ricky in tow. Two big, thick-set, shaven-headed blokes in checked shirts and jeans. 'What the fuck happened here?' said Kev, turning around to look at the house.

'What do you think happened?' said Julie, giving him a withering look. 'It was a bloody bomb.'

'Fuck. Is it the fucking Muslims, havin' a pop at us, like?' said Ricky, his fists gripped into a tight ball as though he could fight the idea of terrorism, the way he could fight a night club bouncer.

'No, it fucking isn't. Shut your fucking mouth and sit down, you couple of total fucking idiots,' she said gesturing angrily for them to sit down. They did as they were told.

'We heard about it on the radio. I knew you were working here so we came right over. They've shut off the road so we parked up on the back lane and came through the woods and across the festival field. That side of the house is a real fucking mess. How many dead then?'

Kev Wells didn't have a subtle bone in his body.

'I reckon two or three. I saw two different people's...bits, like,' said Nick, leaning back on his hands.

'Fuck. Body parts, like?' said Ricky, almost with relish, at the gore.

'If it's only two we'll have been lucky. That room had 10 or more in it most of the time. Jeff was in it a little bit earlier, man.'

'The big man. Where is he?'

'I don't know.'

'He wasn't one of the...'

'I don't know, he might have been...it was hard to tell,' said Nick. He called Jeff again, again it went to voice mail.

'This is the work of the Ironopolis Anarchists, it has to be,' said Julie. 'If you two want to make yourself useful, you can find out who the fuck they are and beat the living shit out of them and then bring them to me so I can beat the living shit out of them as well. The absolute, fucking bastards. Who the hell do they think they are? It's...it's...it's disgusting.' Emotion boiled in her throat. Nick put his hand over hers.

'The Iron what?' said Ricky.

'I told you, Rick. Some nerd online,' said Kev.

'Oh aye. Cunts.'

'Watch your language, big mouth,' scowled Julie, kicking him on the shin.

'Aiyazz. Alright Jules, man. No need for that,' said Ricky.

'No need? I've just been wading through blown up bits of bodies, man. It's the most sodding horrible thing I'll ever see. The least you can do is keep your mouth in check.'

'I'll put the word out, Jules. See what we can come up with,' said Kev, lighting up a cigarette.

'Whoever did this will want to claim responsibility soon enough,' said Nick. 'No-one does this to be anonymous. This is part of something. It's not a one-off. They've targeted this festival for a reason. My guess is that it's symbolic of something they think is wrong. It's a follow-up to the hoax one a few days ago.'

'What's wrong with music, like?' said Ricky.

Nick shook his head. 'It's not a protest against blues music, Ricky. I'm pretty sure of that. It's something to do with Brian and Stevie Salmon, I think,' said Nick, searching to make sense of something fundamentally senseless. 'The tax and that...stopping the festival...'

'Twats.' She said it with a flat grimace.

'Maybe it's the animal rights lot protesting about horse racing. If it is we should be able to give 'em a proper pounding, like,' said Ricky, fists gripped again. 'Got nowt about them, veggies.'

'Rick, man. They've got access to explosives and if they've got access to explosives, they could well have guns as well. So don't go thinking you can bully some weedy, pale-faced bunny hugger. These are fucking dangerous, man.' said Julie, her mouth open, incredulous at her brother's thinking. 'You can be such a stupid prick, sometimes.'

Nick called Jeff again, but it went straight to voice mail once more. He texted him instead. 'Where are you? Bomb gone off at Brian's house.' He walked towards the car park to see if Jeff's van was there, but wasn't able to get a proper look at all the cars before the police stopped him. The whole place was one massive crime scene. Everyone was a suspect. In the distance, talking to two officers, he could see Simon Garbutt, Big Fish's manager alongside another couple of people pointing in the direction of the explosion. Mel Stephens was gesturing dramatically while smoking his cigar. He had his arm around Emily Davids, who had gone to him for protection, almost as though he was a father figure. Stress and fear was written on everyone's face.

Officers began moving amongst the staff taking statements. The festival couldn't go on in the face of this, could it?

Eventually, Mel gathered everyone working on the site together in a semi-circle in a field far away from the house. Everyone was quiet, some smoking, all of them in shock. As they did so, Nick's phone vibrated. The relief that fell from his body almost made him throw-up. It was a text from Jeff. 'Just saw your text. Are you OK? Got called to the hospital. Rita. Bastards.'

'We've lost three,' Mel said, his cigar wedged in the corner of his mouth. 'The three lads in that corner. Three students.' He shook his head in disbelief and the straightened himself up to his full height and puffed out his chest. He looked like a heavyweight boxer. 'But I'll tell youse all this. We're not stopping. Right? This is not going to break us. This festival is going ahead and is going to be best fucking festival we've ever put on because we owe it to those three lads. No fucking terrorist is getting the best of us. Not now. Not ever. I've already spoken to the copper in charge and some top brass in London, they've both said the politics of this is clear - we keep on keeping on. Fuck 'em!! So we go home now, we get our shit together and we come back tomorrow even more strong, right? No retreat, no surrender. Right? Right!'

They all shouted out their agreement. It was spine-tingling. Unity in the face of death and destruction.

The overcast humidity of the day was blown away on an evening westerly breeze, leaving clear skies as the sun went down. Nick and Julie sat in their garden after giving an exhaustive statement to the police. Nature was almost unreasonably lovely in the face of the day's heinous violence.

'Nice to get clean,' he said, almost underneath his breath, a towel around his neck.

She pursed her lips together and nodded as she de-tangled a knot in her wet hair.

'I'll never forget what I saw in that room for as long as I live.' She spoke quietly.

'Aye. It's one thing seeing this sort of thing on the telly, it's another altogether seeing it in person. It's all in abstract, until you're actually there and you see, smell and hear what it does.'

She shook her head. They'd both witnessed it. Words didn't help deal with it.

'I wonder how Rita is? Doesn't sound too good for the bairn, does it?' she said.

'Nope. Though, ironically enough, that call saved Jeff's life. He must have missed it by a minute or two.'

'What was on when the bomb went off? I heard it when we were walking down the stairs.'

'Soundgarden. "Spoonman". Not a bad track to breathe your last to. At least it wasn't "Highway To Hell".' He rubbed his forearm contemplatively. 'The bomb went off in that far corner. I'd just had a brief word with Jeff before I came up to see you. I left my bag there.'

'Where did you leave it?'

'Behind the desk in that corner.' There'll be nothing left of it now. Lucky I didn't have my laptop in it. Normally I would have, but I'd just sent Emily my stuff, so I figured I'd not need it and left it at home.'

'That was right where the bomb went off. You could see the pattern of the explosion up the wall. You must have seen it, even if you didn't register it.'

'Yeah. I suppose so. Awful thought, that. I was there with the fucking thing ticking away right beside me.' He shivered.

She let out a moan. 'I wonder if anyone has put their hand up for this yet? And I wonder what Big Fish and poor Brian make of it?'

'Brian is still at Sandy Lane in the Bahamas, thankfully. If I was him, I'd bloody stay there. It'll break his heart to see what has happened to his lovely Georgian house. The Fish is in London, I think. He had a gig last night at the Apollo.'

'The Apollo? How does he sell that many tickets?'

'People like him, Jules. We don't. But others do. A lot of others.'

'I don't understand that.'

'Comedy is very personal, isn't it? You can't argue for your own taste over someone else's.'

'With him, I can.'

'Aye. There are only so many rape jokes anyone can tell before it sounds like an endorsement.'

'I wonder if he'll come back up. He strikes me as a coward who would stay a long way from any trouble if he could. That sort of bloke has got nowt about him.'

'It's only just over two weeks until the festival starts and he's supposed to be doing the headline set on the comedy stage each day as well as doing some compère work between sets.' He took out one of the green Phenibut pills and washed it down with tea.

'The weird thing is, in a way, I wasn't shocked when it happened. That's stupid; I mean, of course I was shocked, but I think in part of all our brains now, we do half expect it. We've seen these atrocities on TV so often, those bombings in London, 9/11 and all the way back to the IRA in the 70s and 80s. I think a bit of us isn't actually that surprised when a bomb goes off, ' she said, pulling her legs under her.

He nodded. 'I know what you mean. Whenever I see a plane flying over a city, I think of 9/11. Did we do alright, Jules? We did what we could, didn't we?'

'Yeah. I think so. I mean, it was hard to even breathe in that room at first. We got out the only one we could get out and at least he turned out to be alive. Shit, y'know, I've still got grit in between my teeth.' She let out an other groan and rubbed at her eyes, then gave a half snort and a bitter laugh. 'Never thought I'd be

125

wondering around Brian's house in my bra with my shirt wrapped around my face. Sounds like a bad dream.'

'A bloody nightmare,' said Nick.

'Mel was amazing, wasn't he? Proper larger than life hero. The way he took charge and almost didn't seem fazed by it at all,' said Julie.

'Aye. You find out something about a man in a situation like that. I liked what I saw.'

'Yeah, me too. Proper gutsy bloke,' said Julie. 'And you picked up Emily like she was a hand bag.'

'There's nothing to her, is there? Poor lass was petrified.' A car engine dropped its revs up on the road and turned down their track. 'I bet that's Jeff,' said Nick, getting up and walking around to the front of the house.

'How is she?' he called, as Jeff got out the van.

'Fine. Aye. She's fine. False alarm. Crapped myself, but everything's alright. What a fucking day you've had, though.' Nick was going to give him a hug, it was so good to see him, but then Jeff didn't do hugging, so he slapped him on the arm instead. They walked around to the back.

'Hi Jules. You alright?'

'Yes thanks. How's Rita?'

'She's fine. Had a bit of a false alarm. She woke up bleeding and then called me. She's got the all clear though. Turns out it saved my sodding life. I was away about three minutes when that bomb went off.'

'We thought you were a goner, man,' said Nick, sitting down.

'Aye, after I got your text and calls I could tell your brown-eye was twitching about us...'

'I just expected to see some bit of you in that room...I was sure I would,' said Nick, rubbing the corners of his eyes.

'Mel says they've had an email claiming responsibility for the bomb from the Ironopolis Anarchists, plural. No phone call, though. Same demands as with the hoax. They want an end to the festival, an investigation into the Blakeston Estate and Big Fish, only this time they've also tagged on some animal rights stuff. They want an end to horse-racing, saying it's cruel and exploits the animals.'

Nick sat upright and rested his chin on his hand. 'That's not the IA gig, is it? They've never mentioned animal rights before.'

Jeff shrugged. 'Well, you buy into one of these ways of seeing the world and you get a load of other attitudes free of charge though, don't you? It's like astrology comes with crystals, whale music, dream catchers and tie-dyed pants. It's a package deal. A boxed set, to put it in vinyl records parlance.'

Nick pulled his bottom lip up over his top lip. 'I know what you mean, but I'm not sure that's right in this case. Inequality and fair taxation don't usually go with animal rights. It's usually anti-hunting, wearing fur and pro-Smiths records. If animal rights was important to them, they'd have voiced it before now and it's all been about taxation and inequalities of wealth. These demands sound too...'

'...too stupid,' chipped in Julie. 'They are, they're stupid. They've killed people, it doesn't seem likely that the estate's tax affairs are going to be scrutinized because it means they win by violence and that cannot be allowed to happen. And they must know horse racing won't end either. Right or wrong, it's got a long tradition and loads of people really like it, even though I can't work out why.'

'You're right. They're surely not serious, are they?' said Nick. 'No amount of bombing will make any of those things happen. How could it?'

Jeff shrugged and held his index finger aloft as he took a seat. 'Two things occur to me. First, these demands are not from the people responsible for the bomb at all, they're idiots just riding on their coat tails and second, if it is the person or group responsible, they really are proper nutters, to whom we can't assign any logic or rationale. They're just fucked up, vicious bastards with some general grievance against humanity.'

He flicked his long greying hair over his shoulder. 'Either way, it makes no difference, in that the festival is going ahead as a symbolic act of defiance, if nothing else.'

'Have you spoken to Big Fish?'

He nodded. 'He's still in London. He reckons it's "loony lefties". At first he thought it was Al-Qaeda.'

'He's pathetic,' said Julie, turning her mouth down and shaking her head.

'It's probably the only terrorist group he's heard of, apart from the IRA. Mind when I told him who had put their hand up, he was furious. Started off on a big rant.'

Julie went into the kitchen and got a bottle of cheap white wine out of the fridge, unscrewed the top and returned outside with two glasses.

'Will you join me, Jeff?'

'Aye go on. I feel like a proper drink up, actually. Better wait until I get home though. I've only got to drive to Hartburn, so give us half a glass.'

She poured Nick some fizzy water and squeezed a wedge of lime in it.

'Could you get hold of the email they sent Mel, Jeff?' said Nick.

Jeff pulled a stupid face, took out his phone, pressed it twice and then passed it to him. 'I am your humble servant, master,' he said. 'I sent myself a copy of it from Mel's computer.'

'Good work,' said Julie, slapping him on his arm, putting his glass down.

Nick squinted at it. "We claim responsibility for the bomb at the Blakston Estate" - they've spelled Blakeston wrong. "We planted it and detonated it. If you don't want this to happen again we demand an immediate cancellation of the Teeside Blues festival" - bloody hell, they spelled Teesside wrongly, that is absolutely criminal - "an investigation into the tax affairs of Stevie Salmon and the Blakston estate" - spelled wrongly again - "we also demand an end to the cruel, exploitative sport of horse-racing. Yours in violence. The Ironopolis Anarchists". Anarchists. Plural.'

He studied it closely for a minute, plucking at his beard stubble with thumb and forefinger. 'See, the first threat was made over the phone...and then by email.'

'I've got that first email on there, too,' said Jeff. 'Forwarded myself a copy at the same time. See, it's from the Ironopolis Anarchist and it's all spelled correctly, too.'

Nick looked at it. Teesside was spelled correctly.

'Angie took the call, didn't she, Jeff?' said Julie.

'Yup. That time, they called themselves the Ironopolis Anarchist. Single. Deffo. I remember that's what she said.'

'But you've only got Angie's word for that, haven't you?' said Nick, mulling on an idea.

'Uh huh. Why? Do you think she made it up? She invented it or something?' said Jeff.

'No. But she might have got it wrong,' said Nick.

'That's true. She wasn't the sort to be calm under pressure. I mean, she was sweet but...' said Julie.

'...but you wouldn't want her opening the batting for England at Headingley with a sticky wicket and swing in the air,' said Jeff, nodding. 'I know just what you mean.'

She gave a tired laugh at his analogy. 'Totally. I do find it odd that the email has this horses thing tagged on. Tax is their big pressure group thing, unless Angie missed something about animal rights, too. She might have panicked and just not heard them or something.'

Nick drank the water and thought about it. 'No. I'm sure these messages are from two different groups. Being a part of a pressure group is a big thing so they wouldn't spell their own name wrongly. Not even one letter wrong. I think the hoax call and its email are not the real group. How does anyone get in touch with them? The real Ironopolis Anarchists, I mean. The ones that have been campaigning?'

Nobody knew. There was no contact info online, no website or email address.

'The last piece about them was in the *Gazette*. Why don't you call Malcolm Helms up, he's still some sort of editor there, isn't he?' said Jeff. 'He must have a way to get in touch with them. Or he'll tell you how he hears from them. You know Malky from school, don't you?'

'Yeah, yeah...I forgot he went back to the *Gazette*. I've not seen him for a couple of years. We used to run into him at the Boro, didn't we, Jules?'

'Hmm, I always felt he was looking through my clothes somehow. He's one of *those* blokes...' She shuddered.

'Aye, he is a bit sleazy. He does local affairs, politics and that. I've got his number here somewhere.'

He dialled.

'Malky. It's Nick Guymer.'

'Hello stranger. How's thee?'

'Alright man. Yeah. Good thanks. I'm getting married soon, actually.'

'Really? Who'd have you, like?'

'Julie...Julie Wells..'

'Bloody hell. You still with her? How's an ugly get like you a lass that good-looking? You must have a cock like a Python.'

'I sometimes wonder that myself, Malky.' He grinned at her. She poked a tongue out at him

'I know he's saying rude things,' she said. 'He once tried to chat me up in the Incognito when I was 16. Put his hand up right my skirt. Sod. From what I hear, he's not exactly matured since then.'

'She says hello, by the way. I'll tell you why I'm ringing...' He explained what they'd gone through that day. 'I can give you an exclusive interview about it if you want.'

'Top man! Great human interest story. I'll take it.'

'We were first on the scene. You probably won't be able to use it until you get the go-ahead from the authorities, but all the same...the thing is Malky, I need a favour in return.'

'What can I do for you, like?'

'You know you've done interviews with this Ironopolis Anarchists pressure group? How does that work? Do they meet someone from the paper?'

'No mate. No chance. The stuff we've done has all been done by email - to and fro like. No-one has spoken to them directly.'

'So you've no idea who they are or where they are?'

'As far as I know, nobody has. For all I know they're not even based up here. They could be in Vladivostok for all we know. The IP address they used to send the email is, somehow, anonymous. I don't understand all that teckie shit, but they've hidden or masked it so they can't be traced. I even had someone from the terrorism squad come and take a look at it after that bomb threat. He was as puzzled by it as I was.'

'So all the bits we see in newspapers quoting them, they're all done via email, never by phone?'

'Yeah. All of them. We've asked for a number to ring them on. They could give us a pay-as-you-go phone, but they don't even want to do that. The security blokes said they think they're part of a wider network of groups all over the country and into Europe as well.'

'Really? So they're all working on similar local issues?'

'Yeah, always about tax and having a go at rich landowners, that sort of thing. It's not a formal group or anything, just a...what did the fella say now? Err...a union of like minds...that was it.'

'I see. So you don't know anything about them at all?'

'Nothing. They obviously know this area well though and if you look at the details they use in their press releases, they clearly have access to inside information on landowners. They know who to go after and who to leave alone. That Lord Wolviston fella who approved a takeover of some financial institution, pocketed a massive pile of cash in the deal and then almost bankrupted the whole financial institution. He got hauled up and prosecuted late last year and it was the Ironopolis Anarchists who brought that to the attention of HMRC and the FSA. They forced all of that into the public domain. He's one of the few bankers who've been hauled over the coals. That's not guesswork, is it? They know what they're doing, this mob. They've repeated that trick a few times now. All the lords and ladies, bankers and landowners are running scared of them.'

'You couldn't give me the email address they use, could you? If I get anything, I'll let you know right away. Exclusive.'

'It's different every time. The security guy told me that a new one is generated for each mail. It's never been the same twice. But you can have one of them if you like. It won't do any good. The emails we've sent always bounce back.' He read out a string of random letters and numbers @ a seemingly random string of letters and numbers dot some more letters. It was like no email address he'd ever seen before, but he wrote it down, regardless.

'OK. Well, thanks, Malky.'

'Do I get a wedding invite, then? I'd like to see your Julie in a white dress or preferably out of it. No disrespect, like.' He laughed as though Nick would take this as a compliment. He didn't. He was cut from the same cloth as Big Fish.

'We'll be having a party. I'll be in touch, Malky. Cheers.'

Jeff held an index finger aloft. 'I don't get this. They've had a lot of support in the last year, they've had some success exposing people, all the posh rich 'uns are scared of them, so why go from that to bombing? That's mad. All the good work they've done is ruined by killing people and causing destruction.'

'Maybe their leadership changed and they decided on a different strategy,' said Nick.

Julie shook her head. 'Something isn't right about this at all. The plural and singular, the change from research-based campaigns to violence. Do you know where that Angie woman lives, Jeff?'

'Nah. Why, like?'

'I'd like to talk to her about the hoax call. See if she's certain she heard it all correctly. I mean, she was really scatty that day I worked with her and easily flustered. Do you know her surname and what does she does for a living normally?'

'I don't know what she does, Jules, but I saw the list of workers the other day. Her name is Page, Angie Page.'

'Are you sure that was her?' said Nick.

'She's the only Angie on the list.'

Nick got his laptop and entered the name into a search engine. 'Got her Facebook page. Her profile says she lives in Fairfield, where I grew up.'

A couple more searches and he'd found her address on the BT directory. 'She lives on Glenfield Road, right next to Fairfield Junior school, where I went.'

'Let's go round there in the morning before we go to work,' said Julie. 'Have a word with her.'

'Should you be doing that?' said Jeff. 'Maybe better to tell the cops.'

'Bollocks. This is personal. I'm not having someone blow the shit out of us,' said Julie. 'If we can find out who it was, get them banged to rights and stop them ever doing it again, we're going to bloody do that. I'm not hanging around for Plod to get its finger out.'

'Too fucking right,' said Nick. 'One way or another, we're going to fucking well have these bastards, Jeff. No twat puts a bomb under our arse and gets away with it, right?' He jabbed a finger in Jeff's direction.

'Aye. I can understand that. I'm amazed you're so calm, really. All in all. Must be a fucking horrible thing to have to go through.'

'We've had better days, aye,' said Nick, reaching out to take Julie's hand.

CHAPTER 9

'Isn't it weird how places are frozen in your mind at the age you were when you last remember them? This all seems so small, but in my imagination it feels like Glenfield Road is really long and the junior school I went to seems really big in my mind. But neither is true.'

He pulled up and parked on the side of the road, outside of Angie Page's semi-detached house.

'How old is she do you reckon?' said Nick, as they walked up her path to a white front door.

'35 going on 65.'

'That young?'

'Yeah, she was going on about growing up as an 80s kid, so she must be.'

'Married with kids?'

'I don't know. She seem very...conventional, so I imagine so.'

'Yeah, she seemed super straight, didn't she?'

'As straight as they come. Almost painfully so. American tan tights sensible.'

'The sort of woman you can't imagine actually having sex. Do you know what I mean?' he said, grinning at her as he rang the bell.

Julie put on an imitation of Angie's dreary voice, let her raised hands go limp and said, 'Oh no. I'd rather have a cup of nice tea than any of that sort of monkey business.' Nick grinned at her.

A figure loomed up behind the frosted glass.

'Hi, Angie,' said Julie with her biggest smile. 'Sorry to bother you. You remember me, don't you? Julie Wells? We worked together at the festival briefly, like.'

'Yes of course. Hello. And you're Nick, aren't you?'

'Well remembered. I'm terrible with names err...Gloria,' he said, and they all laughed.

'What can I do for you? Oh...what am I thinking? Were you at the house yesterday? What a terrible, terrible thing to have happened. I was mortified when I heard. What is the world coming to? I was so glad I decided to quit after the hoax bomb. Come in, come in.'

They stepped into the narrow hallway of the 1950s-built house. It was very like the sort of place he'd grown up in. It seemed tiny, even though it was a three-bedroomed property. They went through to a small kitchen. A pine table was pushed against the back wall. She filled the kettle and gestured for them to sit down.

'The kids are with their dad for a couple of days, so I've got the place to myself for a change.'

'How old are they?" said Julie.

'Nine and seven. Two boys. They're a bit of a handful. He lives near Ropner Park, so hopefully they'll exhaust themselves running around there. Do you have kids?'

'No. Err...no, we don't,' said Julie. 'We left it a bit late.'

'Being a mother is very rewarding, but also very tiring, especially on your own. It's hard to know what to do for the best sometimes.'

Her voice tailed off at the end of sentences as though she barely had enough energy to complete them. It was a Yorkshire-inflected Teesside accent, related to, but very different from the pure urban Middlesbrough accent, or at least, very different to Nick's ears. To outsiders, it probably all sounded the same. While she had the Teesside habit of drawing out vowels in words, those vowels were flatter and softer than you'd find even just 10 miles further east. It really was pure Mavis Riley out of *Coronation Street*, just as Julie had imitated, a character played by Thelma Barlow, who was born in Middlesbrough, but grew up in West Yorkshire. Maybe Angie had a similar geographic pedigree.

'What can I do for you, then?' she said, leaning with her back to the sink, arms folded, as the kettle came to the boil.

'Well the thing is, Angie. We were at the house yesterday when the bomb went off...we were actually first on the scene.'

She put her hand over her mouth and looked at them with

frightened eyes. 'You poor things. How terrible for you.'

'It wasn't nice. You know when you took that phone call about the hoax bomb...can you remember exactly what they said?'

'Oh...not really. I mean, I told Mel and the police what they said.'

She put instant coffee into the cups and added milk and then added hot water. 'Sugar?'

'No thanks,' they said in unison.

'Did they say they were the Ironopolis Anarchists, plural, or Anarchist, singular?' said Nick.

She looked at him blankly. 'Err...Anarchists. I think. Plural...oh no...it was singular. Yes, singular.'

'Are you sure?' said Julie.

'Yes. Very.'

'The quotes in the press all said Ironopolis Anarchists.'

'Did they? Yes. Well that was it then. Plural, sorry, I'm getting mixed up. Does it matter?'

She was obviously either confused or lying. Her eyes betrayed it, flitting from side to side, from one to the other of them, self-conscious and worried.

'Did you write it down at the time?'

'Err, not exactly. I wrote it down once they'd rang off. I was shocked. At first I thought it was someone playing a joke. Then he said he was serious and to tell Mel Stephens what their demands were.'

'So they knew of Mel?'

'Yes, they did.'

'What was the first thing they said?' asked Nick, trying to not be too aggressive in his questioning.

'The first thing they said was "Listen carefully, we have put a bomb under a horse box outside of the stables." And I said, you've done what? And they repeated it.'

'What did they sound like? Did they have a local accent?'

'They didn't have an accent at all.'

'Were they posh?' asked Julie.

'No. Not posh, not anything. Just a blank sort of voice.'

'And they said, "Tell him to call off the festival",' said Nick. 'Is that all?'

'Yes.'

Julie narrowed her eyes. 'Didn't they make any other demands?'

She faltered. 'Yes. No. I mean. They said something about wanting an investigation into the Salmon's tax affairs and...err...'

Nick glanced at Julie, knowing she was thinking the same thing. Angie Page was lying. She simply was not convincing at all. This was partly because of her wishy-washy tone which lent an insubstantial air to everything she said, but mostly because she seemed unable or unwilling the recall the few details of what you'd think was something so shocking, it'd be burned into your brain. It was such a big thing to happen, you wouldn't forget it like this. Would she really make it up, though? And if she was, why the hell would she be doing that?

'After the call, what did you do?' asked Nick.

'Oh well...I ran downstairs and found Mel and told him.'

'Did you find him right away?'

She nodded and drank some coffee. 'He went mad. He's frightening when he gets mad.'

That much *was* true.

'What time was this?' said Julie, picking up her mug and looking over the top of it.

'About 5pm or a little after. What's this got to do with the bomb going off yesterday?' she said, her eyes fixed on the lino floor.

'We just want to be sure it's the same people,' said Nick.

'It must be, mustn't it?'

'Not necessarily,' said Nick.

'And you decided to quit after that?' said Julie.

Angie nodded, her simple, plain fringe and bob hair cut moved, almost as a single unit.

'Yes. I couldn't face it. I was scared that a real bomb might go off as well. Which it did, obviously. I could have been killed.'

They all went quiet. She looked up from the floor at him. He wiped his lips with his fingers.

'And you had no idea who it was?'

'No. I'd have said if I did.' That was as close to indignant as she got.

They finished their coffee, made small talk while they did and then left. As they got back into the car, Nick let out a sigh. 'Why is she not telling us the truth, Jules? I mean, you felt she was lying too, didn't you?'

'Totally lying and not very well, either. Do you think it's possible that...this will sound mad...'

'...that she made it up? I thought that. But she didn't - Jeff saw the hoax device under the horse box and it was a bomb, just a bomb with no explosive.'

'She didn't make the bomb up, but she might have made the call up. Maybe she put the hoax bomb there?'

'Angie? A hoax bomber? I don't think so, do you?'

'No. Sorry. She's such a wet fart, I don't see her clambering under a horse box for a start.' She scratched her centre parting and scrunched up her face. 'She's an odd one...'

'When you had that day working with her, did she tell you anything about her life? She's obviously divorced or separated from the kids' dad.'

Julie looked out the side window as they headed toward Stockton town centre.

'Jules?'

'I'm thinking, aren't I? I don't remember her even saying she had kids, or a husband or partner.'

'Well maybe she just didn't mention them.'

'Women always mention their kids. It'd be weird not to in the space of four or five hours, especially when they live with you. They're part of your everyday life.'

'Are you saying she's lying about that as well?'

'Oh hell. I don't know. Now I think about it, she was quite secretive about her life, but that means nothing on its own, does it? I tell you what, let's go and ask Mel about what she said to him.

See if he can shed any light. We know she told him, don't we?'

'We know she said she told him and we know he got the email, that's about all we do know,' said Nick, heading toward Norton and the festival site outside of town.

Mel Stephens was using a small caravan as a makeshift office. The whole site was crawling with people in high-viz jackets, the bombed area of the house already secured behind large swathes of plastic sheeting to protect the crime scene from the elements. It took over 20 minutes to get access to the site. Every road in and out had armed guards to protect it.

Nick knocked on the open door. Mel looked up from his position at a cramped melamine table. 'Howay in youse two. You alright today?'

'Yeah. Fine, thanks. I mean, still shocked but...life goes on...or not...err...sorry...you know what I mean,' said Nick sitting down opposite him. Julie perched on a stool leaning against a cupboard in the small two-berth caravan.

'Aye, I do.' Mel looked around him. 'This is like the van we had at Amble when I was a kid. Shitey little thing. About big enough for one fart, but we still got five of us in it. Best bloody holidays I ever had was in that thing.' He let out a sigh and a groan. He was clearly running on empty after the events of the last day. 'So why are you two here, in my well-appointed rabbit hutch?'

'We've just come from Angie Page's house,' said Julie.

'Oh aye? That woman was as much use as a jelly hammer. Totally went to pieces. The exact opposite of youse two and she only had a hoax to deal with.' He shook his head wearily.

'The thing is Mel. We think there's something dodgy about her,' said Nick.

'Eh?'

'We think she was lying to us about the call she got. The bomb threat call. Did she come and tell you about it?'

'Aye. I was out the front and she came running out.'

'When was that?' said Julie.

'The time?' He sat and thought. 'After 5pm...maybe 10 past.

Why?'

'She said it was 5.'

'Well she's got her head in the clouds that one.'

'Is there any way we could find out when she got the call?' said Nick, tapping his nails on the table. 'Phone records maybe?'

'Such a thing must exist, but that's the copper's area of expertise, isn't it? I don't get what you're saying. Are you saying she never got the call and made it all up or something, because there was definitely a device where she said they'd told her there was a device.'

Nick rubbed his face. He couldn't think where his train of thought was even taking him on this. Something was weird about Angie, but maybe she was just an oddball person.

'How did you come to employ her?'

'Are you playing at detective or summat?'

'Mel, we tend to get arsey on Teesside when people try to blow us up. We'd like to find out who is responsible and then sort the fucking twats out, alright?,' said Julie. Mel grinned at that.

'Aye, aye...not unreasonable. She just responded to the ad I put in the *Gazette*. She works at the council and wanted some part-time work. I don't remember much else about her. I never occurred to us that she wasn't telling the truth about the bomb threat. Didn't doubt her for a minute.'

'Did she ever mention having kids?'

'Nope. But even if she did, that sort of shite goes over my head. I mean, I don't give a shit about the private lives of temporary workers. They're here today, gone tomorrow.' He held his hand up and shook his head. 'Sorry, sorry...that was in poor taste...those poor kids that died...' He closed his eyes slowly. 'Poor kids. We've got to get whoever did this banged to rights. Fuckers.' He was quietly seething, his tattooed hands clenching. 'I'll tell you what though, I'd bet my last pound that Angie wifey is not a terrorist. So I dunno what tree you're barking up with her, but I reckon all she did was pick up a phone, someone said there's a fucking bomb under the horse box and she's come and told us. She was shit scared-looking, mind...had gone white as a sheet. Anyway, the coppers will dig her out if she's got a record or something. They've been all through our records already looking for likely culprits and people with grudges. They'll go through the lot like a dose of salts. In fact, I'm bound to need extra muscle 'cos we'll have lost all the big bastards who are fresh out of jail or on the run from something or someone.'

'Alright. Mel. Cheers mate,' said Nick, standing up, his head nearly touching the roof of the caravan. 'Bit small in here, isn't it?'

'I'm having a big fuck-off tent erected for us all to work in and I'm getting me own fucking one as well. Local company is doing it free of charge tomorrow. Everyone's pitching in now. People can't do enough for us. Give the terrorists a kick in the balls and say, "fuck you, you can't stop rock 'n' roll, y'knaw". And rightly bloody so, mind.'

He hi-fived them both.

On the way home Nick pulled in to a parking space on Yarm High Street.

'What are we stopping for?' said Julie.

'We're still getting married, aren't we?'

'Yeah. But not here and now.'

'We need rings though, don't we?'

'Rings? Oh yeah. I suppose so, I forgot about that. It's part of the deal, I suppose. I wear so little jewellery. I don't even think I've got a ring. All I've got is that fine silver chain you bought me and some earrings mam got me about 10 years ago. I've never been a big jewellery wearer.'

'Me neither. It's a foreign language to me is jewellery. I don't really understand it. Let's look at some in the jewellers there.'

They walked up to the small shop's big glass window. 'We can't afford much.'

'I don't want anything expensive anyway,' she said. 'I'll only lose it.'

They looked in the window. 'Is there a tradition when it comes to wedding rings?'

'You're talking to the wrong lass. I haven't a clue.'

'I think we each get a gold ring, don't we?'

'I think so. That's what Freda Payne had in that song, "Band of Gold".'

He put his arm around her. 'Number one in 1970. Those ones are nice. Nine carat gold in two colours - white and yellow.'

'Aye. It's a sort of Celtic design an' all. I like them. Mind, it says his and hers and hers is smaller than his. That's not fair. I want them to be the same size. I'm not having sexist wedding rings. Give us a look at your fingers.' He held them out. 'You've got long, slim fingers, they're thinner than my little stumps. We'll get them then.'

'Sounds good. £260 isn't too bad. I'll put it on the new credit card.'

'May as well. If we get blown up in another bomb, we'll have got them for free.'

He laughed. 'That's good positive thinking that, Jules. Ever the optimist you, eh? Dead, but ahead.'

They got their fingers measured, put the order in and were told to look in in a few days.

'We better get the registry office booked, you know,' said Julie, 'there's probably a waiting list and all sorts of legal gubbins to go through. I'll get that under way tomorrow.'

'Thanks missus.' He reached over and slapped her on the leg.

Within 72 hours of the explosion, the whole festival organisation had decamped to a huge white marquee pitched in the gardens, the sort of thing that the biggest, poshest weddings have for a reception. It had been donated free of charge from a local company and had come with a team of workers to erect it in double-quick time. The festival's determination that the show must go on had received massive support from all over the country, but especially on Teesside, where defiance against what was seen as terrorist bullies was virtually unanimous. Mel Stephens even had to turn away armies of local volunteers keen to help out and keep the show on the road. Electricity, broadband and every other resource they needed had been readied and made available. No band had cancelled, most had sent messages of support. No-one wanted to be seen as giving in.

Mel had appeared on national TV and, in a combative mood during an interview on the 10pm BBC news bulletin, when asked if he had a message for the bombers, had said nothing, had stared the camera down, his big pink tattooed head glowing and then given the V's with both hands in a silent, slow-motion riposte.

This had gone down very well throughout the whole country and briefly turned him into a tabloid press hero with his gesture splashed across the front pages. It seemed a simple, symbolic act of defiance that anyone from anywhere could understand. Giving someone the fingers seemed to be an almost joyously retro insult, straight out of 1970s culture. Mel also insisted on attending the funerals of each of the students murdered. He took it all very, very personally and could be heard on more than one occasion, walking around the festival site shouting to the sky in his solid Geordie voice, "I'll get youse fuckers. Don't ye worry about that. I'm comin' for youse."

The entrance to the driveway up to the house was still behind a police barrier and all workers had now been issued with photo ID to facilitate quicker entry and exit. Nick leaned out of the car window and showed their passes as they turned up to work on another sunny morning.

The marquee had been divided by desks into different areas handling different aspects of the festival. Considering the tragedy that had unfolded earlier in the week, the spirit was upbeat and almost cheerful, driven on by Mel's limitless energy and capacity for swearing. Julie worked the phones in one corner, putting calls through to various other members of the team and in between answering correspondence from suppliers and bands. Nick wrote the websites, press releases and publicity material. The music was still loud. Defiantly loud.

Nick stopped as soon as they entered and pointed at the speaker in the corner which was blasting out something funky.

'That's Little Feat, "Skin It Back".'

'Luckily I feel like I'm a Dixie Chicken today. I'll see you later,' said Julie, pushing her sunglasses up onto her head. She gave him a peck on the cheek and made her way to her far corner desk.

'Yo! Guymer, dude!' Jeff trotted up and hi-fived him. 'How goes it, sugar tits?'

'Good. This all looks amazing. I've not been in for 36 hours and it seems to have all sprung up like a mushroom, almost overnight.'

'I know. It just shows what can be achieved when everyone pulls their finger out and tries to make things happen rather than getting in the way and trying to screw people for an extra few quid, which, I'm led to believe, is capitalism's preferred modus operandi.' He flicked his long hair over his shoulder.

'It is hugely impressive, like. The whole place is buzzing. Out of adversity comes...something...I dunno what.'

'Nope, neither do I, but then I'm not a pseudo philosopher like you, am I? All I know is it's running smooth as silk.'

'Is silk always smooth? A dupion silk isn't. It's got slubs in it.'

'Slubs, you say? I have no idea what a slub even is. That's all I need - a fabric hipster. As smooth as chocolate then and not fruit and nut, before you say. Point is, it's all running to plan and is on time. I just came from the stages. They're mint. PA system is top rank. Can't wait until we open the gates. Have you seen the long-range forecast? It's looking perfect, baby.'

'Baby? You're calling me baby now,' laughed Nick.

'Well, you do wear a nappy.'

'Aye, but only for healthy, pervy reasons, not due to incontinence. Anyway, you can talk, you love a baby's rusk or 12.'

He held a finger aloft. 'Correction. I did like a rusk until I went low carb and lost 75 stone in weight. I'm actually weight-free now. I weigh literally nothing. I'm like a gas or a vapour...'

'...a vapour? Aye, you've given off a few vapours in your time, you, like.'

'Talking of which, I've got the brewery coming with barrels of beer and lager and about 10 million plastic glasses. When you've done whatever it is you're here to do, can you give us a hand shifting in all the cans and mixers and wine and...well, you get the picture.'

'Sure. I can do that. I've just got to find Emily first.'

'Catch you later, then.'

He squinted, looking for her, spotting her coming in holding a cup of coffee, talking to another woman about her own age that she often hung out with at work. He waved and intercepted her.

'Hi, Em. How are you?' he said. She said goodbye to her friend.

'Hello, Nick. I'm OK, I think. How are you?'

'I'm good. I feel...I feel strong.' He put his hand on her cheek. A spontaneous gesture on seeing the worry in her lovely green eyes. But then he quickly withdrew it. It was invading her personal space. She looked vulnerable though.

'Can we go over a couple of things? Work has piled up a bit in the last two days.'

'That's why I'm here. You emailed me, remember? We said we'd sort out the website content.'

'Yes we did. Sorry Nicky, boy. I'm juggling plates on sticks right now.'

'I think you'll find you're spinning plates on sticks - you juggle balls in the air.' He smiled. She was a good kid and had clearly been really upset by the explosion. Nothing in her quiet life to date had prepared her for the horrors of terrorism, understandably enough.

He sat down beside her at her computer and she loaded a screen of the website.

'It's just this bit here. It doesn't really fit around the photos. Can you just edit it by 30 words? And then here, the page describing the food and concession stalls needs updating as there have been two withdrawals and two new ones added. I'll log in and you can do it on my computer, it's much easier. I've got it all set up for working on it at home.'

'Sure. I'll do that now. So how are you then?' said Nick. 'Bearing up? You look...maybe a bit nervy.'

She sighed. 'I'm on auto-pilot really, Nick. I've just been to the doctor about it.' She went quiet as he re-edited the text, then put a small, cold hand on his bare arm. He looked across at her and smiled. She looked so worried.

'How do you cope with something like the bombing? What you saw after the explosion, how do you cope with that? It makes everything seem pointless. I have never, ever, ever been more terrified in my life. Even just thinking about it makes me feel cold. I feel like it's ruined my peace of mind and I don't know how to get back to where I was. Do you know what I mean? It isn't possible, is it?' He put his hand on her leg and patted it.

'No, you can never re-become what you once were after big stuff has happened. I don't think so, anyway. Life isn't all good times though, Em. No-one said it would be and if you think about it, until the last few decades, no-one thought it would be. Certainly the northern working class were brought up to think life would be nasty, brutal and short.' He put his hand on top of hers and squeezed it. 'I'm a bit of an expert in getting through life while feeling messed up.'

'Really? God. Why? Did something terrible happen to you when you were young?'

'Nothing like the bomb. But in recent years I've realised that I've always been a bit adrift in the seas of life; a bit of a loner, mostly because I didn't have a happy home life. My mam and dad didn't get on and then mam lost her mind and it messed me up. It traumatized me on a really deep level and that's why I was a heavy drinker for years, just trying to cover up or drown my feelings of...I don't know...' He let out a small breath of air. 'Drink was the parents I wanted, but didn't have. Does that make sense?'

'That's awful. Poor you.' She put her right hand on his neck, her head sympathetically on one side.

'On the surface, I'd have seemed quite cheerful, but underneath I wasn't, though for much of that time, I didn't even realise what was going on. I would probably have told you I was happy. I couldn't face what was buried deep in me. I'm only just doing so now...so don't do that with this tragedy, Em. Don't bury it down so deep it affects the rest of your life negatively. That'd be my advice.'

'I'd never have guessed this about you. You do seem quite a happy go-lucky sort of guy.'

'Well now, that's 'cos I'm on drugs.' He took a Phenibut capsule out of his checked shirt pocket and held it up at her. 'I've been taking these for a few days. They've really helped me a lot so far. I don't know anything about them, Jules looked them up. They raise my dopamine, apparently. I'm sure they've helped me cope with everything here, as well as my other issues. I've never felt better, even despite everything that has happened. Not, like, stoned, but just sort of even-tempered and the hurt inside that has never left me since I was 12 or 13... that's gone. I don't know where it's gone and I don't want to know and I'm scared it comes back, because the pain would be all the worse for having had it relieved.'

He looked up the website Julie had bought them from and saved it in Emily's favourites.

'Sorry, Em, I'm talking on and on about myself. Selfish of me, that. All I'm saying is try and deal with it. Don't be a noble Englishwoman and swallow it all down.' She looked close to tears, picking at her lips and then nibbling at her nails and fiddling with her jewellery. She sat quietly alongside him while he made the edits. He gave her an encouraging little smile and squeezed her hand again. She didn't seem keen to let go. Maybe she didn't have anyone at home to talk to this about. Maybe she was on her own.

'Right. That's all done. Do you need anything else written while I'm here?'

'Err...yes...I will do. I'm just waiting to hear from someone at *Blues Today*. I'll need a piece for them which they can dress up as content on their website. Also the programmes are being delivered in about 15 minutes, so I need some big strong dudes to carry them from the van into the storage tent.' She smiled at him with her green eyes and squeezed his bicep. 'You seem like a big strong dude.'

'OK, whatever needs doing, I'm here for you. And if you don't mind me giving you one last bit of advice, don't try and suffer this alone...I go to a therapist. I don't even like him really, but it helps to talk about...' He waved his fingers at his temple '...what's in there.'

'Someone said there's going to be counselling available for us all if we want it. My doctor suggested it, too.'

'Well, I'd take that if I were you. It's not weak to admit to not being strong. See, it's even taught me to talk in cheesy aphorisms.'

'Thanks Nicky boy. You're a nice chap. I needed a bit of talking to, I think,' She leaned forward and kissed him on the cheek. She had terrible halitosis. Really eye-watering, probably caused by not eating properly.

'No probs. Can I get you anything? A cup of tea? Here...I baked these earlier.' He took out a Tupperware box of egg, bacon and cheese muffins from his shoulder bag and put two on her desk. 'They're my speciality. They'll get some protein and good fat into you. It'll do you good. There's no wheat in them. Your blood sugar will be all over the place if you don't eat properly. That'll not help your emotions settle down either.'

'You're a doctor and a chef, too?'

'No, I'm just an old git whose been around the block a few times and knows what it's like to go through hard times. I'll get you a tea from the catering van.'

He walked across the courtyard where a big catering truck made three meals a day for the workers and served up as much tea and coffee as was need. He got her the tea. When he'd been really depressed, it was always the small kindnesses that people showed you that helped the most. A kind word here, or an understanding gesture there, went a long way to make things bearable. Sometimes, they'd actually kept him alive. He hoped this was one such small kindness for her.

She'd already eaten both of the muffins when he got back.

'They were bloody delicious,' she said with a happier smile now, the food probably helping her feel a bit better.

'They're a bit nice, aren't they? I could fire them out of a cannon into Jules' open mouth for hours and she'd not get sick of them.'

'Tell her she's a lucky woman. Thanks again, you've been a real sweetie.' She stood up and gave him a tight hug.

Nick and Jeff and four other men were soon moving boxes of bottles and cans from a truck into the two drinks tents. Although it was overcast, they soon worked up a hell of a sweat. Nick took off his t-shirt and wiped his face on a bar towel while the other guys had a cigarette break.

'Jesus Christ, this is hard work, Jeff. You've gone the colour of a Victoria plum.'

'And you look like you've been oiled up for a body-building gig. Are you trying to turn me gay?'

He laughed and put his hands on his hips. 'Yes Jeff, that's exactly what I'm trying to do.'

'Aye, well, I have no objection to the man-on-man sex, it's just the Hi NRG disco music I can't stand. That and the cuddling. I'll have sex with you, but I'm not cuddling, alright?'

Nick laughed and took a drink of water. 'Men are strange beasts. Somehow, the cuddling would be far more intimate than the sex.'

'And we all learned at birth that intimacy is to be feared. Especially in the North. Owee, give us a hand with these boxes of wine. Wine at a rock festival on Teesside - we live in changed times, my friend. Time was the only thing at a festival that looked like wine was piss in a bottle of Tizer, usually thrown at the head of a hapless DJ stage announcer.'

'Tommy Vance used to wear a crash helmet at Reading, didn't he?'

'Aye. Which only made people try and hit him with said bottles of piss. Not rock 'n' roll's finest hour. If anyone does that here, Mel will personally drag them out and insert a bottle of wine into them.'

'Hey, what do you make of that Emily Davids lass? I was just having a word, she seems really upset by everything.'

149

'The one who does the media work? I've not spoken to her that much. She seems like a nice, respectable young woman. Got a little bit of rock chick going on, but she's obviously a nice, well-scrubbed girl. One of those tidy, clean-living middle-class student girls who loves her parents and never wears the same knickers two days running.'

'Aye, she's got that vibe, hasn't she? She's well organised and really friendly. I find myself admiring sensible people more every year.'

'Sensible people used to be the enemy when we were students.'

'Yeah. Recently I keep saying how I now realise that being sensible is a whole gig in itself and it's a hard one to get right, but without those who do, we'd be knackered. We should appreciate sensible people more. They're actually quite exotic, really.'

'But they'd have nothing to entertain themselves with if it wasn't for the irresponsible, arty, creative fuck-ups, would they? The crazies go to the edge so that the sensible types don't have to.'

'That's very true. I remember we'd meet lasses like her at college and they seemed a very rarefied creature. I always felt like I was a big, dirty member of the working class in their presence. Still do, really.'

'A big, dirty member is about right, son.'

'Personal hygiene was never one of my strong points. I do feel sorry for Emily, though. We're grizzled old bastards from the school of hard knocks, but she's not. Suddenly, I feel quite protective towards her.'

'Protective? Horny, more like. She's got it going on and even if you won't admit it, you know it. Have you been alright in your head, like? I mean, you were right there at the shitty end of the stick when it went boom.'

'Yeah. It was shocking - truly shocking - but I've coped well with it. Jules, too. It must be because of all we've been through in life. You just think, fuck, here we go again...but you don't let it grind you down. If you do, you let the bastards win.'

Jeff snorted a laugh, 'You sound just like your Jules there. Aye well, I dunno what to say about young Miss Davids. She's a nice looker, like. I've always found women with a little gap between their front teeth very sexy.'

'That's because you like toothless, poor, white trash.'

Jeff laughed. 'True enough. Anyway, you can talk, you're the one who was mad about Paula Wilcox in *Man About The House* at school. She had the gappy front teeth.'

'Aye, she did. God, I loved her. She seemed kind and lovely, but sexually knowing on the quiet, too. Ideal combo, that.'

Jeff leaned against the van that had brought the drink. 'And that's your Emily lass to a tee, that is. That would make you Richard O'Sullivan or even Sally Thomsett, which is a troubling image. Though actually you could be Richard Beckinsale in *The Lovers*.'

'He was cool, was The Beckinsale. I'll take that.'

'When is your marriage happening, anyway?'

'I dunno, we've not decided on a date. We've ordered the rings, though. I'll need you to give me away.'

'Give you away? Ah, I didn't realise that you were the bride.'

'Jules wears the suit in our house, as you well know. And I'll pull on a pair of tiny white panties at the slightest encouragement.'

' That is far too much information - even for this grizzled old warrior. Bombs I can deal with, you in white panties...just...no, sir! No!'

He turned to see another long-wheelbase van approaching. It was the programmes.

'Shit me. More stuff to shift. C'mon son, no sleep 'til Hammersmith...or in my case, Hartburn,' said Jeff.

They had all just finished stacking the piles of programmes into a storage tent and were taking a rest when Mel Stephens came over.

'Good work, you big ugly gets. Youse lot have put some serious graft in here, so shifting a few amplifiers and mixing desks will seem like a piece of piss.' They all groaned. 'Big Mikey will be over in 20 minutes to get you.'

Nick lay down across two chairs and closed his eyes for five minutes' rest.

'Eeee look at you, all tanned, half naked and sweaty.' It was Julie. He opened his eyes. She leaned over and tweaked his nipples. 'Emily says you've got to go and do some piece for her for *Blues Today*.'

'Couldn't she come and tell me herself?'

'She caught me going on my break and I think she's intimidated by all the male nudity over here. She's not been around as many naked men in her life as I have.'

'Howay Jules, cop a load of this,' said one of the long-haired roadies, holding his big belly and shaking it up and down at her.

'The sad thing is, that's the only thing on you that is big and fat,' said Julie with a laugh. The rest of the roadies cheered. There was nothing they liked better than a good piss-taking at one of their number's expense.

Nick walked over to the marquee with her. 'I'm going to need one of your massages tonight,' he said, 'Every muscle on me aches.'

She handed him his t-shirt. 'Put this on, can't have you driving young Emmy wild with your nudey nakedness. She'll never have seen the like. You know how girly student men are like these days. Barely an ounce of testosterone between them all. I blame all the oestrogen in their food and water.'

He sat down next to Emily. 'Jules says you need me.'

'Yeah. Read this email from *Blues Today*. They only need 500 words or so. You can sit here and do it on my laptop while I go for my break. See that icon on the toolbar, just click on that and upload the file from there. It'll go right into place just like it did on that last thing.'

He knocked out a quick piece on how the echo of British blues boom of the 60s still reverberated today and how the authenticity of the blues spoke to every new generation. Nothing especially original, but then pretty much everything that could said about blues music had already been said. For a simple art form it had attracted a lot of academic interest over the decades. It only took 10 minutes. He could write this stuff in his sleep. He saved the document into a folder labelled 'Content' and then uploaded it as she'd said.

After he was done he wondered if she'd looked at the Phenibut website he'd recommended. Opening up her web browser history, he scanned down the list of websites she'd recently visited. She'd been looking at it half an hour ago. He smiled. It was nice when people took your advice. He meant to click on the link to the website, but hit the one below it by accident. It was blank but brought up a page, all the same. It was white with a black box in the centre. There was no indication what the website was and the URL was just a stream of code.

It had to be a log in and password box. He double-clicked on the top box. A cookie had saved her log in as 'helenwheels' - a song by Wings - and more importantly, had saved her password too. 10 asterisks popped into the lower box. He clicked a 'go' button.

Jesus Christ. Fucking hell. What was this?

CHAPTER 10

You could accidentally stumble across all sorts of weird shit on the internet by accident. He'd once done an innocent search for images of gas masks only to be confronted with something called gas mask porn, which was like regular porn only with people wearing gas masks. Who knew? How do you develop a taste like that? But this wasn't something you could just come across, she must have been issued a password and log in.

The screen looked like the newsgroup looked like in 1997. Long string of threads and posts under various topic headings. At the top a heading: 'Ironopolis Anarchists - Industrial Strength Justice'. He skimmed down the posts. A quick inspection showed it had to be a Darknet group as there were no IP addresses to be seen. They were discussing the bomb threat, the bombing, Stevie Salmon and lots of other festival-related matters. There were discussions on taxation and left wing, revolutionary politics and animal rights. He glanced up to check if Emily was coming back. All was clear, but he knew he didn't have long and that he wouldn't be able to access it anywhere other than on this laptop.

He went to the most recent posts. "This must just be the start. RadLand must be destroyed. They must be shown that the people are the bosses, not them."

One of the regular posters was someone known as 'Volunteer'. In commenting on a long thread about wealthy landowners, most of which was focusing on the assets of the Salmons' Blakeston Estate. 'Volunteer' seemed to be some sort of organiser, posting information about a 'Strategy Meeting' at 7.00pm that evening and calling for 'all IA Leaders' to attend'. Nick got a piece of paper and wrote down a post code given as the assembly point: TS3 9LB. That had to be fairly central in Middlesbrough. He did a quick Google Maps search. It was by the cemetery on Cargo Fleet Lane, the A171.

He glanced up. Emily was coming back, weaving around men

carrying large bits of kit. He shut the browser down, clicked the browsing history and speedily deleted the evidence of his activity, such as it was.

'Hi, Em. That's me done. I've uploaded it for you.' He pushed his hair behind his ears and got up with a smile.

'Thanks Nicky, boy.'

'Right. I'm off. Give me a shout if you need me.'

'Will do.' She reached for his hand and took it in her own. 'And thank you again, for the little chat. I feel much better now. I was stewing in my own juice too much.'

'It's my muffins - doctors prescribe them for depression all the time.'

She giggled, a fluttering light laugh. 'You'll have to come round and eat my muffin, sometime.'

He winked at her and walked away. Muffin? Singular? Was she being rude? She most certainly was. Naughty little Emily. Maybe Jules was right, the ovens with the coolest tops had the hottest ovens.

In the far corner of the marquee, Julie was sitting at her desk, Nick squatted down beside her. She was on the phone, speaking in a very refined version of her normal accent.

'You sound like a proper posh lass on the phone,' he said as she finished the call.

'What can I do you for? I'm very busy.'

'Emily Davids had a weird website on her browser history.' He explained what he'd found. Julie's eyes widened. 'That can only mean one thing, she must be a member of the Ironopolis Anarchists. She *must* be. That sounds like a secret message board. The hidden IP addresses and that.'

He nodded. 'That's what it looked like. And the posts clearly stated that they had detonated that bomb and made the hoax call, earlier. There was no doubt they had done it. But, Jules man, little Emily? She's not a terrorist, not that skinny little kid, is she? She was shit scared when it went off.'

She rubbed her neck and grimaced.

'I dunno, man. God. You don't want to think that. She's such a sweet girl. Or she seems like a sweet girl, anyway. Maybe it's all an act. And you know how idealistic you can be when your her age. You think you know everything and can change the world. I know I did when I was at Newcastle Uni. We were always having demos against Thatcher and all of that. It was great fun. I loved it. And I really did mean it in my own way, but now I can see I was just trying to find myself and mostly I did it for the social life. We had some great piss-ups going down to London to protest one thing or another and it made you feel like you were important. We weren't, of course, and all the protests had no effect at all, but at the time I was convinced we could have an effect. Maybe she's like that.'

'We didn't do much of that at the Poly. I was too busy collecting records and drinking heavily. I seem to remember I signed a petition once. Not sure what it was for...or against. I did go on a Rock Against Racism thing. Massive piss-up, obviously. But that was quite radical at the time. The thing is Jules, I know I'm rubbish at reading people, but I'm not sure Emily is everything she might seem to be. She's been quite flirty with me, I think.'

'In what way?' She looked down at him with arched eyebrows.

He rubbed the stubble on his cheek. 'Words mostly. Double entendres, that sort of thing. In her office just before the explosion, when I was waiting for you, she lifted her dress up and showed me her knickers, just in a silly sort of way...but even so...'

'Did she now? You never said.'

'After the bomb it didn't seem important. She was just having a laugh...messing around. It was embarrassing but I don't mind.'

'I bet you don't. What were they like?'

'Eh?'

'What were her knickers like?'

'Jules man, I don't know. I said I was embarrassed. I put my hands over my eyes. White, I think. Quite, err, y'know, err...small...I think anyway. I looked away...'

She let out a hoot of laughter making a couple of other workers turn and look at her. 'You know fine well what they were like. I bet you can still picture them. I know what you're like, don't forget.' She spoke in a low whisper. She was, of course, correct. 'It's like I said, cold tops have hot ovens,' she said, grinning at him, pinching the skin on the top of his arm. 'She's a sweet young woman on the surface, but underneath she's a volcano of red-hot sex.' She chuckled to herself again, shaking her head. 'It's alright, we'll say no more. You look soooo embarrassed. Ha. Serves you right for making nice young lasses fancy you. So what's this RadLand they're talking about?'

He shrugged. 'I've never heard of it. Look it up, see if you can find it.' She typed it in. 'Anything there?' he said, now unable to get the memory of Emily's underwear out his mind.

'Yeah. There's a RadLand - with the middle L capitalised like you said it was on the message board. It's a charitable trust. Hold on...here it is...they say they "work to alleviate rural disadvantage and poverty". Sounds vague, but noble. The "About" page says they're "a collection of landowners, farmers and rural businessmen". Bah. I hate that word, do they actually mean business *men* or are they using it as a generic term to describe people who own businesses, including women? Very annoying. By the look of it they give out grants for small business start-ups and such. Probably a tax dodge or at least, a way to reduce tax.'

'Ah, Teesside cynicism at its finest there, Jules. Maybe they're just trying to do something good.'

'Bollocks. The names of the people on the board are Lord this, Lady that, an Earl and a Sir. All big landowners, I'd bet. All richer than fizzin' Croesus and all doing the "Here, have some crumbs from my table, you peasant" thing.'

'In some ways I feel like that's worse than doing nothing. You've got millions in the bank and you dish out £200 to a bloke who wants to start a window-cleaning round in rural Yorkshire or wherever.'

'Aye, but they'll be acclaimed for it, won't they?' She clicked on some more links. 'The working class help each other out financially where they can and they give a higher percentage of their earnings to charity and yet get sod all recognition for it and wouldn't expect to, but here...here we've got the Earl of bloody Louth - the head of RadLand - in the *Yorkshire Post* accepting an awards for Outstanding Rural Charity of 2008. He looks like a piss-take...look...' She turned the screen to him to show a photo of a man dressed from head to foot in tweed, sporting a large baggy tweed cap, waistcoat and plus fours.

'Ha ha...he looks like one of Monty Python's "Upper-Class Twits of the Year" from yonks ago. See if you can find anything out about Emily Davids.' His phone vibrated in his pocket. It was Ian Bertram. He walked outside to take the call.

'Hey, Ian,' he said, walking out into the warm, overcast afternoon.

'Nick. Just a quick call. You asked me to let you know if we were offered cash for the gig. Just had a call from Stevie Salmon's manager saying they'll do five in cash and five by transfer. Obviously, I said yes. But this is strictly between you and me. OK? I also know that at least four other bands have been offered some amount of cash. Rumour is YYZ, who are pulling in 40k for this gig, are getting a big cash bonus. But don't tell anyone. I don't want to blow this, OK?'

'Yes. Of course. Thanks for letting me know, Bertie.'

'They're putting us on at 8pm on Friday. Quite pleased. It's a good thing to be involved in - ironically, it's even more high profile because of that fucking bomb. It's turned it into a much bigger deal. What's it all looking like? Good?'

'Yeah. I'm on site now. It's bloody good, Bertie. Top notch.'

'Where you there when the bomb went off?'

'Was I there? I was coming down the stairs with Jules. We were first on the scene.'

'Ooof, shitting hell. That cannot have been pretty. Have they got any idea who did it yet?'

'No. If the police know anything, they'd not tell us anyway. MI5 or MI6 are probably involved. There are rumours that there are security service agents on site the whole time, just to keep an eye on things. Whether that's actually true, I don't know.'

'Blimey. That's some heavy shit. Mind you, it'll probably be the safest place on the planet as a result.'

After he rang off, Nick tugged at his lip contemplatively. Big Fish was obviously pulling some sort of scam exactly the way Mike had said, laundering money through the festival. Greedy sod. How much money do you need? Mike's mantra was right. How much did you need? He probably saw the bomb as a great way to avoid scrutiny. Who in authority would want to question something which had been kept going in the face of wicked terrorism? Far less controversial for HMRC to pick on a few powerless, low-profile, regular members of the public instead. Sadly, that was how things seemed to work. The regular people got a kicking and the rich elite *did* the kicking.

He shouted at Jeff as he walked past. 'Hey, big man!'

Jeff reversed and walked backwards towards him making a bleeping noise as though he was a large vehicle. Nick laughed.

'What can I do for you?' said Jeff.

'Am I still needed on the main stage?'

'Nope. On the acoustic and comedy stage. Owee, I'll go over there with you and lend a hand to shift some PA gear.'

They set off past the big tent, around the back of the house, past the stables, heading towards the smaller field which housed the white, open tent in which was the small stage. A PA system was being constructed.

'Where have all the horses been shipped to?' said Nick, looking into the yard which was surrounded on three sides by stables. Normally, horses poked their heads out curiously as anyone passed by.

'Yeah, they're all temporarily housed at some stables in Thirsk. Not big fans of loud electric blues, horses. They prefer folk music. Though frankly, they probably moved them so they don't have to hear Big Fish's beard jokes. No animal should suffer that.'

'Aye, got good comedy taste, your average horse, I reckon.'

'I can never work out if they're sensitive and intelligent animals or a bit thick,' said Jeff.

'Good buttocks though.'

'Oh aye, they've a good firm, lean buttock. You know what the best thing about being a horse must be?'

'The really massive cock?'

'Nearly. The pissing. Male horse or female horse, it makes no difference. Watch one taking a piss, they clearly enjoy it.'

Nick laughed. 'The horse piss is a powerful, never-ending stream, isn't it? Have you noticed that when they're doing it, they sort of stare off into the middle distance as though lost in a dream.'

'Ha ha. Yeah, they do that. I always thought they were concentrating on the job in hand, or on hoof, possibly. Cats do that as well. Rita's got this white cat, it gets on the litter tray for a piss or a shit and as soon as it's started, you couldn't disturb it with a small thermo-nuclear device. It seems to go into a hypnotic state. I get down on my hands and knees and wave at it, but it can't see me. Then as soon as it's finished, it comes back to consciousness, in much the same way we do after listening to an early Hawkwind album.'

'Oh hey, I just got a call from Bertie. The Big Fish is paying some of his fee in cash, y'know?'

'Is he now?' Jeff pushed his long hair over his shoulders as they hopped over a fence and walked down the field. 'That means he'll be on site with thousands of pounds in cash. That's a sodding security risk, that is. He should have told the security team. Prick.'

'Well he can't, can he? He's got to keep it quiet. If only the managers know about it - and they're in on the scam, after all - then it doesn't get out that he's laundering dirty money, or whatever it is that's going on.'

'We've got five or six bands on each day, collectively their fees are the thick end of 70 grand. I've seen the contracts.'

Nick stopped. 'That's quite a low amount when you think about it for six bands. The headliner should be getting 50 grand at least.'

'Yeah, it is low, I suppose. It hadn't occurred to me. Averages at about 12 grand a band.'

'You've only seen the stated fees then, not the actual fees. If on paper he's paying 70 a day, in reality it could be upwards of 150k, if he's done the same deal with Bertie as with everyone else. It'd mean he'll have 70 grand per day in cash on site. Well over 200 grand for the whole weekend. He probably hasn't done a cash deal with everyone - but even so, he'll have a lot of money on him, on Simon Garbutt or someone, somewhere on site.'

A quad bike zoomed past them carrying two huge blokes to the stage, all muscle and tight t-shirts.

'It's bloody dangerous, that is. If anyone twigs about it, it might attract hard core drug criminals. But...y'know...so what? It's nothing to do with us, is it? If he gets whacked because of it, he gets whacked. No-one will be weeping except maybe his bookmaker.'

Nick said nothing, got to the tent housing the stage and picked up a monitor, putting it onto a trolley as instructed by a roadie.

'I know what you're saying, but the fact is, I really don't like rich people dodging on their tax. I don't mind someone who runs a decorating business taking a few quid in cash, but this is obviously some sort of fraud on a massive scale. He's probably laundering money from all sorts of dodgy schemes or he's laying off cash from the chip shops. Either way, it's stinks. When governments say sorry, there's no money for something like Julie's Teesside Women Centre, that's in part because of people like Big Fish.'

'It's not like it's a bank bail-out job, is it? Just a few thousand here and there.'

'A few? Since when is 200 grand a few quid?'

'But hang on, if he pays fees in undeclared cash, it'll make the festival look even more profitable, won't it? It reduces his costs on the books. Thus more tax will be due on those profits. So he's not cheating HMRC at all. He'll end up paying more than he needs to.'

Nick pulled the black and silver box up to the side of the stage and passed it onto a stage hand, then began the walk back to pick up another from where it had been left by the PA hire company.

'Jeff man, if you think he's doing this to make sure he pays more than his due, you're insane. Like I say, it's all part of a bigger plan to clean up dirty money, money earned without being declared for tax, or from illegal ventures like drugs or knock off fags, or whatever. They'll sell the company on the back of huge profits and get a fortune for it. They'll pay off the tax and walk away clean and even richer.'

Jeff loaded on two more speakers.

'I'm still not seeing the problem. The bloody government screws us every which way, the citizen is entitled to screw them back when he can.'

'He or she, you mean. You're sounding like Big Fish now. It's part of the bigger picture, isn't it? The elite cream it up while we, the sodding poor working class and other associated hangers on, pick up the tab. That's what I hate. It's the politics of it, but more than that, it's just morally wrong for someone with plenty to just greedily hoover up more money, just for the sake of it. How much money does anyone need?'

'But governments just spunk all our money on shit no-one wants or just on being useless.'

'I know, but that doesn't change the principle of it. And anyway, over the years we've benefited from state money. We were educated at Newcastle Poly on a full grant and we both spent plenty of time on the dole not exactly looking for work. The whole of our civic society is paid for from common taxation.'

'Ah, the dole years. I loved them. Got some of my best record collecting done when we had spare time to scour all the junk shops. Remember all those rare records we used to always see?'

Nick was cross with him for not understanding his point, but there was no point in getting uptight. It wouldn't do any good. He let out a groan.

'Oh god, don't. Makes me sick to think of it. The two Trees albums - they're worth a few hundred quid each now. Used to see them all the time.'

'I remember once being in that junk shop on Pink Lane in Newcastle, must have been 1980, and there were three pristine copies of *Five Live Yardbirds* first pressings on blue and black Columbia. 50p each. Why didn't I buy them? I wake up having nightmares about that. You'd pay £250 for one of those now, and don't get me started on Beatles first pressings. They were as common as dandruff.'

'And you'd never have had a chance to even see them if you'd been at work and not dossing around the dole. So you see, public money does have its uses. Taxation money isn't all thrown away. And don't forget when you had your heart attack they kept you alive in North Tees hospital. That doesn't come without a bill to the state.'

'Julie's been bending your ear about this, if you ask me. All this stinks of her.' He said it with a sneer.

'Hey. Shut your mouth,' said Nick, really annoyed now. 'Just because she's got principles, there's no need to have a pop at her.'

'It's all bullshit, man. Julie likes money as much as anyone. She's quick enough to buy designer clothes. Always was. I don't see her in a Chairman Mao suit. That suit she wore on the first day looked expensive. This left wing crap is all a pose. She just likes the sound of it, if you ask me.'

Nick stopped and looked at him.

'Hey, fuck me, Jeff. I didn't know you cared that much about her politics. That suit, for your information, since you've been thinking about it so much, came from an Oxfam shop for about £25. She buys loads of second-hand and vintage clothes to save money. And she's not left wing. It's pathetic that you think about it like that. Really pathetic. You're not thinking straight. She just wants things to be more fair and I agree with her, by the way. It's fucking disgraceful the way this country is run for the benefit of an elite, all the banking shit has only gone to prove that the richest people are totally insulated from failure. We'll put some poor fuck in jail for not paying their TV licence, but not one single banker is going to end up behind fucking bars. And you're trying to tell me that's right? And we're all supposed to be so grateful that the rich don't sod off to the Cayman Islands? You don't have to be Chairman fucking Mao to realise that, son. You're getting blinded by his bloody money, if you ask me. You're onto a loser going into bat for your brother, you know that, don't you? He's nasty bit of work and you bloody know it.' He jabbed a finger at him.

'You don't mind taking his money though, do you?' said Jeff, indignant.

'Hey, if I only took money from people I liked, I'd die of starvation. What am I supposed to do? Stop being pissy about this, Jeff. It's not like you. Don't lie to yourself about what he's like.'

They said nothing else while they were shifting PA gear. After they'd done, Nick fished two bottles of water out of a big ice bucket backstage, handed one to Jeff and took one for himself.

'Cheers,' said Jeff, wiping his pink, sweaty face on his black t-shirt. 'That was hard graft in this humidity.'

'Aye. I bloody hurt all over.'

Jeff drank the water in one go. 'Sorry, like.'

'Eh?'

'Sorry about...before, like. Unnecessary twatishness. I take it back.'

'I should fucking well hope so. You're forgiven. I'll put it down to stress.'

'Aye, even so.' He shook his head. A long drip of sweat rolled down a strand of his greying hair and dripped onto the grass. 'Dunno what I was doing putting your Jules up against El Bloater. Fuck me. That lass saved my sodding life when I had my heart attack.'

'Well, exactly. For all her faults, and god knows she's got plenty, being a selfish twat isn't one of them, as you well know.'

'Sorry mate. I tell you what though, right? He gets under your skin.'

'Big Fish? What do you mean?'

'Being around him a lot, you get used to his world. All the money and the mouthing off at everyone. Easy to lose your...your standards, like. It's a bit like you're King Cock and everyone else is the ungrateful grubby masses. You get totally into that mindset if you're not careful.'

'Well, we'll say nowt more about it, you big shite.'

A very tall, willowly man stood behind the board talking to an engineer.

Jeff looked up. 'That's Simon Garbutt, El Fishio's business partner. Weird looking bloke. He's all legs. Look. See? He's got a normal sized top half and then about five foot of legs. Dunno how he gets jeans to fit him.'

He really was a strange shape. The long, bony legs meant it appeared as though he was walking around on stilts. In his mid 50s, he had very receding blonde hair and a smooth, almost radioactively pink face.

'We saw him with The Fish at LAX and I've seen him around the site quite a lot. Do you know him, then?'

'Aye. Well, I don't know him. But I've spent a bit of time in his company. He's a posh Chelsea boy, isn't he? He'll be having a nosebleed being this far north. He thinks Watford is near the Arctic circle.'

'How did your brother get mixed up with him?'

'God knows. Money attracts people to you, doesn't it? He's alright, but he just seems a bit alien, really. Not our sort of bloke. Show him a rare Soft Machine album and his pulse doesn't quicken. Doesn't even like football.'

'Ironic, given The Fish's common man shtick.'

'What he doesn't mind is his cut of El Fish Boy's considerable earnings. He coins it big style off him.'

'What does he actually do as a business manager? That's one of those catch-all, mean nothing job titles.'

'I haven't a clue. Generates money and invests it, I suppose. Aye aye, he's coming over.'

The tall, angular, loping figure approached them and waved.

'Hello Jeff,' he called out. Jeff saluted. 'I didn't realise you got warm summer weather up here.' He laughed at his own joke.

'Oh aye. Sometimes it gets so warm the whippets have to take off their cloth caps when they get the coal out of the bath,' said Jeff. Nick laughed. The man held out his hand towards him.

'Simon Garbutt.'

'Nick Guymer. Alright, Simon. Welcome to the Costa del Teesside.'

'Ah *the* Nick Guymer?'

'I'm *a* Nick Guymer, not sure if I'm *the* one.'

' Ah don't be so modest, I've heard a lot of good things about you. A top man, I'm told. So, you were Johnny on the spot when the bomb went off. You were in all the news reports.'

Nick shrugged. He hadn't bothered to read them. He didn't want to revisit those moments.

'Modest too. I like it. Classy.' He smiled at him warmly. 'Good man. So, I've seen you around with a blonde woman.'

'That's Julie, my fiancée.' What a strange thing to say. Fiancée.

'Splendid. So, congratulations. When is the wedding?'

'We don't know yet. Maybe in the autumn.'

Simon nodded and smiled at him. 'Fantastic. So, this place looks great. I was looking at the main stage. So, it's like, totally huge, isn't it? I'm really looking forward to it all starting.'

He was well-spoken and accentless; the sort of voice that made Nick feel slightly on edge. He didn't like accentless voices. It was unnerving. How could he not have an accent? Why wouldn't you want one? But more importantly, why would you start so many sentences with the redundant word *so* when you didn't need to? It was a very annoying modern fashion which seemed to have quickly evolved into a verbal tic.

'Are you staying up here?' said Nick.

'Stevie is putting me up at his place in Wynyard. One of his places, I should say.' He tutted and rolled his eyes at the extravagance. 'So, this is all a big investment for us. I wanted to be on site to make sure it all runs smoothly.' He intertwined his ridiculously long fingers together. Nick had never seen fingers that long. It looked as though they should have a third joint.

'Well, the figures Arthur sent me suggested it's going to be hugely profitable,' said Nick. 'That was before the explosion though and all the added expense of security.'

'Indeed. Well, we've had to do that, but it is a bitter irony that the bomb and the deaths have made the whole thing more high profile and even more profitable, especially as we got the TV rights sorted after the explosion. So it's all covered.'

Nick raised his eyebrows, but said nothing. Murder and profits didn't belong in the same sentence as far as he was concerned.

'I mean no disrespect in saying that. It's just a bald truth,' said Simon, holding up a hand. 'Frankly, I wanted the festival called off. It made sense to me to call it off. People are in danger...who knows what else will happen?'

'That was never going to happen,' said Nick. 'It'd have been giving in. Teessiders don't give in - especially not to bullies. We've been pushed from pillar to post economically, we've been down so long it looks like up, to quote the old blues song. It's made the area very resilient and tough.'

'I'm sure it's an admirable quality,' said Simon, idly fiddling with an expensive-looking watch.

'What would have happened if it had been cancelled, Si?' said Jeff. 'Would it have been an insurance job?'

He let out a bitter laugh. 'No, it wouldn't and there was a whole world of hurt for the BF if that had happened. But as it happens, everything is fine, so everyone is happy.'

He squinted and pulled his lips back over his teeth, scuffing at the ground with expensive brown leather shoes.

'So, what are you working on here, Nick?'

'I'm a bit of a jack of all trades. I've been doing social media website and publicity work with Emily Davids and also box humping with the big man here.'

'He's brains *and* brawn, this one, Si,' said Jeff, jerking his thumb at Nick.

'A very useful combination. Hmm, now actually, I can push some work your way if you're available later this summer and into the autumn. So, all things being equal, the BF is touring down under. Did you know he's had the best selling DVD in the last three years down there? So, he's huge with a capital H. We need a full-time social media and publicity person on board. That could be you. It is a bit gruelling, but it'd be a nice little earner for you.'

'Wow. Australia. I've never been there. Could I go with Julie?'

'As long as you pay her way, of course you can. So, I think the money is about six grand gross for the five weeks. We pay your air fare, travel and accommodation, you pay for your food. October to November. It'll be lovely weather too. So, have a think anyway and let me know.'

He smiled again and slapped him on the top of the arm. 'Well, watch out for the Ironopolis Anarchist. See you around,' and loped off.

Nick turned to Jeff and put both thumbs up. 'Oz here we come, mate.'

By the time he got back to the admin tent, Julie was waiting for him, sitting on the edge of her desk.

'Sorry I'm late, Jules. I got caught up in something. Listen, do you fancy going to Australia for five weeks in October?' He explained the offer. She broke into a huge smile and punched the air.

'Yes, get in! We're bloody doing that. Too good a chance to pass up and it's even decent money.'

'I know. It's a grand a week near as damn it.'

'Well, well, well, good old Simon. He might have legs like a stick insect, but he's a good lad, eh.' She gripped her fists together and punched the air again.

'Look, I'm late. I've got to go over to the Boro now to see who turns up for that Ironopolis Anarchists meeting. I've not got time to take you home first.'

'Don't worry, I'll collar Jeff and get him to give us a lift. I'll start sewing corks onto a hat for us.'

Nick left the site at half six and drove into Middlesbrough, taking the A66 and the A171. Cargo Fleet Lane ran roughly south east from the centre of town out into the southern suburbs. He pulled up in a road near to the cemetery and got out, looking at his watch. It was just before 7pm. Would they meet on foot, or come by car? How would he know them? The road was busy but few people were on foot. He walked up to a bus stop and stood, as though waiting. It was right opposite the gates of the cemetery.

Just before the hour, two men in their late 20s with neat, short hair and open-necked shirts came out of a side road and walked up to the cemetery and rested on a low wall. He didn't recognise either of them from the festival site or anywhere else. They stood around talking until 10 past, then walked off.

The number five bus pulled up and two people got off. He stepped back a little so the driver wouldn't think he wanted to get on. As he did so, a figure walked out of the side road he'd parked on, came up behind him and stood 10 yards away, waiting to cross. While the bus was at a halt, he trotted over the road. Initially, Nick didn't register who it was, and who it was certainly hadn't seen him, but as the bus pulled away in a belch of diesel, there he was.

Mike Trent. His accountant. Bloody hell fire.

Nick's heart-beat dramatically increased as his brain tried to compute what he was seeing. Dressed in his usual white shirt and black trousers, Mike stopped by the gates and looked around, then walked inside the gates and along a path. What the hell was Mike doing here?

'How much money do you really need?' Of course. That was Mike's saying. The phrase he often used. And it was all over the Ironopolis Anarchists website from the poster called 'Volunteer'. He said he'd had a tip off about Big Fish laundering money. He said he had inside knowledge, the sort of inside knowledge that the Ironopolis Anarchists had. *Volunteers* was even a Jefferson Airplane record that Mike had in his office. It was Mike. Mike was 'Volunteer'. He was in this group. He was in the Ironopolis Anarchists and they had bombed the house. They were murderers. They'd almost killed him and Julie.

It was too much to comprehend. He couldn't comprehend it. But here he was. There couldn't be much doubt. This wasn't a coincidental meeting. Mike was never even on Teesside. He lived on Ripon Road in Harrogate. He lived a quiet life on his own. He liked his books and his records and watching Harrogate Town. He wasn't a revolutionary. But then, maybe Julie was right, he was another cold top with a hot oven.

There was no way he could follow him into the cemetery without being seen and certainly no way he could get close enough to hear what they were saying. He walked up the road a little so that when Mike came out, he wouldn't see him. He rested against a lamp post wondering if he could get access to Emily's laptop again to log back into their website and take a longer look at it, now that he knew Mike was involved. Maybe Emily would turn up, too. She must be one of them as well. She had access to the secret message board so she had to be. It was all too weird and, on some level, just didn't feel right. While he waited for Mike to return, he called Julie and explained what he'd seen. She was about to go home.

'That's so strange. I've never met him, but you've always said how low-key he is. I mean, I can imagine Emily Davids being involved in some green-type movement - she's the right impressionable age for that. But Mike is your age.'

'You don't know anyone who is a hacker by any chance? I'd love to get access to their message boards again and we can't without Em's laptop.'

'I tell you what I'll do, I'll call our Terry. He's into all this online gaming thing and I seem to remember he did some sort of computing course while he was in jail as part of his rehabilitation. It wouldn't surprise me if he knew someone who was using their powers for evil instead of for good.'

'Good idea. I'm just going to wait for Mike and then accidentally run into him, just to see what he says.'

'OK. It'll be interesting to see what excuse he comes up with off the top of his head. Be careful though.'

As he talked he looked over the road. A man in a blue t-shirt with close-cut blonde hair was looking at him. He was, wasn't he? No. He looked away. He was just hanging around. Nick looked down the road and turned back to the man suddenly. He was looking at him again. Then, at pace, Mike emerged from the cemetery. Nick rang off and walked briskly down Cargo Fleet Lane to intercept him as he crossed over the road. He was within 10 feet of him as he reached the pavement, but he still hadn't noticed Nick. Lost in his own thoughts, he walked briskly, head down.

'Mike! Fancy seeing you here,' said Nick, with a wave, trotting up to him, noting as he did so that the blonde man was now on the phone.

The accountant visibly jumped as though shocked by a loud noise. His dark brown eyes looked at him in disbelief for a second.

'Bloody hell. Hello Nick. You shocked the living daylights out of me. What are *you* doing here?'

'I was just visiting a mate of mine who lives up the road. What are you doing here, more like? You're a long way from home in Harrogate.'

'I had a meeting...' He looked at him. Clearly, he was weighing up whether he was a fellow IA or not. 'I was just meeting up with some fellow accountants.'

'Oh. Right. Often meet in a cemetery, do you? I saw you arrive, but you didn't see me.'

'I thought you said you were seeing a friend. What are you doing, hanging around waiting to see me?' He looked at him suspiciously. 'Who told you to come here?'

'No-one told me,' said Nick, truthfully.

Mike began walking away from him towards the side street where he'd parked.

'Mike? What's wrong? What's up?' He trotted alongside him, then walked backwards, looking at him. 'Is something the matter? Are you alright? You're behaving weird.'

He waved him away with his hand. 'Don't ask me anything.'

'Anything about what? I don't understand.'

Mike reached his blue Nissan and unlocked it. 'I can't say, Nick. I really can't.'

'By the way, you were right about Stevie Salmon, he is paying bands with cash,' said Nick, but Mike didn't seem interested now. 'Are you going to tell me what this is all about it?'

No. Mike wasn't. Without further words he got in the car, started the engine and drove off at speed.

CHAPTER 11

By the time he got home, Julie had made burgers and some sweet potato fries. The house smelled of frying beef.

'By heck, that smells good, Jules.' He threw his car keys on the kitchen table and told her what had happened with Mike.

'You know what they say, the quiet ones are always the worst,' she said, wrapping a couple of burgers in some lettuce leaves and pushing them across the table to him. 'That's what my mam always used to say, anyway. Mind you, our Ricky and Kev were noisy as anything and they absolutely were the worst, so obviously, it's a load of old shite, that. Talking of which, our Terry is on his way over.'

'Oh aye, what did he say?'

She poured herself a glass of white wine and him a fizzy water.

'Reckons he can hack into anything up to and including the Pentagon. He's probably full of shite, like. Lives in a dream world, does our Tez.'

'It's probably the stink from the bins...decaying waste must have a hallucinogenic quality to it.'

She laughed. 'At least he's going straight and he's kept himself in employment on the bins for a couple of years now without going on the rob and he's had a steady girlfriend all year. Jasmin is a lovely lass too, not some hard-faced rat bag. This, when it comes to Tez, is major progress. I found a little bit on Little Miss White Panties, Emily Davids, by the way.'

'Oh yeah? Anything good?'

'Her Facebook page is quite new and there's not much on it except pictures of cats. She doesn't seem to have a boyfriend or if she has she's expunged all trace of them. She's got cats though. Put it this way, she's not a typical 21 year old. I'd expect to find a long digital life trail on Facebook and before that on MySpace or even Bebo, but there's nothing. That's unusual for a university student. It's almost as if she's wiped it all away and replaced it with a bland Facebook page. She might just not be into social media, and actually, the way she's got it all set up is how a lot of women's groups suggest you should run your social media. Keep everything private and don't share much about you or your life, but even so...it makes me suspicious of her. I'm sure she's an IA, but if she is, I'd have thought she'd have been at that meeting. I don't understand where everyone was. What's the point in posting details of a meeting if no-one except Mike goes to it? He must have thought you were an IA too.'

'At first I think he did and then decided I couldn't be. I mean, he knows me. I'm far too scatter-brained and badly organised to do anything that involves research.'

Her younger brother arrived on a noisy 500cc motorbike which sounded like it was on the verge of exploding. They could hear it coming along Aislaby Road before he even turned down their track. Where his older brothers, Ricky and Kev were fair-haired, big, heavy men, Terry was scrawny. The only one of the family to take after his father rather than his mother, he was dark-haired and dark-eyed.

'Now then, young Tezza,' said Nick, greeting him at the door as Terry pulled his helmet off. 'How's you?'

'I'm alright, fella. Jules says you need my computer skills.'

'Aye. I'll tell you all about it.'

He showed him into the back room.

'Blimey, you've caught the sun, Jules,' said Terry on seeing her. 'Proper tanned you, like. I've not seen youse since you got back.'

'That's California for you,' she said, handing him a mug of tea.

'Aw haven't you got any beer? I'm clammin' for a beer.'

'You're on your bike, Tez. You're not drinking while you're on your bike.' She shook her head, arms folded like a disapproving mother. 'We've not even got any beer, anyway.'

'No beer?' said Terry, as though this was almost impossible to believe.

'I don't drink it and his Lordship doesn't drink at all, so all I've got is a Premier Cru Chablis and I'm not wasting that on you, it's

'£20 a bottle and I was given it as a leaving present by someone at Uni.'

'Pity. I work best with a drink on us.' He took a packet of cigarettes out of his top pocket and stuck one in his mouth.

'No you don't. You just think you do when you're pissed,' she said. 'And you're not smoking in here. You can go outside if you need to do that.'

'Aw Jules man, just one tab. It helps me concentrate.'

But she was firm with him. 'No. I don't want my house stinking of fags. I had enough of that growing up with mam. My bloody lungs are probably still coated in tar because of her.'

'I remember when I was a bairn you used to smoke,' he said, a little sulky.

'I just went through a stupid phase. Then I realised I was just following mam's example and that made me bloody stop. You should do the same, Tez. It'll fuck you up, smoking. It will. You know it will.'

Because she was 16 when he was born, Julie had at least tried to mother Terry for most of his life. As he'd been to a young offenders institute and an open prison for theft, it hadn't exactly been successful substitute parenting, but she hadn't given up on him yet. He wasn't a bad lad, not like his older brothers, Terry was just easily led and had been poorly educated as a result. He'd recently got involved with a girl, Jasmin, who seemed like a stabilizing influence on him and had given him something to hang onto in life.

Nick opened up his laptop, cut and paste the web address he'd sent himself from Emily's computer into his browser. It was hundreds of random letters and numbers. It opened up the blank page with the two boxes for username and password.

'Right. The log in was "helenwheels" but I've no idea what her password is. I tried the obvious ones that make the lists of most-used passwords. It was 10 characters, though. There were 10 asterisks on her computer.'

Terry took out a pair of glasses and took hold of the laptop.

'They probably generate new usernames and passwords every day, to stop people like you getting hold of them. This has been re-routed several times, probably from servers in Russia.'

He chewed on his bottom lip in exactly the same way that Julie sometimes did and then scrunched his face up and opened up a blank DOS window and began typing code into it. 'Don't sit around waiting for us to just get access just like that. It'll take us ages. I'll give youse a shout when I've done it.'

'If you've done it, you mean,' said Julie.

'No, I'll crack it. You can crack anything if you go at it long enough. 'Ave you got owt to eat, Jules? I'm starving. I've not had any tea.'

'I've got some burgers and chilli fries leftover.'

'That'll do, like. Ta.'

She brought in the burger wrapped in lettuce, and the remainder of the sweet potato fries. He looked at it in amazement.

'What the fuck is that? It's not a burger Jules. It's got green around it.'

'We don't eat wheat, do we? So there's no bun. Get it bloody eaten.'

He peered at the plate suspiciously and picked up a chip. 'These chips are orange Jules. And they're sweet.'

'You're a food Neanderthal, you. It's sweet potato, isn't it? They even sell them on Teesside these days along with other exotic stuff, like watercress and aubergines.'

'I like it, like, just never had it before. You're dead posh you two, Jules. I dunno where you learn about this shit from. Watching BBC2, probably.'

'We're not posh Tez, you're just a retard,' said Julie, pushing him in the back playfully.

They left him to it and went back into the kitchen. Julie started to load up the dishwasher. Nick came up behind her, put his arms around her waist and pulled her into him, nuzzling into her neck, inhaling her, musky, honey-straw smell. She spun around with a wide smile.

'Aw aren't you nice? Is this your happy pills again?'

He nodded. 'I think so. I feel really good in a way that I haven't for a long time.' He took her hands. 'And you know what?'

'What luv?'

He whispered in her ear, 'I could just rip your pants off, bend you over the kitchen table and give you a right good seeing to.' He pressed into her and she gurgled a loud, woody laugh. The smell of her made his passion rise quickly.

'Could you now? Hmm, I reckon you could an' all,' she said, with a raised eyebrow.

'I definitely could, aye. Do you fancy it?' he said, nuzzling her again. She was so soft and smooth.

'Tez might get a bit of a shock when he comes in for more tea. No brother should see his own sister bent over the kitchen table, stripped naked and doing it doggie.' She gave another low, rumbling chuckle and rubbed his lower back.

Nick laughed and slipped his hands down the back of her pants, feeling her silky, bare buttocks. He began to whisper more dirty talk into her ear, feeling as strong an urge of lust as he'd felt since he was a young man. It was almost overwhelming, his heart racing.

'Eeee, what are you like, you? Stronger and harder than a bad girl's dream. Cool your engines Hoochie Coochie Man and bank it for later. You can unleash as much dirty passion as you've got in you when Tez has gone. Alright?' She squeezed him, pecked him on the lips and went back to loading the dirty plates into the machine. 'Must be strong medicine those tablets, eh. This isn't you trying to get bad thoughts out of your mind again though, is it?'

He stood and thought for a few seconds. 'No, it really isn't. I seem to have replaced diversion sex with proper big, hard, priapic lusting. I'm just feeling very...y'know...horny. Maybe you got me Viagra by mistake.'

'By the state of you, I think I might have.' She flicked at his crotch with a tea towel. 'I'll hose you down with cold water in a minute. Sort yourself, lad, it's all too obvious. I bet you're really just thinking of Emily Davids in her pants. Oh hey, just to take your mind off your trouser department, one thing I forgot to tell you, just before I came home I got an email at the festival from Artie Taylor, remember him?'

'Artie Taylor? No, who's he?' said Nick, rearranging himself and letting his racing heart calm down a little.

'The photographer we met on the plane from LA with the shorty lezza lass, Kaz.'

'Gotcha, yeah,' he said, pouring himself some water from a bottle. His rising passion had left him dry-mouthed.

'He emailed to get two press passes for the Friday.'

'Cool. It'll be good to see those two again. Hey, you know what we should do. We should get him to take some pictures of us...'

'...of us? We've got loads of pictures of us,' she said, dropping a dishwasher tablet into the machine and closing its door.

'Not professional ones. I was just looking into him, he's photographed everyone in rock and roll, blues and country and has done some really famous album cover shots. You know that famous KK May one from 1988? He did that.'

'Ooh, he was a proper gorgeous, sex-on-legs, snake-hipped shag machine, him. Whatever happened to him?'

'He was a major druggie and his life fell apart. There's talk of a comeback sometime though. He's supposed to have been cleaning up but who knows if that's true?'

'He was supposed to have a really huge cock. A proper big old baby's arm.'

'Trust you to remember that, Jules.'

She laughed and gave him a mock indignant look. 'I can't imagine why that was on my mind, can you?' she said. 'But if Artie Taylor is a big photographer, he won't want to do us will he? We're nowt.'

'He might if we ask nicely. Doesn't have to be anything elaborate. Just a couple of good portraits of us together that we can put in a frame. It'd be cool to be shot by him.'

Tez shouted from the back room. 'Jules! Nick! I'm in!'

They bustled into the room and sat down alongside him. There again was the long list of posts.

'How did you do it?' said Nick.

'Secrets of the trade. I'd have to kill you if I told you,' said Terry, pleased with himself.

'Have you hacked into it or used some password-generating software or something?' said Julie.

'Nope. I did it the old-school way.'

'What way's that, like?' she said.

'I guessed her password!'

The three of them cheered.

'It took a few educated few guesses. I went to her Facebook page. I saw she had pictures of her cats. Cats are the biggest thing in some lasses' lives. Chances are she' going to use her pets names in a password somehow. See...' he pointed at her page. A big black cat with a white patch over its eye looked back along side another white cat with ginger splodges on its paws. 'The black one is Pirate, the other is Mr Paws.'

'So which one is it?' said Nick.

'It's both, isn't it? I went through a lot of combos of the name and numbers, then I thought, she'll not want to favour one cat over the other, so if she's used the cats' names, she'll use both. I first went for pawspirate, but it wasn't that, it was piratepaws.'

Julie patted him on the back. 'Bloody hell, Tez, I've underestimated your perception of human nature. Jasmin must be having a good effect on you. Where did you learn to get inside the head of young middle-class student girl's heads?'

'I'm not as stupid as I look. There's loads of clever blokes work on the bins. You learn a lot about life when you're hoying punters' crap around.'

'Do you?' said Nick.

'Do you bollocks,' said Terry with a laugh. 'It was just a lucky guess, wasn't it? I was going to try and hack into their password server, but it's always worth taking the easy route first if you can, like. So you're in. Now, if you're going to use this, remember that anyone else might think you're Emily Davids and second, she might change the password at any time and lock you out, or their administrator will. Also, by the look of it, this is only 12 hours worth of messages. It probably clears down every few hours.'

'Right, well, let's print everything out that's on here so we've got a record of it,' said Nick, connecting the printer to the laptop and opening each message. There were fewer now than there had been earlier.

'Alright, I'll get off, Jules.'

'Thanks, Tez. I owe you one. We'll have a drink-up in the Black Bull sometime.'

When he'd left, they began sifting through the printouts. There were 16 in total posted in the last 12 hours.

Julie read each message one by one. 'They're clearly trying to agree on their next move. Someone called King Hell says, "Let's bomb them to back to the stone age. We have the technology. We have right on our side. This is our moment". Another one says, "Unless we bomb again, no-one will take IA seriously". It's really all about the bombing. Nothing about what was said, agreed or disagreed at Mike's meeting. There are a few people going on about RadLand. Here's one which says, "RadLand are rich bastards, they deserve what's coming to them" and another says, "this has to be just the first strike of many against RadLand"; "we need to devalue everything they own" and another, "they've kept us all under their thumbs for too long. Bomb. Bomb. Bomb". She counted the posters. There are 15 taking part here and all of them are really militant. There really isn't a voice of caution, just more suggestions of who to blow up and where. Clearly, the Salmon Estate and the festival is actually seen as part of RadLand and thus as part of the problem.'

'What is the most recent post, Jules?' said Nick. She shuffled the papers.

'19.18, Volunteer says, "Another big day is coming. A bomb on a bigger stage". That's all.'

'Weirder and weirder. I got to Cargo Fleet Lane just before 7pm.

Mike didn't show up for about 5 minutes and then he went into the cemetery for no more than 10 minutes. I then intercepted him and we had a bit of to and fro for maybe 4 or 5 minutes. That means he was with me when he posted that. In other words, he can't have posted it, not even from a mobile device.'

'Are you sure you've got the times right? It would only take a few seconds to type this.'

'I'm certain. If that was posted at 19.18, Mike didn't post it. So maybe it isn't him. Maybe it's someone else. It really sounds like his voice, though. The words he uses, they're how he speaks.'

Nick sat back on the sofa, tugging at his beard stubble with his finger tips and then began writing a family tree of events and people out, in order to organise his thoughts. Julie lay flat out next to him. Her eyes closed.

'We know a group called the Ironopolis Anarchists have been exposing rich people as tax cheats. We know they're very careful to remain anonymous. Malky Helms told us how they operate. They could be anywhere in the country or anywhere in the world. They've brought six different people to book in the last year or so. There was a hoax bomb threat called in by a man claiming to be the Ironopolis Anarchist or from the Ironopolis Anarchists, Angie can't remember which, afterwards Mel Stephens gets an email from the Ironoplis Anarchist, singular, making demands. Then the bomb goes off and he gets another email, this time from the plural version with the same demands, but with an animal rights element added. We find the Anarchist, singular, has posted messages on various websites going back a year. But the message board is plural. We find that via Emily Davids, who must therefore be a member of IA. A meeting is on the board which only Mike Trent attends, proving he's also in the IAs and possibly goes by the name "Volunteer". Is that everything?'

'There's this RadLand charitable trust. The IAs want to attack them and their assets basically because they're rich landowners. It looks like IA have put this respectable, research-based face forward as their identity, but underneath have been planning something more violent and that's all happening now.'

He rubbed his eyes and groaned. 'Something just isn't right with this, Jules. I don't see Mike being part of this sort of terrorism thing. It's too aggressive, same goes for Emily.'

'Still waters run deep? Or the old cold tops have hot ovens, again.'

'He yawned. Yeah. Maybe. Let's go to bed.'

She turned out the lights and followed him upstairs. 'Mind, my back hurts from sitting at that desk all day, so don't go thinking you can actually bend me over anything. Lying down, I can do.' She yawned. 'I'm really, really good at lying down. You won't take it personally if I fall asleep half way through though, will you?'

As Nick took his early-morning walk, he was just watching a hare nibble a long dandelion leaf with relish when out of nowhere a thought flashed into his conscious mind from somewhere in his subconscious, as though his brain had been working on it all night. When he got back in Julie was poaching eggs and had dressed in torn old jeans and a black vest and trainers.

'Jules, I've had a good idea. You know how we're struggling to make sense of the bomb? Maybe, it wasn't actually meant to explode. It makes no sense because it shouldn't have happened at all. It wasn't meant to happen.'

She put bacon into the frying pan. 'So you're saying someone had a bomb made, but it just went off by accident?'

'Exactly. I know that doesn't answer the question who had the bomb made and why, but it would explain why it went off where and when it did.'

He opened up his computer and searched for a news report on the bomb in the *Northern Echo*.

'See. This report yesterday says it was some kind of explosive with a timer. I reckon that's not worked properly or it's had a dodgy detonator and something has set it off accidentally. Home-made bombs are an imprecise art form. If you don't quite know what you're doing, it's a volatile thing.'

'OK, but who would be carrying a bomb around? No-one has a bomb and doesn't mean to use it.'

She served up the food onto some old blue willow-patterned plates bought from a car boot.

'Maybe whoever was carrying it didn't know they were carrying it? For all it made a big bang, it wasn't that big a bomb. It says here that they think it was designed to be small and very powerful. It would have blown the walls out and not just the windows if it was a proper big IRA 1970s-style one. So it was probably literally quite small. Small enough to be put in a sports bag, but when it went off in an enclosed space it was devastating.'

Julie nodded. 'I like your idea. But it still means someone was planning to use a bomb.'

'It does, aye. And that's not a good thought at all. Though I suppose they may have planned to put it somewhere and then call in a warning so that when it went off, no-one got hurt.' He sat and thought for a bit. 'Yeah, that makes a lot of sense. It would have been the next step up from a fake bomb being found, to a real bomb being found and then, if they still didn't get what they wanted, to explode a real bomb without hurting anyone and then, finally, a proper big bomb which actually kills people. A steady escalation, like. Yeah, that's why killing people makes no sense - they never meant to kill anyone, only to threaten to.'

He cut into his bacon and piled it onto his fork along with egg and tomato. Julie sat looking at him, chewing.

'Nice idea, but you're forgetting that their message board would have some mention of the bomb being a mistake, but it doesn't. I know there are only 12 hours of messages on it at any one time, but even so, they talk a lot about the bomb and no-one even suggests or refers to the fact that it wasn't meant to happen, quite the opposite.'

'Bugger. I forgot about that. You're right. Yeah. Sod it. There goes that idea then. OK, let's try something else.' He tapped on the keyboard of his laptop while he ate.

'What are you looking for?'

'Angie Page...here she is. She's on Facebook. There's something not right about what she told us - we both know that - we didn't both jump to the same false conclusion about her, did we? At the very least she was hiding something. So let's find out something about her.'

'Has she got the Facebook security settings on public?'

'I think there's quite a bit that is, yeah. People should learn how to use the settings properly, you can look right into people's lives otherwise. Christ, she's even got her birthday on the public setting. That's mad. She's got one boy and one girl. The boy is seven, the girl nine. She went to Ian Ramsey, same as us. She's 35 years old and has worked at Stockton Borough Council since leaving school. Kids are cute, look...'

He spun the computer around to show her the two doe-eyed fair-haired kids.

'Aw, yeah. Bless 'em.'

He went back to the computer. 'She's divorced and doesn't seem to be in a relationship at the moment.'

'So she'll have deleted all the photos of her bloke from her Facebook page then. The digital evidence of relationships you've had must be an awkward and even an upsetting thing, I'd think. Imagine trying to purge someone you've fallen out of love with from your online life? It'd be really hard to do.'

'I'm glad we don't have to go through all that. If you were dating, you'd have to keep everything locked down or you might give away that you'd seen three different people that week or whatever. People would make all sorts of judgements on you, otherwise,' said Nick, finishing his food and pouring them both fresh black coffee.

'Oh god, I can just imagine. "Oh she's gone out with him and him and him"...it'd be like that. And blokes could swot up on you and find out all sorts of things if you don't have your settings right.' She pursed her lips together. 'And that's before the whole revenge porn awfulness. People need locking up over that. The whole online thing is one big potential relationship nightmare.'

'What about those people who film themselves having it off and upload it to some porno site? What happens to that when they break up? You're in cyberspace copulating with him forever.'

She covered her face with her hands and shuddered. 'Imagine if you then decided you wanted to be a teacher or something. There you are, chewing on the love bone of some bloke you went out with for a month 10 years ago and the kids would be asking, "Miss, miss, why are you doing that? Is he your husband, miss?" Can you imagine? Oh god. Ha ha.'

'Well, Angie hasn't got anything like that on here. She's clearly only recently divorced. She's not deleted the man from her digital life yet. I've just clicked on 2007 when she joined Facebook and look, the profile picture is her in the arms of a bloke. I bet that's the dad. He's in most photos that year and look, here's an old wedding photo. It's tagged "St. Peters March 2006". He looks familiar to me for some reason.'

The man was fair-haired and handsome in a rugged sort of way. Julie looked at him with narrowed eyes.

'He's a shagger,' she said it with a world-weary cynical sigh. 'She left him because he was unfaithful.'

'How do you know that from this picture?' he said, vaguely incredulous that she could make such a judgement.

She looked at the man in the photo again. 'I can tell the type. Good looking, alpha males like him are ruled by their dick. Trust me, I know. Plenty of women would be attracted to him and he'd not resist them. He's the sort of bloke who should never get married or be in a long-term relationship. Causes pain and upset wherever he goes. Like I say, trust me on this. There are loads of men like him. More commonly known as twats.'

Nick went through her Facebook timeline year by year. The pictures of them together disappeared in early 2008.

'I reckon this tells us they were married in 2006, had problems by late 2007, split up in 2008 and probably divorced late last year.'

He went back to 2007 and looked at the ex-husband again. He was tagged as David Murray. So Angie had reverted to her maiden name after the divorce, understandably. Clicking on his name brought up his Facebook page. His profile was a photo of him on the beach somewhere sunny, stripped to the waist. He look chunky, with big powerful arms, but a flabby, paunchy gut.

'There's your half-naked alpha male, Jules. What do you reckon?' He showed her the screen.

'He's obviously a heavy drinker. You can see it on him.'

'Aye, he's quite fat, especially for a youngish bloke. He must be about 30 in these.'

'Oh yeah, but this isn't him now, I bet. This is the him the divorced him wishes he still was - and let's be honest, he ain't all that in this, is he? I don't like the look of him on any level and he's an odd choice for Angie. She's a quiet woman. This bloke will have bullied her one way or another.'

'He does look like a bully, doesn't he?'

'And he thinks he's much more well-endowed than he really is. Typical of his sort.'

Nick gave a snort. 'I won't ask how you know that, Jules.' He kept clicking through the pictures, stopping at a series of him showing off a new car, standing proudly pointing to a red Audi.

'Good. OK so we're making some progress here. She hooked up with him probably about 10 years ago, had two kids, then married him. He was probably always a domineering, boozing bully, but she managed to get out of the relationship. Good on Angie, I say. I bet that took a lot of strength of mind for her to do that. They see women at the TW Centre that put up with his sort for literally decades and suffer in silence, too scared to leave and just hoping he stops being a bastard.'

'She must still have contact with him because of the kids. She told us they were with him in Ropner Park,' said Nick, still looking at the photos of the man.

'Yeah. We may have underestimated Angie, she might sound like Mavis off *Coronation Street*, but underneath she must be made of sterner stuff. Getting your life back together after a messy break up, especially if he's a bit of a bastard, can't be easy when there's kids involved,' said Julie. 'Means you've got to keep in touch with the father, even though he's probably the last person you want to see.'

Nick rested his chin on his hand. 'I hate blokes like him. I always have, even going back to school. They just think they're it. I especially hated how successful they were at getting girlfriends, as well. That line from the Joe Jackson song, "Pretty women out walking with gorillas down my street", that's about men like this. Why is that? Why don't more women see through them?'

'Most probably do, eventually, when it's too late. They can be charming at first as well...if you're a nice person it's hard to imagine how horrible some people can really be and also you really don't want to believe it. So you lie to yourself about them. Anyway...'

Nick suddenly banged the table, interrupting her. 'That's where I've seen him...'

'What?'

'This bloke. I knew he looked familiar.'

'You know him?'

'I don't know him, but I think he was watching me on Cargo Fleet Lane when I was watching Mike.'

'Watching you? Are you sure?'

'Definitely...he was on the other side of the road and he saw me go up to Mike and speak to him. He looked a bit like Steve McQueen...or at least like what Steve McQueen might have looked like if he'd grown up in South Bank eating parmos and drinking Camerons Strongarm.'

She frowned at him...the lines around her eyes creased in contemplation. 'I don't get that. That's too weird. You must be mistaken, man.'

'Oh god, maybe I am. I don't know, I'm rubbish with remembering names and faces.' Suddenly, excitement rose in his throat again as he looked at the man's Facebook page. 'Good god, one of his Facebook friends is Simon Garbutt.'

'What?!' she stood up in shock. 'How? Garbutt isn't from around here, is he?'

'No. He's from London.' He mulled it over for a minute. 'Think about this. Garbutt handles Big Fish's money. The Fish is rich and his dad is a major landowner, thus could easily be part of this RadLand group that was mentioned on the message board. Garbutt is friends with the ex-husband of Angie who was, effectively, working for Garbutt and took the hoax bomb call. Should we be suspicious of that?'

'I don't know. Should we?'

'RadLand is a group of rich landowners, right? The very sort of people the IA group have been successfully going after, right? So who stands to gain most by blackening the name of the IAs? RadLand does. Garbutt and Big Fish are probably part of the RadLand group. If the IAs are no longer taken seriously because they're regarded as terrorists, that means their investigations will fall on deaf ears.'

Julie sat up straight. 'I get what you're saying. So via Angie, they make up the hoax bomb threat thing and say they're from Ironopolis Anarchists, thus painting them as nutters.'

'Exactly.'

'That makes sense, but the problem is, the IA message board posters all refer to the bomb as being their work. So even if they didn't do the hoax, they definitely did the real thing.'

Nick threw his head back in frustration. 'Oh bugger. You've ruined another perfectly good theory there, by referring to facts. Sometimes facts get in the way of truth, Jules.'

'Very existential. There still might be something in what you're saying, though. It is too much of a coincidence. The ex-husband might be bullying Angie into lying about that phone call for some reason. Does David Murray's Facebook page say where he's from?'

Nick looked at his 'About' info. 'He's local. He went to Sheraton school. He'd have been there in the early to mid 80s.'

'If he went there, his family must've lived around the area...'

'...which means your mam or auntie will know them or know of them or have heard something about them on the estate grapevine.'

'Exactly.' She looked at her watch. 'We've just got time to go over to mam's before work. I'm knocking off early today 'cos I've got that do at the Penny Black tonight.' She got up and threw a pose. 'Tonight, Matthew, I'm going to be Pat Benatar!'

'I wish I could see that.'

'Well you can't. It's a lasses' night out. We don't want our oestrogen cloud dispersed by your turbo-charged, testosterone-fuelled sexuality.'

'Ha ha, my what?'

As they drove along Bishopton Avenue and took a left at the roundabout onto Durham Road, Nick looked in his rear view mirror as they sat at some lights.

'You know what, I've had the same car behind me since we went past Ropner Park.'

She quickly turned and looked. 'Ooh, he's nice looking.'

'The driver?'

'He looks like Steve McQueen in *The Great Escape.*'

'Steve McQueen? Are you sure?'

'Well...no...not really...more like Gordon McQueen, ha ha...that was a good 1970s football reference.'

Nick didn't like this at all. 'He's not following us, is he?'

She looked again as they pulled away. 'He might be.' They went a bit further up Durham Road. 'He's still there.' He took a quick right turn up Redhill Road. It was going totally the wrong direction, but he wanted to see if the black Ford Ka followed. It did. He took a left on Ragpath Lane and drove down to Junction Road then left again. The car was still behind them. At the Horse and Jockey roundabout he went straight on and then took the first left down Easington Road, turning in at the last minute. The black Ka drove straight on along Harrowgate Lane and disappeared. He parked up for a minute.

'Where we paranoid there?' he said.

'You took an odd route, so it did seem like he was following us. But he's gone now...so maybe he wasn't.'

'I couldn't see him properly because he had his sun visor down...and I know this might sound mad...but did he look like David Murray. Angie's David Murray?'

She looked back at him. 'Come on, that can't have been the man we're going to see mam about. No, it was just some fair-haired bloke.'

'He wasn't not like him. '

Julie sat back and thought about what she'd seen. 'I'd need to see David Murray again to say if it was him. He was fair-haired. That's all I can say. C'mon, let's get to mam's.' They drove through the remains of the old Hardwick estate and pulled up outside of Jackie Wells's house just as she was coming out of the front door.

A short, scrawny, wizened woman in her late 60s, she wore a pink hoodie, a pair of blue slacks and white trainers. She looked up at them with the turquoise blue eyes that Julie had inherited.

'Hiya mam,' said Julie, walking up the path briskly.

'Alright Jules. How are you feeling, luv?' she said with uncharacteristic kindness.

'I'm fine mam, you know I'm fine. I haven't been ill, remember? I just lost the baby. You don't have to tip-toe around me any more. You brought us up to get through shitty times, so I'm getting through.'

'Good. Right then. I'll say no more. Now then Nick. Eeee, I was sorry to hear your mam passed away, son.' She put her leathery, claw-like hand on his bare arms, gripped him tightly and shook him. It was a small and unusual act of affection.

'Thanks, Jackie.'

'First Jules and now you. These things come in threes, mark my words. It'll be my bloody turn next. So, to what do I owe this dubious bloody pleasure? I'm just off out.' That was more like the normal Jackie.

As she had come to a halt for more than 30 seconds, Jackie lit a cigarette, narrowing her eyes at them in exactly the same way Julie did when she was focusing on something. 'Owee, then what is it? I'm going 'round our Sandra's.'

'Do you know a family called Murray? They're from somewhere around here. The son is called David. He's in his late 30s. Good-looking bloke, fair hair, beefy sort. Drinker.'

'Why, like?'

'Never mind why. Does it ring any bells?'

She sucked deeply on the Benson and Hedges.

'There was a Glenda Murray that used to go up the club of a Saturday night. She was blonde, like. I think she had a son.' She frowned, trying to recollect. Nick got on his phone and looked up David Murray's Facebook page again.

'It says in his profile that his mam is Betty Murray and his dad was Fred.'

'Eeee, aye, I know them.' She let out a rasping cackle born out of smoking 40 fags a day for over 50 years. 'We used to call them "fretty in bed". Betty and Fred, get it? Ha ha. Aye, they had two daughters and a son. The son was the youngest, went to Sheraton, he's about five or six years younger than you, Jules. Aye, he was a good-looking lad. I'm surprised you never had him, Jules. You went through all the good looking lads around here.'

'No I did not, mother.' She put her hands on her hips and stared down at her, indignant.

'You bloody did. You were well-known for it until you went to university, then you had all the good-looking blokes there.'

'You know that's not true. Stop being a shit, mother. Can't you just be nice to me for once?'

Jackie grinned at her mischievously and winked at Nick. 'I'm just saying that lad was the sort of lad you used to go out with when you were in your teens.'

'Well, he'd have been too young for me, wouldn't he? I went out with older blokes if anything.'

Jackie sucked deeply again and yet just blew out a mere wisp of smoke, seemingly able to retain the vast majority of it in her lungs. 'Aye, I suppose so. So alright then, I know them, so what?'

'What's the son do now? Does he work up here?' said Nick.

'I don't know, but I'll ask San, she was more mates with Betty than me. Fred died years ago. He carked it before he was 60. I'll give youse a ring later, Jules.' She stood and looked her daughter up and down. Julie looked back, then held up a hand and turned away.

'No mam. I'm not staying to listen to whatever you're going to say about how I'm dressed. I'm just working in old jeans and a t-shirt and trainers. I'm not trying to be dressed up.'

'What? I was just going to say you were looking nice. Very slim.'

'No you weren't. You never say that. Not even when you're being nice to me. You're always saying I've got fat thighs or a fat arse, or my tits are sagging or I've got bags under my eyes.'

Jackie rasped another laugh and slapped Nick on the back as they walked out onto the road, whispering in his ear. 'She knows she looks good, she always has, so I have to keep her from getting a big head, y'see. If I was a bloke and she wasn't my daughter, I'd bloody fancy her. Don't tell her that, though.'

'I heard that, mam. Sometimes I think you can't embarrass me any more, mam and then you find a new way to do it,' said Julie over her shoulder as they got back into the car.

Once on the festival site they went to Mel Stephen's desk. He was writing on a huge white board.

'Hey Mel, can we have a quick word?' said Nick.

'If you must.'

'When Emily Davids came for the job, did she have an NI number and everything? She's not working for cash or anything, is she?'

He turned around and looked at him. 'Little Em? Weighs about four stone wet through? Her? Why?'

'Just wondered if she's legit. We're working on an idea.'

'Angie Page will have checked her out, that was her job before she legged it. I'll have the paperwork somewhere. Hang on.'

He went to one of three big filing cabinets and looked under D, pulling out a brown card file.

'Here we go.' He handed it to Nick. Inside was an application form with an address in Marton. A phone number and some details of her Computer Science degree at college. She had an NI number and her date of birth was 25th August 1987. She'd been on the books for three summers, just as she had said. It all looked right. He handed it back.

'Thanks, mate.'

'You going to tell me what this is all about?' said Mel. 'That look on your face says, "No Mel, I'm not." Well get yourselves fucked off then and don't waste any more of my valuable time. You must both have work to do.'

Julie went to work at her desk and Nick found Emily. It was a strange feeling to know something so secret about someone, when they had no idea that you knew. She smiled up at him with her gap-toothed grin as he sat down. She was an unlikely terrorist. Too unlikely.

'Morning, Nicky boy!' she said, bright-eyed, her hair all messy on top, as usual.

'Hello hello. How are you today? Feeling better?' He said, with a little stroke on her back.

'Yes, *much* better, thanks to your chat yesterday. I haven't got any of those pills yet, but you really helped put things into perspective for me.' She patted the seat next to her. 'Come here. I've got a hole I need filled,' she said and then giggled like a teenager at the double-entendre. 'That sounded a bit wrong, didn't it?'

'There's nothing wrong with a bit of mutually consenting hole filling, Em,' he said. She giggled again.

'I think it must have been a Freudian slip...or a cry for help...it has been a while, if you know what I mean.' She rubbed him on the leg as he sat down and smiled right in his face, almost nose to nose. He was far from the most perceptive when it came to body language, but it seemed very like she had suddenly decided to flirt quite openly with him.

CHAPTER 12

'Well, tell me about this hole then.'

She was giggling again. 'Well...it's about this big...' she formed a small oval with her fingers, laughing as she did so. It was definitely flirting and then some. 'Sorry, I don't know what's come over me. Would you like to? Oh dear, sorry.' She put her hand over her mouth.

'I'm not sure you should be saying that to an old dude like me, Em.'

'Oh that's all rubbish. You're not that old. How old are you?'

'48, which makes me 27 years older than you.'

'I'll soon be 22. So that will make it only 26. Anyway, you don't look it. You still look very...err...what's the word...err...very virile...yes...virile. I like older men, anyway. Blokes my age are boys, whereas you sir, you are a man.' She gave his hand a squeeze and shrugged her shoulders.

He felt awkward and he felt that she was awkward at playing this role of bad little good girl, almost as though it was a role she had been given to play or had decided to play.

She checked a couple of screens and then brought up the festival website and pointed to a blank space.

'That's the hole I need filling, there. About 300 words about the history of the site and of this area...' She chewed a little on some gum '...though if you're interested, you can fill the other hole as well...' She widened her green eyes at him a little. 'No one needs to know.' She made a gesture with her head in the general direction of Julie. 'It can be our secret.' She put her hand at the top of his leg and let her fingers press into his crotch. It was almost under the desk, so no-one could see. 'C'mon, say yes. I know you want to. I want to. A lot.' She placed her hand fully on him now and stared into his eyes. 'God, you feel really big.' She chewed slowly, looking at him searchingly, her thin right eyebrow raised. It felt very weird. Partly, because a woman of 21 had hold of his genitals, but also because it seemed so out of character for her to be talking dirty like this. The words didn't sit right with her at all. That's what he felt. That and a bit horny.

He took her hand and tried to lift it off him, but for a moment she didn't release her grip, as though testing his resolution. She certainly had tight hold of all of him.

'Em, this is flattering, it is, really...but you should know by now that I'm madly in love with Jules and that means she has exclusive rights on all my below-the-waist bits and most of the above-the-waist bits too, and probably all of my internal organs as well. It's old fashioned and traditional, I know, but it works for us. Like I say, I'm flattered you asked me and it's nice to have one's wedding tackle gripped so tightly by a good-looking young woman with great hair...but nothing is going to happen between us. Sorry.'

She turned her mouth down, let go, turned away from him and casually said, 'Alright then, it's a pity. You don't know what you're missing. I'm *very* good.' Again, it just sounded odd coming out of her mouth. Maybe it was because it contradicted the impression he'd built up of her. Maybe he'd just got her wrong. It wouldn't be the first time, nor the last. He was notoriously bad at reading people.

'Yeah. Well I can't blame you for trying. I am gorgeous,' he said with as much self-deprecation as he could manage.

'We'll say no more about it, then,' she said, now obviously feeling awkward and embarrassed.

'Fine. I'll just get on with this writing, then I'll go and shift some more stage gear.'

She got up and went to get tea from the truck. He watched her stride out of the tent in black leggings and a long black t-shirt.

He wrote a small colour piece and uploaded it to the website. It was all done by the time she returned.

'That's all done, Emily. I'd better go and help out the three hairies.'

'Thanks Nick. Sorry about...before.' She half closed one eye and looked at him sideways with an embarrassed hunch in her body language. 'Do you forgive me?'

'Nothing to apologise for, nor to forgive.'

'I don't know what came over me.'

'I almost did,' he thought, but didn't say it because he knew it'd make her giggle and her giggle was a little annoying. She smiled and shrugged, still awkward.

She was a nice lass, seemingly the very embodiment of that word. Polite and respectful, she'd barely even sworn around him before. She was the last person he'd have expected to come on to him in this way. It wasn't just some sort of false modesty, women didn't fancy him like that, they never had and there was no reason why anyone should now, especially not a lass who was so much younger. It all seemed like she was playing a role rather than being herself. He wondered whether she was alright. Was she having some sort of breakdown? Then again, he really was a poor judge of people at the best of times. Maybe this was just how 21-year-old women went on these days, or maybe they always had and he'd just never been on the receiving end of it before now.

It was a long, hard day's work carrying lighting rigging from a truck to the main stage; he stood by the big tent, taking a rest, waiting for Julie to finish at 4.30. Emily seemed to have gone so there was no chance of an awkward scene.

'You look exhausted,' said Julie, blinking in the bright afternoon sun and putting on her Ray Bans. 'Did you get it all shifted? I saw you on my lunch break stripped to the waist, carrying lots of tubular metal.'

'It was scaffolding for the lights to go on. You don't realise just how much construction has to be done for something like this to go ahead. It's not like putting a gig on at a venue when you've got some sort of structure in place. Here, there's nothing and it all needs building up from the ground. But it'll all get done one way or another. We're not far off it all being done.'

'The phones never stopped and I sat down to 87 emails this morning. It took me until early afternoon to clear them all. I could do with some help really. Mam called. Sandra says David Murray lives in Hartburn now and works for some financial adviser in the Boro called Harman and Garbutt.'

'Garbutt, eh?'

'Yeah, that's what I thought. I looked at his Facebook page again, but wasn't sure he was the bloke in the car. I'd need to see him again...it's hard retaining an image of someone in your head, isn't it?'

'Very interesting info, though. As Simon works in London and on the road with Big Fish, I bet David Murray runs that financial advice company in Middlesbrough. How it relates to Angie and that hoax bomb threat, I'm still not sure. If you want some more weird, I'll tell you what happened to me with Emily this morning.'

He drove out of the site and onto Darlington Back Lane, heading west and then south towards Yarm.

'What happened with Emily, then?' she said, lowering the window.

He told her. She immediately burst out laughing.

'The cheeky mare. Ha ha...I'd like to have seen that - not her and you - I mean, the look on your face when a young lass like that is giving it the "Come on big boy, give it to me" routine. Ha ha. I bet you nearly shat yourself. Ha ha.'

'Well, I'm glad you're not jealous and you're not far wrong. I froze. I didn't know what to say for a minute. How do you politely remove someone's hand from your meat without making a fuss?'

'I dunno. Whenever I've grabbed one, the bloke always seemed happy enough for me to do it. My iron grip has not been rejected yet.' She grabbed hold of the gear stick suggestively, laughing. 'Did you firm up?'

'Not really,' he lied. 'It was all really odd. Have I got her wrong, Jules? She's a nicey nicey girl, her. I'm sure she is.'

Julie shook her head and looked at him wryly. 'Her trying it on with you doesn't make her not nicey nicey does it? She was just looking to have it off with you. Those two things are not mutually exclusive.'

'But surely to her I'm an old git. I'm 27 years older.'

'You're probably a father figure to her.'

'Oh bollocks, am I nowt. And if I was, that's even more wrong.'

'Well, what else could have been going on, then?'

'I've been thinking maybe the Ironopolis mob told her to seduce me for some reason. We know she's one of them. She might want to find out if I am. Or maybe if I'm in RadLand. I mean, I do know Big Fish and Jeff's my best mate and we were in LAX with him...maybe she thinks I'm on their side.'

Julie burst out laughing uproariously now. 'She's not Mata bloody Hari. She isn't going to get some top secrets out of you during pillow talk, is she? If you ask me, she's just a horny lass with a crush on an fit older bloke who's spent half of his time around her half naked. Don't overthink it. Sometimes women just want a good old-fashioned shag. There doesn't have to be a reason beyond that. You've been working together on stuff and you can be quite charming an' all.'

'I'm not charming. I wouldn't know how to be charming,' he protested.

'That's exactly why you're charming.'

He looked at her disbelievingly. Maybe she was right. He was hardly that experienced in such matters, whilst Julie most certainly was. Even so.

When they got home, he made some beef salad for them whilst Julie got ready for her karaoke night out at the Penny Black. He sat out in the back garden as the day cooled down. It was totally quiet except for bird song. As he sat, he saw movement and a white flash across a field on the edge of the strip of woodland that ran east on one boundary. At first he thought it was a dog, or another animal, but then realised it couldn't be because it was too big. There was another flash. It was a reflection of the sun off glass or a mirror or something. He strained his eyes to see who it was, but they were too far away so he went into the kitchen and got his bird-watching binoculars. Standing at the back door he focused them where he'd seen the flash of light. Squatting down against a low hedge was a man in a green army shirt and combat trousers. He was looking at him through an even bigger pair of binoculars. Nick walked down the garden to get a clearer view of him, looking back at the house as he did so. Julie was standing at their bedroom window. She was naked after her shower. She waved and, laughing, grabbed her breasts and squashed them up against the window. He walked back in, calling up the stairs.

'Nice show Jules - but I think we've got a Peeping Tom. He just got a good eyeful of you.'

She came down. 'You're kidding me.'

'I saw him out by the woods, down by a hedge. He had binoculars.'

'The cheeky sod. Eurgh, he wasn't knocking one out, was he?'

'No, he wasn't pleasuring himself. He didn't even try to hide when I looked at him through my binoculars.'

'I wonder how long he's been doing that? I'm always wandering around in the nip. I never thought for a moment someone would be 100 yards away spying on me.'

'Yeah, but we're out most of the time and you usually get dressed for bed after dark and in the bathroom after a shower in the morning, so he got very lucky today. He'd have to put hours and days in just for a quick glimpse of flesh, so maybe he's just an innocent birder or wildlife photographer. Should we report him?'

'Nah. We're just being paranoid again. Don't do anything unless he's there again. He might be innocent, like you say. I have seen birders down there before. There was a red kite over the woods once.' She smoothed out her old ripped jeans and a fitted white shirt and at her centre-parted hair. 'Do I look alright?' She turned around in a circle.

'Jules man, you must know by now that you look good. You always do. Well, I think you do anyway.'

She sat down at the table and picked at the salad.

'You know I've always felt insecure about how I look. Don't believe what mam says. I'm always worried I'm either being too prim or too "tits oot". All my life I've always overdone it or underdone it one way or another.'

'Well you don't look either of those things to me. You look cool. Like a blonde Pat Benatar ready to make your Yoko Ono-style animal noises alongside some classic rock tunes. Oh hey, I forgot to mention this a couple of weeks ago, but there'll be a lass at this do called Shawn Yeadon. I went to school with her. She was in my year. I met her in town a couple of weeks ago and we went for a coffee. She works for a women's charity in the Boro and said she was at the last karaoke evening you went to. She vividly recalled your stellar performance. I told her to say hello.'

'Oh aye? What does she look like?'

'About your height and size. She's got fair-blondish hair, blue eyes.'

'Huh, so she looks like me then...oh, is this that one you told me about? The one you were daft on? OK, we'll have good gossip about the teenage you and how you now drive the young chicks wild.' She winked at him.

'Please don't, Jules. That would be so embarrassing. And don't do that all-girls-together thing of talking about...y'know...downstairs bits...you'd hate that if men did the same thing about your doo-dah.'

She laughed loudly. 'Aw it's your turn to go all coy. What do you know about what women talk about when we're together, anyway?'

'You can't miss what they talk about when there's 12 of them in the pub together. Most of it is filthy and involves tape measures and baby oil. I'm all for the sisterhood until there's 12 in a pub drinking Bacardi Breezers, all dressed in bright pink t-shirts on a hen night.'

'Oh god, I hate all that as well. Don't worry, all your secrets are safe with me and with Emily Davids left hand now as well, sadly.' She put on her boots. 'I promise not to disclose anything too personal or intimate to your big old crush. Right. Give us a lift over there, then. I'll get a cab back. I will endeavour not to get utterly shit-faced, come home, strip naked and sit on your face. I can't promise though, so don't say you've not been warned.'

Once Nick was back home after dropping her off at the estate pub, he flopped down and put his feet up in his music room, lined with shelves of vinyl albums, to listen to Rush's *Moving Pictures* album and have some tea. He liked Julie going out with her mates. Sitting in pubs was a bit boring when you didn't drink and he was more than happy to sit at home playing albums instead, but he was also keen that they didn't become one of those couples who went everywhere together and always did the same things. She liked a booze-up from time to time and when she came in from a night out with a few drinks on her, she was often in a very amorous, adventurous mood and really funny with it. For some reason drink seemed hard-wired into her libido, so it all added a bit of spice to life. Also, she wouldn't want him to witness her terrible singing and dancing and making a fool of herself. But it was a strange thought to picture her talking to Shawn. The big romantic regret of his life talking to the big love of his life. What would they make of each other?

He put the album on, took a drink of tea and checked his emails. His heart leapt. There was a message from Mike. It had been sent half an hour ago.

'Nick, I really need your help. Call me asap.'

There was a mobile phone number. He dialled. It was answered immediately.

'Hello?'

'Mike? It's Nick.'

'Nick. Thanks for calling me. Where are you?'

'At home.'

'Can we meet somewhere discreet?'

'Why don't you come here? It's in the middle of the countryside. We've no neighbours.'

'Are you sure?'

'Of course I'm sure, Mike.' He gave him directions and then sat on a bench at the front of the house to wait for him. He can't have been far away because within 20 minutes he heard a car engine drop revs up on the Aislaby Road and turn down their rutted old track. The blue Nissan came to a halt behind his BMW. Mike Trent got out with a heavy frown on his forehead. He advanced towards him with his hand held out.

He turned around and took a 360 degree view of the surroundings. The accountant was really tense, letting out a brittle breath of air.

'Can I get you anything?' he said. 'I'd offer you a drink if you weren't driving. You look like you could use one.'

'Thanks. Just some water please. Nice place you've got here. Lovely spot.'

'Aye, it is. We just had our first Peeping Tom out in the fields at the back, though. Had binoculars and everything.'

'What?' Where? Show me.' He looked at him with panicked eyes.

Nick led him out the back and pointed to the line of trees.' He was just over there. I only saw him because of the sun reflecting off his binocular lens.'

'Was there only one person?'

'Yeah. Why? I'm sure it's nothing, man. It was probably a bird watcher.'

Mike didn't answer. He blew out air and walked back into the kitchen. Nick poured him some cold sparkling mineral water.

'So where do we start, Mike? What's going on?'

He sat across the kitchen table from him.

'After Cargo Fleet Road, can I ask you to tell me exactly how much you actually know about the Ironopolis Anarchists?' said Mike, rubbing his hairy arm.

Nick weighed up the situation. Better to keep some things back. Don't put your cards on the table all at once.

'I don't know anything really, beyond what is in the public domain already. When I ran into you, you looked shocked, then scared and then practically ran away from me. It all seemed weird.'

'Was it just a coincidence that you were there?'

'I was just visiting a friend. You never come to Teesside, so I was obviously surprised to see you there, but then I once ran into a school friend in a coffee shop in Los Angeles, so these things do happen. You looked concerned about something. I didn't know what to make of it. You were acting weird, just like you are now.'

'Are you sure you're telling me the truth?' said Mike, his voice raised now, almost making the question a demand. He drummed his fingers on the table twice.

'Yes. Look Mike, I'll be honest, I want to know who the bomber is. They nearly killed me and Jules. I want those responsible for it to be caught. As it seems to be the Ironopolis Anarchists who did it, then I'd like to know who they are...but that's as far as it's gone.'

'Look, I know you don't have a friend on Cargo Fleet Lane, but I'm going to tell you something that can't leave this room. Right? Can I trust you with that?'

'Well. That's a choice you'll have to make.' He sat back, arms folded.

Mike pointed to himself. 'I set up the Ironopolis Anarchists and I'm one of the working group.'

Nick feigned huge surprise, raising his eyebrows.

'I won't bore you with the hows, whys and wherefores. The problem is, as you know, we're supposed to have done this bombing and the truth of the matter is, it wasn't us and I need to find out who the hell really did do it.'

'Are you totally sure your lot didn't do it?' said Nick, thinking of their message board.

'Yes. Totally. Anyone claiming it is, is just trying to bring us down and devalue what we've done so far.'

'Who would do that?' he asked.

'That's what we don't know. There are ideas, rumours, theories, but no-one really knows. Obviously, it must be someone with a lot to lose from our investigations. That points to rich and powerful people. There's a group called RadLand, we think their members own a lot of land around here, though we're not sure exactly who is in the group. It may be them. Have you heard of them?'

'Yeah. They're a charity. They help our rural businesses with grants. Is that a front?'

Mike pouted his lips. 'Honestly, we don't know. There are some very wealthy and powerful people involved and some have things they'd like to keep hidden.'

Nick nodded. 'So why tell me this?'

Mike cleared his throat. 'Firstly, cards on the table, right? There are those who think you are the bomber.'

'Me? Eh? Who thinks that? How could it be me? It nearly killed me!'

'There's no better alibi than that, is there? Look, I can't say much. You turned up for some sort of meeting on Cargo Fleet Road, didn't you? You were meeting someone.'

'No I didn't, I...'

'I know you're lying, Nick. Like I said, I know you don't have any friends there.' Nick went quiet and folded his arms again, reluctant to say too much. Mike went on, 'I know you. I know you quite well after all these years and I know you wouldn't get caught up in this sort of thing, no matter how it looks. I'm trusting that my opinion of you is correct. No matter that you put your bag down on the very spot the bomb went off. I trust you and I trust that was just a terrible coincidence along with a lot of other coincidences. Others do not. If you can help me out, it'll prove to them you're on the right side of this.'

The annoyed him. 'Fuck off, Mike, I'm not justifying myself to anyone. Who are these others?'

'I can't say. And I don't expect you to be happy about this. But like I say, you can help me and trust me, it'll help you.

Nick shook his head. 'Go on then, what do you want me to do?'

'Look, the Ironopolis Anarchists have so far exposed six major landowners as tax avoiders, but more than that, we exposed them as corrupt people who pretend to have the interests of the land and of the country at heart, but don't at all. We have another five in our sights. These people are at the heart of the establishment of the country, they own vast tracts of land, they sit in the House of Lords, they employ lots of people and pass themselves off as custodians of the countryside and as responsible, respectable people. But they're nothing less than thieves and vagabonds. They don't pay their fair share, they dodge and weave through our tax laws, they're rich, but pay their workers terribly and above all, they protect and grow their assets. They're greedy and utterly self-interested, but they're also so well-connected with government and the civil service that it's hard for anyone to take them on. They are The Establishment. They have controlling interests in media outlets or at least, they have the ear of proprietors, so they can muster opposition to anyone seeking to limit their activities. That's why we've had to work so strictly anonymously. It's meant they can't fight back against us because they don't know who we are or where we are, or who to look out for in their organisations. That's how we've got under their radar and how we've got hold of incriminating evidence against them. They know they can't prosecute us because it'll give publicity to our investigations. Discrediting us is much easier.'

'And this is why you asked me about Big Fish paying cash?'

'Yes. How we work is we get sympathetic people like yourself to keep an eye open on the ground, but often without knowing that they're actually helping us. It's a nationwide thing. I'm just running this region. We have contacts in law firms and accountants and even an estate manager who all feel these people need bringing to account. The financial crisis last year only made people feel more strongly that a rich elite plays fast and loose with our lives and then demands we bail them out of their recklessness. But crucially, none of them know who we are or what we're doing. Just as you didn't.'

Nick nodded. 'Tell me this then, did the Ironopolis Anarchists actually make the first hoax bomb threat?'

'No of course not. That was nothing to do with us either. We're not terrorists. Before I ask you to help me, tell me why you went to see Angie Page.'

'How do you know we went there, like?'

'You just told me.'

205

Shit. He'd fallen for the oldest trick in the book,

'Look, Mike, we just wanted to hear from her what the bomber actually said. She seemed confused about whether it was the Ironopolis Anarchists or Anarchist.'

'Why does that matter?'

'Well it's inconsistent. Your group is plural, but the hoax call was singular, as was the first email Mel got. But the email from the group claiming responsibility for the real bomb was plural.'

Mike looked confused and nervous. 'I'm sure that spelling is not relevant, Nick. It's sometimes hard to know if someone has said the "s" on a word, isn't it?'

'I don't know...I was just exploring ideas. Angie took the bomb threat call, so she's an important player in this.'

'I don't think so. She just answered the phones at the festival, that's all. Listen, like I say, you can help me...and in doing so help yourself. How well do you know Emily Davids?'

Nick paused before answering. Why did he want to know that? Was he testing him to see if he knew she was a member of IA? Did he suspect she was in IA, but not actually know? They were each blindly dancing around each other here and it was ridiculous since, presumably, they both wanted the same thing - to find those responsible for the explosion.

'I've been working with her for a couple of weeks. I like her a lot. She's a nice lass. Is she in your group?' said Nick, narrowing his eyes at Mike who remained inscrutable.

'I don't know that she is, we're anonymous to each other.' He stared at the table and began fiddling with the pepper grinder. 'Are you *sure* you don't know anything about her?'

'I know she's interested in me. Physically, I mean.'

That seemed to get his interest. 'Is she now? Why is that?'

'Why? Because I'm a red hot piece of man meat, me, Mike. Why else?' He held his arms out wide and snorted a laugh. 'Look, I don't know, do I? Maybe I'm a father figure to her. Some lasses like older blokes. I'm not interested in her though, obviously.'

Mike nodded. 'I'll come back to her in a minute. Can you just explain a few other things to me, just so I've got things clear. You know Stevie Salmon quite well?'

'More's the pity, aye.'

'And his father?'

'Brian is good bloke. Me and Jules like him. He's a sort of friend, really. Albeit, one we don't see very often.'

Mike raised an eyebrow.

'And the son, Stevie, he's paying you?'

He said it like it was an accusation. 'Well, sort of. The company running the festival is owned by Stevie, they're paying us for working at the festival, yeah. Well, they're paying Julie. I've not had any money yet.'

'Why not?'

'Because I work freelance and the amount of work for me is variable, so I'll just put an invoice in after it's all over and get paid out later.'

'But Jeff and Julie are on the payroll?'

'Yeah.'

'Uh huh.' He nodded. 'We've known each other long time, Nick. You'd tell me if you were involved in something, wouldn't you? You wouldn't do something stupid, would you?'

That just really bloody annoyed him. 'For God's sake, Mike. This is so stupid. Stop asking me these bullshit questions. If I *was* "involved" in anything, I wouldn't tell you now, would I? Do you think I'm going to confess something to you? I don't understand any of this. I'm not "involved" in anything, for the record. The only thing I'd like to do is find out who the hell nearly blew me and Jules into a thousand pieces. That's not that unreasonable, I reckon. To be honest, mate, if you're training up for a new career as a detective, then you're shite at it.' He folded his arms once again and stared at him.

Mike just ignored him and took out his phone, skimmed a few screens and showed him a picture.

'Do you know him?'

It was a very distinctive person. A long, full-length shot.

'That's Simon Garbutt. Stevie Salmon's business manager. Strange looking bloke. All legs.'

This admission made Mike raise his dark eyebrows. 'So you *know* him?'

'I've met him, but I don't *know* him. He has also offered me some work on tour in Australia with Big Fish in October.'

'Did he now? What do you make of him?'

'He was alright. Not my sort. Starts his sentences with "So" too much.'

'What?'

Nick waved it away. 'Nowt. He's alright, but he's the sort of bloke I have nothing to do with and whose whole value system I don't really understand. He's all about profit, money and business. And he has that London way about him. You know what I mean? Like he's the sophisticate from the big city slumming it in the flat-cap strewn wastelands of the north. A typical London Wanker. You know what that means, right?'

Mike nodded. 'Yes, I do. Sorry for the all the questions, I'm under a lot of pressure, Nick. I need to find out who is framing the IA for these bombings and find out who is responsible before any more bombings happen.'

'Why don't you issue a denial to counteract the accusations, then?' said Nick. He sat back in his chair and looked at Mike while he thought about a response. He did look very stressed. Stress usually came from feeling powerless. Maybe he knew someone in the Ironopolis Anarchists was responsible, but just didn't know who. Because of the anonymity of the group to each other, there was no way he could be certain it wasn't one of their number.

'A denial would have no weight without me or someone else appearing in public and we can't do that because our anonymity is crucial. If we just send out a press release saying, it wasn't us, we're no further on. The public want answers. They're inclined to believe that whoever is accused of it really did do it. Us saying we didn't do it wouldn't dislodge that notion, so it's a waste of time.

We need to find out who it actually was and prove it. Now, you were in LA with Stevie Salmon and Simon Garbutt, weren't you?'

'I was in LAX with them, not in LA.'

'Are you sure you weren't in LA with him?'

'Fuck off, Mike. I know who I've met and where. The trouble with everyone being anonymous is that no-one is accountable for anything they say and do, thus innocent people like me and Jules get slandered by them without an ability to defend ourselves. What does it matter anyway even if I was on holiday with him, god forbid. What business is it of anyone?'

Mike picked up the pepper grinder again and rolled it in his hand.

'Do you think I had something to do with the bomb, Mike? You do, don't you? You think because I know all the people involved, that I was in LA with Big Fish, am friends with his dad and I'm working at the festival that I'm somehow I'm a suspect? I should throw you out of here and I would if it didn't look like you might break down weeping. You're so tense that your arsehole is up around the back of your neck. What are you doing? Testing me to see if I'm lying? I'm not lying, Mike.'

This was no good. It was time to stop all this skirting around each other, it was doing his head in. He was no good at keeping secrets at the best of times.

'OK, I'll tell you absolutely everything I know. Everything. Right? I'm sick of trying to hold one thing or another back. It's too much like hard work. Here's the thing, somehow Emily Davids has access to the IA message board, so I assume she's an Anarchist. We've logged onto it here, too. It's full of plans to bomb RadLand people and other stuff which clearly shows the IA group did the bombing. I saw the postings on there from "Volunteer" and thought they sounded like you. So when you turned up on Cargo Fleet Lane, I already knew you were an IA and I knew you'd seen that meeting time and post code on the message board. Hadn't you? Hadn't you, Mike? Just nod if you can hear me. But no-one else turned up there except you and me. There, that's me done.

Right?'

Nick got up and paced around the kitchen, furious. 'You're the one who is fucking well behaving weirdly. I'm suspicious of you. You're the one in the terrorist group. Not me. I didn't have a bomb in my bag, I just put my bag right by where it went off, that's all. I'm not a bomber and you can have me and this whole place tested for explosives or whatever.'

Mike nodded. 'Thanks Nick. Thanks for your honesty. All I can say is, yes I did see that meeting notice. This is a complicated business and I'm not the one called "Volunteer". So let's just to go back to Emily Davids, that's where I need your help. Could you talk to her and find out exactly what she knows about Ironopolis Anarchists and the RadLand charity?'

'Mike, she's a student. Not a terrorist. Not little Em.'

Mike paused and traced an imaginary line on the kitchen table.

'That might be what she'd like you to believe. Her father is actually the Earl of Louth.'

'Really? Oh wow.' He sat back down. 'Oh, I *see*. He's RadLand's head honcho, isn't he? I saw him online, Jules found him. Bloody hell. He looked like a right prick. So you think she's working for him?'

Mike nodded and bit his top lip. 'Nick. The IA didn't plant that bomb, nor the hoax one. I'm not sure she's in IA even if she does have access to a secret message board.'

'But Mike, you've contradicted yourself. You don't know who you all are. One of you could have done it. You just don't know. You just *hope* it wasn't.'

Mike ran his fingers over his cropped hair. 'Alright, alright. Bloody hell, man, I'm trying to do you a favour here.'

'Sorry to get pissy with you, but you know that's the truth,' added Nick.

Mike coughed and tried to compose himself. 'Like I say, there are important people who are not...shall we say...inclined to look upon you favourably. Helping me find out more about Emily Davids will help allay those suspicions. If she's sweet on you then she may open up more readily.'

'Which important people?'

'I can't say. You can surely guess.'

He had to mean security service or police.

'OK, I'll talk to her and see what I can find out. She doesn't know that I know she has access to the message board. But tell me Mike, why do your "important people" think I'd do something like this?'

'Money. You're both in debt and skint and have bills mounting up, I'm your accountant, remember?' He got up. 'Let me know anything you find out, please Nick. Use this email address.' He handed him a card. 'Forgive me, Nick. I know this is odd.'

That was a bloody understatement.

Julie returned at just before midnight, putting her head around the bedroom door and waving, a big grin on her face. 'Don't worry, I'm not mortal, just a bit tipsy. What are you up to? Looking at porn on your computer?'

He closed the laptop. 'I've been researching RadLand, or trying to anyway. Haven't found out much. I had a visit from Mike tonight.'

'Really? Wow. Hold on, I need a wee.'

He looked at the notes he'd made. She came back with her old jeans unbuttoned and began to undress.

'So what did Mike want?'

He explained the visit. 'He was very weird, Jules. Kept saying there were important people who thought I might be responsible for the bomb. I told him we'd seen the IA message board, but he was still making out they were innocent, more out of hope than anything else, I think.'

'How odd. I'm not sure what to think. That message board couldn't be clearer.'

'Yeah, I know. He was very cagey. So did you have a nice night?'

'Yeah. Not as pissed and raucous as the last one. The karaoke machine broke after a couple of numbers so we just sat around drinking and talking all night.'

'How many were there?'

'Twelve in total. I played darts for a bit with your Shawn woman. What a lovely lass she is.'

'Oh yeah? You liked her?'

'She was really, really nice, aye. Throw us me pyjamas. Ta...yeah she's quite a gentle soul from what I could tell. Went to the Open University. Nice sense of humour. Very down to earth.'

'So you got on well?'

'Yeah, we did. Really well. I invited her round here for a meal and a few drinks.'

That was a strange thought - Julie and Shawn being mates. It felt like two separate worlds were colliding. Julie got into bed beside him and gave him a kiss on the cheek. She smelled of booze.

'I can see why you fancied her all those years ago.'

And why he still did, he thought, but didn't voice. 'Yeah? Why?'

'Well, she seems a genuine sort of lass and you don't meet a lot of them, do you? She was a bit cagey maybe, probably because of having gone through a lot of relationship shit at various points...but life does that to you, doesn't it? I bet when she was a teenager she was more open and that's probably why she got hurt and messed up by unsuitable blokes. I'm sure she's really good at her job.'

'Yeah, I think you're probably right about all of that. So you spent a lot of time talking about me?'

'A bit. She said you were funny and a bit of a sensitive sort as a kid. I wish I'd known you back then as well. Wouldn't it have been odd if we'd got together when you were 18 and I was 15?'

'Going out with a 15 year old when you're 18 would have been weird. Only the odd boys did that. Those three years are a big gap at that age.'

'True.'

'Also, I've seen pictures of you from back then and you were so far out of my league. I'd never have dared speak to you even though you're three years younger. You looked like the sort of girl

I'd have lay in bed giving myself blisters over in a frankly unhealthy manner.'

She scrunched up her face. 'Euwww. Moving swiftly on...what else did Mike say?'

'You know Emily Davids?'

'Not her again, I'm sick of hearing her bloody name.'

'Mike said her dad is the Earl of Louth, the mega rich landowner.'

She sat up and looked at him in surprise.

'He's the man who set up RadLand,' said Julie. 'He was the Upper Class Twit of the Year, remember? Good god. That's a bit weird. So she might be working for her dad...spying on IA or something?'

'He wanted me to find out how much she knows about both the IAs and RadLand. He seemed to think she wasn't an Anarchist but I don't know why because they're all anonymous to each other, so he can't know for sure who is.'

'Well she has access to that board, so as far as I'm concerned she is an IA. That's surely a fact. So she must have done work for them and know a lot about them.'

'Sort of, except when we looked at the board, she hadn't posted anything. She wasn't taking part in the debate. Maybe we just missed her posts, though. It does clear down every 12 hours. She's a puzzle though, isn't she? We do need to find out more about her.'

She sat looking at him, breathing heavily through her nose.

'Are you thinking what I think you're thinking?' she said.

'That depends on what you think I'm thinking.'

'I think you're thinking you should accept her proposition of sex.'

CHAPTER 13

'Good grief. No. No I'm not saying that, Jules. I can't believe you'd think I would.' He was genuinely surprised at her.

'Sorry. My old male mistrust reflexes.' She looked away from him.

'I do think I should see what I can get out of her, though. I'm not sure how. If she does fancy me maybe I can use that in some way. Gods knows how, though. Obviously, I'm not going to have sex with her. I'm sure she doesn't want to anyway, she was just putting that on to get in my good books. She wants to get something out of me. Maybe she thinks, or at least is entertaining the idea, that I planted the bomb, just like Mike does. Maybe that's been discussed on the message board and we just haven't seen it.'

'But why does he think that?'

'Primarily because it went off where I put my bag as well as all those other coincidences that link us to Big Fish, his manager and the festival. Also we're skint and need money.'

'That's just mad. How do you prove you didn't leave a bomb somewhere?' She let out a big sigh. 'Who would pay someone to do that anyway, and why?'

'Maybe some sort of insurance scam?'

She frowned heavily and rubbed her eyes. 'What, like burn down the pub to claim the insurance? That kind of scam? That'd mean Big Fish or Brian had paid you to damage their own house. That's just daft as well. They're loaded, they don't need money. Brian loves that house, anyway. Nah. It's not an insurance scam.'

'No. It doesn't work, does it? Well they can't prove I did, because I didn't. Everyone is just suspicious of everyone else at the minute. We're all paranoid. That's why I've got to get the truth out of Emily. Mike reckons it'll help me prove I'm not guilty. We need to know where she fits into this. She's the only one who connects the blues festival, the Ironopolis Anarchists and RadLand all together. She's the lynch pin, if you ask me.'

'Do you actually reckon she could be the bomber?' said Julie, applying some moisturiser and laying back on her pillow. 'She was shit scared when it went off. Paralysed with fear. You had to carry her out.'

'She was, but that doesn't mean it wasn't her, does it? It just means she was shit scared of the devastation it caused. Honestly? It wouldn't be the biggest shock if it was her.'

'OK, if you think it'll help catch the bomber...but I'm only going to say this once, Nick Guymer. I know what men are like, even you. You're prone to think with your cocks, especially if someone comes on to you strong. But you should know this - it's one strike and you're out. Faithful means faithful. Got me? So don't go getting tempted.'

'I wouldn't, man. You know I wouldn't. You *do* know that, don't you?'

She ran her fingers through her hair and fixed him with steely glare. 'I know exactly how easy it is to get a man into bed. I didn't make that 3,000 number without not learning how easy it is, even with men who have strong relationships. Put it out strongly enough and most men, not all, but most, will respond. It's like you're programmed to do it. Sex is a powerful lure, at least it is until you've done it; it's then that the regrets start. So think on. I'm not giving you a free pass. That's all bullshit. It's about respect. Understand?' She didn't let her eyes move from his. His stared back at her knowing that if he looked away it would make him seem untrustworthy.

'Of course I do. And I don't need a sexual politics lecture, Jules. You know I'm not like that. I've never been like that. I've always been faithful to anyone I've had even the briefest relationship with and I've been like that my whole life.'

'Well...technically that's not true, is it? You went out with Shawn when I left Harrogate.'

'Did she just tell you about that? We'd split up by then, though.'

'Had we? I'd left. But if you remember, we'd agreed to meet up to try and work something out. Only you never really wanted to meet up or were unable to and so we drifted apart. So we hadn't broken up properly.'

'Me and Shawn just went out three times...I didn't think of it as being unfaithful because I knew we were over...and for the record I never had sex with her...she wanted to...I sort of did...but sort of couldn't because I was so messed up after our break up, plus I was really drunk. It was a bad time...she was lovely and I really wasn't.'

'I know...she said what had happened, which was good of her...healthy...for the sake of openness and honesty if we're going to be friends. I think she thought I'd already know, which obviously I didn't and I'm not saying I should have known. It *was* a very difficult time for us both and you'd always been fond of her. I do understand, like. All I'm saying is things can easily happen in the right circumstances and I don't want it to. I love us being together and I love how we are with each other and I don't want any stupid thing to spoil it and it easily could. Very easily.'

'Neither do I. And it won't. This isn't a normal thing though, is it? It's not me sneaking off to shag someone. I'm sitting here telling you about it and frankly, I'm a bit pissed off that you think I'd even entertain any of this if it wasn't such a big deal. I have absolutely no desire to have it off with a 21-year-old student; I do however, want to find out who the hell tried to blow us up and to stop them trying to do it again.'

'I know what you're saying and I know you're not lying. But if you're trying to tell me that a lass like that squeezing your dick doesn't make it hard, then I don't believe you, and that's when the trouble starts.'

'There's a difference between mentality and physicality though, isn't there?'

She lifted a finger and pointed it him, eyebrows raised. 'See, right there, that is the mind set of the man who has an affair - or a woman, for that matter. What you're saying is it's all physical, not mental or emotional, therefore it's alright to do it.'

'But that isn't what I was saying at all, Jules. OK, I won't say anything to Emily.' He held up his hands. 'I don't want to fall out with you over this.'

'No. I want you to get her confidence and find out what she's up to. Mike is right, she might open up if she thinks you're interested in her. People do. Therefore it might help us get the people responsible for the bombing, or stop another bombing. I'm just telling you this to get it stuck in your head, good and proper. You might be older than me, but in a lot of ways you're much younger, much less experienced and much less worldly-wise. You often don't realise what you've got involved in until it's too late. You get out of your depth with people.'

'I know that Jules. I'm not saying I'll be any good. I probably won't be. I'm shit at interpersonal relationships at the best of times. But I have to try.'

'Good. Well, I'm glad we talked about it.' She brushed his hair of his forehead. 'You know I wouldn't be worried if you weren't so bloody sexy.'

'I'm not in any way sexy Jules. I'm a messed-up, scruffy git. Don't say that. It's embarrassing.'

'Not to yourself you're not, but to some women, you are. I know that for a fact. On top of that, you're a proper horny sod at the moment. Those happy pills seem to have put extra lead in your pencil. You're not far short of insatiable when you get going. You're putting me to shame.'

He shook his head. 'I just feel hugely awkward now.'

'Alright, we'll say no more about it. Let's get some sleep.'

As usual, she dropped off well before him. He lay on his back thinking about what she had said. He felt like he'd spoken honestly, but part of him felt like she was totally right and that there was a point at which resisting the sexual advances of someone you found attractive was really difficult. It was one thing to say you wouldn't when the likelihood of it happening was minimal, but when you were fairy certain it would, how did you handle that? You had to keep focused on the bigger picture. Life was so much more than a few minutes of sex, but it could be ruined by those few minutes of sex. That was the truth of the matter. It was about projecting forward and stopping yourself indulging in short-term pleasure; about not being so self-focused and selfish. He knew if Julie had sex with another bloke, for which there would be a lot of volunteers, it wouldn't exactly fill him with joy. It would, no matter how fleeting or meaningless, feel like a huge betrayal and the thought of it was awful, appalling, even. There was a physical commitment to each other, as well as an emotional and spiritual one, that needed preserving. It was typical of Julie to address this though. Not for the first time in their lives together, he felt like she was the adult and he the child.

As he made breakfast for them the following morning, he put BBC Tees on the radio, wondering if there was any news at all about the Boro signing a half-decent player in a bid to get out of the Championship at the first attempt and just as importantly, getting rid of players on big wages they could no longer afford. Manager Gareth Southgate was widely thought to be on the verge of the sack, after taking the team down. But no such decision was forthcoming. He liked Southgate, but he was in an increasingly diminishing number in that regard.

'Morning,' said Jules, ruffling her hair and yawning as she sat down at the table.

As she did so the local news came on.

At an early press conference, Alan McFadden, head of the investigation into the terrorist bombing at the Teesside Blues Festival said they had significant leads and were closing in on the group that call themselves the Ironopolis Anarchists and who have claimed responsibility for the explosion which killed three people. Security at the festival site is high, but organiser Mel Stephens says it will be the safest place on earth.

They cut to a reporter who pointlessly repeated the same information in a slightly different order, but left it in no doubt that the security services were close to making Ironopolis arrests.

He poured coffee for them. Julie chewed at her bottom lip. 'I was thinking, if Emily is not in the IA group, that means their secret communication system has been breached by her, which means their wall of anonymity is breaking down and it's all falling apart,' she said.

He pulled on a grey t-shirt and an old pair of jeans. 'Right, come on you,' he said, standing by the door. She put her bag on her shoulder and kissed him on the lips.

'You don't look much like a gigolo, mister.'

'I don't much feel like one.' He took two Phenibut capsules from the bottle and swallowed them.

As Julie drove out of Yarm towards Stockton, she noticed a black Ford Ka pull in behind her. The man behind the wheel was neat and fair-haired.

'I'm sure that black car behind us was the one following me the other day.' She glanced up in her mirror again. 'It is, it's Steve McQueen. Bugger, I can't really see him properly, he's got the sun visor down again. Have a look, is it actually David Murray?'

Nick turned to look. 'I think this bloke has shorter hair. I think. Oh, it must just be a coincidence. He'll live on the route somewhere. That's all.'

As she got to Darlington Back Lane just before the turn off for the festival, the Ka overtook them and took off into the distance. As Julie parked the BMW at the festival site, she turned to him. 'So what's your plan?'

'All I'm planning to do, is take Emily somewhere nice and quiet, let her think I'm interested in her and make her feel like I'm on her side. And then see what I can get out of her about her dad, the IA message board and RadLand.'

'Good. Be charming. Listen to her and ask her questions. Women love men who listen to them, 'cos we're not used to it. OK?'

'What you're saying then, is be a decent, sensitive human.'

'Exactly. As opposed to the git you are normally.'

'And if she gets naked and sits on my face, I'll just hold my breath and close my eyes, right?'

'Well, that's what you've always done with me.'

They both laughed, but both were nervous and on edge. It was such a weird situation.

'Right, let's do this thing then,' he said, patted her on the backside and strode into the tent. Emily Davids was sitting at her desk, flicking through her phone. She looked up as he approached and smiled her gap-toothed, girlish smile.

'Morning, Nicky boy,' she said. 'Before we start work, I just wanted to say sorry about yesterday...I made a fool of myself.'

He saw his chance and sat down next to her, putting his hand on her shoulder, he turned to her. 'No need Em. And I was thinking, I might have been a bit hasty.'

'What?' She looked at him with the green eyes, initially not grasping what he was saying.

'I was thinking about what you said. Maybe we should go somewhere for lunch and...you know...talk about it.'

'Oh. I see.' She looked awkward. Maybe she'd had second thoughts. 'Err...well yes. Let's do that. As I...err...said yesterday, no-one needs to know.'

'Yes, discretion would be good.' He smiled a smile that was far too wide. Too keen. Over the top. 'I do like you Em, it'd be nice to get to know each other a bit more...y'know...intimately.'

He had always been rubbish at chatting up women and had already run out of something to say. Out of nowhere, his mothers' voice came into his brain with a clarity that was so sharp, it couldn't have been more audible if she was standing next to him. *"Just be yourself, our Nick."*

Where did come from? Was she with him? It sounded like she was with him. Was he going mad, as mad as she had gone? Was he hearing voices? He had to glance over his shoulder just to make sure she wasn't actually standing there.

'OK. Shall we nip out and get an early lunch, after we've finished the latest press release and sent it out to the media?'

'I'd like that. Yeah.'

She smiled at him with delicate, thin lips and let her tongue rest between the gap in her top teeth.

He began work. As he typed, she sat beside him, chewing a pencil and looking at her screen. With her small frame, physically, compared to Julie, she was insubstantial to the point of skinny yet still had something really attractive about her, something that was more to do with her personality than her physicality. She gave out more than she took. Yeah, that was it. Just like Julie in that respect.

He sent her the press release he'd written.

'There you go. I've just highlighted the current releases by some of the bands that are playing and put links to their websites.

'Thanks. I don't know any of them except Jill Jamieson on the acoustic stage. I saw her at Latitude last year.'

'Any good?'

'I didn't like her. She was too wispy and...you know...self-indulgent. I mean, OK, you're miserable, shut up about it.' She laughed delicately. 'That probably sounded harsh, didn't it?'

'She's not my cup of tea either, for what it's worth. But I'm an old geezer. I'm not her target demographic.'

'You're always saying you're old. 48 isn't that old, it really isn't. It's not as though you've gone to seed. You're not fat or anything. You could do with a good hair cut, though.' She giggled her lightweight, flowery laugh again. 'Sorry.'

'No you're right. I'm a scruffy git and I always have been. I've got fine hair though...it's like baby hair. You can't do anything with it.'

She pushed at it with her fingers. 'Oh, it is fine, isn't it? Very soft. You're not balding, though.'

'I'm not hairy y'see. My mate Jeff has this theory that the less hairy you are, the less likely you are to go bald.'

'Haven't you got any hair on your chest?'

'A little now, but I was well over 30 before anything really grew in. Not a proper man y'see. Not enough Y chromosomes, or is it X?'

'This fashion for men waxing their chests and their other bits is horrible, I think. Why would you do that? It's as though they're trying to pretend they're not men at all.'

'Jules always says that. She calls this obsession with defoliating the human body, pubic fascism.' No no. Christ don't mention Julie. You don't mention the wife if you're having an affair. It made Emily look awkwardly at him. She said nothing and typed something instead and then looked back to him.

'Shall we go and get something to eat then?' she said.

'Sure. We can go in my car.'

'Great. You go out to the car park, I'll follow you in a minute. It's the old BMW, isn't it?'

He waited for her in the car feeling nervous or was it a little excited? Both. He licked his dry lips and put Radio 2 on. They were playing some hysterical wailing which was trying to pass itself off as soul music. It sounded like noise made by malfunctioning software. He switched it off immediately. Within five minutes she opened the passenger side door and got in.

'Right...we can just go to mine, if you like. In Marton. I can rustle us something up.'

'Fine. I like the sound of that. You give me directions.'

'Oh it's easy to find. It's on Stokesley Road right beside Stewart Park. Do you know that?'

'Very well, aye. It's a nice well-to-do bit of Middlesbrough.'

'It's a bog standard semi-detached house. I was just renting it while I was at uni. My dad paid for three years upfront so I'd not have to think about it. I'll be moving out later this summer, I should think.'

He took off towards the A19, taking it south to the A66 east, turning off on the A172 south.

'So tell me a little about yourself, Em. How did a nice clean girl like you end up in this dirty part of the world?'

'I really like Teesside. I know people say it's shit because the economy is so poor, but I think the people are brilliant. So much nicer than where I'm from...'

'Where's that?'

'Well I was born near Louth in Lincolnshire, but my parents got divorced when I was 11 and I went to live in Dulwich Village in London which is just the most...' she snorted air of disgust out of her nose. '...just pointlessly snobby, stuck up, pretentious fucking place...pardon my French, but it really is. You won't know it...but trust me...don't go there. Because you're northern, they'd think you work down a mine and eat ferrets or something. I came up for an open day at Teesside University and loved it. That's how I ended up here. You're from 'round here, aren't you? I think you said.'

'Yeah, I grew up in Stockton.'

'You have a really lovely accent. I love how people around here talk.' She gave a generous smile at him.

'We'll have to make you an honorary Teessider.'

'I would *love* that. I have no plans to move away. I'd like to get a job in the area, maybe get a flat instead of the house. I don't know why I'm living there, really. Where do you live, again?'

'We've got...I live just outside of Yarm.'

'Oh Yarm is posh, but in a nice way, unlike Dulwich fucking Village.'

'Yeah, it's quite divisive really. Some people think it's where all the local snobs live, others feel it's just a nice old town with good shops. I think that's why some want to make it part of North Yorkshire. They think it makes it more posh and less infected by Teesside's more down-market image, which only fuels those who think it's full of snobs, of course.'

'And what do you think?'

'To me Yarm is part of Teesside and I wouldn't want it divorced from that because I think, perhaps controversially, unlike North Yorkshire, Teesside is very cool because it's a mythic sort of place. It's not on any map. You can't tell where it stops and starts because there are no official boundaries. It really only exists in the hearts and minds of the people. I love that about it.'

She let out a feathery, quiver of a laugh and patted him on the thigh. 'You've a big romantic streak in you, haven't you? I've noticed that.'

'Have I?'

'Yeah. It's really nice. Unusual. But nice.'

They arrived at a semi-detached house on the main road. It had mock Tudor features on the front. All very respectable and a long way from the usual student-style flats.

'Have you heard anything more about the Ironopolis Anarchists - the people who planted the bomb?' she said, as she parked up. 'I can't believe the police haven't caught them yet.'

'Nobody seems to know who they are,' he said. 'Have you any idea who it might be?'

'Me? How would I know?'

'I wondered if they might be students,' he said.

'They might be, but I've not heard anything if they are. It's amazing that in this day and age they've managed to remain anonymous. I was wondering if someone else was responsible, but just pretending to be the Ironopolis group?'

'Yeah, that had occurred to me too. Do you think that's likely?'

'I don't know. What do you think?' she said. This was a bit like the dancing around each other that he'd done with Mike. Someone was going to have to make the first move here.

'My mate Jeff, thinks another group is trying to blacken their name to discredit them. Given they've attacked rich people over their tax affairs, maybe that's a direction to look in.'

She got out and unlocked the front door. Two cats came trotting up the hallway to them, meowing.

'Hello Mr Paws, hello Pirate,' she said, tickling them. She threw her keys onto a table. 'I'll just be a minute. I'm just going to get out of these jeans. It's so hot. Put the kettle on if you like, let the cats out the back.' She ran upstairs.

The kitchen looked out over a small garden which was mostly grass and rose bushes. He unlocked the door and the cats ventured out into the sun and lay down next to each other. A cork board had various timetables and notes from University pinned to it along with pizza and curry house menus. He filled the kettle and clicked its button, then pulled open the kitchen drawers quietly looking for anything that would link her to RadLand or the IAs, but nothing leaped out at him. It was as if she was just living on the surface on the house.

After five minutes he heard her coming downstairs. He found two mugs on the draining board. 'Coffee OK?' he said, as she came in.

'Yes. White. No sugar.'

He glanced at her in the doorway. She'd changed into a loose, above the knee plain white cotton dress.

She stepped into the kitchen in bare feet and leaned into him, putting her hand on his cheek, her breath soft on his lips, she kissed him, pressing her small soft lips to his. Nothing else. No tongue. Just the pressure of lip on lip. It was a small act, but one of real intimacy. This was dangerous. She took his right hand in her left and placed it between her legs. Clearly, she now wasn't wearing underwear. She felt warm, hot even. Her pubic hair, soft and fine. He didn't do anything, just held his hand there, pressed to her with her own hand. Keep your fingers still. Taking his hand away would be a rejection, but doing anything was clearly a sexual act. His breath and heartbeat quickened.

He had to find a way not to have sex with her, but not to embarrass or deny her so rudely that she shut down. Her previous hesitancy and shyness seemed to have evaporated in the car, as though it was an opaque mist she surrounded herself with in public, a mist which her hot passion had now burnt off.

'Em. You don't have to do this, you know.'

'I want to. Don't you, Nicky boy?' She slid her fingers under the waistband of his jeans, popped the top button and pushed them down over his hips.

'I do. Yeah...but...'

'Well then. Let me just take this off.' Before he could find the words to say not to, she had pulled the lightweight dress over her head and was naked. He looked down at her small breasts curving to a point and a stiffened dark pink nipple. How did you stop this? Like Julie had said he would be, he was really out of his depth as she pushed his jeans down further.

'Oh my god. Look at you,' she said, staring down at him, then tracing the outline of his lips with the tip of her index finger after wetting it with her tongue. 'I really want you in me.'

He rested his hands on her bare hips, just to put them somewhere. This was the trouble with being a man, right there and then he wanted nothing more than to have sex with this lovely woman. It was exactly as Jules had said, it's like men are programmed to do it. Mix all the right ingredients together and there you go. And for a few minutes it would be all-consuming and end in orgasmic pleasure, certainly for him. In isolation, it didn't seem like it could be that serious a thing to do. It was just a bit of fun, a physical pleasure, not a spiritual commitment. It was nothing to do with what he and Julie had between them. It was a very easy story to tell yourself...but it was just a story.

After that orgasm any amount of trouble would start. It couldn't be undone and even if it remained his secret, it would infect his life quite profoundly forever. This short act of pleasure had the potential to make both he and Julie very unhappy. It would be selfish and it just wasn't worth it for a few minutes of pleasure.

Yet physically, he was, in a very primal way, geared up to respond, geared up to just do it and do it now. The rutting animal was at war with the civilised human. We've developed a self-aware sophistication that is at odds with our own bodies. We've invented a culture and set of mores that our bodies don't always understand and it gets us into trouble; the battle between these two things being the grist to all human existence. If he hadn't been on drugs, if he had still been in the psychic pain over the miscarriage, if he'd been hurting inside as he had been until recently, he might have made a different decision in order just to flood his brain with endorphins and wash away the hurt. But not now. His body was 100 per cent ready for sex with Emily Davids, but his mind wasn't. He made his choice. Back away from the naked woman.

'Come on, Em...It's lovely to have you flatter me like this, but you and I both know something else is going on here. Why don't we talk about it? I mean, I've been around the block a little bit, and you're not this kind of lass...picking an older bloke up and having sex with him. It's not your way. I can tell. Come on, let's have a nice chat. I'm rubbish at sex anyway. I'd only disappoint you.' His self-deprecation seemed to ease the awkwardness.

He hoisted his jeans up and picked up her dress. 'You can put this back on if you like and I'll get that coffee.' She looked genuinely disappointed, her small mouth turned down, she let out a sigh, frowned quizzically at him and scratched one of her small buttocks.

'I don't understand. I thought this was what you wanted and you've got me all wrong if you think I'm putting on some sort of act. This is me,' she pointed to herself, still naked.

'And it's totally lovely but...'

'...but you can't be unfaithful to Julie, can you?'

'No.'

'But you want to?'

'Yeah, well, no. Sort of.' Any way he said it sounded bad in one way or another. 'Like I say, I'm flattered.'

She laughed a little and shook her head. 'Flattered? It's just sex, Nicky boy. You're making too much out of it. Far too much. We make each other come and that's it. It's not a lifetime commitment or anything. It's just lust.' She slid the dress over her head.

'Yeah, well, I tend to do that.'

He poured hot water onto the coffee granules, quite pleased at how he'd got out of the situation without it being massively insulting, but knowing he had to maintain a level of intimacy with her in order to have a chance of her opening up to him. He took the mugs in to the front room, setting them down on a small table, he sat on one end of a large blue sofa and patted the cushion next to him. Keep being nice. She was nice. Were it not for all the complications, being there with her would have been nice.

'Owee, sit down Em, let's talk, eh.'

She pulled her legs up underneath her and sat alongside him. He put his arm around her shoulder and she leaned into him. Her hair smelled of something floral, lavender possibly. Her bones were only just under the surface of her skin. There was no padding on her at all.

With a little sigh, she looked at him. 'So explain to me why we are here if not to bonk each other senseless?' she said with a watery smile. 'I'm sorry if I offended you or something. I don't know what I did wrong. I don't understand what you thought was going to happen. I thought it was all very clear. Did I misunderstand?'

'You didn't offend me and don't be daft, you did nothing wrong. It's my fault. Shall we put our cards on the table?'

'I guess so,' she said, slightly puzzled. 'What cards are those?' He looked down at her; the dress was up around her hips, revealing her small patch of brown pubic hair. It was very distracting. He looked in the opposite direction.

'OK, so you tell me first, what do you want to know?' he said.

She cocked her head on one side. 'Excuse me?'

'You asked me here to find something out, didn't you?'

She giggled a little. 'I wanted to find out what you were like in bed.'

'Come on, Em. I'll tell you my big secret if you tell me yours.'

'I've just seen your big secret.' She giggled again, annoyingly, almost childishly. He let out a sigh.

'OK, I'll go first,' he said. 'I know who your dad is. I found out online. And I know he runs the RadLand charity and that the Ironopolis Anarchists really don't like them.'

She stood up and wandered across the room, briefly looking out of the window, returning to sit facing him, cross-legged on a large embroidered pouffe. Her position exposed herself and left absolutely nothing to the imagination. Was she still trying to test him or something? If so, it was starting to get wearing.

'Em. I'm not being funny, but could you put some underwear on? I'm getting a right eyeful here.' He nodded at her crotch. She let out another extended giggle, briefly leaned back on her hands, spread her legs as wide as she could, rubbed herself with her right hand index finger a couple of times, made sure he'd seen absolutely everything and then skipped out of the room, returning a minute later wearing her jeans and top from before. Nick drank some coffee. He was dry-mouthed and his head was spinning as his blood kept flooding from his head to his groin and then back to his head.

She settled down next to him and patted his stomach. Leaning into him, she put her face right up to his, talking quietly. 'OK, look. I'll be honest with you. First things first. I really, really just wanted to make love. I don't have any other ulterior motive than that. I really like you. I fancied you from the first time I met you. It's called lust, Nicky boy. Right? So whatever else you might think was going on, that's where I'm coming from.' She pecked him on the lips and sat back. 'But yes, that is my father; it's no secret, though I have little to do with him or with mother these days. We're very different people. I don't see eye-to-eye with them about almost anything. But...you are right about one thing...I have something else I need to say.'

Leaning her elbow on the back cushion of the sofa, she looked at him.

'It was me who put that meeting on the Ironopolis Anarchists' message board that you saw on my laptop. I thought it would be interesting to see who turned up. There now, that's surprised you, hasn't it?'

Bloody hell. It had. That would definitely make her an IA and not working for her father or RadLand. Was it true, though?

'How did you do that?'

'I'm a computer nerd, aren't I? I know how to hack into systems like theirs.'

'Wow, but how did you even know where to look for the board?'

'I did it from that email they sent to Mel after the hoax bomb. I got hold of that from the festival Intranet. From that I found their server and a massive hole in the back door. I set up an account on it, but masked it so they didn't know I was on there. It sounds complicated, but it was easier than I thought it would be.'

'It sounds like very advanced IT work.'

'I used to go out with a hacker when I was 16 and I've been interested in it ever since.'

'So you're not actually in the Ironopolis Anarchists yourself, then?' he said.

'No. I'm not. Honestly, I'm not. Are you, though? Look, while we're being honest, I really wanted us to...you know...but I really thought you were one of the IAs and you might talk to me about it.'

'No. Of course I'm not. Really, I'm not. I didn't plant the bomb either, in case you've been entertaining that idea. How did you know I looked at your laptop?'

'You thought you'd cleared your browsing history, but that's far from comprehensive. You can still find the info on the system if you know where to look and how.'

'So you planned that I'd access it?'

'As much as I could. I didn't know when you would, but I thought it'd happen. Didn't it occur to you that if I'd wanted to keep anyone out of that page, I'd not have stored the log in and password? I assumed at some point, if you had the opportunity, you'd have a nosey around because I thought you were one of the anarchists. You can tell me if you are, I won't tell any one else.'

Nick pulled at his lip and shook his head. She knew he'd accessed it on her laptop, but not at home. He still had that secret to keep.

'I just thought you'd been careless.'

'Don't be silly. I knew right away that you'd seen it.'

'Mike, my accountant, turned up at that meeting you posted as well; he's an IA.'

'Mike? Was he the dark-haired man with a beard that you talked to?'

'Yeah, how do you know that?'

'I was there, silly. You didn't see me, though. I was parked on the corner of the next street down in my Mini. I saw you at the bus stop and I saw that man go into the cemetery and then you went after him when he came out. I didn't see what happened after that.'

'So that's why you thought I was in IA?'

She nodded. 'Until about 10 seconds ago. You, him and the blonde-haired chap who was hanging around.'

'I forgot about him. Who was he?'

She shrugged. 'I don't know. I just assumed he was involved. Maybe he wasn't. Didn't you know him?'

'No I didn't, but as I said, Mike is in the IAs. He told me. I'm really not, Em. Do you believe me?'

'OK, I believe you. I'm certainly not. I'm not *in* anything. I've seen the Ironopolis messages for a couple of weeks now and I can tell you that they definitely planted that bomb. There's no-one saying they didn't. No-one is saying that anyone else did it,' she said and Nick knew that really was true. 'Has Mike told you the IAs are innocent? Because they're not.'

'Yes he has. Interesting. All the postings I saw were all about attacking RadLand again. They see the bomb they planted as a successful attack on them, but when I spoke to Mike he seemed to think that RadLand or someone was trying to set up them up. Trying to frame them for the bombing. He was adamant IA didn't do it, though he can't know that for sure.'

'Well the message board totally contradicts that and he obviously knows what the board is saying. He's lying to you and trying to cover up the extent of his own involvement. The IAs hate RadLand.'

'Have you told your dad? Mike thought you might be working for him and RadLand.'

She shook her head. 'I don't want to worry him. What can he do, anyway? It might all be internet hot air. You can't go through life looking for bombs in every room, can you? That's no life at all. But no, I'm not working for him or anyone else except Mel Stephens.'

That was a glimpse of a more mature Emily. It was to be hoped she didn't reveal it too often because it was really attractive. Much more so than the giggling girl.

'And you're not close to your dad?'

'No. No, I'm not. Neither him nor my mother. They're not my favourite people, I don't like the lives they lead or where they lead them. As I said to you earlier, I like it here. I can totally see why this Mike guy thinks RadLand might be a malign force...I really can...there are rich and powerful people in their ranks, but RadLand isn't some sinister organisation, it really isn't. It's a bunch of in-bred chinless idiots and their even more in-bred chinless offspring - some of whom I grew up around - but despite that, in their own way, they mean well. They might well be cheating the system one way or another, but they're not evil. I'm sure of that. I'll tell you what you should do. You should go and interview my father. See what you make of him. I'd love to know. When you meet him you'll see what I mean. He's an old fart and lives in this rarefied, protected rural world, but he's not a bad man at heart. I just don't want to live the life that he expected and wanted me to live. I'm not going marry a farmer and have eight children, go to gymkhanas and make jam for the WI.'

'That's entirely understandable,' said Nick with a grin.

'So do you have any idea who uses that message board?' she said.

'Not a clue. IA are all unknown to each other, so none of them know who the others are. So no-one knows who is doing what. We know Mike uses it, but that's it.'

'I thought loads would turn up to my fake meeting but they didn't, so maybe there could be a split between them. Some peaceful, some violent?' she said.

Nick nodded. 'Since you hacked the message board, can't you tell where they're all posting from?'

'I'm working on that. It's a bit above my pay grade, I'm afraid. It's bounced all over the place, probably from East European servers. I'll keep at it though.'

'Have you told the police that you have access to the board?'

'Have you?'

'Answering a question with a question, eh?'

'Sorry. I'll be honest, I'm worried to tell anyone in case they come after me. The IAs might be anywhere, including in the police force. I was only two floors up from the last bomb. I don't want to be any closer next time. They obviously have lots of connections in all walks of society in the just the same way my father does. Who knows what they'll try next.'

'I know what you mean. I'm getting paranoid as well, not least because my accountant seems to think I'm capable of an act of terrorism. He actually asked me to ask you about RadLand and everything. He said it would prove to "important people" - whoever they are - that I'm not actually responsible. Well, I'm glad we had this talk, Emily. You've told me the whole truth, haven't you?'

She held her hand on her heart. 'Honest. Yeah. I want to know who is behind all this as much as you, Nick.'

'Come on then, we'd better get back to work.'

'You didn't have to go along with my little afternoon delight plan to get me to talk, you know,' she said, calling the cats in. 'You could have just asked me straight.'

'I suppose so. I thought you had a lot to hide, though.'

She locked the back door. 'And you thought the promise of sex might loosen my tongue? '

'Something like that.'

She giggled and shook her head. 'So naïve. It's very endearing, really,' she said as though she was the one who was 48. 'Though, in truth, I did think the same about you. I thought you might confess to being an IA during the throes of orgasm.'

'And it turns out that a nice chat over a cup of coffee was all that we needed to do. Me and you - we're not good at this subterfuge and spying lark, are we?'

She let out a fluttering laugh. 'No. Maybe we've watched too many movies.'

'Yeah, this is real life on Teesside, not some LA cop thriller.'

She closed the door and locked it. 'You could never mistake

Middlesbrough for LA, could you?'

'Not unless you were on some very good drugs, no.'

Twenty minutes later, as he parked up on the festival site, he said to her, 'If you hear or see anything about RadLand or the IAs, will you let me know?'

'Of course I will. We're still mates, aren't we, Nick? Even though you were admirably determined not to be seduced by my limited charms.' She grinned at him, her pink tongue tip poking between the gap in her front teeth again.

'Totally, yeah. Just because I'm not in the market for getting naked and exchanging bodily fluids doesn't mean we can't be friends.'

She placed her small hand and little fingers on his bare arm. 'Cool. I'm glad. And if you do ever fancy a good time, you know where I am. I'll be happy to, y'know, oblige you, especially now that I know what I'm missing.' She pulled up and down his arm as though it was a different part of his body, gave her light, fluttery laugh and got out.

Later that day as Nick drove home with Julie, he went over what had happened in detail, for the sake of honesty not wanting to miss anything out. She sat impassively as he did so.

'Did you ever come on to a bloke as old as me when you were 21?' he said.

She sat and thought as they drove along Yarm Road. 'No. I had a couple of one-night stands with blokes who were 10 or 15 years older than me, but not 27 years older. But then, older blokes were much older back then, do you know what I mean? I reckon if I was her, in this day and age, I might have tried to pull you as well. Just a guess, but I reckon you wouldn't have been off-limits.'

'Yeah? How weird.'

'Yeah, I'd have been like her and assumed an older bloke could give me a good time. Mind, I'll say one thing, she's a cheeky cow, doing it under my nose.'

'So you're OK with it, though? I've told you everything right down to the gynaecological details. '

'I could have done without those. Euww. I do feel weird about it. It feels really odd and my instinct is to slap her hard.'

'Yeah. Sorry. I didn't know what to do really...'

'And you obviously enjoyed it...'

'...well...'

'...don't bother denying it.'

'I wasn't going to. I mean, it's sort of a natural thing, getting a bit aroused in that situation. I don't have much control over it. It goes up and down on its own accord. It's like when you really want to sometimes you just can't, no matter what you do and then when you're not fussed, it rears up and wants attention. The penis has a mind of its own. I have no idea what makes it do what it does. But, crucially, I'm perfectly able to control what I do it about it. So that's what I did.'

She let out a sigh. 'Ooh aren't you clever?' she said, understandably acidic. 'I'm just saying, I'd rather it hadn't happened. You're *my* special secret rutting animal.'

'I still am and I always will be.'

She twirled a strand of her around her finger and looked at the split ends. 'I know, but you're a bit of a dark horse, you, and I like it that way.'

'Well at least we did actually find out *some* important stuff. We found out that she isn't a member of the Anarchists, even though we thought she was, and she admitted hacking into the message board and putting that meeting on there. I'm amazed she was there and I just never saw her. She thought I was an IA and she now knows that I'm not. To be honest, I think she was telling me the truth about everything. I trusted her.'

'Hmm. She could have been lying. Would you have known? Your brain was starved of most of its blood, wasn't it?' She gave him an arched look. That was all too true.

They had just got home and Nick was taking some steak out of the fridge for their tea, when Julie called out to him from the living room.

'Quick! Come and see this!'

CHAPTER 14

He ran through. The TV was showing local news. The first image he saw was of a man being bundled into the back of a police van under a grey blanket. The voice-over said,

'...the man arrested is believed to be a 50-year-old Harrogate accountant, Michael James Trent.' Nick's stomach dropped. *'He is being questioned over the Teesside Blues Festival bomb and is believed to be a main man in the Ironopolis Anarchists, who have claimed responsibility for the bomb which killed three people.'*

No wonder he'd been acting so strangely and had been so tense. He must have known the net was closing in on him. Nick went to his laptop and brought up Emily's log-in page, entered the password again. It let him in. 'Tez was wrong, this isn't changing the log in and password every so often,' he said. She joined him to look at the previous 12 hours of messages, but as soon as he logged on, it was obvious that everything had been deleted.

'They've been wiped.'

'By IA or by someone else?' said Julie.

'Who knows? Shit. What do we do?'

'I can't see what we can do. We know almost nothing and what we think we know, we don't know is really true.'

'I feel like I should trust Mike to be a good guy, but that might be stupid of me.'

'Is he married?' said Julie.

He thought for a moment. 'I just don't know. He lives on his own, I think.'

'You must know. He must have mentioned his wife or partner.'

He thought again. 'No. He hasn't.'

'Or you didn't pay attention.'

'That is possible, but if he'd mentioned her a few times I would have taken notice eventually. Most blokes at some point say something like, "I'm not sure the wife would like that"...or that sort of thing. He never has.'

'Is he gay maybe?'

'You've met him. Does he seem gay?'

'Not in the slightest, but my gaydar is far from perfect. The point is, he's a mystery man.'

'Yeah, but he's not a terrorist, is he?'

She shrugged. 'He could be. Reading people's minds is impossible sometimes. Look at Emily Davids, we both thought she was a goody goody middle-class girl, turns out she's a raving nympho. You could not tell that by looking at her or talking to her. I couldn't anyway.'

'Me neither. There's nothing to indicate that under the quiet middle-class respectability lies a woman with a voracious vagina,' said Nick.

She laughed. 'That sounds like some sort of carnivorous plant.'

'Meat eating, certainly,' he said, quietly. She snorted and punched him on the arm.

'The stupid thing is, in the little time I've spent with her, I've always liked her. She's thoughtful and intelligent and has nice manners,' she said.

'I think she is like that. You said yourself just wanting to have it off with someone doesn't make you not nicey-nicey. It's not like she's breaking anyone's trust, is it? She's single.'

'Hmm. I should listen to myself sometimes. I talk sense.'

Nick didn't sleep well that night. It had been such a stressful, emotional day. The image of Emily Davids was burned into his synapses and the fact that Mike was under arrest imbued him with a sense of worry. It was hard to think of him in that context. He'd always been such a quiet, steady man. Emily and Mike both hid their passion well. That was the key thing. You were off the radar when you didn't make a fuss. You didn't shout about your passions, you just went about doing your own thing and only disclosing your real nature to people you trust to be in sympathy. That must be what the other IA people were also like. Beavering away, not suspected. They could be anyone.

He was up at 6am for his early walk, taking a different route this time, straight up the long avenue of trees and standing for 10 minutes watching another hare devouring big dandelion leaves. They had a magical quality to them, hares. They looked like they were thinking about things. Rabbits were just impulsive and silly, but hares would sit and look around themselves and contemplate the morning.

'I just saw a beautiful hare,' he said to Julie as he came in. She was frying two fillets of salmon for their breakfast. 'I wouldn't mind being a hare.'

'You've not got the thighs for it. What was its name, do you think?'

'It looked like a Larry. Larry's always have long, loping legs.'

She laughed and served up the food. 'If I was a hare I'd like to be called Bunny, just to confuse everyone.'

Her phone chirped into life - the opening riff to Pat Benatar's 'Best Shot'.

'Who's that so early? I hope it isn't mam. Huh, don't recognise the number. Hello?'

She stared into the middle distance. 'Yes it is. Hello, Angie. This is an early call. No, we're always up early...we're just having breakfast. No, it's alright.' She paused again to listen. 'Yes of course I can. What's this about, Angie?' Her face suddenly dropped and the pink in her cheeks turned an off white. 'Yes, I will. We'll be there within the hour.'

'What?' said Nick, chewing a mouthful of fish.

'That was Angie.'

'Yeah, I guessed that.'

'She's just told me she's a member of the Ironopolis Anarchists.'

He dropped his knife in shock.

In the car on the way to Angie's house in Fairfield, Nick tried to make sense of Angie's confession.

'So tell me what she said again.'

'All she said was Mike being arrested had changed everything. That she was a member of the IA and that she needed help and didn't know who to turn to. Given how secretive they are, it's a huge thing her asking me for help. Being anonymous is so important to them. I think she asked me because we'd been asking her all those questions and she sussed out we were trying to find out what really happened. She probably thinks we know a lot more than we really do.'

'OK, let's think for a minute what this means. Her ex-husband David Murray, works for Simon Garbutt, who manages Big Fish's money. There's no way they're members of IA, is there? '

'No. They won't be in a group fighting rich people. So we need to know once and for all, did she get a bomb threat or not?'

'And we need to know if David Murray is our Steve McQueen and has been following us. I'd also like to know if it was him on Cargo Fleet Lane that day.'

She was waiting for them at the door, arms crossed, a cardigan wrapped around her, her hair in the neat bob.

'I'm so glad you came. I didn't know who to turn to, but you obviously have some sort of idea about what has been going on,' she said as they walked up to the door.

She sat them down in the back room. It was a plain room with blank walls. Neat and tidy to the point of featureless.

'As I said to you on the phone. I'm one of the Ironopolis Anarchists. I know it seems odd. I'll give you the history if you want, but I'd rather get to the crux of the matter.'

'Yes do, please,' said Julie.

'I just don't understand how this Mike Trent person has been arrested. If, as they were saying in the news, he's an IA, then our security must have been breached somehow and that means I and everyone else are in real danger. Someone is out to get us, I'm sure.'

'Mike actually came and told me he was an IA,' said Nick.

'Did he? How odd. Y'see, I don't know him. I had never even heard of him. I've never even seen him before. We're all anonymous to each other.'

'He was worried the net was closing in on him, I think. I found out that your message board had been accessed by an outsider.'

Angie looked frightened. 'Really? Oh god. I think RadLand is behind this. They've paid their sympathizers in the police to arrest him. They've already successfully blamed us for the bomb by claiming responsibility for it on our behalf, when I'm sure it was them who planted it. How can we fight back against that?'

'That's also what Mike speculated, but Angie, tell me honestly. Did you really get a call saying there was a bomb?' said Julie, leaning forward, the palms of her hands on her knees. 'You didn't make that up under duress, did you?'

'Yes, of course I took the call. Obviously, you didn't believe me when you came around before, that much was clear. I don't know how to prove it to you, but I did. It scared me badly. I knew we wouldn't bomb anyone, so I knew from the start that someone was trying to frame us, frame the IAs. All sorts of paranoid thoughts went through my brain. That's why I quit. I'm sure it's RadLands. Most of the people we've been working on recently are in some way related to RadLands. They're so rich and powerful. I genuinely think they'll stop at nothing.'

'And you don't know any other IA people?' said Nick, feeling that, like Emily, she was being very sincere.

'Like I said, none of us know each other. I've never met any other member, not knowingly anyway.'

Nick explained about how Emily set up a meeting on the message board and what had happened.

She shook her head. 'No, no, no that doesn't make any sense. No-one has ever posted anything like that, I would have seen it. I check it every day at least once. No-one has ever posted a meeting. There have been no meetings. You can't have been logged into the right place.'

He explained what it looked like and how he'd accessed it.

Angie held her hands up. 'Honestly, I've never, ever seen a message board like that. I have no idea what that was, but it wasn't the one we use. We don't have names assigned. The system allocates us a random number every time we log on. Look, I'll show you.'

She took an iPad from the arm of the sofa and loaded a page, typed in a username and a password and then put it under his nose. 'See? This is where we communicate with each other.'

They crowded around it. She was right. It was entirely different to the one Emily had hacked into. Messages from randomly numbered users were stored on it and they documented discussions between 9 or 10 people over the last few months. That day they were all discussing Mike's arrest and were along the lines of "is he really one of us?". Some were paranoid that he was a stooge who was being set up by the powers that be, to take the rap for the Ironopolis Anarchists. Some said it was the work of RadLand. It was obvious that they had no idea even if Mike was one of their number and certainly no idea if he'd decided to go rogue and bomb the festival or was part of a RadLand scam. Confusion reigned, but the one thing that was for certain, it was a very different board to the board Emily had hacked into and on which he and Julie had read so many bombing plans.

'Who set this up?' said Nick.

'I don't know. It already existed when I joined. I got a phone call from someone anonymous who gave me a log in and password and that's what I've used ever since.'

Nick shook his head and rubbed the point of his chin, tugging at the stubble, thinking it over.

'How well do you know Emily Davids?' he said.

'Personally, I don't *know* her. I've run into her a few times in the short time I worked on the festival site. That's all.'

'But you know who she is?' said Julie.

'I know she's the daughter of a big landowner in Lincolnshire. One that we've been doing some work on, as it happens. The Earl of Louth. He heads up RadLand.'

'Some posts on that other board say RadLand are, for want of a better word, evil,' said Julie. 'Do you think that's right?'

'Not all of them. Some are smug and self-satisfied, certainly. But the RadLand trust fund does good work and no-one can say otherwise. The Earl of Louth who heads it is typical landed

241

gentry. Has a bit of a liberal conscience, wants to do some good, but is driven primarily by preserving his wealth and power. As indeed most of us would be. I have found nothing we can use against him. But others in RadLand are far less clean and it is them I'm worried about. It's not the whole organisation, just some elements. They really scare me.'

They sat and looked at each other for half a minute, then Nick spoke. 'One - someone in IA really did do it and called in to admit it or two – someone pretending to be in IA called in. Now, given the demands that were made along with the claim for responsibility, the calls to stop the festival and especially that animal rights one tagged on, does that sound like the sort of thing anyone you've ever seen on your message board say?'

'No. That's why I think it's a set up. We have never, ever, touched animal rights. We have only worked towards what I call fairness issues. We've been very single-minded about that. That demand is totally not what IA is all about. Violence, stopping the festival, calling for anything - none of that is our thing. We're a research group.'

'How do you actually work on a project, Angie?' said Julie.

'We'd agree online what we were doing, who we were looking into and then go about our business individually and report back on specific dates, usually the first and the middle of the month. Work would be pooled into a document that was then prepared by one volunteer. We'd then all sign off on it before it went to the media. That's how it has worked for 18 months now and it has worked really well.'

'How did you get involved in the first place?' said Julie.

'It was odd. I work at the council on databases. In my spare time I also work for a children' s charity which combats poverty and I also do work for Unison on low pay. Someone had seen my work and must have thought I was a sympathetic soul. I got an anonymous email one day asking if I'd like to help them, but that it would be totally anonymous and no-one would ever find out. Well, to my mind, the things the rich and powerful have got away with...well...forever...it's wrong. Plain and simple. Wrong. And the ordinary people have to pick up the bill for these people's reckless and corrupt behaviour one way or another. Children suffer poverty and their life chances are put in jeopardy, all because of their irresponsible behaviour and I don't see why that should be the case. There's plenty to go round if those with the most were not so...so damn selfish! I don't see how anybody could think it is wrong to expose people who sought to deny the public their rightful share of taxation. But I can certainly see why the rich and powerful would want to stop us doing that.'

For all she had a plain, lilting, insubstantial voice and defensive body language, underneath the cardigan she was clearly made of sterner stuff and seemed driven by a strong sense of morality. Right there and then Nick liked her, he really liked her. She was another warrior in the sensible army. It was the sensible people like Angie who had their shit together who could hold the abusive elite to account by virtue of their rigorous thinking and simple dedication. What a wonderful woman, entirely without self-regard or ego. She just wanted to do what was right and see justice done. A proper decent Teesside citizen.

Julie leaned over and grabbed her hand. 'You are so right, Angie. I'm with you 100 per cent. We'll help in any way we can. It's the least you deserve.' Angie managed a weak smile.

'But now, I'm so worried that the police are going to come here and arrest me. If they've found this Mike person is in IA, they might find me too. I'm scared that we've all been set up somehow. I would never do anything to hurt another person and I was utterly appalled when that bomb went off. I want nothing to do with any group that would do such a thing.'

'Don't worry Angie. You haven't done anything wrong, so they can't have evidence that you have,' said Julie, reassuringly. Nick didn't voice it, but immediately thought that planting evidence to 'prove' her guilt or anyone else in the Ironopolis group's guilt, would not be hard to do. If someone wanted to shut them down, that is exactly what they would do. Given Mike's arrest, and given his paranoia that exactly this sort of action was in the pipeline, it seemed to him that her fears were entirely justified. It was also the sort of thing a group of rich and influential people could make happen. There was enough evidence that elements in the police could be persuaded of almost anything, if the money was right.

Julie drove them away from Angie's house.

'I proper love her,' said Julie as they headed down Greens Lane. 'She's total class. I'm sorry I ever had a bad word to say about her. I got her totally wrong. She's got a core of steel, that one. Made all the hairs on my neck stand up when she was saying about how the rich had got away with things for so long.'

Nick called up Emily Davids.

'Em? Hiya. Are you at work? Have you got your laptop with you? Good. I need you to do something for me when I get in...no...ha, ha...not that. Sorry.'

He rang off.

'She's a cheeky get, her,' said Julie. 'I know what she said.' He grinned.

'Can't blame her for trying it on. I am, by your own confession, a rutting animal.'

She gave a snort and nodded her head to one side. 'Well, I can't say I wasn't the same way at her age...not sure I ever begged anyone to slip me a length quite so much though, not least because, frankly, a woman is better off with the love of her own fingers than she is with most blokes.'

He burst out laughing. 'That's unusually crude for you, Jules.'

'Sometimes I just feel really cock-suckingly crude, me, like.' She poked her tongue out at him. As she drove up Norton High Street towards Junction Road, she looked in her rear view mirror. A black Ford Ka was two cars behind.

'I swear that's Steve McQueen in that car. Again. We're being followed by him again. That's three times now,' she said.

'He probably just lives around here. He probably thinks we're following him. Teesside is a small area, you can see the same people a lot. Calm down Jules. I'm not sure it's even the same man. We're all getting too paranoid.'

'Yeah, I'm probably just being paranoid.' She slapped her herself on the forehead. 'Oh shit. We'd better just nip home and get my car.'

'Why's that?'

'I've got loads of passes to sort out - it's a ton of work, I'll be working later than you. No point in you hanging around. If we go in separate cars, you won't have to wait for me and you can go and see if the wedding rings are ready.'

'Actually, that's a good idea because I'm going to see if I can speak to someone at RadLand. Do an interview with them, see if I can find out who is in the group and what exactly it is that they do,' said Nick, finding them on his phone. 'Might as well start at the top, with the Earl of Louth.'

He sent an email to the contact address on the website asking for an interview with the Earl, saying it would be run in the *Yorkshire Post*. When you emailed anyone in any organisation it could take hours, days, weeks, even months for them to reply, so he didn't expect to hear anything quickly. However, just as they were pulling into the festival parking area, half an hour later, his phone rang.

'Hello?'

'Is that Mr Nick Guymer?' said a crisp, porcelain accent.

'It is.'

'Hello, Mr Guymer. I'm Fiona Miles, secretary to the Earl of Louth. You've just emailed us to request an interview to discuss RadLand. Can you outline your ideas a little for me?'

'Well, it seems to me that a lot of landowners have been under fire in recent months from various groups who accuse them of greed and tax avoidance and such. Yet, RadLand, from what I know, does a lot of work in the rural communities. So I thought it'd be good to find out more about what it is you do.'

'Well, that's very refreshing. I think we can accommodate you, Mr Guymer. Charles will be happy to give you half an hour of his time. When would suit you?'

'As soon as possible,' said Nick.

'How about you pop down to Louth Estate Manor in an hour or so? Is that far too soon? We have a window.'

'No, that's fine.'

'I'll email you directions.'

'Thanks, Fiona.'

'Very good. We look forward to seeing you.'

After a quick coffee, he sped down the A1 to the M62, taking the M18 and then the M180 east to the coast of North Lincolnshire. These were the flat lands south of the Humber. It had a bleakness the way Teesside did, only somehow, because its economy was based around the fish processing, it lacked the same grand architecture of industry. Aesthetically speaking, industrial estates full of big metal boxes, filled with people in hair nets did not match up to the flaming chimneys and knotted digestive tract-style piping of the chemical and steel industries that hugged the Tees.

Taking the A16 south out of Grimsby he headed into open countryside around Louth, taking a minor road off into the Lincolnshire Wolds. The Manor House was a plain name for a very grand early Georgian country home. He pulled up at a pair of 12- foot-high wrought-iron gates into which a family crest was set, presumably the Earl of Louth's. He got out and pressed an intercom buzzer. Fiona Miles's voice barked out.

'Can I help you?'

He introduced himself and the gates opened automatically. It was like being granted entrance to the lair of a spy or something. The long, curving gravel drive crunched under the tyres of the BMW as he rolled up to a large set of black double doors, set into a classical, columned porch. So this was were Emily Davids grew up, was it? Wow. This was proper privilege. And quite something to reject, too. Big respect to Em.

The door opened as he got out and a middle-aged woman in a quilted green gilet and a pair of green corduroy trousers appeared as though out of 'English rural middle-class' central casting.

'Mr Guymer?' she said with a repressed smile.

'Hi. Thanks for inviting me over, this is a smashing place,' he said, automatically slipping out of his Teesside accent and into something far less pronounced, immediately feeling like a traitor in doing so.

This was a scaled-up version of Brian Salmon's house on the Blakeston Estate; as though someone had multiplied everything by a factor of five. He was led into a large Georgian drawing room.

'Charles will be with you soon. I've let him know you're here. Now, a coffee, perhaps?'

'Yes please. Black, no sugar.'

He sat down on a firmly padded red and gold 18th-century sofa, if indeed they were called sofas in the 18th century. The walls were, in the typical country house style, covered with paintings of stern people, presumably relations going back a few hundred years. No piece of furniture seemed to be newer than about 1780. This wasn't just posh, it was thoroughly Upper Class. Nice to look at, but stuck living in the past. It felt as though he'd gone back in time. This sort of place resisted change and sold that resistance to the people as the preservation of the nation's heritage and history, but really, it didn't want to change, because all of its money and power were wrapped up in it. They were not primarily custodians of historical buildings, but actually, on the quiet, something much more vulgar; they were preservers of wealth and power.

One noticeable thing was that there were no photos of family anywhere. There was however, a large photograph of a dog in a gilt frame. Maybe that illustrated his priority for affection.

She returned with two lovely, thin white bone china mugs of coffee and set them down on a low table. As she did so, a man in his early 50s came in. He was wearing a blue shirt and pinkish-red trousers with brown leather shoes. What is it with the rural posh bloke and the pinkish-red trousers? It was sort of uniform for a certain class of people.

'Nick? Welcome to Louth Manor House,' he said, in a voice that boomed around the large room. He advanced on him, hand outstretched. Nick got up and shook the large, soft paw.

'Thanks for having me down here...err...do I call you Earl?'

He laughed. 'Charlie will do. That's m'name. No standing on ceremony here.'

Fiona left them on their own and they sat opposite each other in large armchairs.

Nick took out his iPod, plugged in the microphone and set it to record.

'Gosh, that all looks very hi-tech,' he said in a plummy voice. It was as though he was 93, not 53. They were virtually the same age, but Charlie seemed to be from a different era and certainly a very different culture.

'So why don't we start by you telling me about RadLand and what it does?'

Charlie could talk. He was well used to the sound of his own voice and also used to people having to listen to him. He launched into a 10-minute explanation about their work, which, when all said and done was small gifts of money or grants to help start new rural businesses. Nick nodded patiently. It quickly became clear that while the money did some local good, it was also part of their overall tax strategy which saw them put a lump sum into a charitable trust, invest that money on the stock exchange and then pay the returns out the following year, to various good causes and individuals. There was nothing illegal about it, but it showed just how rich both he and the others involved were, that they could afford to put aside several million. And really, underneath it all, it wasn't actually generous at all. They were not spending a penny of their own money, the capital remained untouched, they merely spent the income. It made them appear generous, but a poor person who donated £1 of their minimum wage to a charity was giving away more money than Charlie was. There were probably other more complex tax advantages of setting up a trust, too. It certainly kept the capital invested in it out of HMRC's way.

After a long soliloquy, he paused for coffee and Nick jumped in.

'Oh, I met your daughter, Charlie. Emily works at a festival I'm working at on Teesside.'

'Oh really. How interesting. I don't see much of Emily. She's her mother's daughter. Brought up in London. How is she?'

'Very well. She's a nice girl. I like her a lot.'

'She's a very independent girl. Knows her own mind. Always has. These days she refuses a penny from me. I admire that. She's very hi-tech, I'm told. She has a sister who lives in London. I don't see them as much as I'd like.'

It seemed obvious to Nick that they were not a close family in the slightest. There was no affectionate talk of each other, no interest in their lives, nor much knowledge about them either. Equally, there was no real hostility. It was more like they were strangers.

'Do you have a list of the members of the RadLand Trust?'

'Err...yes...it's not a secret. Because it's all a charity, it's in the public domain.'

'And you set it all up, I understand?'

'Yes and I invited some others to be part of it. It seemed the least I could do. Banks and so forth are not interested in helping the little chap. A lot of the people we help just can't get funding from anywhere else. Often it's just a few quid for a bike or a computer. It doesn't always help them, but at least it gives them a chance and we have had some success stories.'

He took out his phone and dialled a number, spoke to Fiona and asked her to bring a list of RadLand Trust members. She turned up within a couple of minutes and handed Nick a printout of some 24 names. He glanced at it quickly. All members of the great and good.

'Charlie - I notice Brian Salmon, who owns the Blakeston Estate and stables, isn't on here. I thought he'd have been keen to help. Do you know him?'

'Yes, yes, indeed I do. Damn good fellow. He offered his support, but he has a little thing of his own going on in Durham and Teesside. Similar sort of set up. He keeps it quiet that he's involved. So there was no point to him coming in with us really.'

'I didn't know that. Good old Brian.'

'Indeed.'

'And his son Stevie isn't on here, either? He's done so well for himself, earned a lot of money.'

'So I believe, but...he's not our sort. Sorry, that sounds frightfully snobbish, it wasn't meant to. I just mean, I'm not sure he shares our values and Brian was good enough to gently guide me away from him and his team, on that basis.'

'I can imagine that. For what it's worth, I dislike Stevie Salmon a great deal. I just assumed he'd be involved though, as they're one of the richest families in the north. Have you ever met his business manager, Simon Garbutt, or a colleague of his, David Murray?'

'The names sound familiar, but no, I don't think we have. Probably been at some social event, nothing more.'

'What do you make of the recent financial crisis?' said Nick, searching for a bit of the man's politics.

'Appalled. We've gone from a situation where financial institutions were pillars of civic society, to seeing them as nothing more than bookmakers, worse probably. It's a terrible state of affairs.'

There was nothing to disagree with him, there.

'And what's your view of how some people in society have come under scrutiny for their tax affairs?'

'Well I think it's perfectly reasonable. If you've broken the law, you deserve everything that's coming, if you ask me.'

'In my region there's been a group called the Ironopolis Anarchists who have been instrumental in investigations into a few rich landowners. Are you worried some group like that looks into your affairs?'

'No no. Personally, I've nothing to hide. I suppose I would say that, wouldn't I? People might not approve of what I do, or of people like me, but I comply fully with all HMRC requirements. I pay all my taxes in the UK. I can't speak for all our members, though. I'm sure we've got a few bad pennies. To be honest, we're not a group as such. We barely meet once a year. I keep everyone informed about matters, but some on that list I haven't ever even met.'

That didn't sound like an organisation that might turn to terrorism.

'But it must worry you if people lose faith in the system and feel that a rich elite runs things for their own benefit, while the rest of the people work harder and harder for less and less. We had this bomb at the festival and people think that's the motivation behind it.'

He side-stepped that. 'What worries me is people losing faith in the system, breaking it and not having anything to replace it with. Revolution is all well and good...but then what? I'm not sure how to resolve it all really. I have a responsibility to the house and the estate. If I just gave it all away, I'm not sure it would, in the long run, make a better world.'

After an hour, Charlie drew matters to a close.

'I do hope you can put a broadly positive piece together, Nick. I do think RadLand is a force for good and I'll admit, people like me are not exactly flavour of the month right now, but I'd like people to know more about it and in the future, perhaps some of them can benefit from it.'

He walked him to the car. Just one man and his secretary in a house with over 30 rooms. It was ridiculous really. 'Would you like me to pass on a message to Emily?'

'Err...tell her...tell her I hope she's being a good girl and to call me once in a while.'

Driving away, Nick was torn between two states of mind. He'd wanted the Earl of Louth to be a twat. He was called the Earl of Louth for a start. He wanted to meet a chinless Tory idiot who was intent on screwing the state out of its due taxation and who thought the poor people were just feckless losers. But he wasn't like that, despite appearances to the contrary. OK, he was born into vast wealth and land, and he was probably a Tory, but you respond to people on a human level and although he was literally and symbolically representative of much that was wrong with Britain, he seemed a decent enough bloke. It all proved that life was always more shades of grey, rather than black and white.

When he got back to the festival site at 3pm, he recounted his visit to Julie.

'So you don't think he's some sort of terrorist plotting to overthrow the IA group to stop their work?'

'Nah. He's just a rich dude with land. I actually now think the whole paranoia about RadLand is way off base. I can see why Angie and Mike are uptight about them, given their investigations, but it's just the paranoia talking, there's nothing to suggest RadLand are guilty of anything other than of wearing awful trousers. Charlie seemed OK. Looked like an idiot in his pink pants, but then who am I to give fashion tips? He also wanted nothing to do with Big Fish, which puts him well up in my estimation. Incidentally, you know we assumed Big Fish would be in RadLand, but he's not. Reading between the lines, I think he was rejected for being a bit rough...ironic really, given his pampered upbringing.'

'Maybe RadLand is, by and large, a force for good then. Angie said it was, but that there were some rogue elements she was scared of. It's harder to dislike, let alone hate people when you meet them, isn't it? When it's all in isolation and they symbolise something, it's easy to, but when you can see they're just people with feelings like we have feelings, it's impossible to be like that. He might be smug and a bit greedy, but it doesn't make him a murderous bastard or anything, does it? I make the exception with Stevie Salmon, though. I really hate him...that's a harsh thing to say, I suppose. Hate is a big word, but if I mean it about anyone, I mean it about him.'

He went to get one of the massive beef hot dogs they served at the catering truck. As he did so he was intercepted by Mel Stephens.

'Have you heard? They charged that bloke with the bombing. Get in!' He gripped a fist and punched the air. 'I hope they stick a bomb up his arse for what he did here.'

'I hadn't heard that,' said Nick. Mike was charged? What did that mean? Surely the police didn't think he was guilty - he couldn't be guilty, could he?

'I just got a private call from the force to let me know. Really fucking pleased, now all I need is for the Health and Safety inspector to give us a clean bill of approval and get the missus to give us a blow job and my day will be perfect.'

'They charged him really quickly,' said Nick. Far too quickly. He went back to the admin tent and told Julie.

'I wonder if the message board is talking about this?' she said. 'Let's get Emily to have a look, I don't want us to log on, in case it looks dodgy. We're already under suspicion.'

Emily was sitting at her desk, she looked up at him with bright eyes as he approached, her smile dropped a few notches as she saw Julie.

'Hi guys,' she called out, breezily.

'Hiya. Listen Em, this is important. I want you to log into the IA message board.'

She glanced from Nick to Julie. 'Why?'

'I'll tell you in a minute. Just do it please,' said Nick. Julie gave her a flat smile.

She opened her laptop, went to the log in screen and entered her details. It opened the message board. But it was still blank. The page was totally empty.

'That's weird,' said Emily. She opened a command window and began entering a string of code. Letters and numbers and other symbols spilled down the page. She leaned forward and pointed to some numbers. 'It was deleted from this IP address, which, I would imagine, is in some distant exotic place like the Ukraine. A lot of the servers used for anonymous boards are in Eastern Europe. I'll just check.'

Her small fingers tapped away at speed on the keyboard, her brown eyebrows knitted together in a frown. It all looked like a numerical jumble. She paused and tapped at the screen with her nail.

'I was wrong. The IP is in Yarm on the Aislaby Road.'

'What?! That's where we live,' exclaimed Julie. She narrowed his eyes at her. 'You're not pissing me around, are you Em?'

'Of course not. Look. This is the IP number here... and here is where that IP address is...' She tapped at a blue dot on her screen, a mile out of Yarm, right beside the track that led down to their house. 'These things are never 100 per cent accurate. They're often a house or two out, but as there any no other buildings around there except this one - is that your house?' She pointed at a Google Earth satellite image.

'Yes that's it,' said Nick. 'But we didn't delete anything.'

She sat back and looked at him squarely. 'Well you might think you didn't, but you must have done.'

'What? How?' said Julie, her face set in an impatient scowl.

'Someone might have hijacked your computer and instructed it to log in and auto-delete everything on the board. But to do that you'd have needed to be able to log into the message board and you could only do that on this laptop.'

'Oh, my brother worked out your password in 20 minutes,' said Julie acerbically, as though it was a criticism of Emily. 'We've had access to the board on Nick's laptop since then.'

Emily nodded and gave a quick grin at her. 'I actually knew that. I could tell. I looked into the server log and saw your IP when you accessed it.'

'You cheeky little sod,' said Julie, as though Emily had violated her privacy.

Nick banged on her desk, making her and Julie jump. 'You accessed the server log? Did you note any other IP addresses that had logged on?'

'Yes of course. I told you the other day, they were all masked. However, I have done some work on them since and lo and behold...' She took out a piece of paper with numbers on.

'Where were they from?' he asked.

Emily's eyes flicked from him to Julie, back to him, back to her, back to him. Darting at speed.

'Emily! Tell me. It might be important,' he insisted.

'There were only three IP addresses used to post the previous 12 hours of posts.'

'But that doesn't make sense, there were at least 15 posters on there when we looked,' said Julie. 'Were they all living in a couple of houses?'

Emily tapped on her keyboard and brought up a map with the IP locations on. 'You can see where they are. I saved a map with them on. Two are on Teesside and one is in London. But these are almost certainly accessed via mobiles, so it's not like we can be sure these are home addresses that they've been used at.'

'Why not?' said Julie.

'A wi-fi network assigns your phone a common IP address when you go online, that is usually randomly chosen by the access point or router that broadcasts the signal, so that variable also makes it virtually impossible for someone to guess which IP address you have been assigned. You've also got to remember that wi-fi routers act as a hardware firewall for your phone. Typically they randomly assign you only a local IP address and then route the outbound traffic to a modem, which is the only device on the network which has a unique, traceable, and geo-specific IP address. That's the IP numbers I hoovered up. But these will never be identified by the phones used, so it's very unlikely anybody could track the phone user that way either. Basically it makes the user anonymous. Even if you got hold of their phone you couldn't match it to the IP numbers here...but it does give you an idea where the IP used at the time is. But you've got to bear in mind, it could be someone just standing outside of someone's house, not the person in the house.

'Christ, you know your teckie shit, don't you?' said Nick.

'I told you, I love technology and how it works. It's what my degree is in, after all,' she said.

'One thing is clear though - there were a maximum of 3 posters posting, but apparently 15 different posters, so they were taking on other identities to make it appear there were more involved than was the case,' said Julie.

'Yes, that's really significant. In actual fact, given when posts were made, it would have been possible for one person to post all of them if they travelled around a little bit. If you like, I can look at your computer and see if it has been compromised.'

He took the laptop out of his bag and handed it to her. 'We've only accessed it on my machine,' he said.

She flipped it open. 'Oh look, you've got some letters rubbed off from overuse. Let's see now which ones, p,o,r,n,o,g,r,a...'

'Alright Emily, this really isn't the time for joking around,' said Nick.

She grinned up at him. 'Sorry. OK, leave it with me. I'll look up its skirt and see what I can find,' she smiled at them both.

'Thanks. I just came back from seeing your dad, by the way.'

'Oh, that's a strange thought. What did you make of him?'

'It's a different world that he lives in, isn't it?'

'I told you, didn't I? Now can you see why I don't want anything to do with it?'

He nodded. 'He said to call him once in a while and hoped you were being a good girl.'

'Ha, some hope. I might struggle with both of those.'

Nick ignored that. 'OK, I'll check in with you later. By the way, why did you choose "helenwheels" as your log in? It's a song by Wings. You're too young for Wings' music.'

'I really like Wings. I generally like older things...' She stopped herself mid-sentence and almost laughed, looking out of the top of her eyes at them and to her credit, went a shade of raspberry.

Julie put her hand on Emily's head and ruffled up her hair quite aggressively and then gave her a little push. 'You're clever kid, but trust me, you're not nearly as clever as you think you are,' she said, turning and walking away to her desk.

CHAPTER 15

Nick glanced at her as they walked, she was muttering under her breath. He put his arm around her shoulder. 'Owee, lass, it's all cool.'

'More like school than cool, if you ask me. I don't need that sort of shit at my age. Silly little mare.'

They sat down at her desk she turned on the computer. There were still 22 emails to answer and six voice mails.

'The show goes on, I guess,' said Nick. 'Is there anything I can do?'

'Give me an hour to clear this. Don't go over and work with her, right?' He wouldn't have dared to.

'Nah, I'm going to find Jeff.'

He gave her hand a squeeze. In fairness, if he had to work around a bloke who had got naked and had had a damn good go at seducing her, he'd feel very queasy about it, so her tetchiness was more than understandable. Relationships could be so much messier than the beds they were consummated in.

Jeff was walking across the field from the main stage with a roll of wire over his shoulder. Distinctive even at great distance with his long hair flowing in the summer wind, Nick went down to meet him halfway. They stood looking out across the fields.

'Hey man. Jesus, every day this place looks different. All the toilets are here now, I see.' He pointed to rows and rows of Portaloos in the distance.

'Aye, and all the car-parking is good to go. The stage is about as ready as possible before the bands get here. To all intents and purposes the site is done. I'm just going to fix some fencing down at the perimeter edge that runs alongside the main road. You want to help? Just got to knock in some extra posts. We pick them up from the maintenance unit at the back of the stables.'

'Sure. Happy to help, big man. Anything to keep me out of the big tent.'

'Why's that, like?'

He gave him a brief resume of the Emily/Julie scenario. Jeff's bushy eyebrows shot up as he told him what had happened at her house in Marton.

'You're like one of those Buddhist monks who have such self-control that they can walk on hot coals or stick needles in their feet. How did you manage to resist a naked lass like her? She's ripe young fruit that Emily lass.'

'It wasn't that hard...'

'...I bet it bloody was!'

They both laughed.

Jeff continued. 'But seriously, dude, you must have the will-power of a saint. You've got a chick like that ready to open her wings and fly, as popular music's vernacular might have it...seriously, no-one could resist that. I'll be honest, there's no way I could. Are you sure you really did and you're not just trying to tell yourself a lie, to make yourself feel better?'

'Nah, man. The key is projecting into the future. Thinking outside of the now and to what life would be like after you've...you know...'

'...blobbed it, as my shop lad, Lukey, would say.'

'Very poetic. Aye.'

'I've always thought you were a woman, really. You think and act like a woman, you do...thinking about the consequences of your actions? Very female, that.' He squeezed Nick's chest a little. 'You've got nowt up top though, luv.'

'Yeah, this is no time for messing around though, man. Bigger shit is going down.' He explained about Mike's arrest and what Angie had told them, as they picked up two fence posts and a big mallet.

'Sounds to me like Mike has been bullshitting you to some degree. This dual messaging system...that is weird.' They walked to the outer perimeter of the site to where the land backed up to Darlington Back Lane. Two holes had been dug for extra fence posts to reinforce the boundary. Nick put one of the extra posts into the hole and took hold of the mallet to knock it into place. Jeff was standing looking into the middle distance, his index finger aloft.

'I reckon he did it.'

'Who did what?'

'Mike. He did the bombing.'

'Bollocks he did. He's an accountant, he's not a terrorist.'

But Jeff's finger was still aloft. 'That is where you are wrong my priapic but monk-like friend.' He twizzled two long strands on his beard. 'Think about it, he asked you about looking out for Big Fish making cash payments, I reckon he set the whole group up. He recruited people. He organised and arranged meetings. He did everything. The reason he's been arrested is because he is responsible. He must be.'

'There's one big flaw in that. To be responsible, he'd have to have been here, on site, and left the bomb. But he wasn't, was he? We've never seen him here.'

But Jeff wasn't having that. His finger shot up again and he cocked his head on one side. 'Ah...but...not necessarily, he could have planted it in someone's bag or had someone working for him do it. Think about this seriously. He could have planted it in your bag. Don't look like that at us. He could have. Your bag went up in that boom. Ever thought of that? No. By the look of you, you haven't.'

'I'm looking shocked, because I can't believe you're giving me all this crap, Jeff. If I'd had a bomb in my bag, I'd have noticed it. I take my stuff out of it every night and I'd have noticed if there was a bomb in there, trust me. It's not some massive deep suitcase, it's just a standard nylon record shoulder bag.'

Jeff shrugged. 'OK, man...but I think one way or another, it's all down to him, even if he didn't plant the bomb. He must have known there were two boards, for a start. One they all used and one that the extremists used, the one Emily hacked into.'

'Maybe so, but I don't see why he or any IA would want to do that.'

'It's a double bluff, isn't it?' He dropped the mallet and post and fencing and waved a hand into the Teesside summer air. 'They plant a bomb, then say they're being framed by this RadLand group - that's what Mike and Angie said, but what they're really doing is fitting up RadLand to make it look like they're the terrorists. It's part of their plot to bring down their biggest enemies, RadLand. Brilliant. Yeah, yeah...I've cracked it.' He held his arms aloft like a footballer.

'Nice theory, Jeff. I'll give you that. Trouble is this, they haven't publicly said they were being framed for the bomb, have they? When I asked Mike about why he hadn't, he said no-one would believe them, that they might break their cover if they went public with a denial. In fact, for their denial to have any weight, they'd have to. So they chose not to. So, like I say, nice theory, but it just doesn't fit. If anyone is being set up, it'll be as Angie fears. Some RadLand people are trying to get their enemies busted. That is far more likely. That being said, I've just been down to see Emily's dad, the Earl of Louth, and he was decent bloke; what's more, the list he gave me of RadLand members doesn't include Big Fish.'

He gave him a summary of his trip to Lincolnshire.

'But RadLand can be both a socially responsible charity run by a decent bloke and a vicious organisation trying to mess things up for their biggest critics. They don't have to all be working together, do they? It could just be a couple of extremists in their group.' said Jeff. 'Big Fish not being in their number could be significant. If he was one of them, they'd not target the festival.'

'That's very true. Let's face it, nothing discredits any cause better in the eyes of the general public than some sort of terrorist activity. No matter how right you are, you can't make your case after you've blown up three innocent students. And RadLand really are the ones under attack from IA, they're the ones with everything to lose if the IA pick them apart. So it does make sense, at least on one level. But having met Charlie boy, I just don't think he's like that. He's a stuck-up, posh rich snob in silly trousers, but that's about it.'

'Hold that post while I give it a seeing to,' said Jeff, picking up the mallet.

'I was wondering if I could get to see Mike? I want to know what he says about what we've found out.'

'Well, they've charged him, so he'll be on remand, probably in Durham jail. He'll be allowed visitors surely. And you've got good connections with the police, through Col Harcombe. So if anyone can get a visit sorted, you should be able to.'

'Aye. Actually, I'm going to try and fix that now.'

He let go of the post and looked on his phone for Colin Harcombe's personal number. The DI of Cleveland Police was a good mate to have. He dialled, looking out across the open countryside while Jeff kept bashing the fence post.

He picked up after five rings.

'Hello, Nick. Are you well?' said Colin Harcombe in his clipped, crisp, rather old-fashioned tone.

'Fine, thanks, Col. And you?'

'I'm taking a bit of a holiday at home, but the garden is proving harder work than the policing of villains. And how is Julie?'

'She's good, thanks.'

'I heard you lost the baby. Bad business. Send her my best regards.'

Nick smiled broadly at the use of Colin's favourite expression. There was something reassuringly grown up and sober about him. He was another one of the sensible people that weirdos like him needed to run the world.

'I will. She'll appreciate that.'

'I take it this isn't a social call, though.'

'Not exactly. Mike Trent, the man arrested for the bombing of the Teesside Blues Festival today, he's my accountant.'

'Good god!'

'I can't really go into details yet, Colin, but I think he may be innocent and I need to speak to him. Is there any chance I could get to see him wherever he's on remand?'

The phone distorted as Harcombe blew into it. 'Let me make a couple of calls. If it wasn't you...the answer would be no. But after the business with the Tees Digital murders, I'll see what I can do. We owe you a favour as I recall and I trust this is all in the greater pursuit of the rule of law?'

'Totally, yes Colin. Thanks.'

'I shall call you on this number. OK? Good man.'

Jeff handed him the mallet and put the other fence post in its hole. 'Your turn. How's Col? Did he say "bad business" by any chance?'

'Just once. He's a top bloke, is Col. Gives you faith in humanity. Another General in the sensible army.'

'In the what?'

'Nothing. Just something I've been thinking about recently.'

'He's firm but fair. Like a strict teacher who you end up really respecting. Hard gig to pull off, that. I always feel he's judging me harshly. Like I've not quite lived up to his standards somehow.'

'Well he's going to make a call or two. Hopefully, I can get in to see Mike.'

They finished the fencing and walked back up to the catering truck for a bottle of iced water as the sun came out from behind a heavy sky that threatened a rain storm.

'I've got one last theory,' said Jeff, draining the bottle in one long gulp. 'The Emily Davids lass. She says she hacked in and set up her own username and password. How likely is that really? How about her and Mike being in cahoots somehow?'

'To do what?' said Nick, looking down to the marquee and seeing Emily sitting at her desk, on the phone.

'To make it look like this RadLand group is after them. A diversion tactic to take the heat off.'

Nick groaned and rubbed his face. 'No, no, that's not on...they only told me and I've not told anyone else...so they've gained nothing by the deception, other than to trick me. No. That's all bollocks. Also Emily is big giant computer brain as it turns out. I totally believe she could do the hacking. She's currently looking at my laptop, to find out how it wiped the IA message board.' He explained what she'd said about IP addresses.

'Bloody hell, she's a proper Pointdexter. But you've forgotten one thing, fella.'

'What?'

'She's looking under the bonnet of your laptop, that means she'll find out what you've been looking at.'

'So what? She's not interested in news about the Boro's transfer targets, I'm sure.'

Jeff cocked his head on one side and pulled a crazy face. 'No, no, no, my pretty...I was thinking of something more X-Rated even than the Boro. The small matter of a chap's hand exercise inspiration.'

'Oh. That. That's all cool. I'm not bothered about that.'

'But she'll shop you to Jules just to embarrass you, even if she's not fazed by whatever sick perversion you've been scrutinizing.'

'It's cool, because I don't look at porn, Jeff. I've told you this before. You might not believe me and I might be the only man on earth with a computer who doesn't, but I don't. I've seen it in the past on exactly two occasions, both times prompted by women to do so and it makes me feel really uncomfortable. I don't like it aesthetically or politically. Thus, there's nowt for Em to find.'

'You liked that *Emmanuelle* film we saw at the Classic cinema when we were 16. That was porn.'

'I was 16, Jeff. I'd never even seen a naked woman in real life. We thought page three in the *Sun* was exciting. So of course I liked it. Doesn't make it right. Mind, it was tame soft porn by internet standards, I'm sure.'

'Oh, aye. No bodily fluids spilt.'

'See, I just can't understand why anyone would want to witness that. I'm really squeamish about it. I feel awkward seeing blokes naked in the locker room at the sports club, let alone having it off on my computer screen. What's the attraction in watching that? And anyway, the physical act - the in and out thing - it's not much to look at, is it? It's 90 per cent how it feels, not how it looks. It's not like watching a Pink Floyd mind-blowing laser show or something. To be honest, sometimes I feel sorry for women even having to endure it.'

'God, you don't half overthink things, you do, son. Jules would tell you just the same. I'm surprised you can even bring yourself to do it with her, if you feel like that. I think your aversion to heterosexual porn is because you're afraid you're gay. That's it.'

Nick laughed. 'Am I? Maybe I am. I did once share a bed with a gay bloke when I was 17 when we stayed over at a mate's house - didn't know he was gay at the time. He started talking dirty to us.'

'Ha, ha, ha...what did you do?'

'I'd had eight pints of Theakston's Best Bitter so I did what any 17-year-old boy would do, I passed out in a stupor before anything happened.'

'Would you have given it a go?'

'Maybe, just to see what it was like, but alcohol robbed me of my big gay chance.'

'Who amongst us has not said that? At least if you have it off with a bloke, you're with someone who is familiar with all the equipment. An expert, really. Most 17 year old lasses wouldn't have known what was what, back then.'

'Hmm, well, I think Jules did. She got an A in Biology.'

Jeff shook his head. 'Well, with this no porn stance, it just proves that you're definitely some sort of exotic Buddhist monk, you. A life of denial and abstinence. You'll let me know when you see God, won't you?'

'I sure will. I bet she's a groovy chick.'

'Aye. If God doesn't look like Grace Slick in 1968, or Stevie Nicks in 1981 - with the top hat, mind - I shall be very disappointed.'

'You and me both, sunshine.'

Nick was hungry again after the physical exercise and went up to the food truck, got them two cheeseburgers, sans the bun. He handed it to Jeff wrapped in a napkin.

'Thanks man. Listen, I remember a while ago, you said that there was some confusion between using a singular and a plural on Anarchists. The bomb threat was singular and so was the first email to Mel. But the IAs themselves call it by the plural...'

'...yeah? So what? Mike thought there was nothing to that.'

'Well, maybe the singular is one group and the plural is another. There are different groups saying different things. One lot spells it wrong, one spells it right,' said Jeff, devouring the burger in three bites.

Nick finished his more slowly. 'Yeah. One of those emails was littered with bad spelling actually, but I'm not sure where it takes us, other than to say that whoever wrote it can't spell.'

'Which rules out Mike or Emily, doesn't it? You'd know if they couldn't spell, because you've worked with both of them.'

'Actually, that's a great point, man.'

Jeff rolled his eyes up into his head, leaving only whites showing and held his hands out in front of him like a blind man.

'I see things, no-one else sees,' he said in a mock horror movie voice. Nick laughed and turned to look at the marquee again. Simon Garbutt was walking out of it, his stick-like long legs eating ground up, his body seemingly balanced on top.

'That bloke is such a physical freak,' he said.

Jeff turned around to look and as he did so, some gears dropped in Nick's brain, the machinery of recollection whirred in his subconscious and spat out a memory.

'Jeff! Fucking hell!'

'What? You've not got the shits, have you? You'll never get from here to the Portaloos in time.'

'No, man...when we met Simon Garbutt down by the acoustic stage the other day, he mentioned the Ironopolis Anarchist, remember? Anarchist - singular, not plural. He'd just offered me that job in Australia so I didn't think of it at the time. The only other times we've heard the singular were the bomb hoax call and the email to Mel after that. Ever since, it's been Anarchists.'

'Garbutt? He's not got the balls for that. He's a London Wanker, not a London Bomber,' said Jeff.

'Where does he stay when he's up here?'

'The Teesside International Hotel. Nice and handy for the festival site. It's what, two miles away?'

'And where does he live in London?'

Jeff took out his phone and looked at the address book. 'Mount Street in Mayfair, right by the Connaught Hotel. He's got a big flat there.'

'Have you been in it?'

'I stayed over once. The Fish was doing those warm-up dates, before his last big tour. I said I'd go down and pretend to laugh at him. Not that it was necessary, he killed it. People were rolling in the aisles, not that there are aisles in a comedy club...Garbutt wasn't there, though, El Fishio had the keys.'

'Right, come on.' He tugged at Jeff's sleeve and ran over to Emily's desk.

'Em? You know Jeff, right?'

'Of course. Hiya.' Jeff doffed an imaginary cap.

'Those IP addresses that the posts to the IA message board where made from, you said they were made in London and on Teesside. Can you show me where?'

'I can indeed.' Her delicate fingers tapped at speed on the keyboard and she brought up a Google map with three red flags on it. 'The London one is along this street...it says 71, but it could be either side of that...in fact, it could be in the hotel. Like I said before, it's probably a mobile device that's just been used there and anyone can stay in a hotel, can't they? ' She tapped her nail on the screen on the words *Mount Street* and the Connaught Hotel. Nick looked at Jeff and flashed his eyes wide. 'The Teesside ones are here and here.' She pointed to one in Stockton. 'Again, these are mobile devices. This one seems to have been used in Ropner Park, and this one somewhere out in the countryside, west of here, possibly in a lay-by or again, at this hotel. That's a big posh one as well, isn't it?'

It all made sense to Nick. Ropner Park was where Angie said her ex, David Murray took the kids. The rural one was 80 metres from the Teesside International Hotel. Home to Simon Garbutt when he was up here. Excitement rose in his throat. This was the break they'd needed. He was sure.

'Are you alright? You've gone pink,' said Emily, amused. 'I'm still working on your laptop, in between doing festival work. I think you downloaded a very sophisticated trojan and that's what's done it. Has your computer been running slowly?'

'Yes, sometimes.'

She nodded. 'That'll be it. It's basically gone to the IA board logged in and deleted everything, probably in the middle of the night when you weren't using it.'

'A Trojan was a popular contraceptive when we were kids in the 70s,' said Jeff. 'I always thought they should've made an out-sized one called the Trojan Horse.' He spread his arms wide as though delivering a joke on stage to an audience. 'Come on...that's better than any of Le Grande Poisson gags.'

Emily giggled. 'You've got comedy genes, Jeff.'

He pulled at his jeans. 'Aye, I know. They don't fit us very well, like. I was a fat get, y'see, Em, and I still have the fat get's wardrobe.' She giggled again, but Nick was mulling this information over, staring into the middle distance.

'Come on, Jeff...thanks, Emily...see you in a bit.'

He tugged at Jeff's shirt and led him towards the back of the marquee, past rows of people on phones, looking at spread sheets and photographs, adding up numbers, talking animatedly, having arguments and laughing, to where Julie was working on the phone.

'I bloody love that Emily,' whispered Jeff into his ear. 'She's got the flattering laugh.'

'Eh? The what?'

'The flattering laugh. One of those laughs that feels like she's really much more entertained by your jokes than she probably really is. I love that. Makes an old man feel good. Are you sure you didn't accidentally take any photos of her naked?'

'Shut up, man,' he said, as they were in earshot of Julie who had just finished a call. She looked up at them with her arched eyebrows.

'Yes? I'm busy. Very busy. It's alright for some lolling around eating and having a laugh,' she said, giving them a stern glare.

'Jules, listen. I'm onto something, right?' He explained about the IP addresses and Garbutt.

'It's a good start but we need proper evidence, though. Like Emily says, anyone can use a mobile device in a hotel. Just because he's been near those locations doesn't mean anything.'

'In fairness, I've been near each of those locations myself in the last few weeks,' said Jeff. 'When I think about it, like. So if you want to prove it is Garbutt, you need something more concrete. You said there were spelling errors in the email - what were they again?'

'Blakeston was spelled without the "e" and Teesside with only one "s" - which is bloody criminal,' said Nick.

Jeff raised a finger, 'And, think about it, not a mistake many from this region would make. It annoys the hell out of all of us. But it is the sort of mistake a London Wanker *would* make.'

Nick pointed to him. 'Good thinking. So we need Garbutt to write those words down and see if he makes the mistakes.'

'Leave that to me, I'll try and sort it, now,' said Jeff. 'I'll catch you later.' He marched off, flicking his hair over his shoulder and waving at Emily as he left the marquee.

'Go and get us some coffee and a bottle of water will you, luv,' said Julie. 'I'm parched and busier than a very busy thing.'

He wandered up to the catering truck and took a look around. The site was all but done and ready to go. It was hugely impressive and almost impossible to believe none of it had existed a few weeks ago. It was as though a village had been built up from scratch. He felt proud to have played a part in it and, bombs or no bombs, was still looking forward to the music starting. As he stood in a queue at the catering van he could see Jeff in the distance talking to someone. It wasn't Garbutt. Jeff knew everyone, everyone knew Jeff. He was so distinctive, even after having lost 75 pounds, that he couldn't walk far across the site without someone stopping him to talk.

It was hard to see what even the most twisted mind could have against this celebration of the blues in all its many forms. It was a music that was all about the resilience of the human spirit in the face of the trials and tribulations that life brings. It was about emotion and belief and even faith. In essence the blues spoke of what it was to be a human being. Why would anyone be against that? He let out a low, internal moan. Not for the first time, it was both disappointing and wonderful to be a human, all at the same time.

He turned to look at the Georgian farm house. The scar where the bomb had gone off was still wrapped in plastic sheeting to protect it from the elements. No. It wasn't about blowing up the festival or the house. It can't have been. It was surely a symbolic act, not a literal one. Someone was making a point about something. Jeff was shaking hands with someone else now. A blonde guy who looked annoyingly familiar. He took a few paces nearer to get a better look at him, then walked back with Julie's coffee and water. Emily looked up and winked at him extravagantly as he went past. The admin tent was buzzing, with phones ringing and the low chatter of people sorting stuff out.

As he sat down, as his brain was prone to do, it suddenly belched out a clear thought, apropos of nothing, as if it had been working on something without his knowledge. An exclamation came out of his mouth. Julie looked at him, surprised.

'Have you got wind or something?'

'Can you find Angie's ex, David Murray, on Facebook?'

She did so. 'There you go. Why do you want to see him again?'

'That's who it was that I've just seen with Jeff. He's here now. I couldn't place him. But it's definitely not the bloke who was in the Ford Ka that we thought was trailing us. That's a relief. Garbutt's partner following us was freaking me out. I'm just too bloody paranoid.'

'When you think about that IP thing, it'd mean Garbutt would be involved in bombing a festival that he's set to make loads of money from, wouldn't it? I don't think he'd do that, so I think this IP business is a distraction or at least, it isn't him.'

Nick sat back, arms folded, sucking on his bottom lip, deep in contemplation, rolling different combinations of events over in his mind, whilst she went back to work. What he was struggling with was the fact that killing people with a bomb was a huge deal and only crazy people did it, people really dedicated to a political or religious cause. Greedy, rich people didn't do it, landowners didn't, anyone with anything to lose didn't. Why would you? Even though capitalist protesters had form for kicking off, destroying shops and having rucks with the police, they weren't big on bombs and certainly not on bombs that would only kill students. It left no-one credible to plant that bomb, so that could only mean one thing; it wasn't meant to be planted at all.

Everyone involved in this had been so busy suspecting each other of being some kind of terrorist, that the fact that it was all some sort of accident had been overlooked. Trying to work out who wanted to kill whom, was a total distraction, more important was to work out who wanted to look like a violent terrorist, not who actually *was* a violent terrorist. When you considered that things became more clear. Yes. Yes they did. Much more clear.

'Penny for your thoughts,' said Julie, sitting back, turning off her screen for a minute and taking the lid off her coffee.

'The more I think about this, the more I'm convinced that the bomb went off accidentally. We said ages ago that it was at a time when there were the least people there, it was in place where it did less damage than it might have done almost anywhere else and it killed people who were innocent students. It turned everyone into one big unified team that would not be beaten down by an act like this. That can't have been the objective. A proper terrorist crazy would want to kill as many as possible. We realised that soon after it went off, but we've got distracted from the fact.'

They sat amidst the comings and goings, just thinking.

'How about this as an idea?' said Julie, doodling on a bit of paper. 'It wasn't either IA or RadLand. It was someone who wanted to paint *both* of those groups in a bad light. They wanted both to appear guilty, so they set up the second board as a home for loony ravings, knowing it would get hacked or even encouraging it to be hacked and that the word would get out that IA was to blame. Then they called in claiming responsibility for the IAs knowing, not just that they hadn't done it, but that the IAs would think RadLand was to blame because they'd been working on them. They had tried to frame them using their money and power. In actual fact, like you said after meeting Champagne Charlie in Louth, RadLand is innocent. IA is innocent. It's all the work of a third party.'

Nick sat back and looked at her and began to clap. People looked around at him.

'That's brilliant Jules. That explains it. Emily said the hole through which she hacked the server was "huge". It's like they left it for someone like her to find, just as you said. But who's the third party?'

As she spoke, the slight figure of Emily Davids approached the desk, cocked her head at them, apologetically.

'Hi...hi there guys, I'm sorry to interrupt...but I thought you should know this as soon as I dug it out.'

'What is it, Em?' he said.

'You know I said it was a trojan that removed all the info from that server? Well, I was right. But it was more complicated than that. Quite a beautiful bit of malware, really. When it had wiped the server, it sent an auto-email to Scotland Yard's anti-terrorism section, as though from the server, saying who had wiped it. An actual email which said the Ironopolis Server was deleted by Nick Guymer and it gave your home IP address. It is purporting to be a security feature of the server - a bit like how your computer can start its video, to film who's stolen it - it's kind of like that.'

'Hold on. That means they'll think I wiped a terrorist group's server. That's not a good thing, right?' said Nick.

'If I hadn't found it on your computer, it'd be a terrible thing because basically it looks like you're guilty of covering up terrorist activity. Fortunately I can prove you're not, if called upon to do so. Also, you didn't actually download the trojan, it was uploaded from a memory stick. Must have happened when you left it unattended - probably here, I'd think.'

'What? So someone just wandered along and stuck in a USB stick and uploaded it?' said Nick.

Emily nodded. 'I'm afraid so. Then it went about its malicious work.'

'Well it's a big relief that you found it, then,' said Julie. 'Thanks Emily.'

'No problem. One other thing though - it obviously means someone has really got it in for you. This was designed to frame you specifically and no-one else and given they uploaded the malware here, and everyone here has to have a pass of some sort...'

'...and I handle all the passes here...' said Julie, pointing at her computer.

'...you're looking at someone who works here trying to stitch you up. Not a nice thought.'

'Bastards,' said Nick, looking around at the seven or eight other people in the tent. Just because you're paranoid doesn't mean they're not out to get you.

His phone vibrated in his pocket, making him jump. Somehow the two things seemed related. He drank a bit of water to calm himself. It was Colin Harcombe.

'Nick. If you get a move on and go to Thistle Green station in Stockton, you can see Mike Trent there for 10 minutes. Be there by 5.30pm. Local plod isn't much involved in this. I've had a word. Said you're a good chap, etcetera. Seems there's a lot of...shall we say....complexity. Strictly, off the record, MI6 are in control.'

'MI6? Really? In control of Mike's arrest?'

'In a manner of speaking, yes. I shouldn't say any more. I haven't been fully briefed due to being on leave - but this is a big deal. Some top brass around. Bad business, terrorism. Can't be having it. Be careful Nick. Try not to hit anyone in the face too hard, unless you really have to, I know what you're like.' Pleased with this joke, he laughed his odd, mechanical laugh and rang off.

'Are you coming into town to the station? I'm meeting Mike there. They must be holding him in the cells. I assumed they'd have sent him to Durham or somewhere similar on remand.'

'I can't, man. I'm too busy. I've got to print all these passes off and laminate them. There's about 50. I'll be here for another hour or two at this rate.'

'Can I come?' said Emily, eagerly. 'I've never been in a police station.'

'I don't think that's a good idea, do you?' said Julie, scowling at her and dragging him away from her.

He leaned over and gave Julie a kiss on the cheek. 'You make your own way home in your car. Don't wait for me. I'll call you.'

'You can't. My battery is flat.'

'OK. See you Emily,' he said, striding out of the marquee.

'OK, Nick. Don't worry. It'll all be OK. I'll get it cleaned up.' She pointed to the laptop but was now talking to a girlfriend she hung out with on site. He put his thumb up, his brain allowing him to see her standing there naked. Lovely.

'Well, this is a weird situation, Mike,' he said, as his accountant came into a small, windowless room at the police station. He shut the door behind him. 'Are we being left alone? I assumed there'd be a guard on the door to stop you making a run for it, not that you could get far, I suppose.'

Mike looked at his watch. 'I don't have a lot of time, Nick. What did you need to see me about?'

Nick looked sideways at him. 'You don't have a lot of time. Why? Are they sending you to a jail?'

He ignored the question. 'What did you want to talk to me about?'

'After you came to see me, we've been doing a bit of digging around and we think it's not your lot who did and it's not RadLand either.'

'So who is it, then?' His stare was hard and unforgiving. Then again, if you were looking at the rest of your natural life in jail it'd focus your attention a bit.

'Ah, we're not sure. We don't know for sure. But the crucial thing is, I don't think the bomb was deliberate. It wasn't exploded on purpose. It was to be used to scare, not to kill. So we're not dealing with killers, not with loony terrorists, but someone who was going to use the bombs to extort money, maybe, or for some other reason. When the bomb went off, the demands that were made were done as though they were the Ironopolis Anarchists, but I don't think that's anything to do with what they really wanted. They were making the best of a bad job at that point, so they tried to paint your lot as nutters, hence the addition of an animal rights element. Then they set up a second message board and posted incendiary things on it to back that up. They left a big loophole so it could easily be hacked from information in the emails they sent. And that's what Emily did.'

'Woah, woah, you're going too fast. So you're saying it's nothing to do with IA or with RadLand?'

'Nope. It's the only theory that works, Mike. But I think whoever it is, works on the festival site or has regular access to it.' He told him about the uploaded malware and server.

'Look...Nick...I haven't been arrested. I'm not here under arrest.'

Nick looked at him squarely. 'You've not been...I don't get it.'

'I'm not authorized to tell you much. The only reason you're here, is because of DCI Harcombe's call. I'm not under arrest, we just want it to look like I am.'

'Who's we?'

'MI6.' He licked his lips and looked up from the table. 'I'm working for MI6. I have been for most of this year.'

Nick felt like looking for hidden cameras. It was a joke, surely.

'So you're a spy? Really, Mike? Bloody hell, was accountancy getting a bit dull?'

'There's no time to go into details. Everything you've said is very interesting and it will be important information for the team to collate. I'll ask you to write it all down before you leave. The problem is now a little more pressing. They've just got intelligence that there are three more bombs going to be brought onto the site or created on the site. They might even be on site now. They might even have been there since the start of construction.'

'How do you know this?'

'MI6 have just found who supplied the detonators used on the first bomb. It was really unusual, sourced from the Ukraine. It was a known dealer in London. He sold four. One has been used, there are three more. These are probably small explosive devices. We have to find them.'

'Why is this happening? What do they want?'

'We don't know. It's a total mystery. Our best guess is to blackmail Stevie Salmon. I've been arrested to try to take IA out of the equation. Maybe it'll stop them because it proves I'm not the bomber if another goes off when I'm in custody. It's a desperate move to try and get them to make a mistake. I think the malware uploaded to your computer might be a late attempt to make you appear involved.' He chewed at his beard. 'The three remaining devices, if they've been made, might just go off any time and anywhere. There could be carnage at the festival. It doesn't bear thinking about. We've got to find those detonators or the explosives or both. There's going to be a big security sweep this evening and again in the morning, before the gates are opened.'

Nick nodded. They went quiet for a few seconds. 'I still can't quite believe you're up to your neck in all this, Mike.'

'Neither can I. I'm looking forward to getting back to the day job. Doing VAT returns suddenly looks like a nice, easy lifestyle. I'm sorry...when I came to your house, I felt you were involved. It all made sense to me. I know now you weren't. I should have trusted you.'

'Yes, you bloody should, and you should've taken notice of me when I said that the use of the plural and singular of the word "Anarchist" is really important.'

'You've talked about that before, but I can't see how it's significant. Does one letter "s" make such a difference?'

'We'll soon know, Mike. We'll soon know.'

Nick returned to the festival site. It was winding down for the day. Roadies and PA people milled around the main stage. Someone played a bit of guitar very loud: the riff from Van Halen's 'Unchained'. Drums were hit. Microphones spoken into. The gates were due to open at 9.30am. It all had to be ready. It was profoundly sinister to think that somewhere here there were three explosive devices. What the hell would happen? How were they going to handle this? Surely if they didn't find them they had to call off the festival? They couldn't risk it. Even if it'd look like terrorism had won. Hopefully, the security sweep would uncover the devices or the important component parts of them.

The admin tent was deserted, except for one of the three hairies, who was looking at a computer.

'Alright, Nick?' he said, looking up. 'You looking for your Jules?'

'Aye. Have you seen her?'

'She's away home, mate. Left about 10 minutes ago. Jeff's gone as well.'

'OK, cool. All set for the big day tomorrow?'

'All set, man. Something will go wrong though. It always does. These gigs are always about damage limitation, once they kick off.'

Not literally, hopefully. He nodded and made his way to the car park. Might as well get off home too. Emily must have split as well.

He'd just got to the BMW when there was a voice in the distance shouting. He ignored it. Probably Mel bawling at some one for doing something wrong. Then there was a piercing scream. He stood and looked around. Emily Davids was sprinting towards him, coming from Mel's office tent. A few paces behind her was Mel himself - unable to keep up. She was screaming his name. What the fuck?

He ran towards her. 'What is it? What is it?' he shouted. 'What's wrong?'

'There's a bomb!!' She let the words out between gasps of air.

'What?! Where?'

'It's in Julie's bag...' She came to a halt, hands on her leg, panting. 'I just...I just hacked it...another auto-email to Scotland Yard from your computer...she's gone...she's carrying a bomb...it's a set up...no time to explain.'

Mel came up behind her...he spat out a huge gob of saliva. 'She's not answering her phone. Must have it turned off.'

'The battery is flat. She just said earlier.'

'We've got to find her! Where was she going? Think, man!' Mel shouted. Nick's brain froze in shock.

'Just...err...just going home...I think. Em - this bomb - is it going to explode? Is it a hoax? What is it?'

'It's real. It's going to go off soon. Like, really, really soon! They're trying to make it look like you're the bomber. Get going, Nick! Find her!'

CHAPTER 16

'We'll go in my jeep', said Mel. 'You take the route you'd normally take to Yarm...Darlo Back Lane, Yarm Back Lane, right?'

'Yeah, yeah.'

'We'll go via Stockton High Street in case she's stopped off there. Right. Get fuckin' gannin'!!'

Hands pouring with sweat and his mind racing to make sense of this information, he floored the accelerator on the BMW; turned off Darlington Back Lane, screeched the tyres down Yarm Back Lane and headed east on the A66. Pedal to the fucking metal now. The old lumbering beast of a car did its best, shuddering at 90mph just as he reached the A135 turn off for Yarm. He braked hard at the roundabout and took a right, screeching past the Premier Inn. She couldn't be far away. Desperate to see any blue car, every vehicle seemed to be silver or white or black. Nothing. Get out of the fucking way! There was no room to overtake, the traffic relentless as he went through Eaglescliffe at a steady 28 mph, his heart racing. Past the Bluebell, over the bridge crossing the Tees and curving left into Yarm High Street. Where the fuck was she? Had she gone somewhere else? No. She always goes straight home...maybe not this time...where was she? Where? 'Come on, Jules. Come on...where are you?' His mind was burning up in a desperate panic.

His eyes scoped the dozens of cars in his vision, for one that looked familiar. C'mon Jules....c'mon darlin', c'mon, where are you? Where are you? It felt like if he only thought about her hard enough, he could transmit a signal to her brain. She was near. He was sure she was near. Rows of parked cars, but no old Peugeot 206. She must be at home.

There it was.

Parked up on the cobbles.

She'd stopped to get some shopping. It was Thursday. Late night shopping. She'd have her bag with her. Oh, fucking hell. She was in a shop or a supermarket. He flung the car up onto the pavement with people shouting at him and blaring horns and ran towards the Peugeot trying to work out where she was. He stood, sweat running down his face looking around frantically. Where was she? What was she doing? They'd just done a big shop, they didn't need food. They didn't buy anything else, they were so skint, there was no money for anything else.

Where? Fucking where? 'Juuuulllieee!!!' He screamed her name as loudly as he could looking around him, rotating in a circle. Shouting and shouting it again. Some people looked at him, probably thinking he was a drunk. He tried to keep calm, tried to keep on top of his panic as he scanned up and down the High Street. There was a screech of tyres further up the High Street and a slamming of car doors. It was Mel and Emily.

Then he saw her. There! In burst of painful recognition, he saw the long loose curl of her hair. His heart shot up into his throat with a painful urgency. She was in the jewellery shop. She was picking up their wedding rings. Of course she was. He sprinted faster than his feet had ever moved, charging into the small store. The shop assistant screamed as he dashed in, clearly thinking it was a robbery of some sort.

'Your bag. Where is it?!' he yelled. She looked back at him not comprehending, her eyes wild and confused.

'Where is it?!' he yelled again, looking around the shop. It wasn't on her shoulder or on the counter. She raised her hand and pointed to the car. As she did so, there was a loud explosion and the sound of shattering glass.

Out of sheer reflexive instinct he jumped on Julie, knocking her down to the floor, covering her with his body to protect her from the fragments of window glass that exploded into a rainstorm of lethal shards. Outside, the old Peugeot was engulfed in flames, a tower of orange fire and black smoke reaching fingers into the summer sky. Alarms, sirens and car horns droning made a cacophonous soundtrack to the scene of devastation. It was appalling and yet as he lay there, sweat running in streams down his face onto the back of Julie's head, he felt nothing but relief. She was alive.

Now there were only two detonators left.

'Yeah?' said Nick, into his phone, looking bleary-eyed at his bedside clock. It was 5.58am.

'Nick. It's Mel.'

'Alright, mate...what's going on? Are we starting a festival today or not?'

'Good news. First, we've just got the OK to go ahead today. The official line is that it was a faulty fuel pump on the car that sparked the explosion. Right? No retreat, no surrender, that's the MI6 line. They're doing a sweep of the whole place now and...'

'...she's fine thanks, Mel,' he said, interrupting the Geordie, turning to look at Julie, lying next to him, still fast asleep, her jaw slack, a thin crust of drool in the corner of her mouth.

'Eh? Oh aye. I knew she would be. She's as tough as a donkey's cock, that one.'

'Is that especially tough, like?'

'Listen smart arse, I'm telling you something important. They've found another detonator.'

'Really? Shit. Where was it?'

'Portaloo number 33. Taped in the cistern. So they're going through the rest to try and find the last one. These bomber twats can't do anything without the detonators. It'd be nice if we found the explosive as well, mind. So, I need youse two in as agreed at 8.00am, might as well get up now and put the kettle on for your missus. You've just got time for a quick shag as long as you don't waste time on foreplay, then get in here. We're ready to rock 'n' fucking roll.'

Julie, eyes closed, said, 'Trust me, the first part of that sentence is not going to happen.'

It had dawned cloudless with a little low mist drifting across the fields around the farmhouse. As Nick walked the perimeter of the field, stopping to smell a wild rose in the hedgerow, it couldn't have been a better morning to have a blues festival. He was excited at the thought of the it finally getting under way, but also scared shitless about the possibility of another explosion. He climbed onto a fence and looked towards the Cleveland Hills and caught himself whistling. His blues were still being held at arms length by the pills and better still, he hadn't had a proper depressive episode for about two months. And now, bombs or no bombs, he was whistling. In the same way that the occasional good night out couldn't cure a depressive of their depression, something terrible happening couldn't just make you depressed when you were not depressive. As bad as yesterday had been, he still felt strong.

Slowly but surely, it felt that he was climbing out of the mental hole he'd lived in since his teenage years. He'd thought change wasn't possible, indeed for most of that time he'd never even entertained the fact that change was even necessary. Even the times when he did want to be different, he'd assumed the way he was, was the way he was; that it was set and you just had to live with that setting. But it hadn't been true and god knows, he wished he'd found that out much earlier in life.

The most remarkable thing about not being depressed and not having the blues, not having that deep hollow ache inside, was that it was utterly unremarkable. He'd sometimes fantasised about being happy and wondered what that was really like. He'd managed it in short glimpses only. But now, with the aid of the Phenibut he just felt normal. Not woo-woo happy, not sad or down. Just on an even keel. Sane, even. It was both strange and yet not strange at all.

'I'll really miss that Peugeot, y'know,' said Julie, as he drove them to the festival site for an 8.00am start. 'I nursed it through 15 years of trouble and strife. I'm only glad I didn't bother servicing it earlier this month when it badly needed doing.'

'No. That would have been a right waste of time, wouldn't it? Still, you can enjoy getting a replacement car with the insurance money. What do you fancy?'

'I've been thinking. This old Beamer is a workhorse. We can keep this going for 10 years more yet. BMW's go on forever. There are plenty on the road over 30 years old.'

'Well, if you can keep servicing it and healing its broken bits, I'll keep on driving it. Don't understand the obsession with new cars. Get one that works and stick with it. That's my policy.'

'If this is the work horse, we should get something more fun. How do you fancy getting an old Porsche?'

He burst out laughing. 'Yeah, right.'

'I'm serious. I can probably pick up a totally shagged-out mid 1970s 911 for a few grand. It'd have to be post 1975, anything before that will be rusted to buggery.'

'What, so you mean you buy something that basically doesn't work and then do it up?'

'Yeah. I can beg, borrow or steal parts from Sid's garage in Hardwick. If I get the book and do some online research I can get it roadworthy. I've always fancied one and the old ones are way cooler than the new ones anyway. We'd probably not do any long distances, it'd just be for tooling around Teesside and going up into the Dales.'

'OK, man, if the insurance money covers it, then you do what you want.'

'Well, I got that Peugeot when I was a young thrusting career girl who thought she was sensible. Now I'm hooked up with a nutter, I've no job, no money, no pension and no prospects and someone is trying to blow me up and make us look like terrorists. Happy days, eh.'

'An ideal time to get yourself an impractical sports car.'

'I think so. You've de-sensibled me, Guymer, or rendered me senseless, one of the two.'

'Much like what your holiday underwear and broccoli farts have done to me.'

She laughed and patted him on the leg.

They were both wearing their bright lime green festival t-shirts, issued earlier that week so all workers could spot each other.

'Fluorescent lime green suits you, Jules. It works with blonde hair and faded blue jeans.'

'At least they gave me a women's tee and not some huge tent-like thing. It ain't your colour though, kid. Gives you a pukey pallor.'

'I know. Mam always said I suited green, but I don't think she meant this sort of green.'

'Just as well it's not a fashion show then...eeee god, the traffic is bad already.'

It was starting to build up as they got near the site. They turned into a specially designated staff gateway which had six security guards on the gate, along with several soldiers within shooting distance. They showed their photo ID while their car and bags were given a rigorous once over, with an Alsatian sniffer dog given free run at it. Once clear they parked up near the house.

Nick looked around. The early arrivals were already in front of the main stage, the campsite in the distance had a rainbow of tents being pitched in the field and cars parked in long ranks. It was happening. Just as planned. The directions, the signs, all the of the instructions. They were all being used. It was fucking on. Nick gripped his hands into a fist. It felt like a win.

He looked at Julie excitedly, she looked back with bright turquoise eyes. 'I'd better get to my desk and make sure I'm up to date with everything and get all those backstage passes ready. I'm set for a day meeting rock stars. Ace!'

'I'm going to take some photos around the place and pump up some social media content with them and then I'll go and find Jeff to see if he needs any muscle.' He grabbed her around the waist and pulled her into him, kissing her full on the lips. 'I shall see you later, wife-to-be.'

'Ha ha...alright, hubby-in-waiting.'

At 8.30am there was one final big meeting held in another marquee which was to be used as a green room for bands and hangers on to eat and drink in. A bar was still being constructed as all of the main admin staff sat around in a circle. Mel Stephens, resplendent in a half-mast, white boiler suit, red 20 eye lace-up Doc Martens and an acid green bandana, marched in, arms aloft.

'People! I bring great news! The last security sweep has found the missing detonator in Portaloo 187. We are now officially 100 per cent bomb free!! Get in!!'

Everyone cheered and followed his lead in applauding. What a bloody relief. The exhalation of air was palpable. Everyone looked at each other with a shared feeling of total relief. Thank god. Now they could properly relax and enjoy it.

'Now, I won't keep youse long. I know you've all still got work to do. First thing is, I just want to thank each and every one of you for a magnificent bloody effort these past weeks.' He pointed a finger at them, turning in a circle around the table. 'Best fucking team anyone could want. The best of British right here in this room.' His pink face glowed, as he pointed with both index fingers at the ground. 'The way you've stayed on board, no matter what shit has been thrown at us, has made me bastard, fucking proud. Youse have grafted on in the face of adversity. No backing down...but it's not over yet. So we keep on keeping on, so we make sure we deliver the best fucking festival anyone has ever delivered. Right?!'

'Right!' chorused everyone.

'I can tell you that there will be undercover security here all weekend. I don't know who they are. No-one knows. They'll come in with regular ticket holders. However, this man here to my right who I know some of you have already encountered, is Harry Lee. He's from...actually I don't know where he's from. Where are you from Harry?'

He turned to a tall, broad, balding blonde man in his late 40s.

'MI6,' he said with a flat smile.

'MI fucking 6? Shouldn't that be a secret?'

'If it had to be, I'd not have told you, Mel.'

Mel Stephens laughed. 'Smart arse. Alright. So, as you probably know, Harry here is de facto head of security. We've got the private contractors, Northern Power, on the ground for muscle, and we've got stewards and we've got regular plod here as well as the undercover boys...and now we've got the fucking Durham Light Infantry, or whoever the fuck the army lads are.'

'...and girls,' interrupted Julie, pointing at him.

'Aye, aye, and girls - or should I call them wimmin', Rosa fucking Luxembourg?' He said it with a big smile on his face.

'What do you know about Rosa bloody Luxembourg?' laughed Julie.

'Never you bloody mind, I know enough. I'm only surprised Hartlepool United haven't sent some of their fucking psychotic defenders to kick the shit out of would-be terrorists as well. Harry knows everything security related. He's co-ordinating it all from a desk in the big tent. If you have any suspicions about anything that might be a security risk, anything at all, let him know. No complacency. He'll give you all his contact numbers. Call him any time of the night or day. He's Robocop, he doesn't sleep. Do you want to say anything, Harry?'

The MI6 man stood up and held his arms out wide.

'Just a quick word. Go about your business as you would normally. As Mel said, we've found the detonators and there is no way anyone could bring explosives onto this site now. There were none here this morning and it is literally impossible to get any in. So we're clear. But as Mel says, anything at all suspicious, come to me or any security or police officer. Despite finding the detonators, we will still be on the look out for unusual packages.'

Mel Stephens stood up again, having re-lit his cigar and jammed it into the corner of his mouth. 'OK. You heard the man. Now, remember, those of you who are team leaders in this operation, make sure you're always available and that all your people can get hold of you at any time. Don't be a smart arse and try to sort something out that you know you can't sort out, communicate with each other at all times, help each other out and come and get me if you absolutely bloody well have to.'

He went around the table reminding everyone of their duties, pointing at them each in turn with thick forefinger, full of energy, excitement and humour.

'Nick and Emily, please make sure we're knocking endless shite out on social media all day long. I say that, like I even know what social media is. You do. Make sure everyone knows what is going on and make it interesting. The Three Hairies - you guys make sure your labour is sober at all times. I don't want stage hold ups because we're a few men light due to someone being pissed. Don't look at us like that. I know you're professionals, I'm just reminding you to keep on top of the drinking. Jeff. Your mob is important. Keep the bands happy as they arrive, get them to where they need to be efficiently and give yourself enough time to get them from the green room to the stage. If we lose eight minutes on every band, we'll overrun by an hour and incur a shit load of fines - remember that. Matty - stage security - I don't want groupies noshing the fucking bands or roadies backstage or anywhere else. That shit is old. No call for it in this day and age. They've got all day, every day to release bodily fluids into strangers. So for the short time they're on duty at my festival, everyone behaves properly. Got me? And I want the whole backstage area as clean as a nun's bra. Make sure it is. No vomiting, no sex, no nudity, no pissing. We don't want it, so come down hard on anyone who steps over the line. Jules. Make sure everyone has all their correct passes, right? That's going to be your main job, that and not getting fucking blown up.'

There was a loud laugh at that one. Gallows humour, very bloody northern. Strong. The vibe was positive and upbeat. After the last team member had been reminded of their duties, he said,

'Right. Remember to wear your lime green festival t-shirts at all times. I know most of you look shit in them, but it's important we can all see each other and let's face it, no other fuckers will be wearing lime green t-shirts. I'll shut the fuck up now. One last thing. This is important. Have a bloody good time. Enjoy yourselves. You're getting paid to put on a music festival. This Is A Good Thing! A good thing for you and me and the punters and for humanity! Yes?! It stands against all that terrorist bullshit. So don't forget to boooogie!! Now get out there and make this bloody thing happen youse bunch of ugly, fucking gets!!!'

He punched the air and clapped his hands above his head. Everyone followed his lead, whooping.

As they dispersed, Julie pushed her sunglasses onto the top of her head and turned to Nick.

'He does a good speech, doesn't he? I got proper goosebumps there.'

'Aye. I nearly fucking cried. Top-notch boss to work for. No-one wants to let him down. All for one. No elites. Everyone working for everyone else. This is how it should be in life. I bloody love it.'

They hi-fived.

He got a coffee from the staff catering truck and began taking photos. As he did so, a small two-man helicopter came into view from the south, setting down on the far side of the house beyond the stables. A helipad had been marked out for ferrying in people who would only travel by helicopter. Security guards and sniffer dogs searched every arrival.

There was a great buzz of excitement about the place. A big centrally located clock said it was just 8.45am. The first band wasn't on until noon, but already the PA system on the main stage was cranking out music for the first arrivals. Jonny Lang's *Lie To Me* album. Superb. Smoke was already rising from some of the early starter food stalls, who had begun cooking up breakfast; the smell of hot fat drifted on the breeze, mingling with brewing coffee from the backstage catering truck. It was a village being populated right before your eyes; a temporary community springing up like a desert flower after rain. There was something almost biblical about it as people disgorged from cars or came on foot and wandered into the fields, looking around and taking it all in, sharing a cigarette or maybe something a little more herbal. It was an all new, fresh creation, a new birth, but one that would last just three days and then pass into folklore and the collective memory.

To create something like this from the ground up was a

testament to Mel Stephen's organisational and motivational skills as much as anything. As he zoomed past on some sort of electrically powered dune buggy that he was using to get around the site, Nick took a quick photo of him. He looked like something from a Freaks circus.

Another helicopter came in across the fields and landed behind the stables. Man, this was something. What a gig to happen on Teesside. He got a big prickle of excitement up his spine. Even the New Age wankers in yurts and people massaging chakras couldn't spoil it.

He leaned on a fence at the back of the main stage field and watched people come in and find a spot on which to spend the day. Some wanted to be near the stage, others were happy to just hang out around the outskirts.

'It's not bad, is it?' Nick turned around. Jeff was standing behind him, drinking coffee from a litre thermos mug. He raised his bushy eyebrows.

'It's bloody brilliant. Just to see it all coming together. And you know what I've liked so far...seeing people smiling and laughing as they go about the site. Y'know, just mates, friends and lovers mingling around, all up for the gig. It's just such a positive thing, isn't it? Music is such a beautiful thing, the way it draws us together.'

Jeff raised an eyebrow at him. 'Bloody hippy. They won't feel so happy when they use the bogs in 10 hours time.'

'Aye, but it's better than when we went to Knebworth to see Zeppelin, remember?'

'Ooof, using those bogs was like peering into the bowels of hell itself.'

'It was just a huge trench of effluent.'

'I assumed an awful lot of people opened their bowels because Chas and Dave were first on the bill,' said Jeff, laughing at the memory.

'I ended up pissing in a bottle. Using those toilets once was enough. No 18-year-old boy should have to witness such horrors.'

The helicopter that had just come over took off and took a flight path right over them, over the admin tent and out across the main stage heading back to the airport; which despite being awkwardly renamed in 2004, as the inappropriate and faintly ludicrous Durham Tees Valley Airport; would forever be known as Teesside Airport by the people in the area who actually used it, largely because it was on Teesside and it was an airport.

Nick went to the admin tent, waving at Julie in the far corner, laminating passes. He plonked himself down at the first desk he came to and began uploading photos to the festival Facebook page. He had just finished his first upload when Ian Bertram came striding over, all long hair and tanned, leathery face.

'Bertie! How goes it, man?' said Nick, extending his hand.

'Good, Nick. By god, this place is amazing.'

'It's all running like clockwork just now. How did you get here? The roads must be choc-a-block by now.'

'I just flew in by chopper. Big Fish has got his available at the airport. Only a two-man job, but very useful. The fucking band can come via road though. Ha, ha. We're not on until 8pm, so they've plenty of time yet. Mind, they virtually stripped me naked and put their hand up my arse. Talk about tight security.'

'Yeah, well, some bad shit has been going down. But the show must go on. I heard the crew doing sound checks yesterday, it all sounds really good and they've got a big screen with three cameras, so it'll all look really good.'

'Cool. I've got a positive feeling about this, especially as I'll be picking up an actual big bag of cash from Mr Salmon later.'

'He's still going ahead with that, despite everything?'

Bertie nodded. 'I spoke to him this morning. It's all set.' He rubbed his hands together.

'Not even bombs can get in the way of avoiding tax, I guess.'

'In this world, the money talks louder than anything, even louder than explosions. Right, I'd better go and press the flesh. I'll see you later, man.'

Nick took a photo of him for the Facebook page and uploaded

it. His previous posts were already attracting a lot of likes and comments. This was the modern currency of acceptance. Maybe it was a million miles wide and a millimetre deep, but you couldn't ignore it.

Emily soon came in her finest rock chick regalia, resplendent in a cropped Led Zeppelin t-shirt, pierced belly button, some skin-tight black leather-look leggings, an armful of silver bracelets and high-heeled boots. She began uploading pictures she'd taken of the food stands. Nick would've complimented her on how she looked, but didn't want Julie to overhear him.

'Wow, it's nice to see you and Julie, Nick. After yesterday. Bloody hell. I shit myself when I saw that email. But now everyone is having a great time,' she said. 'I'm so excited that we all made this happen. For all of the horrible things that have happened, it's still been the best thing I've ever been involved in.'

'Yeah. It is brilliant. Thanks for saving our lives, Emily. I don't think I've ever said that to anyone before.'

'That's alright Nicky boy. I can't have you being blown up, not before I've had my wicked way with you anyway. That'd be a waste of good meat.'

He pushed at her and laughed. Backstage, all through the administration areas and out into the fields, everyone was all smiles. The vibe was unmistakably positive.

The first band on were a local act called Trouble Is... Nick took some photos of them as they waited in the green room to be led by to the stage by Jeff and his team. They were nervous as hell.

The guitarist said, 'Bloody hell, it's packed out there.'

He was right. Both the main stage and the acoustic stage were now full to capacity and still there was a steady stream of traffic and people joining the throng. Julie came in with backstage lanyards for them all.

'You're supposed to wear these at all times, but you can take them off on stage. Nothing looks less rock 'n' roll than a laminated plastic card. Lanyards do not rock,' she said, handing them out to the band. They took them dutifully more like school boys than

Rock Gods.

The music kicked off right on time. Trouble Is... were nice and loud and though a bit clunky and occasionally out of key, got things off to a good start, with some people even doing something that might be not have been actual dancing, but which was certainly vigorous moving for so early in the day.

One band after another arrived by road or by helicopter, were shown into the green room, issued with their passes, fed and watered, led to the stage, played and then began the more important business of hanging out and having a good time.

It was amazing to see how all their plans and all the organisation clicked into place. Even Mel seemed pleased with how it was going. The whole place was scoured for explosives on an ongoing basis.

'I think everything is going to be alright y'know,' Nick said to Emily as they finished uploading some band reviews to social media.

'Yeah, I do as well. And you've not been arrested or blown up for wiping a terrorist message board by the security services, which is always good.' She laughed and drank from a coke can after pouring in a miniature of vodka.

'It's always good to not be arrested or be de-constructed via explosives. God, I'm really hungry again. Do you want anything?'

'Can I get a foot long?' she said, as she typed. 'Ha ha...sorry. That wasn't yet another plea for sexual intercourse.'

'Just as well. I can't manage a foot, Em. I don't think any man can.'

'Well bring me a nice fat beefy eight incher in a bun then...I know you can manage that.' She gave him a cheeky look, her tongue tip curved up to her top lip.

He scuffed her on the back of her head playfully. 'Wash your mouth out with soap, young lady.'

There was a long queue for food. As he waited Simon Garbutt walked past him, head down. He seemed to be talking to himself.

'Hey Simon!' said Nick, cheerfully. 'Isn't it brilliant?' He gestured around him.

'So, yeah, it's going well. Amazingly well.'

'Big Fish must be pleased. Is he compère on the acoustic stage?'

Garbutt nodded. 'He's actually going on the main stage in an hour. So, you don't want to miss what he's going to do.'

'Oh yeah, what's that?'

'Wait and see. You'll really not believe it. You really won't.' He laughed, shook his head as though genuinely astonished. 'Can't believe he agreed to it, really. I'll see you later then, Nick.'

Suddenly, a thought leaped into Nick's brain.

'Oh hey, mate, can you just write down the address of your company? I'll need to send in an invoice next week and I don't know the full address.' Nick took out one of his business cards and a pencil stub out of his back pocket.

'Sure. Between you and me, you can add a nought on if you like, Nick,' he said as he wrote. He winked and handed him the card and pencil back and strode away. 'See you in Australia.'

'Hey you,' said Julie, galloping up to him. 'Are you eating again?'

'Aye, I've got a tapeworm, I think,' he said, putting the card in his back pocket. 'I'm getting a foot long for me and Emily.' He held up hand. 'No jokes please, Miss Wells. Do you want one? They're all beef. Mostly anus and eyes, I think, of which I'm a big fan, especially yours.'

She wagged a finger at him and laughed. 'Don't be naughty. I haven't got time. I'll get something when I knock off. Hey, guess who I just sorted out with a press pass: Artie Taylor, the photographer from the plane. He's here with Kaz.'

'Ah, that's cool. Hopefully I'll see him backstage.'

'They'll be in the pit with all the other snappers and cameras. Man, he's so rock 'n' roll. I quite fancy him. In another life I'd have been all over his bones like gravy on Yorkshire pudding. He's all windswept and grizzled like he's been on tour since 1969. The things he must have seen. This probably seems quite tame.'

'Ha, ha. You're a lustful wench, you. He might struggle to buy any drugs here, if they're into that. The security is so heavy that I'm certain no dealer will risk it and anyone bringing anything in will be picked up by the sniffer dogs.'

'They seemed happy enough to go to the green room bar for vodka. Now, I'm just waiting on a couple of the last bands coming in and once I've got them sorted out, I'm all done. Then I'm going to have a big drink up and a dance and then when we get home I'm going to rut on you like your back ain't got no bones. You'll be begging for mercy!' She drummed out a beat on his chest with her index fingers, laughing.

'Am I on a promise?' he said.

She laughed and danced off-beat to the sound of a band cranking out 'Bad to the Bone' from the stage.

'Consider yourself promised. I've prepared the holiday underwear and everything. It's gonna be a proper big session, right, so save some energy for it. You up for that?'

'Give me about 10 seconds and I will be.' He looked down at his crotch. She yelped a laugh. 'OK Jules, you're on.'

'I will be, aye. On, over, under, sideways, down.' She lifted an eyebrow at him.

'You get big points for a Yardbirds reference in a sexual context.' She skipped off happily and he took the hot dogs back to Emily.

'There is simply no way to eat these with dignity and without it looking like you're engaged in oral sex,' said Nick, holding the long floppy tube of meat.

She held hers out, resting in the middle of a split bun. 'Goodness me. That's almost erotic.'

He looked at it. 'Nah. Only if you've got a bread-based vagina which, let's face it, would get soggy quite quickly.'

She began to laugh, choking on her food as she did so. 'Oh shit. Don't do that.' She drank from a can of boozy coke and sat back. 'You're so funny sometimes...a soggy vagina indeed. I'm not sure that'd be a bad thing at all.'

He finished the hot dog and got his camera. 'Right, I'm off to the main stage to take some shots of Big Fish.'

Emily raised her finger. 'Ah, yeah. I got an email about that from Simon Garbutt...he says it's going to be something big and...err...he uses the word *incredible*. I simply can't believe Stevie Salmon would do anything incredible, other than in an eating competition, maybe.'

'Why don't you come with me? You've hardly seen anyone yet. Have you got much left to do?'

'Just Facebooking. I can do that side stage on my phone.'

'Owee then. Have you ever been backstage at a gig?'

'Are you asking if I'm a groupie, Nicky, my boy?' She said it with a raised eyebrow and laughed loudly. 'None of your business.'

'Righto. I will not pry into your soggy vagina.'

She laughed, looked over her shoulder, to see if Julie was at her desk - she wasn't - put her arm around him, leaned in and gave his balls a gentle squeeze. 'Oooh, you had your chance to do that, Guymer and I daresay you'll have the chance again, sometime...if you're lucky,' she said into his ear in a throaty whisper.

'You're a randy little sod, you, aren't you?' he said, laughing and pushing at her playfully.

'Only with you, Nicky boy. Only with you.' She was a bit pissed now.

There was a pathway from the admin area to the main stage, defined by long rows of metal fencing that ran down the side of the main field and curved around to the backstage area.

'It feels like we're celebrities,' said Emily, ruffling her hair up as they walked down, security guards posted at intervals nodded at them as they passed. With her reflective round sunglasses and very, very tight leather pants and high-heeled boots, she looked like a rock star who might be playing the gig. Some members of the crowd clearly thought she was Someone and took photos of her as they passed.

'Nick! Nick! Over here.' He looked around at a woman calling his name from alongside the fence that ran down the side of the main field. A familiar face looked back at him. Dressed in a light grey hoodie, white top and jeans, was Shawn Yeadon. She waved at him, smiling.

'Shawn. Hey there lady,' he said, coming to a halt. 'You go ahead, Em. I'll catch you up.' She nodded and walked on. 'Now then. I didn't know blues was your thing.'

'It's not really, but I wanted to support the festival after everything that happened with that awful bomb. Did you hear about the car explosion as well? I thought, oh my god it's another bomb, but apparently it wasn't.'

The details of the people involved hadn't been released to the media.

'I heard something about it, yeah. It's all running like clockwork here, though. Are you here on your own?'

'I came with my youngest lad. I just spotted you at a distance. Did Julie tell you we had a good old chat the other night? She's great fun. I'm sure you two are very well suited. Two sides of the same coin, I think.' She touched his hand, affectionately. He put his hand over hers.

'She said you'd got on well. You should come over and have drinks sometime.'

'I will. I'd like that. How are you feeling now? You seemed a bit down when I saw you in town.'

'I took your advice. Your good, sensible, Shawny advice. I got some pills. They've really helped me. See I always knew you were good for me, one way or another.'

She smiled and nodded. 'I don't know about that but I'm glad to hear it. You deserve to be happy. Well, you'd better get on. You look very important with your badge and camera and everything.'

'I'm not important really. Just a dogsbody really but it's good fun. Great to see you, Shawn, and thanks...'

'What for?'

'Just for being your solid, sensible self.'

'That makes me sound very boring.'

'Not at all, man.'

He leaned over the fence and kissed her on the lips and then ran to catch Emily up, his heart full of one more drop of joy for having done that.

On the main stage Evie Dale was playing some slow blues on an old green Telecaster.

'I love her,' said Nick, walking up behind Emily, who was doing something on her phone.

'Is she a bit like Bonnie Raitt?'

'Yeah, totally.'

'I've got the *Nick of Time* album. It's a lovely late-night record. If you were at my house, we'd make love to that record.' She patted him on the backside affectionately.

'Would we indeed? Well that'd be very tasteful.'

'I do taste good,' she said, giggling again.

He laughed and pulled her into him in a little embrace, just happy to be backstage at a summer blues festival on Teesside. How brilliant was this?

It was a superb view from the side, out across the stage and into the crowd. And it was loud. Evie Dale introduced their final song, a lovely funky slide guitar number. Someone tapped Nick on the shoulder as he watched Emily dancing to the music.

Jeff made a face at him and gestured to follow him.

'What is it, Jeff?' he said, as they stood behind a baffle screen backstage, which reduced the volume from the PA.

'You might think I'm crazy here, but I think something is going to go down.'

CHAPTER 17

'Eh? What do you mean?'

'Something weird is happening.' He put his hand on Nick's shoulder and leaned in his ear. 'Look at those two blokes just behind that stack of drum cases at the side of the stage. Right? Then look at the fella in the black t-shirt behind the amps. Now look at the three blokes in black t-shirts on the other side of the stage standing together.'

Nick narrowed his eyes. He could see the men he meant.

'What's wrong with them? What's the problem?'

'I saw them all arrive together about half an hour ago. They're not here to work for me or any of the roadies. They're not normal punters. They're not in a band. So who are they?'

Nick frowned.

'They've got the backstage passes though...look, lanyards with purple ribbons like ours.'

'I've just spoke to Jules in the Green room, she didn't give six blokes in tight black t-shirts any passes. They must be fakes.'

He looked back to them. They didn't look like thugs or anything. In fact they were lean and wiry, but they were all dressed the same - tight black fitted t-shirts and tight black skinny jeans.

'I know everyone working on this stage. We've all sweated bullets together for weeks and I don't like that I don't know who they are so I'm going to ask them and get their story. Will you ride shotgun for us?'

Nick nodded and held a fist up to him. Jeff walked up to the two blokes by the drum cases and tapped one of them on the shoulder. Nick stood close and looked at him as he turned. He was a pretty lad with long eyelashes and pink lips. He was no physical threat. He could put him down with one good right hander.

'Excuse me mate, I'm just doing a security check. Can I look at your passes please?' said Jeff, not giving the bloke an option and scrutinizing the lanyard. Nick looked over his shoulder. His name was Jason Cantino. 'And can I see yours too, mate?' said Jeff to the other guy, who was a little older. He was Tim Ronson. 'Did you get these from the admin tent?' said Jeff.

'No mate. Simon Garbutt gave us them,' said Jason.

'Oh, aye. What are you doing for him?' said Jeff, looking down his nose at them, suspicious.

'Can't say, mate,'

'You can tell me, I'm Big Fish's brother, Jeff.'

'Ask him then. He'll be here any moment now.'

Jeff pulled Nick to one side and leaned in his ear. 'They're not proper passes. They're fakes quickly knocked up on a printer. Not photo ID. Just the right colour ribbon, that's all.'

'What the fuck are they doing?'

Jeff looked over his shoulder at them. 'I don't know, but I don't like it. I'm going to get security.'

'Too late, here's Big Fish now. I'm sure it's OK, man. They're not terrorists, are they? They've not got any room for bombs in those skinny jeans, there's barely room for their balls.'

Jeff snorted. 'True. Alright, but keep an eye on them.'

The large and distinctive figure of Big Fish came waddling backstage dressed in huge combat pants, big black boots and a black 5XL t-shirt on which, written in bold white letters was his mantra "Talk To The Beard." The beard itself looked especially red and explosive, surrounding his chin like a huge, dense cloud of ginger snap biscuit crumbs. He must have back-combed and blow-dried it to make it extra bushy. As usual he had two or three people around him. Who they were and what they did wasn't clear, but they were always around. His latest girlfriend, a predictably busty, blonde woman in a cocktail dress who looked like the sort of lass to lead darts players up to the board in the big tournaments, followed a subservient 10 paces behind.

Nick went back to Emily, who looked over at him and shouted, 'What was that about?'

He shrugged. 'Nothing much.' She grinned at him, happily dancing on the spot again as Evie Dale wound up her set.

Big Fish was beaming, pulling big expressive faces at anyone's eye he caught, his face pink from the sun. The hangers-on stood looking around, a bit bored, clearly no fans of top notch blues. The cans of strong white cider each of them held was a better indication of their cultural preferences.

Evie Taylor and her three band mates thanked the noisy crowd, took their bow and ran offstage.

'They were superb, I want to play slide guitar like her,' said Emily, putting her hand in Nick's back pocket and her other hand on his belly. 'Who's on next?'

'He is,' said Nick, pointing to Big Fish as he strode past them onto the stage, arms aloft. There was a huge, noisy cheer as he emerged and walked up to the central microphone stand. A few began chanting immediately, 'talk to the beard' over and over. The star had arrived. That's what it seemed like.

'Now then...'ow are we doin' boys and girls?' He tugged on his beard dramatically and even that got a huge cheer. He nodded up and down at them all as if giving his approval, arms out wide again, like he was embracing his audience. 'Aye, not bad for a big crowd of ugly Teessiders, like. Lasses, feel free to show me what you've got. The beard needs some love.'

On cue, three girls near the front pulled up their t-shirts to reveal white, wobbly, blancmange breasts, laughing with, or at each other, as they did so. Some parts of British culture will always be a 1975 episode of Benny Hill.

'Ah I see we've got three lovely Roseberry Toppings here...gotta love titanic Teesside tits,' he said. 'You know the reason we have so many cooling towers here on Teesside? Because our women are so damn hot! That's why.' That got a really huge cheer. A couple more women pulled off their tops as though this would prove the veracity of the big man's words.

'So anyway, thanks for coming...I hope you're having a good time.'

In a way, you had to admire him. Years of playing gigs had given him near-perfect timing and he absolutely commanded the stage with his huge presence. For a quite stupid man, he had a quick mind, able to pick up on reactions and spin them back to the audience. His humour was crude and low-brow but, as Julie had often said, you underestimated him at your peril. On his home turf, in his own environment, he was unbeatable. He knew exactly what he could and couldn't get away with. It was ironic that for a man so selfish and self-focused, a man who could insult you without even realising it, he should be so good at judging his own comedy. But then it was his art form and he'd honed it over 20 years or more, and here, his home crowd bloody loved it and bloody loved him.

'People say we've got chips on our shoulders up here...well of course we do...we need something to go with the fuckin' parmos, don't we?'

That brought a second huge roar from the crowd. He tugged on the beard, beaming almost manically from left to right.

Simon Garbutt walked up and stood alongside Nick.

'Alright Simon. He's not short of fans, is he?' said Nick, nodding at the stage.

'He's a big fat fuck.' He spat the words out, his eyes expressing fury and contempt. He'd been so laid back before when he's written the address on the business card for him, now he seemed to be full of simmering fury. Nick felt in his back pocket and took out the card Simon Garbutt had written the address on. He looked at it. As he did so, his heart leaped up into his mouth with such power it felt like it would burst out of his eyes. Simon Garbutt had written 'Big Fish Ltd, Blakston Estate, Norton, TS20 5ZQ Teeside.' The exact same misspelling as the bomber's email.

Simon Garbutt was the bomber.

But then it all happened so quickly. So shockingly. The three guys in black t-shirts that had been standing and watching Big Fish sprinted onto the stage, pulling on balaclavas as they did so. One of them picked three pistols from inside a drum case. From across the stage they were joined by the other three black t-shirts, also now wearing balaclavas and carrying semi-automatic rifles.

They ran up to Big Fish brandishing their weapons. There were screams from the audience, some thought it was a joke, others realised it wasn't and began to run away from the stage. This was no joke. It was deadly serious. Big Fish turned to look at these interlopers, his eyes registering shock.

'What the fuck do youse lot think you're...' he said, his voice picked up by the stage microphone, but it was too late. One of the men carrying a rifle, hit him in the face with butt, knocking him to the ground.

'Don't worry...none of you will be hurt...' said the man who'd been standing next to Nick to the crowd. 'We're from the Ironopolis Anarchists. You might have heard of us. We blew that house up!' He pointed across the field to the building.

The fuck you did pal, that was Simon Garbutt. Nick looked at Big Fish's manager, he was staring with a smirk on his face. What the hell was this?

There were boos and a lot more screams now as more people backed away from the stage, seeing the guns the men had.

'Nick!' Jeff shouted. He turned around and ran back to Jeff. He was holding a baseball bat towards him. 'Take it.' He held another in his other hand. Nick grabbed it.

'What the fuck can we do? These people have got guns, we can't rush them, we'd get mowed down before we got across the stage, Jeff.'

'Any chance you get, just fucking hit them.' That was all Jeff had to say. He was clearly terrified. Emily had got right to the side of the stage and wore the same scared look she'd had on the stairs when the bomb had gone off. He gestured at her to get away from the stage, he couldn't bear her getting hit by a bullet. Where was Jules? He looked around but she was nowhere to be seen. She was probably still in the admin area. Thank fuck for that. Something was going to have to be done here and there was no way it was going to end nicely. One way or another, blood was going to be spilt.

He ran at a crouch to the side of the stage and stood next to

Garbutt.

'Did you know about this?' he said, but Garbutt was acting very weird. He had his arms folded, his face now set in a sneer. 'We've got to do something, man. They might bloody well kill him,' said Nick.

'He's a fat fuck. Let him die. His career is over,' said Garbutt, laughing.

'Is this all your idea? Is this part of your plan? Just like blowing up the house was, like blowing me and Jules up was, just like uploading the virus to my computer? You fucking prick!' He shouted at him, pushing Garbutt in the chest. 'When this is done, I'm fucking 'avin' you, son.'

'Piss off, you Northern know-nothing toe-rag.'

The security teams were all streaming to the stage now, running from the gates and other points across the site, but it was too late. They couldn't risk storming the stage. The six Ironopolis Anarchists owned it, each of them armed. One minute there had been music and laughter and the next, this. Everyone was stunned. It was hard to believe it was happening at all.

Nick only knew he had to save Stevie Salmon from this if he could. Salmon was a twat but he didn't deserve to die. Whatever the situation with Garbutt, that's what needed sorting right here, right now, but you couldn't fight six guns with a couple of wooden bats. Whack one or two and they'd take you out.

Big Fish got to his feet as another man stepped up to the microphone. He didn't seem to be bleeding from being hit with the butt of the gun, but he did look stunned, staggering a little as he stood up, shaking his head like a boxer that had got up off the canvas to avoid being counted out.

One of the black t-shirt men spoke into the mic. 'We're here to demand that you, Mr Salmon, pay more tax and stop being so rich and successful,' said the man at the mic.

What? What shit was this? There were a lot of boos now and a big space had opened up within 40 feet of the stage. A lot just stood and watched, open-mouthed from a distance they thought might be safe from any discharged guns. It was awful and yet compulsive.

The gunmen surrounded Stevie Salmon in a semi-circle, pointing their weapons at him. Bloody hell. They were going to execute him. They were turning their guns on him and were going to slay him like a big fucking Teesside whale. Nick twirled the bat around in his hand, looking for any chance to get in there and take these bastards down, but it was too far and there were too many of them.

Big Fish stared at the guns one by one. He wiped his mouth, then shook his head and spoke into the microphone.

'Yerjokinarntya? Talk to the fucking beard, son.' His legendary catchphrases defiantly echoed into the air and were received with a purring roar of affirmation from the front of the crowd to the back.

Suddenly, he grabbed the rifles out of the hands of two of the men and pointed them at their heads.

'This is my stage and I'm the fucking gaffer round here. So...dance, monkey boy, dance...'

He fired each rifle into the air with two loud cracks. With that, the six Ironopolis Anarchists threw down their guns, gathered into two lines of three, the PA struck up playing Middlesbrough's 'Pigbag' song and the six would-be terrorists began a synchronized dance in time to the music. A fucking dance routine!!

What in all the holy hell of fuckdom was this? Nick looked around, utterly astonished at what was unfolding. His whole body was tense, holding the bat at shoulder height, just looking for a moment to strike one of the terrorists, 'terrorists' who were now doing high kicks and wiggling their backsides.

It had all been a massive joke. A huge prank. Of course it was. A tasteless, gigantic, beyond belief piss-take. He'd scared everyone senseless. Nick looked at Jeff, he was mouth agape staring with eyes that simply couldn't comprehend this outcome. This was harder to believe than the stage being invaded by terrorists. He shrugged at Nick and held his arms out wide, the bat resting against his leg now.

Emily on the other hand had run back to the side of the stage and was laughing and wildly shaking her ass to the music, really getting off on it. She seemed to have adjusted to the situation much quicker.

As people pushed back to the front of the stage, it was clear the crowd absolutely adored it as well. They cheered and clapped along as Big Fish, a presumably mock rifle in each hand, patrolled the front of the stage, holding them aloft and conducting the chanting. It was a cacophony. Bad taste or not, they loved him for it. Bloody loved him.

'Did you know about this, Simon?' said Nick.

He was puce-faced now.

'Know about it? It was my fucking idea, you fucking arsehole. Stupid shit that I am. I thought it'd fucking ruin him, but look at the stupid fucking idiots...they only love him more...'

The crowd were bouncing up and down and singing in time to the 'Pigbag' tune, 'Talk to the beard...yerjokinarntya...talk to the beard ...yerjokinarntya...talk to the beard, beard, talk to the beard, talk to the beard, beard, talk to the beard.'

It was utterly, utterly surreal.

Garbutt grabbed the baseball bat from Nick's hands, jabbed him in the chest with it, knocking him two steps back and ran onto the stage.

'Jeff! It's Garbutt. Everything, the bombs...it's all Garbutt!!'

'What the fuck is going on now?' said Jeff from a few paces behind him. 'What the fuck is happening? Is this another sodding joke? Am I tripping or something? Is any of this fucking real?'

All the locks dropped in Nick's brain. It was all Garbutt's doing. The bombs, the threats, the message board. He had tried to ruin Big Fish by getting the festival called off and sticking him with all the costs, but he'd failed. Not even trying to blow him and Julie up had worked to stop the festival or frame them as bombers. It had all failed. So he had suggested a joke so tasteless and horrible it'd surely bring Big Fish down. But he'd failed in that as well. Big

Fish was no mere mortal. Right there and then, in front of 15,000 Teessiders, he seemed larger than life itself.

Garbutt hadn't understood what people were like on Teesside. Hadn't understood that they loved someone who took the piss, more than anything else. Hadn't understood that when life is tough for a lot of people for a lot of generations, they develop a gallows humour and are anything but precious, their self-deprecation only boosted by their pride in that self-deprecation. Yeah, Big Fish's joke was in the worst possible taste, but it was immediately and without question understood as a celebration of the area's resilience; an acting out of the region's gutsy 'fuck you, son' spirit. Big Fish was taking the piss out of terrorism and out of terrorists and almost by extension, out of anyone who wanted to see the area put down. Sod whether it was tasteful or not. Sod whether that was really what the big comedian was trying to do; for once in his big fat life, purely by accident, he had done something worthwhile and it had all been Garbutt's invention.

Garbutt sprinted across the stage and bore down on Big Fish. He took one big swing of the bat whilst on the move and launched it into the comedian's head with a gut-wrenching, sickening crack of wood or bone. The noise was picked up by the stage microphones and amplified at 100 decibels. The crowd cheered loudly, clearly thinking it was still part of the act. Big Fish went down vertically and with the heaviness of a man who has lost consciousness. The stage emptied as all the dancers ran to get away from Garbutt, who was now swinging the bat around him like a lunatic. They knew it wasn't a joke.

Now he really did have to save Big Fish's life. Another blow like that would kill him if he wasn't already dead. Nick sprinted towards Garbutt at full tilt, but Garbutt saw him coming.

The lanky manager turned on the Fish again as he lay prone on the floor and gave him another crashing blow on the back of the neck. Jesus Christ. The security teams ran onto the stage to stop the beating, but Nick was ahead of them.

He let out an unholy howl from the back of his throat as he ran and leaped at those long, brittle legs, two-footed, turning on his side with his back to Garbutt's baseball bat to protect himself as he did so. It was a vicious sliding tackle, the like of which had been outlawed by the FA for years, but which all true football fans want to see back in the game. Nick had grown up watching the master of the violent lunge, the king of the psychotic leg-break, Mr Graeme Souness, dishing out retribution with a fierce blood lust on a 1970s Saturday afternoon, so it came to him instinctively. A second nature born of cold, Bovril-infused Saturday afternoons at Ayresome Park. Some things just never leave you. Go over the top of the ball, only there was no ball, just Garbutt's unfeasibly long and very snap-able legs. His boots had hard wood soles. They would hurt at this pace. Even as he left the ground, illuminated by a strobe of flash lights from photographers, he knew it was going to be messy.

The bat came down on his shoulder and neck just before his feet connected with Garbutt's shins, but as soon as he connected with him, he knew he'd hurt him and hurt him badly. The crack of bone wasn't audible, but he felt it vibrate up his right foot. The power of his run up sent Garbutt flying with a yell of pain, his feet up into the air, waving the bat impotently as he fell backwards, the whole of Nick's weight and power knocking him to the edge of the stage. It was all the opportunity the security team needed, smothering Garbutt, followed swiftly by paramedics to treat Big Fish, who was bleeding from a wound on his head.

Jeff and Emily ran up to Nick as he lay prone. 'Are you alright, fella?' said Jeff.

'That was fucking incredible!!!' screamed Emily, hysterically. 'You totally fucking nailed him! Awesome! Just awesome!! Whooo!!' She punched the air and stood over him, arms aloft and started gesturing to the crowd shouting 'C'mon!'

He felt his shoulder, it was bruised, but he'd had worse. He got to his feet and got his breath. The crowd was in total uproar, somewhere between horrified, shocked and amused. A line of stewards formed in front of the stage as they dragged Simon

Garbutt away. Nick leaned in towards him and yelled into his face.
  'So...you spell Teesside with two "s"s, you London Wanker!'

CHAPTER 18

The rest of the festival was held in blazing sunshine until Sunday night when the T-Bone Boogie Band brought the curtain down. On Monday morning there was one final meeting of all the staff. Although there was still a lot of work to do dismantling everything, it was the last day for all the admin staff.

'Have you seen the latest bulletin on Big Fish?' said Jeff as Julie packed up her desk.

'No, we were late up,' said Nick.

'Vital signs are good, but he's still in a coma.'

'Funnily enough, that's how I always felt when I saw his act,' said Nick.

'I can't believe I missed all the fun,' said Julie, standing hands on hips.

'You didn't see any of it?' said Emily, packing away papers into a big shoulder bag. 'It was totally brilliant in every way.'

'I saw nowt. First I was sorting out passes, then I was in a bloody Portaloo right over in the far field. I heard them chanting "talk to the beard" but by the time I got out and got back to the main site, it was all over. You can't see the stage from over there, so I missed you doing your best Souey.'

'He was class, like,' said Jeff. 'It was like seeing the 1974 Big Jack promotion side Souey. Primo violence delivered with ruthless efficiency. Pure brill, it was.'

'I have no idea who any of those people are...' laughed Emily, '...but it was a great thing to see. You ran and jumped at him all in one fast movement. I've never seen anything like it. Awesome, I hope it's on film.'

'Aye, he's Hong Kong bloody Phooey this one,' said Jeff, tying his hair back.

'See, I don't know who that is either,' said Emily, shrugging. 'You're all so oooold!'

They all howled in protest at that, laughing as they did so.

Julie bit her lip. 'Eeee god. I hope he's alright though. I mean, I can't stand the big idiot, but even so...'

'Don't waste too much emotion on him, he wouldn't expend any on us. Maybe a few blows to the head is what he needs to forget his shit material and come up with something better,' said Jeff. 'Mind, if it's to be his last gig, then what a last bloody gig. They were worshipping him as though he was a morbidly obese god. I'll never forget that as long as I draw breath.'

'Buddha was morbidly obese, wasn't he?' said Nick.

'Yeah, he was The Great Fatsby, was Buddha,' said Jeff.

'Vegetarian y'see. His diet was all rice, lentil and beans. It's all carbs, that,' said Nick with a laugh.

'Aye, he's even got proper tits, probably due to eating so much oestrogen-rich soya,' said Julie.

Emily giggled. 'He has, hasn't he? Much bigger than mine,' she said.

'To be fair, Big Fish's breasts are more due to vast consumption of potato-based comestibles, lager and buckets of triple chocolate fudge ice cream; none of which are guaranteed to deliver enlightenment, even if you sit under a Bodhi tree whilst hoovering them into your holy gob,' said Jeff, to everyone's amusement.

'We shouldn't be critical of the obese, they've got enough on their plates,' said Julie with a grin. 'See, telling rubbish jokes about vulnerable people is easy, isn't it?'

'Well, that's me all packed up and ready to go,' said Emily. 'Can someone carry this box to my car for me, it's really heavy?'

'I'll do that for you,' said Nick, picking it up.

'Thanks, Nicky boy. Well, I shall really miss you all,' said Emily, fluffing up the feathery bits of her hair and grinning. 'I'll certainly never forget any of this or any of you, for one reason or another. It's been totally brilliant.'

Jeff gave her a hug. 'Nice to have met you, little Em. If you ever need a job in a record shop, selling second-hand vinyl to odd men who shouldn't really be out on their own, you know where to come. Minimum wage and as many Leo Sayer records as you want.'

'I might take you up on that. I like Leo Sayer - actually no I don't, I don't even know who Leo Sayer is - but I'll need a job before the end of the summer.' She giggled at her own joke, as she often did.

Julie held out her hand firmly and gripped hers. 'Good luck, Emily.'

'Thanks, Jules. You've been great - all things considered...well...y'know,' she grinned impishly at her, looking out of the corner of her eye, ducking down a little apologetically, whilst still laughing. 'It's all rock 'n' roll, isn't it?'

'Aye, I suppose so. And thanks for saving me life, like. As a reward I'll give you a little tip - don't let too many strange men get in your knickers, eh.'

'Ha, ha, ha....you're welcome. OK, I won't...though, actually, Jules, you *know* I probably will...ha, ha, ha.' Julie had to laugh, too.

Nick carried the box out to the car park. She opened the boot of the old Mini and he put the box in.

'Thanks. We might see each other around. I am staying on Teesside,' she said.

'Thanks for everything, Em, it's been, like...just really great fun working with you. As I often say, Teesside is a small place and you always run into people you know, sooner or later, so I'm sure we'll find each other in the same place at some point.'

She nodded. 'Come here then. Indulge me.' She put her arms around his waist and pressed herself into him and leaned back. 'You've got my number, haven't you?'

'I have, yeah. And you've got ours?'

'Yeah.' She pecked him on the lips, pulled away, went around to the driver side and pulled open the door. She stood looking at him in her full rock chick gear again, ruffled up her hair and put on the round sunglasses.

'My door's always open for you, Nicky boy. You know that...' she paused and look at him with a big smile, her tongue, as ever, resting between the gap in her teeth, '...my door and my legs...' She let out a squeal of laughter, amused with herself again and waved a hand.

He waved as he watched her drive away, feeling that this would not be the last he saw of Emily Davids and that without doubt, that was a very good thing.

Later that evening, Jeff, Nick and Julie sat in the beer garden of the Black Bull in Yarm. It was still a warm summer day.

'We've been so lucky with the weather,' said Nick, putting down a white wine each for Jeff and Julie and his own fizzy water.

'Rain forecast for tomorrow,' said Jeff. 'That'll be a relief. Feels weird if we get more than four days of good weather.'

'Did Rita not fancy coming for a drink?' said Julie.

Jeff shook his head. 'To be honest, I think she thinks you'll be going on about left-wing politics all night. I've told her you're not really like that and are more likely to be talking about bodily functions, underwear and obscure records by Taj Mahal on the...' he pointed at Nick.

'...Direction label. Great label, Direction. Yellow and black. All those early Taj Mahal albums are on it.'

Jeff applauded. 'What woman could resist knowledge like that?'

'I'll be off then,' said Julie getting up as if to go. They laughed. Nick's phone vibrated.

'Huh...it's an email from Artie Taylor, the photographer. "Here's one for your archives" he says.' He opened the attachment to the email. It was a photograph. A photograph of him in mid-tackle on Garbutt, his right boot connecting with the long shins. He must have taken it from just in front of the stage. Nick showed it to them.

'That's brilliant,' said Julie. 'You look like some sort of Kung Fu master. You're actually in mid-air and Garbutt's leg is bending backwards as you give him the full Souness. Fantastic. Artie must have been right by the stage. Loads of people had backed away. But not him, obviously.'

'The man's a pro. Walks towards trouble rather than away from it. I bet he got loads of great shots,' said Nick.

'So what did they say at the hospital, Jeff?' said Julie.

'Just that the Big Kipper will, probably, be alright. He came out of the coma this afternoon. He's not got too much internal bleeding in his head, so when it all settles down he should be OK. Ironic really, as you could be forgiven for thinking he's been in a vegetative state for most of his life.'

'The thing is, he'll face a full HMRC audit when he's got better. That whole cash scam he was running - 100 per cent correctly predicted by Mike - Garbutt has confessed to all of that,' said Nick. 'Will he do jail time for it, do you think?'

'Will he bollocks,' said Julie. 'They'll slap him on the wrist, fine him and let him off. The rich always get away with things like that. His dad will make sure of it. I like Brian but money is power in this country, and land with money is even more power.'

Jeff nodded. 'That, my Communist lady friend, is almost certainly bound to be true.'

'Col Harcombe texted me before we got here,' said Nick. 'Garbutt has been charged. He's puked his guts totally on everything.'

'So he's put his hands up for the two bombs and the detonators?' said Jeff.

'Yup and for the hoax call and for creating the IA message board, all the messages on there and for uploading the trojan to my computer. The only thing genuine thing online from the Ironopolis Anarchists were those early postings that we found on various websites. The real group were always plural and not singular, but Garbutt didn't spot that for a while and used the singular to begin with. He even called in the first hoax as the Ironopolis Anarchist. Mike told the truth, he was never "Volunteer", it sounded like him, but it was just Garbutt using similar language purely by coincidence.'

'What a shit,' hissed Julie. 'He must have been getting desperate to try to frame us. He put that virus on your computer and then the bomb in my bag thinking we'd be going home together. We'd have been killed and everyone would have thought we'd been the bombers, blown up by our own bomb after trying to get rid of the message board. Thank god that Emily found the hidden auto-emails to Scotland Yard on your computer.'

'What did that actually say?' said Jeff, taking a drink.

'It was fired out of my Hotmail account at 6.20pm and auto-filed into the trash. Emily was working on it at the time and noticed the programme fire up on its own. She sussed out right away what had happened. Thank god she was so well educated in computing. She dug out the email, told Mel and then came and found me right away. It had both of our names and said the we were the Teesside Blues bombers and that the next explosion will be Thursday 7.00pm and the bomb was in a blue canvas shoulder bag in a BMW. He wanted the police to know for sure it was being carried by Julie in my car. He set the timer for 6.49pm, thinking it would paint us as being blown up by our own faulty bomb, but he hadn't realised you were in your own car and would go home alone.'

Julie shook her head. 'The man must be a psycho. Thankfully he was quite shit at being a terrorist. What had we ever done to him?'

'It was just 'cos we were around the place, wasn't it? We were nearby the first one. All the reasons Mike, and by extension MI6, were suspicious of me, were the same reasons Garbutt thought would make us look guilty once we'd gone boom,' said Nick, watching as house martens dipped and swooped above them, catching summer flies. 'He thought it would draw a line under the whole thing and mean that although Big Fish hadn't been ruined, he'd at least got away with it.'

'Yup, the bombers had been killed. He'd live to fight another day and bring him down at some later point,' said Jeff.

'I should've guessed what was going on earlier; I feel stupid now,' said Nick, sipping at the ice-cold water. 'Big Fish was always on the phone with Garbutt arguing. Twice Fish was moaning about insurance costs and Simon even mentioned how BF would take a bath, if it had to be called off. We even saw them arguing in LAX, didn't we, Jules? We almost got to it, but until I saw how he'd spelled Blakeston and Teesside, I just didn't see the whole picture.'

'So Simon's idea was to get the festival called off due to terrorist threats. How would that have hurt Big Fish?' said Julie.

'It would have invalidated the insurance policy that Simon had had drawn up specifically to exclude acts of terrorism,' interjected Jeff. 'He sold that idea to the BF as a cost-saving measure, leaving more profit for them...the BF greedily agreed to it, thinking there was zero chance of terrorism on Teesside.'

'...which meant the BF would have to pay all the costs, but refund all the tickets, when it all went tits up,' said Nick.

'And that would have killed him financially because on top of the costs, he'd probably get sued for compensation, by bands or organisations that had committed to those dates and thus couldn't get any other work...the whole thing would have escalated. I mean, normally, everyone involved would just walk away. But everyone knew Big Fish was loaded, so they'd have squeezed him dry,' said Jeff, sipping his wine.

'Look at you holding that glass by the stem, like you're a connoisseur,' laughed Julie.

'I'm a sophisticate these days, me. So did Colin say anything else?'

'Yeah, see the thing is, Garbutt had had enough of Big Fish. He'd been ripped off once too often by him, so he hatched a plan to ruin him. I don't know the exact details yet, but that cash they were paying bands with, that was part of some big financial scam they had been pulling for months. He'd been booking gigs in LA and New York and bringing cash back in with him. I mean, no wonder he looked like he was crapping himself when we saw him in LAX. He was probably carrying 20 or 30 grand on each trip, exactly as Mike said when I first met him. Garbutt was supposed to get some of that cash, but Fish had, according to what Garbutt has told the cops, informed him last month, that actually he was getting next to nothing. That was the root of the whole plot to bring him down.'

'Where had he got that cash from then, any idea?' said Julie.

'God knows. Mike said to me once that he probably banked it in the Caymans and then flew from there to South America and then to the USA with it. There's all the chip shops as well, don't forget; that's all cash, too. Thing was, he probably thought he could mess Simon around indefinitely, because they'd conspired in so many dodgy deals. He didn't reckon on Garbutt going postal like that,' said Nick.

'I bet the cops will be busy for months unravelling his financial affairs,' said Julie.

'Oh aye. Col said it was "a bad business from top to toe",' said Nick. He put on the policeman's stern voice.

Jeff put his index finger in the air. 'What amazes me is that Garbutt managed to convince all of us and the police and MI bloody 6, that the Ironopolis Anarchists or RadLand were responsible for the bombs. That was very bloody clever, the way he muddied those waters by using the false message board. He knew that the real IA had to have a secret way to communicate with each other, so he created one. MI6 had hacked it as well, which was how Mike knew about the meeting on Cargo Fleet Lane, but they hadn't a clue Emily had set it up. Garbutt must have been delighted when that happened because he knew it was being taken seriously and it just confused everyone, which was exactly what Garbutt had wanted. He wanted it to be discovered and be hacked. In some ways he was very smart.'

Nick agreed and drummed out a beat on the table with his index fingers.

'Cleverly, he wanted us all to think it was a secret community board. Only us, Mike, MI6 and Emily knew about it, but we just hadn't told each other. He probably didn't actually know how many knew about it, but it was a great way to disseminate false information. It worked because it kept all attention away from him and falsely turned it into an IA vs RadLand debate. And you know, he *was* getting away with it. We had some of the pieces in place, but not all of them. If it wasn't for the address he wrote and then freaking out with the baseball bat...'

'Shouldn't we be calling him the Battered Fish now. Ha ha. BF: battered fish, get it?' laughed Julie.

'You should sell that joke to him when he recovers. It's better than most of his,' said Jeff.

'Yeah, well, Garbutt got everyone paranoid, didn't he? We thought Emily was a terrorist, she thought I was, Mike thought I was. I thought Mike was. Angie Page probably thought we were and we thought she was a liar and we certainly thought her husband David Murray was following us. I even thought he was spying on me when I met Mike in the Boro, but that was just some random bloke and not him at all. That's what paranoia does to you. It turns out Murray was blissfully unaware what was going on, even though Garbutt was uploading those messages to the board whilst walking around Ropner Park with him and his kids,' said Nick.

'If you think about it, you see people standing around all the time and think nothing at all about them. But as soon as you get paranoid, everyone seems guilty of something,' said Jeff, topping up the wine glasses.

'Which is why I thought that bloke was spying on us with binoculars,' said Nick. 'But he really was just a birdwatcher.'

'A birdwatcher who saw my sagging bare breasts,' added Julie.

'Let's hope he's a tit fancier then, eh. Boom and indeed boom,' said Jeff, arms wide. 'C'mon, give me some love.'

'Ha, very good,' said Julie. She continued, 'You'd think he'd have got the spelling right in the email though, wouldn't you? All that Teesside with one "s" business...'

'...yeah, well, he did by the second email, either by luck or judgement. Turns out, it worked in his favour because we ended up thinking it was two different groups,' said Nick. 'He got lucky there. That animal rights addition he put in though, that was stupid. He should've stuck to the original demands for the sake of consistency and not tried to make it seem even more extreme. Mind, I was 100 per cent right about one thing, that bomb was never meant to go off. That was just part of the plot to make sure the festival was called off by scaring everyone. But because he was just rubbish at setting it up, it went off by accident. That changed everything.'

'Where he really went wrong was that he really didn't reckon on the nature of Teesside people,' said Julie. 'He thought no-one would want to go to it once there'd been a bomb, whether it was found or went off, but of course Teessiders wanted to come to it even more, just to give a giant "fuck you" to the terrorists. Typical arsiness, that. Makes me very, very proud, like.'

'It just goes to show one thing,' said Nick. 'Never underestimate the sheer bloody-mindedness of Teessiders.'

'Southerners have been doing that for bloody years,' said Jeff, as they clinked their glasses together in a toast.

Ten days later, Nick and Julie stood at his mother's grave in St Andrews churchyard beside the pretty Anglican church in Sadberge where she was buried.

'It's nice to have a place to come to see her,' said Nick, laying a small bouquet of butterfly lavender, her favourite flowers, on the fresh earth. A headstone would have to be made, when they had enough money.

'She liked being here in the village. It's a nice quiet place to end your days, I think,' said Julie, looking around the churchyard.

They stood in silence. House martens swooping around the church made a high-pitched twitter.

'It's weird having how you feel inside change, y'know,' said Nick, as they watched the birds.

'Does it feel like you're a different person?'

He paused and thought for a minute. 'No, not really. For me, it feels like being the person I was a long time ago. It's like a return to home after being away. Something like that, anyway.'

'That must be really fizzin' odd. I can't even imagine it. It's class that you feel like you lost your blues though. Really class, like.'

'It's such a relief not to feel like that. It is literally like having a weight lifted from your shoulders. Thanks for the pills, Jules. That's what has done it. Even if I have to take them for the rest of my life, it's better than the alternative.'

'It's so sad your mam couldn't have recovered years ago, though. Poor old lass.'

'I've been hearing her voice, you know,' he said, taking Julie's hand as they walked up to the path that ran down to the road from the church. 'Really sharp and clear in my head. Quite a few times.'

'Really? That's weird. What does she say?'

'Mostly just to be myself.'

She made a small noise in agreement. 'Well, that's good advice.'

'Yeah. It is. I think she means to be the self I was when I was little. When I was her "laughing little boy". That might be a bit harder. I want to be, though. I want to be that nice happy boy again. I left him behind when I was 13. I want to see if I can find him.'

'If you think about it, though, she knew you from the start of your life, she knew you before the world made its mark on you. You can never go back to being that lad again. Life naturally takes you away from that. You can't undo all of the things that have happened.'

He smiled. 'No. Maybe not. But I think we can reconnect with our untainted little selves more than we do. I still have so many unresolved feelings and emotions, around her and my dad and my upbringing. The illness took mam away from herself and from me, and it took me away from myself as well. But...but...I think, hopefully, with the help of the drugs and everything else, I'm just starting to understand how that happened and where that old self might be.'

'Good. But don't go changing too much, I love the loony Nick. Don't forget. He's the man I'm marrying.'

'Don't worry. I'm not going to turn into a sensible. Not even after we're married. I've never been one of those, not even when I was a baby.'

'09-09-09 is a brilliant date for a wedding. I think we should have the reception in the garden. Mam will get drunk and make a show of me, if we have it anywhere else. She's been seeing this new fella, Conrad. He's a builder. Bit of a rogue by all accounts, so if they're still together by then, she'll probably be all over him. I'm feeling a sense of dread already.'

'She's in her late 60s. You'd think she'd have given up all of that. They're not, like, doing it, are they?'

'We Wells women have a powerful lust for men. It's not easily quenched, not even by old age...as you will find out yourself when you're in your late 60s and I'm still tugging at you for some naughty. We'll be up to at least 10,000 by then, if we put some effort in.'

He laughed a little. They stood by the front of the church for a moment. It was such a beautiful summer morning. A robin flew down onto the pile of fresh earth under which his mother was buried, looking for worms and insects.

'Rest in peace, mam. God knows, you deserve a good rest from the hard life you had,' he said, inside his head.

And in that quiet rural Teesside moment, her voice returned to him one last time, clear and affectionate and now infinite.

"I loved you so much, our Nick, my happy little boy."

'I loved you too, mam, in my own way. I really did love you. I still do.'

THE END

About John Nicholson

John is a well-known football writer whose work is read by tens of thousands of people every week. He's a columnist for Football365.com and has worked for the Daily Record, The Mirror, Sky and many other publications over the last 14 years.

Other John Nicholson Books
published by Biteback Publishing

We Ate All The Pies -
How Football Swallowed Britain Whole (2010)

The Meat Fix -
How 26 Years Of Healthy Eating Nearly Killed Me (2012)

Books in the Nick Guymer Series
Published by HEAD PUBLISHING

1. Teesside Steal (2013)
2. Queen Of The Tees (2013)
3. Teesside Missed (2013)
4. DJ Tees (2014)
5. Teesside Blues (2014)

Kindle/Paperback

http://www.johnnicholsonwriter.com